HOW TO SELL
A HAUNTED
HOUSE

Fiction by Grady Hendrix

Horrorstör

My Best Friend's Exorcism

We Sold Our Souls

The Southern Book Club's Guide to Slaying Vampires

The Final Girl Support Group

Bad Asstronauts

Nonfiction by Grady Hendrix

Paperbacks from Hell:
The Twisted History of '70s and '80s Horror Fiction

These Fists Break Bricks:
How Kung Fu Movies Swept America and Changed the World

HOW TO SELL A HAUNTED HOUSE

GRADY HENDRIX

BERKLEY | NEW YORK

BERKLEY
An imprint of Penguin Random House LLC
penguinrandomhouse.com

Copyright © 2023 by Grady Hendrix
Penguin Random House supports copyright. Copyright fuels creativity, encourages diverse voices,
promotes free speech, and creates a vibrant culture. Thank you for buying an authorized edition
of this book and for complying with copyright laws by not reproducing, scanning, or distributing
any part of it in any form without permission. You are supporting writers and allowing
Penguin Random House to continue to publish books for every reader.

BERKLEY and the BERKLEY & B colophon are registered trademarks
of Penguin Random House LLC.

Library of Congress Cataloging-in-Publication Data

Names: Hendrix, Grady, author.
Title: How to sell a haunted house / Grady Hendrix.
Description: New York: Berkley, [2023]
Identifiers: LCCN 2022026268 (print) | LCCN 2022026269 (ebook) |
ISBN 9780593201268 (hardcover) | ISBN 9780593201282 (ebook)
Subjects: LCGFT: Novels.
Classification: LCC PS3608.E543 H69 2023 (print) |
LCC PS3608.E543 (ebook) | DDC 813/.6—dc23/eng/20220606
LC record available at https://lccn.loc.gov/2022026268
LC ebook record available at https://lccn.loc.gov/2022026269

International Edition ISBN: 9780593547731

Printed in the United States of America
1st Printing

Interior art: abstract paper background © Zeitgugga6897 / shutterstock.com
Book design by Laura K. Corless

Amanda,
You are with me everywhere,
I see you where I go,
You surround me always,
Even though
I know
Exactly where I buried you.

Chapter 1

Louise thought it might not go well, so she told her parents she was pregnant over the phone, from three thousand miles away, in San Francisco. It wasn't that she had a single doubt about her decision. When those two parallel pink lines had ghosted into view, all her panic dissolved and she heard a clear, certain voice inside her head say:

I'm a mother now.

But even in the twenty-first century it was hard to predict how a pair of Southern parents would react to the news that their thirty-four-year-old unmarried daughter was pregnant. Louise spent all day rehearsing different scripts that would ease them into it, but the minute her mom answered and her dad picked up the kitchen extension, her mind went blank and she blurted out:

"I'm pregnant."

She braced herself for the barrage of questions.

Are you sure? Does Ian know? Are you going to keep it? Have you thought about moving back to Charleston? Are you certain this is the best thing? Do you have any idea how hard this will be alone? How are you going to manage?

In the long silence, she prepared her answers: *Yes, not yet, of course, God no, no but I'm doing it anyway, yes, I'll manage.*

Over the phone she heard someone inhale through what sounded like a mouthful of water and realized her mom was crying.

"Oh, Louise," her mother said in a thick voice, and Louise prepared herself for the worst. "I'm so happy. You're going to be the mother I wasn't."

Her dad only had one question: her exact street address.

"I don't want any confusion with the cab driver when we land."

"Dad," Louise said, "you don't have to come right now."

"Of course we do," he said. "You're our Louise."

She waited for them on the sidewalk, her heart pounding every time a car turned the corner, until finally a dark blue Nissan slowed to a stop in front of her building and her dad helped her mom out of the back seat, and she couldn't wait—she threw herself into her mom's arms like she was a little kid again.

They took her crib shopping and stroller shopping and told Louise she was crazy to even consider a cloth diaper service, and discussed feeding techniques and vaccinations and a million decisions Louise would have to make, and bought snot suckers and diapers and onesies, and receiving blankets and changing pads and wipes, and rash cream and burp cloths and rattles and night-lights, and Louise would've thought they'd bought way too much if her mother hadn't said, "You've hardly bought anything at all."

She couldn't even blame them for having a hard time with the whole Ian issue.

"Married or not, we have to meet his family," her mom said. "We're going to be co-grandparents."

"I haven't told him yet," Louise said. "I'm barely eleven weeks."

"Well, you're not getting any less pregnant," her mom pointed out.

"There are tangible financial benefits to marriage," her dad added. "You're sure you don't want to reconsider?"

Louise did not want to reconsider.

Ian could be funny, he was smart, and he made an obscenely high income curating rare vinyl for rich people in the Bay Area who yearned for their childhoods. He'd put together a complete collection of original pressing Beatles LPs for the fourth-largest shareholder at Facebook and found the bootleg of a Grateful Dead concert where a Twitter board member had proposed to his first wife. Louise couldn't believe how much they paid him for this.

On the other hand, when she suggested they should take a break he'd taken that as his cue to go down on one knee in the atrium of the San Francisco Museum of Modern Art and propose. He'd been so upset when she said no that she'd finally had pity sex with him, which was how she came to be in her current condition.

When Ian had proposed, he'd been wearing his vintage Nirvana *In Utero* T-shirt with a hole in the collar that had cost him four hundred dollars. He spent thousands every year on sneakers, which he insisted on calling "kicks." He checked his phone when she talked about her day, made fun of her when she mixed up the Rolling Stones and The Who, and said, "Are you sure?" whenever she ordered dessert.

"Dad," Louise said. "Ian's not ready to be a parent."

"Who is?" her mom asked.

But Louise knew Ian *really* wasn't ready.

Every family visit lasts three days too long, and by the end of the week Louise was counting the hours until she could be alone in her apartment again. The day before her parents' flight home, she holed up in her bedroom "doing email" while her mom took off her earrings to take a nap and her dad left to find a copy of the *Financial Times*. If they could do this until lunch, then go on a walk around the Presidio, then dinner, Louise figured everything would be fine.

Louise's body had other plans. She felt hungry now. She needed hard-boiled eggs now. She had to get up and go to the kitchen now. So she crept into the living room in her socks, trying not to wake her mom because she couldn't handle another conversation about why she wouldn't let her hair grow out, or why she should move back to Charleston, or why she should start drawing again.

Her mom lay asleep on the couch, on one side, a yellow blanket pulled up to her waist. The late-morning light brought out her skeleton, the tiny lines around her mouth, her thinning hair, her slack cheeks. For the first time in her life, Louise knew what her mother would look like dead.

"I love you," her mom said without opening her eyes.

Louise froze.

"I know," she said after a moment.

"No," her mom said, "you don't."

Louise waited for her to add something, but her mom's breathing deepened, got regular, and turned into a snore.

Louise continued into the kitchen. Had she overheard half of a dream conversation? Or did her mom mean Louise didn't know she loved her? Or how much she loved her? Or she wouldn't understand how much her mom loved her until she had a daughter of her own?

She worried at it while she ate her hard-boiled egg. Was her mom talking about her living in San Francisco? Did she think Louise had moved this far away to put distance between them? Louise had moved here for school, then stayed for work, although when you grew up with all your friends telling you how cool your mom was and even your exes asked about her when you bumped into them, you needed some distance if you wanted to live your own life, and sometimes even three

4

thousand miles didn't feel like enough to Louise. She wondered if her mom somehow knew.

Then there was her brother. Mark's name had only come up twice on this visit and Louise knew it ate at her mom that the two of them didn't have a "natural" relationship, but, to be honest, she didn't want a relationship with her brother, natural or otherwise. In San Francisco, she could pretend she was an only child.

Louise knew she was a typical oldest sibling, a cookie-cutter first child. She'd read the articles and scanned the listicles, and every single trait applied to her: reliable, structured, responsible, hardworking. She'd even seen it classified as a disorder—Oldest Sibling Syndrome—and that made her wonder what Mark's disorder was. Terminal Assholism, most likely.

When people asked why she didn't speak to her brother, Louise told them the story of Christmas 2016, when her mom spent all day cooking but Mark insisted they meet him for dinner at P. F. Chang's, where he showed up late, drunk, tried to order the entire menu, then passed out at the table.

"Why do you let him act like that?" Louise had asked.

"Try to be more understanding of your brother," her mom had said.

Louise understood her brother plenty. She won awards. Mark struggled through high school. She got a master's in design. Mark dropped out of college his freshman year. She built products that people used every day, including part of the user interface for the latest iteration of the iPhone. He was on a mission to get fired from every bar in Charleston. He only lived twenty minutes away from their parents but refused to lift a finger to help out.

No matter what he did, her parents lavished Mark with praise. He rented a new apartment and they acted like he brought down the Berlin Wall. He bought a truck for five hundred dollars and got it running again and he may as well have landed on the moon. When Louise won

5

the Industrial Designers Society of America Graduate Student Merit Award she gave the trophy to her parents to thank them. They put it in the closet.

"Your brother is going to be hurt we have that out for you and nothing for him," her mom had said.

Louise knew that her not speaking to Mark was the eternal elephant in the room, the invisible ghost at the table, the phantom strain on every interaction with her parents, especially with her mom, who hated what she called "unpleasantness." Her mom was always "up," she was always "on," and while Louise didn't see anything wrong with being happy, her mom's enforced happiness seemed pathological. She avoided hard conversations about painful subjects. She had a Christian puppet ministry and acted like she was always onstage. The few times she lost it as a mother she'd snap, "You're embarrassing me!" as if being embarrassed was the worst possible thing that could happen to someone.

Maybe that's why she was so certain about her decision to have this baby. Becoming a mother would allow her and her mom to share something just between them. It would bring them closer together. She suspected all the things that annoyed her about her mom were exactly the things that would make her an incredible grandmother.

As Louise brushed eggshell off the counter, she thought that shared motherhood might form a bridge between them, and gradually the walls Louise had needed to protect herself would come down. It wouldn't happen overnight, but that was okay. They'd have a lifetime to adjust to each other's new roles—a daughter becoming a mother, a mother becoming a grandmother. They would have years.

As it turned out, she got five.

DENIAL

Chapter 2

The call came as Louise desperately tried to convince her daughter that she was not going to like *The Velveteen Rabbit*.

"We just got all those new library books," she said. "Don't you want—"

"*Velverdeen Rabbit*," Poppy insisted.

"It's scarier than *The Muppet Christmas Carol*," Louise told her. "Remember how scary that was when the door knocker turned into the man's face?"

"I want *Velverdeen Rabbit*," Poppy said, her voice firm.

Louise knew she should take the path of least resistance and just read Poppy *The Velveteen Rabbit*, but that would happen over her dead body. She should have checked the package before letting Poppy open it, because of course her mom hadn't sent the check for Dinosaur Dig Summer Camp like she'd promised, but she had randomly sent Poppy a copy of *The Velveteen Rabbit* because she thought it was Louise's favorite book.

It was not Louise's favorite book. It was the source of Louise's childhood nightmares. The first time her mom had read it to her she'd been Poppy's age and she'd burst into tears when the Rabbit got taken outside to be burned.

"I know," her mom had said, completely misreading the situation. "It's my favorite book, too."

The book's emotional cruelty made five-year-old Louise's stomach hurt: the thoughtless Boy who abused his toys, the needy toys who pathologically craved his approval no matter how much he neglected them, the remote and fearsome Nana, the bullying rabbits living in the wild. But her mom kept picking it for her bedtime story, oblivious to the fact that Louise would lie rigid while she read, hands gripping the sheet, staring at the ceiling as her mom did all the voices.

It was a master class in acting, a star turn by Nancy Joyner, and getting to deliver this performance was the real reason her mom kept picking the book. By the end, they'd both be crying, but for very different reasons.

"Does it hurt?" asked the Rabbit.

"Sometimes," said the Skin Horse. "When you are Real, you don't mind being hurt."

Louise had dated a girl at Berkeley who had that exact quote tattooed on her forearm and she wasn't surprised when she found out that she gave herself tattoos with a sewing needle taped to a BIC pen.

The Velveteen Rabbit confused masochism with love, it wallowed in loneliness, and what kind of awful thing was a Skin Horse, anyway?

Louise wouldn't make the same mistake with Poppy. There would be no *Velveteen Rabbit* in this house, even if she had to fight dirty.

"You're going to hurt the feelings of all those new library books," Louise said, and instantly Poppy's eyes got wide. "They're going to be sad you didn't want to read them first. You're going to make them cry."

Lying to Poppy felt awful, pretending inanimate objects had feelings felt manipulative, but every time Louise did it she felt less guilty. Her mom had manipulated them throughout their childhoods with impossible promises and flat-out lies (*elves are real but you'll only see one if you're absolutely quiet for this entire car ride*; *I'm allergic to dogs so we can't have one*) and she'd vowed to always be honest and straightforward with her own child. Of course, the second Poppy turned out to be an early talker, Louise had adjusted her approach, but she didn't rely on it nearly as much as her mother. That was important.

"They're really going to cry?" Poppy asked.

Dammit, Mom.

"Yes," Louise said. "And their pages are going to get all wet."

Which, thank God, is when her ringtone activated, playing the hysteric escalating major chords of "Summit" with its frantic bird whistles, which meant the call came from family. She looked at her screen, expecting it to read "Mom&Dad Landline" or "Aunt Honey." Instead, it said "Mark."

Her hands got cold.

He needs money, Louise thought. *He's in San Francisco and he needs a place to stay. He's been arrested and Mom and Dad finally put their foot down.*

"Mark," she said, answering, feeling her pulse snap in her throat. "Is everything all right?"

"You need to sit down," he said.

Automatically, she stood up.

"What happened?" she asked.

"Don't freak out," he said.

She started to freak out.

"What did you do?" she asked.

"Mom and Dad are in a better place," he said.

"What do you mean?"

"I mean," he said, and carefully put his next sentence together. "They're not suffering anymore."

"I just talked to them on Tuesday," Louise said. "They weren't suffering on Tuesday. You need to tell me what's happening."

"I'm trying!" he snapped, and his words sounded mushy. "Jesus, I'm sorry I'm not doing it the right way. I'm sure you'd be perfect at this. Mom and Dad are dead."

The lights went out all over Northern California. They went out across the bay. They went dark in Oakland and Alameda. Darkness rolled across the Bay Bridge, and Yerba Buena turned as black as the water lapping at its shores. The lights went out in the ferry building, the Tenderloin, and the Theater District; darkness advanced on Louise, street by street, from the Mission to the park to her building, the apartment downstairs, the front hall. The entire world went black except for a single spotlight shining down on Louise, standing in her living room, gripping her phone.

"No," she said, because Mark was wrong about things all the time. He'd once invested in a snake farm.

"They got T-boned on the corner of Coleman and McCants by some asshole in an SUV," Mark said. "I'm already talking to a lawyer. He thinks because it was Mom *and* Dad we're looking at a huge settlement."

This doesn't make any sense, Louise thought.

"This doesn't make any sense," she said.

"Dad was in the passenger seat so, you know, he got it the worst," Mark continued. "Mom was driving, which she totally shouldn't have been doing because, dude, you know how she is at night and it was pouring down rain. The car rolled and it sliced her arm off at the shoulder. It's horrible. She died in the ambulance. I find knowing these details makes it easier."

"Mark . . ." Louise said, and she needed to breathe, she couldn't breathe.

"Listen," he said, soft and slurred. "I get it. You're where I was earlier, but it's important to think of them as energy. They didn't suffer, right? Because our bodies are just vessels for our energy and energy can't feel pain."

Louise's knuckles tightened around her phone.

"Are you drunk?"

He immediately got defensive, which meant yes.

"This isn't an easy call for me," he said, "but I wanted to reach out and tell you that everything is going to be okay."

"I need to call someone," Louise said, feeling desperate. "I need to call Aunt Honey."

"Call whoever you want," Mark said, "but I want you to know that everything really is going to be okay."

"Mark," Louise snapped, "we haven't spoken in three years and you get drunk and call and tell me Mom and Dad are . . ." She became conscious of Poppy and lowered her voice. ". . . are not doing well but it's okay because they're energy? It's not okay."

"You should have a drink, too," he said.

"When did it happen?"

Silence on his end of the phone. Then:

"Those details don't matter . . ."

That triggered her internal alarms.

"Yes, they do."

He made it sound casual.

"Like yesterday around two in the morning. I've been dealing with a lot."

"Forty-one hours?" she said, doing the math.

Her parents had been dead for almost two days and she'd been walking around like nothing happened because Mark couldn't be bothered to pick up the phone. She hung up.

She looked at Poppy kneeling on the floor by the piano bench whispering to her library books and petting them, and she saw her mom. Poppy had her mom's blond hair, her delicately pointed chin, her enormous brown eyes, her undersized frame. Louise wanted to swoop down, gather her up, bury her face in the sweet smell of her, but that was the kind of grand theatrical gesture her mom favored. Her mom would never think that it might scare Poppy or make her feel unsafe.

"Was that Granny?" Poppy asked, because she adored her grandmother and had learned to recognize the family ringtone.

"It was just Aunt Honey," Louise lied, barely holding herself together. "And I need to call your grandmother. You stay here and watch one episode of *PAW Patrol*, and when you're done we'll make a special dinner."

Poppy bounced up. She was never allowed to use the iPad by herself, so the exciting new privilege distracted her from her sad library books and from who'd been on the phone. Louise got her settled on the sofa with the iPad, walked to her bedroom, and closed the door.

Mark had made a mistake. He was drunk. He had once invested thousands of dollars in a Christmas tree factory in Mexico that turned out to be a scam because he had a "gut feeling" about it. Louise needed to know for sure. She didn't think she could stand it if she called home and no one answered, so she called Aunt Honey.

Her fingers wouldn't go where she wanted and kept opening her weather app, but finally she managed to make them tap on Aunt Honey's number in her contacts.

Her aunt (great-aunt, technically) picked up on the first ring.

"What?" she barked through phlegm-clogged vocal cords.

"Aunt Honey," Louise said, then her throat closed and she couldn't say anything.

"Oh, Lulu," Aunt Honey croaked, and those two words contained all the heartbreak in the world.

Everything went very quiet. Louise's nervous system made a high-pitched tone in her ears. She didn't know what to say next.

"I don't know what to do," she finally said, her voice small and miserable.

"Sweetheart," Aunt Honey said, "pack a nice dress. And come home."

Louise's mom also had a pathological inability to discuss death. When their uncle Arthur had a heart attack and drove his riding lawn mower through a greenhouse, she'd told Mark and Louise that she and their dad were going to Myrtle Beach for a vacation, then parked them with Aunt Honey. When Sue Estes's older sister died of leukemia in fifth grade, Louise's mom had told her she was too young to go to the funeral. Her friendship with Sue was never the same after that. Louise's mom had claimed to be allergic to all pets, including goldfish, for their entire childhoods, and it wasn't until Louise got out of grad school that her mom revealed she'd simply never wanted anything in the house that might die.

"It would have upset you and your brother too much," she'd explained.

When Louise had Poppy, she vowed to be honest about death. She knew that stating the facts plainly would be the best way for Poppy to understand that death was part of life. She would answer all Poppy's questions with absolute honesty, and if she didn't know something they'd figure out the answer together.

"I'm going to Charleston tomorrow," Louise told Poppy that night, sitting on the story-time chair beside her bed, in the glow of the plastic goose lamp. "And I want you to understand why. Your grandmother and grandfather had a very bad accident." Louise saw safety glass exploding, metal tearing and twisting. "And their bodies got hurt very badly. They got hurt so badly that they stopped working. And your grandmother and grandfather died."

Poppy shot up in bed, smashing into Louise like a cannonball, wrapping her arms around her ribs too tight, bursting into a long, keening wail.

"No!" Poppy screamed. "No! *No!*"

Louise tried to explain that it was okay, that she was sad, too, that they would be sad together and that being sad when someone died was normal, but every time she started to speak, Poppy wiped her face back and forth against Louise like she was trying to scrape it off, screaming, *"No! No! No!"*

Finally, when she realized Poppy wasn't going to stop anytime soon, Louise eased herself up onto the bed and held her daughter in her arms until Poppy cried herself to sleep.

So much for explaining death the healthy way.

Louise held Poppy's feverish, limp body for hours, wishing harder than she'd ever wished before that for just sixty seconds someone would hold her, but no one holds moms.

She remembered her mom holding her in her lap while they sat in Dr. Rector's waiting room, where it smelled like alcohol swabs and finger pricks, distracting Louise by telling her what all the other children were there for.

"That little boy over there?" her mom had said, pointing to a six-year-old picking his nose. "He picked his nose so much that all he can smell now are his fingerprints. They're getting him a nose transplant. And that one chewing his mother's purse strap? They accidentally swapped his brain for a dog's. That little girl? She ate apple seeds and they're growing apple trees inside her tummy."

"Is she going to be all right?" Louise asked.

"Of course," her mom said. "The apples are delicious. That's why they're here. They want Dr. Rector to plant some oranges, too."

Her mom remembered everyone's birthday, everyone's anniversary, everyone's first day at a new job, everyone's due date. She remembered every single cousin or nephew or church person's entire life calendar like it was her job. She wrote notes, she dropped off pies, and Louise couldn't remember a single birthday when she hadn't picked up the phone and heard her mom singing the happy birthday song on the other end.

That was all over now. The cards on every occasion, the phone calls on every birthday, the Christmas newsletter going out to however many hundreds of people—none of it would ever happen again.

Her mom had opinions. So many opinions that sometimes Louise felt like she couldn't breathe. *The Velveteen Rabbit* was Louise's favorite book, you should never throw anything away because it could always be reused, children shouldn't be allowed to wear black until they're eighteen, women shouldn't cut their hair short until they turn fifty, Louise worked too hard and should move back to Charleston, Mark was a misunderstood genius simply waiting to find his place in the world.

All those opinions, all her crafting, all her notes and phone calls, her constant need to be the center of attention, her exhausting need to be liked by everyone, her mood swings from euphoric highs to depressed lows, it made her mom who she was, but at an early age it also taught Louise that her mom was unreliable in a way her father was not.

Louise had never seen her dad upset in his life. In middle school she'd recorded *Nirvana Unplugged* over the video of his paper presentation at the Southern Regional Science Association. When he found out, he'd taken a long moment to absorb the information and then said, "Well, that'll teach me to have a big head."

When she wanted to know about electricity he'd showed her how to use an ohmmeter and they'd gone around the house sticking its test probes into wall sockets and touching them to batteries. She'd used her

Christmas money that year to go to RadioShack and buy Mims's *Getting Started in Electronics*, and she and her dad had taught themselves to solder, making moisture detectors and tone generators together in the garage.

Louise slid out of Poppy's bed, careful not to wake her, and crept into the kitchen. There was something she needed to do.

She stood in the dark and scrolled through her contacts until she found "Mom&Dad Landline." She looked away while she got her breathing under control, then touched the number.

They still had an answering machine.

"You've reached the Joyner residence," her father's recorded voice said in exactly the same rhythm she'd heard for decades. She knew every pause, every change in inflection in this entire message. She mouthed along with it silently. "We're unwilling or unable to answer the phone right now. Please leave a clear and detailed message after the tone and we'll call you back at our earliest convenience."

The machine beeped, and across the country, in her parents' kitchen, Louise heard it click to "record."

"Mom," Louise said, her breath high and tight in her throat. "Dad, hey. I was just thinking of you guys. I wanted to call and say hi and see if you're there. Mark called tonight and . . . if you're there . . . if you're there, please pick up." She waited a full ten seconds.

They didn't pick up.

"I miss you both and I hope you're okay and . . ." She didn't know what else to say. "And I love you. I love you both so much. Okay, bye."

She went to hang up, then pressed the phone to her mouth again. "Please call me back."

She hit disconnect, then stood alone in the dark. A sudden sense of certainty filled her entire body and a clear voice spoke inside her head for the first time since it had told her she was pregnant with Poppy:

I'm an orphan now.

Chapter 3

Leaving Poppy with Ian turned out to be a disaster. Poppy clung to her neck at the airport, refusing to let go.

"I don't want you to go," she wailed.

"I don't want to go, either," Louise said, "but I have to."

"I don't want you to die!" Poppy wailed.

"I'm not going to die," Louise said, unwrapping Poppy's arms from around her neck. "Not for a long time."

She started transferring her to Ian.

"You're going to go away and never come back!" Poppy hyperventilated, clinging to Louise. "You're going to die like Granny and Grandpop!"

Ian took Poppy, put one hand on the back of her head, and pressed her face to his chest.

"You said they d-i-e-d?" he asked.

"I had to say something."

"Jesus, Louise. She's five."

"I—" Louise started to explain.

"Just go," Ian said. "I've got her."

"But—" she tried again.

"You're not helping," he said.

"Bye, sweetie," Louise said, trying to kiss the top of Poppy's head.

Poppy pressed her face into Ian's chest and Louise wanted to say something to make it all better, but all she could do was pick up her bag, turn her back, and walk away toward the big door marked *All Gates*, feeling like she'd failed at being a mother, wondering how she'd screwed this up so badly, trying to remember how her mom had explained death to her. Then she remembered: she hadn't.

She felt slow and stupid boarding her flight. She kept wanting to apologize to everyone.

I'm sorry I can't find my boarding pass, but my parents are dead.

I'm sorry I stepped on your laptop bag, but my parents are dead.

I'm sorry I sat in the wrong seat, but my parents are dead.

The idea felt too big to fit inside her head. It was the thought that blotted out all other thoughts. Before takeoff she Googled "what to do when your parents die" and was overwhelmed by articles demanding that she "find the will and executor," "meet with a trusts and estates lawyer," "contact a CPA," "secure the property," "forward mail," "make funeral, burial, or cremation arrangements," "get copies of death certificate."

She wondered if she was supposed to cry. She hadn't cried yet. She felt like she'd feel better if she cried.

Whenever Louise didn't know what to do she made a list. As a single mother with a full-time job, lists were her friends. She opened Listr on her phone, started a new list called "To Do in Charleston," and hit the plus sign to create the first item, then she stared at the blank line for a long time. She tried to herd her thoughts into some kind of order, but they kept slipping away. Finally, frustrated, she closed the app. She tried to sleep but it felt like fire ants were crawling all over her brain, so she pulled out her phone again, opened Listr, hit the plus sign, and stared at the first blank line until she closed it again.

At some point the plane got cold and her head dropped forward, then snapped back, then she opened her eyes and felt sweat cooling on the back of her neck. Rivulets of sweat tickled her ribs. She didn't know what time it was. The girl next to her was asleep. A flight attendant walked by fast. The pilot made an announcement. They were landing in Charleston. She was home.

Louise walked off the plane into a world that felt too bright, too loud, too hot, too colorful. Palmetto trees and pineapple logos and walls of sunny windows and giant ads featuring the Charleston skyline at sunset all burned into her grainy eyes.

She rented a little blue Kia from Avis and drove over the new bridge to the SpringHill Suites in Mount Pleasant. SpringHill Suites processed her into their system right away and suddenly she found herself standing in a putty-colored room with peach highlights, a pineapple-patterned bedspread, and a print of palmetto trees on the wall.

She looked down at her phone. Mark still hadn't called or texted even though she'd left him two messages the night before. Technically she'd hung up on him, but he had to cut her some slack because, after all, their parents had died. She looked at the lack of missed calls from Mark and felt disappointed but not surprised. She even felt a little relieved. She could handle it if he just showed up at the funeral and they shared a few stories, then went back to their separate lives. They had too much history to suddenly develop any kind of relationship now.

It wasn't even noon. She needed to do something. Her palms itched. Her skin felt clammy beneath her clothes. She wanted to get organized. She wanted to get things accomplished. She had to go somewhere. She needed to talk to someone, she needed to be around people who knew her mom and dad. She had to get to Aunt Honey's.

She got in her Kia and headed down Coleman toward the Ben Sawyer Bridge, and as she passed the hideous new development where the old Krispy Kreme used to be, she realized that she was about to drive through the intersection where her parents had died. The closer she got to the corner of Coleman and McCants, the more her foot eased off the accelerator, her speed dropping from thirty-five to thirty to just over twenty-five. She had one more traffic light. She should turn and take the connector to the Isle of Palms, but then it was too late and she was there.

Every detail leapt out at her in extreme close-up: shards of red plastic taillight scattered across the asphalt, safety glass catching the sun, a plastic Volvo hubcap crushed flat in the entrance to the Scotsman gas station. Her throat closed tight and she couldn't force air down past her chest. All the sound dropped out and her ears went *eeeeeee*. The sun got too bright, her peripheral vision blurred. The light changed. The driver behind her tapped his horn. Automatically she made a right-hand turn from the left-hand lane, not even looking for oncoming traffic, realizing as she did that someone might slam into her. She didn't care. She needed to get away from this intersection where her parents had died and see the house where they had lived.

No one hit her. She made it onto McCants and her heart rate slowed. Her chest unclenched as she came around the corner of their block, and as if a curtain was going up, she saw their old house.

Seeing it with fresh eyes, Louise saw it as it was, not dressed in its history and associations. Their little single-story brick rancher had been fine when their grandparents built it in 1951, but as the years passed, the houses around them added additions and screened-in back porches and white coats of paint over their bricks and glossy coats of black paint over their shutters, and every other house got bigger and more expensive while theirs turned into the shabbiest house on the block.

She pulled into the driveway and got out. Her rental car looked too bright and blue next to the dry front yard. The camellia bushes on either side of the front step looked withered. The windows were dirty, their screens blurry with grime. Dad hadn't put in the storm windows yet, which he always did by October, and no one had swept the roof, where dead pine needles clumped into thick orange continents. A limp seasonal flag showing a red candle and the word *Noel* hung on the front porch. It looked grimy.

The first blank line from Listr appeared inside her mind and filled itself out: *Walk through house.* She'd start here. Do a walk-through. Assess the situation. That made sense, but her feet didn't move. She didn't want to go inside. It felt like too much. She didn't want to see it so empty.

However, being a single mom had made Louise an expert at doing things she'd rather avoid. If she didn't rip off the Band-Aid and take care of business, who would? She forced her feet to walk across the dry grass, creaked open the screen door, and grabbed the front doorknob. It didn't turn. No keys. Maybe the back? She walked around the side of the house where the yellow grass faded to dirt, unlatched the waist-high chain-link gate, banged it wide with her hip, and slid through.

Mark's lumber sat abandoned in the middle of the backyard, a pile of once-yellow pine faded to gray. Louise remembered how excited her mom had been when Lowe's dropped it off for the deck Mark had promised to build back in 2017. It'd sat untouched ever since, killing the grass.

Not that there was much grass to kill. The backyard had been a blind spot in their family, a big weedy expanse of dirt and whatever mutant grass could survive without watering. Nothing significant grew out back except for a ridiculously tall pecan tree in the middle that was probably dead and a twisted cypress in the back corner, which had gone feral. A wall of unkillable bamboo separated them from their neighbors.

Louise grabbed the rattling old knob on the back door to the garage and her heart stopped. She expected it to be locked, but it turned beneath her hand and opened with a familiar fanfare of squeaky hinges. She made herself step inside.

Shadowy cousins and neighbors and aunts crowded the garage, drinking Coors the way they always did on Christmas Day, Bing Crosby playing on a boom box, the women smoking Virginia Slims, adding mentholated notes to the pink perfection of roasting Christmas ham. Louise's eyes adjusted to the gloom and the phantoms faded and the garage looked twice as empty as before.

She walked up the three brick steps to the kitchen door and froze.

She heard the muffled voice of a man speaking with confidence and authority from somewhere inside the house. Louise stared through the window in the middle of the door, peering past its sheer white curtain, trying to see who it was.

The brick-patterned linoleum floor unrolled past the counter separating the kitchen from the dining room and stopped at the far wall, where her mom's gallery of string art hung over the dining room table. Its plastic tablecloth got changed with the seasons, and right now it was red poinsettias for winter. The JCPenney chandelier hung overhead, the china hutch pressed itself into the corner, the chairs kept their backs to her.

The man continued talking from inside the house.

She could see a small slice of the front hall with its green wall-to-wall carpet but no people. A woman asked the man a question. Was Mark in there with a Realtor? Was he already taking stuff? Louise hadn't seen any cars parked outside but maybe he'd parked around the corner. He could be sneaky.

She carefully turned the latch. The door cracked its seal, then swung open, and the man's voice got louder. Louise stepped inside and eased the door closed behind her, then crept forward, ears straining, trying to figure out what he was saying. Details registered automatically—her mom's purse sitting on the end of the counter, the answering machine blinking its red light for *1 New Message*, the smell of sun-warmed Yankee Candle—then she reached the dining room and stopped.

The man's voice sounded big and small at the same time and Louise realized it came from the living room TV. Her scalp tightened. She looked into the front hall. To the left, it got dark, leading deeper into the house. To the right was the living room, where someone was watching TV. Louise held her breath and stepped around the corner.

Hundreds of her mom's dolls stared at her. Clown dolls on top of the sofa, a Harlequin wedged against one of its arms, German Dolly-Faced Dolls crowded a shelf over their heads, a swarm of dolls stared through the glass doors of the doll cabinet against the far wall. On top of the doll cabinet stood a diorama of three taxidermied squirrels. The TV played the Home Shopping Network to two enormous French Bébé dolls sitting side by side in her dad's brown velour easy chair.

Mark and Louise.

That's what her mom had called them when she bought these ugly, expensive, three-foot-tall dolls, with their hard, arrogant faces and coarse, chopped hair.

No matter where you two go, I can keep my precious babies with me forever, she'd said.

The girl sat stiffly in her layered summer frock, arms by her sides, legs sticking straight out in front, strawberry-stained lips puckered into a pout, eyes blank, staring at the TV. The boy wore a navy blue Little Lord Fauntleroy jacket with a white Peter Pan collar and short pants, and his blond hair looked like it had been hacked into a pageboy with a pair of dull scissors. Between them lay the remote. They'd always creeped Louise out.

She looked down the hall but didn't see any other signs of life—the bathroom door was open, the bedroom doors were closed, no lights were on—so she made herself pluck the remote from between doll Mark and doll Louise, trying not to touch their clothes, and turned off the TV.

Silence rushed in around her, and she stood alone in the house full of dolls.

Growing up, her mom's dolls had mostly faded into the background. If a friend came over and said something like, "Your mom has a lot of dolls," Louise would say, "You should see her puppets," and then she'd show them her mom's workroom, but mostly they went in one eye and out the other. A few times, however, like her first Thanksgiving back from college, or right this minute, she really noticed them. At those times, the house felt too crowded with dolls; there were too many unblinking eyes staring, sucking up all the oxygen, watching everything she did.

She tried to look anywhere else and immediately saw her dad's aluminum medical cane lying on the wall-to-wall carpet in front of the TV. It was the only thing out of place in the entire room. It should have been with him in the car.

After he'd retired from the Economics Department at the College of Charleston, her dad kept finding ways to return to campus, and a year ago he'd been walking across the quad to an advisory committee meeting when a student shouted, "Professor Joyner!" and threw him a Frisbee. He'd jumped to catch it—a spectacular leap according to everyone who saw it—but the problem came with the landing. Even then, the doctors thought the real damage was done when the golf cart from public safety arrived and ran over his leg. The end result: a trimalleolar fracture and an ankle dislocation that cut off the blood supply to his foot. Three plates, fourteen pins, one bone infection, and three surgeries later they'd let him out of the hospital. Then came eight weeks of non-weight-bearing recovery, four weeks with crutches, then a CAM boot and cane for another eight weeks. While wearing the CAM boot he developed pain in his right hip, which required more PT, more MRIs, more talk of surgery.

All told, he was out of action for ten months, during which time their mom gave up her puppet ministry to sort out his pain pills, take him to PT, do PT with him, spend time with him so he didn't get bored. Their dad had never even had a bad cold as far as Louise could remember, so this had been a seismic disruption. When Louise flew home he looked like he'd aged twenty years in a month, going from restlessly retired to complete invalid almost overnight.

He must have been watching TV when they got in the car that night and they'd forgotten to turn it off, which did not sound like her dad at all because he followed everyone around the house all the time turning the lights out after them. He must have dropped his cane, which seemed unlikely because she didn't think he could walk very far without it.

Louise's knees popped as she squatted to pick up the cane, and that's when she saw the hammer. It lay on the other side of her dad's easy chair. She got on her hands and knees to pick it up and saw the long chip of raw yellow wood along the edge of the coffee table. It looked like it had been made by the hammer.

The cane, the hammer, the TV being on, the dolls in her dad's chair . . . it all felt wrong. She looked at the dolls. Whatever had happened, they'd seen it all, but they weren't about to tell.

Louise propped her dad's cane by his chair and placed the hammer on the kitchen counter before heading down the hall to the bedrooms, her feet bouncing on the green nylon wall-to-wall carpet woven for durability and sculpted into lily pads. She passed Mark's closed bedroom door, then stopped at her mom's workroom. It sat between Mark's and Louise's bedrooms, more of a large sewing room really, and over the door she'd tacked a card that read *Nancy's Workshop* in cursive with a rainbow. Every night, while Mark and Louise fought over whose turn it was to clear the table or load the dishwasher, their mom retreated behind this door. She'd come out to say good night or to tell them bedtime stories, but for years Louise fell asleep listening to her mom's sewing machine chugging away on the other side of the wall, smelling the burning-plastic stink of her hot-glue gun.

She hesitated, her hand hovering over the doorknob, and decided she wasn't ready to face it yet. She turned and continued down the hall, then her attention snapped into focus and she stopped. Something felt off.

She scanned the walls with the eyes of an expert art appraiser, taking in the endless family photos in big frames, little frames, round frames, rectangular frames; her mom's art (lots of her mom's art); framed diplomas; framed programs from Mark's high school plays; framed class pictures; framed graduation pictures; framed vacation pictures: the Joyner National Portrait Gallery as curated by their mom.

Something felt wrong. The silence of the house stretched her nerves tight. Then she realized she didn't see the string.

They used to tuck the white string that pulled down the attic stairs behind a corner of a picture of her dad receiving an award from the National Economic Freedom Forum, otherwise it bonked you in the head when you walked by. It was gone. Louise looked up and her shoulders twitched. High in the shadows someone had done an ugly job of nailing the attic hatch closed, hammering every piece of scrap wood they could find over it and hacking off the pull-down string at its base.

It reminded Louise of the one zombie movie Ian had made her watch where people boarded up their windows to keep the zombies out. Had the springs broken and this was her dad's terrible attempt at repair? Were there raccoons in the attic and he'd done this to keep them from getting into the house? Had taking care of her dad been too hard for her mom? Had the screens gotten dirty and had raccoons gotten in the attic and this was the best she could do? Louise felt guilty for not noticing things were getting this bad.

Standing under the boarded attic hatch made her nervous, so she headed for the end of the hall and her parents' closed bedroom door, and stopped when she saw the big vent at the end of the hall. Its grille had fallen off, exposing the big square chopped into the drywall. She picked up the vent cover and leaned it against the wall. Had the raccoons in the attic gotten into the ducts? Had squirrels?

It felt wrong. The boarded-up hatch, the busted vent, the hammer, the cane, the TV. Her mom's purse on the end of the counter. Something had happened right before her mom and dad had left their house for the last time. Something bad.

Her parents' closed bedroom door and her old bedroom door faced each other and she decided to finish her walk-through and get out of there. She reached for the knob to her parents' bedroom door and stopped. She'd open it and the room would be empty and that would feel too final. She turned and pushed open her old bedroom door instead.

Her dad had converted it into his computer room long ago. The ancient family Dell stood on her old desk, awash in a sea of her dad's paperwork and bills. Louise automatically started to sort them. She couldn't remember how many times she'd sorted out her dad's desk. Almost every time she came home she hadn't been able to sleep until she'd gotten his desk in order, and every time she came back it had reverted to her dad's cryptic system of filing by piling.

Her movements slowed as she realized that this time his desk wouldn't revert. This time, the papers would stay where she left them. Her dad would never scramble his paperwork again. She'd never get another out-of-the-blue, impossible-to-understand text from her mom full of random emojis and arbitrary capitalization. No more spontaneous presents for Poppy in the mail.

Louise dropped the bills back on his desk and looked at the shelves over her bed: her Wando yearbooks, the lanyard with her Governor's School ID, her Pinewood Derby trophy from Girl Scouts, and her old stuffed animals. Red Rabbit, Buffalo Jones, Dumbo, and Hedgie Hoggie stared down at her from their shelf. She'd outgrown sleeping with them when she was five and moved them onto this shelf, where they'd become a constant, silent presence in her life. They looked so patient. They looked like they understood.

She pulled Buffalo Jones down and hugged him to her chest as she curled up on her bed, wrapping her body around his soft, uncomplaining presence. She buried her face in his white fur. He smelled like Febreze, and she felt a pang that her mom still took the trouble to keep him clean.

She'd loved these guys so much as a kid, practicing her splinting techniques on them when she was working on her first-aid badge for Girl Scouts, insisting her mom kiss each and every one of them good night even after they'd moved to the shelf. They didn't feel cold and silent like her mom's weird dolls. They felt like old friends waiting for her to come home.

Whenever Louise got anxious, her dad always said, *You know, Louise, statistically, and there's a lot of variance in these numbers, but in general, from a strictly scientific point of view, everything turns out okay an improbable number of times.*

Not this time, she thought. *This time, nothing's ever going to be okay again.*

She hugged Buffalo Jones tight and felt something break inside her chest and tears built behind her eyes, and she grabbed onto that feeling and let it carry her away as she realized that, finally, she was going to cry.

In the living room, the TV turned itself on.

Chapter 4

. . . five easy Flexpay installments," a man said, his voice full of excitement. "Or a onetime payment of $136.95 gets you this beautiful, hand-crafted Scarlett O'Hara collectible doll, with her green velvet party gown, her hoop skirt, and this beautiful display case at no . . . added . . . cost."

Louise's body went rigid.

"That's an amazing deal, Michael," a woman cheered. "These dolls are moving fast, so if you want this incredible offer for this onetime price, you need to call now."

Louise made herself stand up. She forced herself to walk to the door. She realized she still had Buffalo Jones in her arms so she put him back on her bed, then peeked around the corner into the hall. Empty.

It's on a timer. The programming has a bug. Just go out there and turn it off.

She drew her head up, pretending to be annoyed so she didn't feel scared, and walked toward the living room fast, the TV getting louder with every step. She entered the room and saw the Home Shopping

Network playing for the blank-faced Mark and Louise dolls in her dad's easy chair. She snatched the remote off the chair and turned the TV off.

The room full of dolls held its breath. She tossed the remote back onto the chair and stayed for a moment, making sure the TV didn't come back on again. The Mark and Louise dolls looked snotty and bored, but of course she knew she was projecting that onto them. Dolls didn't change their expressions.

She should get going to Aunt Honey's. She turned and headed back to her bedroom. She'd grab Buffalo Jones and bring him home for Poppy. She could show him to her when they FaceTimed and—

". . . want you to see this face, because it has the cool touch of porcelain but it's actually crafted from high-quality vinyl . . ."

Louise froze halfway down the hall, shoulders hunched. She felt herself flush with irritation and embraced it so she didn't feel her fear wriggling underneath. She spun on the balls of her feet and marched back to the living room. The Mark and Louise dolls hadn't moved. They stared straight ahead at the TV. Louise snapped it off with the remote, then knelt beside the television and yanked its plug out of the wall.

In the sudden silence, the dolls felt restless. The ones pressing against the glass doors of the doll cabinet felt like they'd just stopped moving. One of the German Dolly-Faced Dolls on the shelf looked like she'd frozen in the middle of lifting one arm. A clown on the back of the couch looked like he could barely hold in his giggles. They were patient. They were sly. They outnumbered her.

She had to do something to show herself (*them*) she wasn't afraid, so she grabbed the giant Mark and Louise dolls by their arms and lugged them into the kitchen, then out the door to the garage. They were heavier than she expected. She found a clear space on one of the big plywood shelves that wrapped around two sides of the garage and sat them on it.

Her tiny thrill of victory disappeared as the Louise doll's hair began to quiver. The Mark doll's hair started to vibrate. His whole body shook until he tipped over on one side, and the air throbbed now, so loud the garage rattled, and Louise turned into the noise and saw through the slit windows on the door the front grille of a giant red truck coming right for her, stopping just inches before it crushed her Kia. It sat there, rumbling.

She walk-ran back through the house to the front door, turned the thumb lock, and stepped outside to see a flatbed truck in their driveway with an enormous red dumpster on top with *Agutter Clutter* painted on its side. Behind it, a busted little Honda pulled up and parked on the edge of the grass, and men in white paper hazmat suits got out.

The truck engine shut off with a metallic rattle and in the sudden silence she heard a crow caw. A big man in street clothes swung down out of the cab and came toward her holding an aluminum clipboard in one hand.

"Agutter Clutter," he said. "You the homeowner?"

"I'm . . ." Louise didn't know exactly how to answer this question. Her parents were the homeowners. Her parents were dead. "I am."

"Roland Agutter," he said, holding out his hand.

Louise put her hand in his and he gave it a squeeze.

"I'm sorry," Louise said, pulling her hand away. "You're here for?"

"Clearing out the property," Roland Agutter said. "I understand that what you've got here is a classic hoarder-type situation, but don't panic. We've seen worse, believe me. What we do is we start at one end of the dwelling and move forward like a big broom, pushing everything out the front door and right into the truck. End of the day, you'll see our taillights disappear and you won't believe it ever looked like such a dump."

"This is my parents' house," Louise said.

Roland seamlessly switched tacks.

"Their lives probably got too big for the property," he said. "Seen it a million times. You'll want to do a walk-through before we start to make sure everything valuable got to their new place."

"They died," Louise said.

It was the first time she'd said it to a stranger. The words felt like rocks in her mouth.

"The Lord takes the best first," Roland Agutter said. "You can depend on my boys to be dainty as lambs. What we do, see, if we come across anything that looks like it has personal value, we put it in a plastic bag and leave it on the porch. You'd be amazed how many baby teeth we find. People don't always want them, but we still like to put them aside because they're technically human remains."

Louise looked at his boys. They did look dainty: three small Latin men with immaculate haircuts, standing in the driveway around their banged-up Honda, wearing white hazmat suits unzipped to their waists, ghost arms dangling behind them. One of them seemed to be in the middle of telling a really good story.

"Who hired you?" Louise asked.

Roland flipped open his aluminum clipboard.

"Joyner," he read. "Mr. Mark Joyner."

"I'm his sister," Louise said.

"Oh, yeah. He said to see you about payment."

"There's been some confusion," Louise began.

"Uh-oh," Roland said. "That's not good."

"Because we don't want everything our parents owned pushed out the front door like a broom and all our baby teeth left in a plastic bag on the porch. Our parents died three days ago, so if my brother told you to come here and throw everything away, then there's been a misunderstanding."

Which was when Mark's truck pulled up.

She and Roland watched him fuss with something in the passenger seat, then get out, slam his door, and walk across the dead lawn toward them. Seeing Mark always shocked Louise because it never matched the eternally sixteen-year-old Mark inside her head.

The Mark in front of her had a receding hairline and his gut had gotten bigger since the last time she'd seen him. He wore a King Missile T-shirt he'd had in high school, but it couldn't be the same one even though it was dirty enough to be, and he wore a flannel she thought he'd owned then, too. The biggest difference from the Mark in her memory were his terrible tattoos. A lopsided cartoon anchor on his left forearm copied from their dad's brother. An infinity sign that ended in a writing quill on the inside of his right forearm because he claimed to be a writer, even though there was no actual evidence for this. *Foxy* in sparkling cursive on the inside of his left wrist for Amanda Fox, his high school sweetheart and former fiancée, when they'd gotten back together after a breakup.

He had a pair of slot machine cherries on the side of his neck and the Japanese characters for (supposedly) *You will succeed in everything you do* running up the outside of his left calf. Beneath that King Missile T-shirt was a barcode from a pack of Marlboro Reds over his belly button from when he'd quit smoking, a phoenix at the base of his spine for when he'd gotten a job at Charleston Grill, *Amanda* on his right ankle from when he and Amanda Fox had gotten back together again, and a yin-yang symbol made of dolphins on his chest after he'd gone swimming with dolphins in Key West.

Louise felt petty, but the way her brother looked embarrassed her.

"Daylight's burning and there's a bunch of junk to dump," Mark told Roland, then gave her a glance. "Hey, Louse, you made it."

No hug, no handshake, no mention of their mom or dad.

"That 'junk' is everything Mom and Dad owned," Louise said. "We need to go through the house before you throw everything away."

"These guys are on the clock," Mark said. "I mean, I'd love to pore over Dad's 1984 tax returns and laugh and cry and tell family stories, but some of us have jobs. If you want, we can smudge it out with some sage afterward and get rid of all the bad vibes."

Roland's workers in their white hazmat suits turned to watch. Louise hated feeling like she was onstage but Mark took after their mom. He loved drama.

"Mom's dolls might be worth something to a collector," Louise said. "And the C of C probably wants dad's research. We can't let some random guy throw it all in the trash."

"I'm actually a fully bonded removal specialist," Roland said.

"I'm going to put the dolls on eBay," Mark said. "And Dad's last paper was on the economics of private railroads in the growth of the South Carolina textile industry from 1931 to 1955. I think the world can somehow stumble on without it. Right now, I need Roland's guys to help me get my lumber out of the backyard and into my truck. You think they can help me out?" he asked Roland. "It'll take five seconds."

"Mark," Louise said, putting all the love and patience and shared childhood memories she could muster into her voice. "You can't take everything Mom ever made, and all Dad's work, and family photos, and scrapbooks, and diaries, and clothes, and jewelry, and puppets, and dolls and throw it all in this guy's dumpster."

"They're pros," Mark said, turning to Roland Agutter. "You're not going to throw away anything valuable, right?"

"Anything we find that looks like it has financial, emotional, or legal value, we leave in a plastic bag on the porch," Roland Agutter said. "I told her that."

"But you might miss something," Louise said, and turned to Mark, trying to feel like the adult. "This is hard, Mark, but I'm here for two weeks. There's no hurry. Let's go through the house together, then have these guys come back."

"Listen, Louse," Mark said. "That house is Afghanistan. Once we go in, we're never getting out. How do we know what to throw away?

We don't. We're too close. And it's fucking spooky. These guys are here, they have the deposit, they know to box up all the dolls, so let's get her done. Clean break."

"I know you're upset and overwhelmed—" Louise started.

"Just because we shared a bathroom for fifteen years doesn't mean you know a thing about me," Mark cut her off. "My yoga instructor knows more about me than you do."

"You do yoga?" she asked, thrown.

"I've got a practice," he said. "Off and on. The point is, I knew you'd do this. I knew you'd show up and start telling everyone what to do."

"I'm not telling everyone what to do," Louise said, taking a breath.

"You're telling Roland not to go in the house," Mark said. "You're telling me we have to clean out the house together." He turned to Roland Agutter. "She's like Flossy Bossypants, right?"

"I don't know who that is," Roland said.

"One of my mom's puppets," Mark said. "Modeled after my sister." He turned back to Louise. "I'm handling this."

"Flossy Bossypants is not modeled after me," Louise said.

"According to Mom she is," Mark said. "Look, I know you need to be in charge, but I've taken care of this."

"Mark," Louise said, "let's slow down. We'll go to Aunt Honey's, okay? Everyone's out there. We can talk about the funeral."

"Stop telling me how to deal with things," Mark said. "Things are dealt with. I dealt with them."

"I think maybe I should get going," Roland Agutter said. "Give you folks some time to work out—"

"There's nothing to work out," Mark said. "Everything is worked out. Let's start filling bags."

"Thank you so much for understanding," Louise said to Roland Agutter.

"You've been three thousand miles away," Mark said. "While I've been here dealing with Mom and Dad being dead, so you don't get to suddenly parachute out of your nerd plane and start barking orders."

"Mark!" Louise barked, then immediately felt embarrassed. She took a breath and lowered her voice. "We need to calm down and have a real conversation before we clean out the house. We need to talk about arranging their funeral, all that stuff."

"I took care of their funeral," Mark said.

"We should have it on Sunday so everyone can come," Louise said. "They're at Stuhr's, right? I think Constance has a friend who works there."

"We're scattering their ashes at the beach Tuesday," Mark said.

"No, we're not," Louise said.

"I already arranged it with Daniel," Mark said.

"Who's Daniel?" Louise asked, feeling slow on the uptake.

"The funeral dude who ran Mom's credit card and is giving me their cremains on Monday at four thirty so we can scatter them on the beach Tuesday in a Hindu sunrise ritual based on the Asthi Visarjan."

"You're not doing that."

He walked across the yard toward his big red F-150. Not knowing what else to do, Louise followed. She felt full of helium. Her feet barely touched the yellowed grass. Mark opened the passenger door and took out a sheaf of green-edged forms. Louise floated to a stop in front of him.

"I had to drive up to Columbia to get the death certificates early this a.m.," Mark said, shaking the thick forms. "Thirteen of them. Cost me forty-eight dollars and that's not including gas, but Daniel said you need them for pretty much anything once someone dies and I could either drive up there now or wait a week. He tried to upsell me on a fancy urn when I signed the cremation contract but we're scattering them on the beach so the freebie's good, thanks. Learned that from Dad."

Louise looked at the contract with its receipt stapled to the front and the sheaf of death certificates and she thought about her parents' bodies in a refrigerator somewhere, and Mark signing a contract for them, haggling over their urn, and all of a sudden the front yard felt very far away.

"You can tell Aunt Honey it's at Station 18 at seven thirty a.m. Tuesday if they want to come," he said. "Get there early, 'cause I want to catch the outgoing tide."

"You can't scatter Mom and Dad's ashes on the beach," Louise said, finally finding her voice. "It's not legal. I don't even think they want to be cremated."

"A, it is legal, I Googled it," Mark said. "B, they didn't say what they wanted so I had to decide what to do because I was here and you weren't, so I did."

"I called you back twice," Louise said.

"After you hung up on me," Mark said. "I'm upset, too, but I'm not hanging up on people."

"You can't cremate people against their will," Louise said, and her temples gave a single blood-filled throb. She tried to hold on to her calm. She'd had so much calm a minute ago. "They have burial plots."

"No, they don't," Mark said.

"Yes, they do," Louise said. "Mom took us to see them. More than once. She had that fixation on making sure all of us wound up buried next to each other."

"Okay," Mark said. "My bad. So we'll sell them. Or, if you're going to be all uptight about it, we'll split the ashes and you can bury your half and I'll scatter mine."

"These are our parents!" Louise shouted, the first time she'd shouted at an adult maybe ever. "They're not a doughnut! You don't split them in half."

"Okay, folks," Roland Agutter said, behind them. "Why don't we all settle down and—"

"Stay out of this!" Louise snapped, never taking her eyes off Mark.

"You have no right cremating Mom and Dad and I'm not letting you dump them in the ocean. Dad didn't even like the beach!"

Mark shook the paperwork harder at her.

"I've got the death certificates and you don't," he said. "This is happening, Louse. So get on board or get out of my way."

"Give them to me," Louise said.

"Hell, no," Mark said.

"I'm the executor of their will," Louise said.

"You got any proof on you?" Mark asked, and when she didn't answer he said, "If you can't show me that in writing, then you can go get your own certificates in Columbia."

He stepped around her, addressing Roland Agutter.

"Let's get my wood out the back before y'all get started," he said.

Louise looked at the sheaf of papers in Mark's hand, dangling by his side

you need them for pretty much anything

and she snatched them out of his hand.

Mark turned, his mouth open in a perfect cartoon O, and for a single second she felt a sense of triumph, then she saw his expression go dark.

She turned her back as Mark came for her, hunching over the paperwork. His arms snaked around her body, grabbing at the forms. She ducked beneath his arms and tried to dodge around him, but he grabbed the paperwork with both hands and pulled. She pressed her thumbs and fingertips into the paper, holding on tight, feeling the contract begin to tear.

"Stop it," he panted, breathless.

"You stop," she panted.

She felt the paperwork sliding out of her grip. She felt certificates beginning to rip.

"You're tearing it!" she said.

Over Mark's shoulder, one of Roland Agutter's guys had his phone up. Louise really hoped he wasn't filming them. His phone moved, tracking the action. He was filming them.

Mark was stronger than her. He was going to get the paperwork and she'd be shut out and he'd go to the beach and dump their parents in the ocean and this wasn't what normal people did and all she wanted was for him to just stop and take a breath and do this together in a way that made sense. The way she wanted to. Her knuckles cramped as the papers slid another inch. She felt their fibers stretching.

Using everything she had, Louise stepped forward, sucked all the moisture from the inside of her mouth, and spat in Mark's face. It sprayed out in front of her in a big white cloud and Mark let go of the paperwork and swiped at his lips with both hands.

Louise darted around Mark and raced for the front porch. Her foot slapped down on the concrete pad and she turned, holding the paperwork to her body. Mark started across the lawn, furious.

"And that's a wrap," Roland said, stopping Mark in midstride. "We don't get involved in family squabbles."

"We're not having a family squabble," Mark said, turning on him.

"I've already got the deposit," Roland said, "so you won't lose anything, but it'll be next Tuesday before I can get back out. That should leave y'all plenty of time to work out your issues."

"We don't have any issues," Mark said, trying to keep his eye on Louise at the same time.

While someone was still there, Louise started across the grass to her car, keeping Roland Agutter between herself and Mark.

"How much to do it now?" Mark asked Roland, taking out his wallet. "I'll pay whatever."

Roland Agutter opened his mouth wide and pointed to a gray front tooth. "You know how I got this dead tooth? Getting in the middle of a family squabble."

"See you Tuesday," Louise called as she passed Roland Agutter, then sprinted for her car as Mark came after her.

Louise yanked out her keys, putting the Kia between her and Mark, and pressed the unlock button on the fob. Mark reached for the passenger-door handle as Louise slid into the driver's side, slamming her door shut and mashing the lock button at the same time. The locks chunked shut all around her as Mark began jiggling the passenger-door handle.

Louise couldn't help herself. She leaned over to the passenger seat, looked out the window at Mark's red face, and . . .

Chapter 5

. . . I said 'Suck it,'" Louise admitted to everyone. "And I may have flipped him the bird. I kind of went blank. But he was going to throw everything away including Mom and Dad if I hadn't shown up."

Louise looked down at the creased and mangled death certificates sticking up out of her purse. Through her peripheral vision she watched her cousins, Constance and Mercy, their mom, Aunt Gail, and, finally, Aunt Gail's mom, Aunt Honey. She waited for them to pass judgment.

"What a raging a-hole," Constance proclaimed.

"Language," Aunt Gail warned.

Everyone waited for Aunt Honey to give an opinion. She'd outlived her entire generation and showed no signs of slowing down. She still dyed her hair blond, and every morning she put on full makeup. She wore a ring on every finger even though she had to rub her swollen knuckles with Vaseline to slide them on.

"This is my house," Aunt Honey said, "and I don't want anyone calling anyone else an 'a-hole' when what they mean to say is 'asshole.' That includes you, Gail. Say what you mean, or get out."

"Mark's a total asshole," Constance revised.

No one argued. Louise tried to relax. She hated losing control, but maybe she'd only been a little over the top? Aunt Honey let out a long sigh.

"He was such a talented little boy," she said.

Louise remembered Mark's plays. She didn't know if he was talented or not but he'd certainly been in a lot of them. Her mom felt deeply validated that Mark had gone into theater like her. She ran lines with him when he got the part of Dopey in *Snow White and the Seven Dwarfs* even though Dopey didn't have any lines. She attended every performance and gave notes. They all had to dress up for his opening nights like they were gala premieres.

"He went downhill after he dropped out of BU," Mercy said. "One of my girlfriend's daughters said all they do at BU is party and d-r-u-g-s."

"I know what drugs are," Aunt Gail said, skinny and angular, perched on the edge of her chair like a large heron, hands folded in her lap, wearing a black turtleneck with the words *Praise Him* bedazzled in gold on the front.

"Mama's on drugs?" Constance asked in mock horror.

"If you've got drugs, share," Aunt Honey barked.

Mercy and Constance laughed with their grandmother. Aunt Gail pursed her lips. They all had the same strong jaws and pointed chins as Louise's mom, the same small bones (except for Constance—where did Constance come from?), the same sense of humor. She had been worried things would be different without her mom here, but family stayed family.

"I'm getting some wine," Mercy said, standing up. "Who else?"

"Me," Aunt Honey said.

"Just a little," Aunt Gail said, holding her thumb and forefinger an inch apart.

Mercy headed for the kitchen.

This felt familiar, at least. In San Francisco, people only grudgingly uncorked a bottle of wine at parties and they always had multiple nonalcoholic options. Here they just assumed you were drinking the second you sat down, and for that, Louise was grateful. She wanted the wine to help her ignore the feeling her mom was going to come in the front door any minute.

She and her cousins had spent entire summers in Aunt Honey's banged-up beach house when they were kids, but coming back for the first time in two years made Louise see every carpet stain and notice how much the outside needed paint. Aunt Honey's skin hung looser from her neck and jaw. Aunt Gail's hands looked like bundles of sticks tied together with blue veins. Her cousins had webs of lines around their eyes and Mercy's neck had gotten thin and stringy and reminded Louise of what she saw when she looked in the mirror. Constance, on the other hand, was almost six feet tall and still looked as thick and substantial as someone who got in fights at bars.

"Louise." Aunt Honey snapped her fingers to get her attention. "What's your brother's number?"

"I've got Mark's number, Meemaw," Constance said before Louise could pick up her phone.

"Dial him and give it here," Aunt Honey barked, pointing at her portable phone on the massive sideboard by the kitchen door.

"You don't have to do that," Louise said. "It's fine."

"It is not fine," Aunt Honey said as Constance got the phone. "My sister's only child—"

"Except Freddie," Aunt Gail said.

"My sister's only child, except Freddie," Aunt Honey corrected herself, "has died. I don't care if you never talk to your brother again, you two are going to act civil this week. There's a lot to discuss and he's going to get his fanny over here and discuss it."

The thought of having to be in the same room as Mark right after their fight made Louise feel light-headed, but she didn't know how to stop Aunt Honey, so she watched helplessly as Constance dialed and put the phone in Aunt Honey's hand. She pressed it to one ear and held it there for a long time.

"Why is your brother such a dickhead?" Constance said under her breath to Louise, which made her feel better.

"Mark!" Aunt Honey shouted. "That's right, you'd better pick up when I call . . . Don't you sweet-talk me. Listen . . . Listen! Your sister is sitting across . . . I don't care . . . I *don't* care. You're going to get in your truck and drive over here because we have to plan their service . . . You have *not* planned their service . . . You do that and you'll need to toss my dead body in the water first . . . Mark? Mark. *Mark!* Get your fanny over here now."

She hung up.

"He's on his way," she said.

"I don't know why he's acting like such a child," Constance said.

"Because that's exactly what he is," Mercy said, coming out of the kitchen with a wine bottle and a bunch of iced tea glasses. "He's thirty-seven years old and still works in a bar."

"Whoever heard of scattering your parents' ashes on the beach?" Constance asked. "People swim in that water."

Mercy began filling glasses way over the halfway mark.

"Children tee-tee in that water!" Aunt Honey said, outraged. "Fish! Dogs! It's a toilet bowl!"

"Mother!" Aunt Gail said, radiating disapproval.

Aunt Honey took a breath through her nose and let it out.

"The one blessing in all this mess is that your mother is finally with Freddie," she said.

"Amen," Aunt Gail said.

Everyone took a quiet drink.

Uncle Freddie had been Louise's mother's brother, who stepped on a rusty nail barefoot when he was five, got lockjaw, and died. Her mom had been seven and because of Uncle Freddie, Mark and Louise had never been allowed to go outside barefoot. Ever. Even on the beach her mom made them wear tennis shoes. Even in the water.

"Now, *he* was a wonderful child," Aunt Honey said. "Friendly like you wouldn't believe and smart, oh! He was smarter at five than anyone in this room and handsome— Lord. Cannons always made handsome boys. The girls have to make do."

"Thanks, Meemaw," Mercy said.

"If I showed you a picture of Freddie you'd agree," Aunt Honey said.

Louise knew what it was like to grow up in the shadow of a younger sibling who sucked up all the air. She'd always thought that should have made her and her mom closer, but whenever she tried to talk to her mom about Freddie, she changed the subject.

"Who's writing the obituary?" Aunt Honey asked. "You got to pay the paper if you want more than one of those little-bitty boxes that are too small to read."

"What happened the night my parents died?" Louise asked Aunt Honey.

Everyone watched Aunt Honey to see how she'd handle this.

"Dwelling on it won't help," she rasped, sitting back in her chair.

"It'll help me," Louise insisted. "I went by the house today. They left her purse on the counter, the TV on, and my dad's cane on the floor because they were in such a hurry to leave. What happened?"

"You don't need to be thinking about none of that," Aunt Honey said.

Her mom's entire family couldn't discuss death. After Uncle Freddie died, the story went, Louise's grandmother gave away all his toys and clothes, then burned his pictures and made everyone swear never to mention him again. She said she couldn't raise one child while mourning another. According to Aunt Honey, it wasn't until she died that anyone acknowledged Freddie had even existed. Louise would not live that way.

"I need to know," she insisted.

"She wants closure," Mercy said.

"Meemaw," Constance said in a warning voice.

"All I know," Aunt Honey said, outnumbered, "is your mother called me Wednesday night in an uproar and said she had to take your father to the hospital because he had some kind of attack."

"What kind of attack?" Louise asked.

"All I could make out was your daddy had an attack and she couldn't wait for an ambulance. I told her, 'Nancy, it's raining cats and dogs, you've got no business in an automobile. You dial 911.'"

"Was it his ankle?" Louise asked.

"I think she said it was an attack," Aunt Honey said, confused for a moment. "I wish I'd argued harder about that EMS."

"Meemaw," Mercy said, "you can't argue with someone when they're upset. Especially Aunt Nancy."

"The next thing you know," Aunt Honey said, "your brother calls and tells me they've been in an accident."

"Did he say anything about what the police said?"

"Just that it happened," Aunt Honey said. "And that's that."

A silence spread through the living room.

"What did your mother want to do about flowers?" Aunt Gail asked.

"I don't know," Louise said, trying to make herself care about flowers.

"They'll want gladioli," Aunt Honey pronounced. "Don't you think so, Gail?"

"White lilies," Aunt Gail said. "I'll talk to Robert Wheeler. He did the arrangements for Mary Emma Cunningham's funeral, the ones with the little pineapples in them."

They began to talk about flowers and obituaries and who needed to be called and Louise felt small and safe, sipping her wine, surrounded by these loud women doing everything for her. She marveled at how easy they were with each other, how they got along so unselfconsciously, how different they were from her and Mark.

"Are y'all selling the house?" Mercy asked, snapping her out of it.

"Mercy!" Aunt Gail said.

"It's what everyone's going to ask," Mercy said. "Prices around here are sky-high. Meemaw could sell this pile and get a million, easy."

"Worldly possessions thou shalt not store up," Aunt Gail said.

"I'm not selling this house and neither is Louise," Aunt Honey said.

"It's her house," Constance said.

"My sister would turn over in her grave," Aunt Honey said.

"I'm only here two weeks," Louise said, trying to head off conflict. "I'm going to clean it out first and then decide."

"Your mother grew up in that house," Aunt Honey said. "That land belonged to your grandfather back when Old Mount Pleasant was nothing but farms."

"Do you need any help with it?" Mercy asked, turning to Louise, and Louise couldn't tell if it was a real offer or a mandatory family gesture.

"That's okay," Louise said. "It's not that much stuff. But thank you."

"Well, let me know if I can do anything," Mercy said.

"And don't give Mark any of that money," Constance told her.

"She's not selling it!" Aunt Honey barked.

"The easiest thing to do is sell," Mercy said. "Money divides in two easier than real estate. I've seen too many families tear themselves up over a house after someone dies."

"You sell that house and someone's going to tear it down and put in a big old tacky mansion," Aunt Honey said to Louise. "Is that what you want to have happen to where you grew up?"

"We have to see their wills first," Louise said, trying to change the subject.

"The Old Village is changing," Mercy tried to explain. "Houses are going up whether we like it or not."

"My sister wanted that land to stay in the family," Aunt Honey said.

"Because it would increase in value," Mercy said. "They should sell before the bubble bursts."

"This is not an appropriate conversation, y'all," Aunt Gail wailed. "Their bodies aren't even in the ground."

Constance sat up straight.

"Mark's here," she said.

Everyone stopped talking and looked at the front porch. Heavy steps shook the stairs as Mark came up. Louise didn't feel ready for this. She didn't want to see him so soon. She drained half her glass of wine. That helped. The screen door swung open and Louise saw Mark's shadow. She tried to compose herself. He knocked on the front door at the same time as he opened it.

"Hey, y'all," he said.

"Look who's here!" Mercy said, and ran over and gave him a hug.

Aunt Gail followed, and so did Constance. Louise was astonished at how quickly they could shift gears.

"Your mother was such an inspiration," Aunt Gail said, kissing him on the cheek. "Always doing, always active. Her ministry wasn't appealing to me, but it suited her. And your father was a saint."

Louise felt grateful they were making him feel welcome, getting him to lower his guard, giving her time to prepare. The three of them brought Mark over to the circle of chairs, and Mark leaned down and pecked Aunt Honey on the cheek.

"You're late," she grumped.

Mark nodded to Louise. She nodded back. He sat on the sofa, taking Mercy's seat.

"You want some wine?" Mercy asked.

"A lot," Mark said.

Mercy poured and when Mark reached out to take his glass off the coffee table his eyes stopped on the death certificates sticking out of

Louise's bag. Louise saw him hesitate for a moment, then settle back and take a big gulp of his wine. She decided to rip the Band-Aid off.

"We should discuss what happened," she said.

Aunt Honey cut in.

"You talk too much," she said, then turned to Mark. "Now, I want to be real clear: you are not tossing your parents in the water."

Mark raised his glass again. They all watched his throat work. When he lowered it the fight seemed to have gone out of him.

"I'm not Louise," he said. "I'm not going to fight all y'all."

"Your parents are going to have a service at Mount Pleasant Presbyterian, the way your mother would have wanted," Aunt Honey said. "She's going to be buried at Stuhr's next to her brother and her parents, then we'll have a reception back here."

"A big funeral is nice for everyone," Aunt Gail said.

"Except me," Mark said. "I wanted to organize something special, you know, call the FCP—"

"You had a chance and you blew it, brother," Constance said. "You're going to put on a suit and come to the funeral and act normal."

Mark looked down at his glass. He didn't say anything, but after a second, he shrugged.

"Fine," he said.

"Gail," Aunt Honey said. "I need you to get your coffee urn back from Layla Givens."

"I'll make ambrosia," Constance said.

"It's not a wedding," Aunt Honey said. "No ambrosia. We'll do a pound cake, a fudge cake, and cookies."

"How many people is it?" Constance asked.

"Probably a hundred but we'll know tomorrow," Aunt Honey said. "Gail, call Lucy Miller and tell her we'll need two sandwiches: egg salad and pimento cheese."

"But what're we going to eat?" Mercy asked.

"I'll fry chicken," Aunt Honey said.

"That's a lot of work, Mama," Aunt Gail said.

"Well, I'm not sending my niece and her husband away with store-bought," Aunt Honey said. "I would if Mrs. Mac was still around, but she's long passed."

"Oh, her chicken was good," Aunt Gail said.

"Who was Mrs. Mac?" Mark asked.

"Mrs. Mac was a lady at the downtown Piggly Wiggly where they put up those ugly condominiums," Aunt Honey explained. "She worked in the deli department and made the best fried chicken. No Charleston funeral used to be complete without a platter of Mrs. Mac's. It's the only store-bought you could serve and still hold your head up."

"I always liked Aunt Florence's chicken better," Mercy said.

"Florence cooked buttermilk chicken," Aunt Honey said. "Mrs. Mac made country-fried."

Louise didn't understand what was going on. Were they really discussing the differences between fried chicken cooked by two women who'd died decades ago? She felt like she wasn't following the conversation.

"Mom made great fried chicken," Mark said, and the room got awkward.

"Pour me a little more of that wine," Aunt Honey told Mercy.

Constance checked her phone. Aunt Gail started to say something, decided there was nothing to say, and took a sip of wine. Mark forged ahead, oblivious.

"I always liked that it was different," he said. "With the almonds in it and the Cajun spice. Was that a family recipe?"

What family? Louise thought. *The Manson family?*

Their mom didn't have a feel for food. She approached her kitchen the way a bomb squad approached a ticking paper bag. She needed a timer to cook pasta, her rice was always mushy or burned, sometimes both at the same time, and her casseroles never came together, but the cult of Southern motherhood insisted she provide meals for her family, so she distracted everyone from her shortcomings by embracing exotic recipes she tore out of magazines. Mark and Louise grew up on greasy potatoes moussaka, zucchini pancakes that tasted like baking powder, jet-black chili spiked with chocolate sauce, salads splashed with blueberry vinegar and banana-infused oil instead of Wish-Bone dressing like everybody else. Women talked about their mother's cooking in the quiet, tragic whispers they reserved for somebody dying of cancer.

"Your mother always marched to the beat of her own drummer," Aunt Honey said.

"Right?" Mark continued, not letting go. "I always thought it was cool when she brought sour cream cabbage or tuna curry casserole to Thanksgiving instead of the same old stuff."

Louise looked at him, sticking up for their mom's cooking, and it struck her how close they must have been. He did theater like her, he lived in Charleston, he'd grown up with her puppets, which Louise had always tried to avoid. She wanted to offer him an olive branch. They shouldn't be fighting like this.

"Hey, Mark," Louise said, and everyone turned, grateful for the change of subject. "You should organize the service."

"Lulu . . ." Aunt Honey began.

"No," Louise said. "Mark knows what Mom would want better than the rest of us. He should do it. If he thinks they would want to be cremated, then they'll be cremated. If he has ideas about what Mom would want at the service, then he can plan it."

"It's happening at the church," Aunt Honey insisted.

Louise stood up.

"I've had a long day, so I think I'm going to go," she said, closing the subject.

She looked at Mark across the coffee table, and somewhere in his face, behind the bad tattoos, the thinning hair, and the jowls, she saw the little boy she grew up with.

"I don't need your pity chore," he said, incapable of lowering his guard.

"You'll do it better than I would," she said. "Good night."

Mark didn't know how to fight someone who wouldn't fight back. Louise felt serene.

"Yeah," he said. "Okay. Cool."

"Stay for supper," Aunt Honey said, looking genuinely distressed that she was leaving. "People have been dropping off food for two whole days. I've got a cheese casserole I can heat up from the Methodists where they laid out little cheese nips on top in the shape of the cross."

"I think I'm just going to call Poppy and go to bed," Louise said.

"I'll walk you out," Constance said.

They went down the stairs together and across the front yard. Up and down this block of Isle of Palms, rich Yankees and downtown lawyers had built hurricane-proof McMansions and hermetically sealed glass cubes. In the midst of them, Aunt Honey's old beach house stood out like a haunted mansion. One of the few original Isle of Palms houses left, it was an enormous pile of weather-beaten white boards with tin window awnings, balanced on creosote pilings over a yard that was mostly sand and cockleburs. When she died, Louise thought, someone would just tear it down and build another McMansion on this lot.

"You really should let Mercy help you with the house," Constance said.

"It's fine," Louise said. "It's really not that much stuff."

"I don't mean to clean it out. You know she's the biggest Realtor in Mount Pleasant? She'd appraise it for you."

That took Louise by surprise. In her mind they were Aunt Gail's children and any jobs they had were play jobs.

"What would she charge for something like that?" Louise asked.

Standing in the early evening gloom, Constance gave her a look.

"Lulu. We're family."

She reached over and pulled Louise into a hug, and Louise stiffened and tried to pull away, but Constance tightened her grip until Louise had no choice but to surrender, and all the strength drained out of her body and for a moment she let her cousin hold her up.

After a minute, they pushed away from each other and the two girls stood, studying each other's faces. Constance reached out and tucked a piece of Louise's hair behind her ear.

Why hadn't Louise seen her cousins more? Why had she let herself fall out of touch with these Amazons, these goddesses, these girls, her family?

"Are you okay?" Constance asked.

"No," Louise said. "Yes? I don't know."

"I know things are tense with you and Mark," Constance said, "but y'all don't want to split up over money."

"There's nothing to split up," Louise said. "That ship has sailed. We both like our space."

"You don't get space from family," Constance said. "He's your brother."

"It's different for you and Mercy," Louise said. "She's normal."

"Mercy's a fruitcake," Constance said. "I once wore a magnet in my underpants for two weeks to make her happy because she told me it would realign my electrical field. Mark's no weirder than the rest of your family."

That took Louise by surprise. She didn't think of her family as weird. People thought her family was weird?

"I don't think we're weirder than any other family," she said.

"Trust me," Constance said. "You guys definitely are."

Chapter 6

e are not weird.

    Louise drove off Isle of Palms repeating that to herself.

    My family is not weird.

Okay, the dolls. And her brother was well on his way to becoming a local character, which was obnoxious, but she was normal, and her mom was as normal as a woman who bought seventy yards of puppet fur at a time could be, and her dad practically defined the word *normal*. He didn't buy presents for people but instead gave cash because, as an economist, he believed the recipient would purchase the most optimal gift for themselves. Was there a more dadcore thing to do?

We are not weird.

Some moms played handbell at church, some moms sang in the choir, her mom had a Christian puppet ministry that kept her active until her dad's ankle forced her to retire. It actually brought in decent money, so in a way all her puppet building and script writing and self-promoting made more sense than women her mom's age who played bridge or became obsessive bird-watchers or rode endless miles on their SoulCycles.

She came off Sullivan's Island on the Ben Sawyer Bridge and watched the light change over the marsh, fading from dark purple to pitch black on either side of the road, and thought:

We're as normal as every other family.

Her mom and dad hadn't been abusive, they weren't alcoholics, they didn't cheat on each other or slam doors. They were like millions of other totally normal parents across the country who went to their normal kids' plays and choir concerts, dropped them off for soccer and swimming lessons, drove carpool to Girl Scouts, and attended graduations.

Her dad was a little quiet, but he kept their mom from floating away. And Mark had been a nightmare as a teenager, but lots of teenage boys went crazy when hormones hit. She and Mark didn't interact, not because of some intense trauma but just because they were different people with different priorities. Like he'd said, they'd shared a bathroom for fifteen years; it didn't mean they had to be best friends for the rest of their lives.

Her mom had a need to be in the spotlight, but that was just how she grew up. And she had another side, too. Louise remembered a ride home from the airport one year, windshield wipers going, Dad driving, when he'd said:

"You may notice your Mom's a little down when you see her. She'll be all right by tomorrow."

"What did Mark do?" Louise asked.

"It's nothing to do with your brother," her dad said, hands at ten and two on the wheel, looking straight ahead. "Your mother just has some dark days every now and again. You never knew your grandparents. They may have died young, but they cast a long shadow. Sometimes it gets the better of her."

Louise knew that after Freddie died her grandparents had shipped her mom around like an unwanted Christmas fruitcake. First they shipped her upstate to Uncle Arthur, then to Aunt Honey on the beach, and finally to anyone who'd take her in. At seven years old, Louise's mom had learned to fit in anywhere. She'd learned to be cute and precocious and adored. She'd been the special guest in so many families that she started thinking being in the spotlight was normal.

Then her dad died. His dry-cleaning business caught fire, and when he ran back inside to save the register the ceiling collapsed on him. Nancy had been eleven. Her mom had stopped going anywhere except church and she'd kept Nancy home to take care of her until she died four years later, made prematurely old by the loss of her son and her husband.

Night pressed in on the windows of Louise's car, and the silence weighed down on her. She wanted to FaceTime Poppy. She wanted to turn on the radio. She didn't want to drive through the intersection where her parents had died again.

She took a left onto Center Street and decided she'd drive by the house, make sure everything was okay, then cut through the Old Village instead of going down Coleman. She drove past the same trees she'd passed her entire childhood, the stop sign at the end of the block that marked how far they were allowed to go alone when they were kids, then where the house with the cactuses out front had been torn down and turned into a McMansion, and the Everetts' old house, which had been gut renovated, and the Mitchells' place, which belonged to a new family who'd added a second story, and the Templetons' house, which had been torn down, and where someone was now in the middle of building two houses on their lot.

Are y'all selling the house? Prices around here are sky-high.

The minute Louise's dad turned seventy she'd forced him to sit down and go over his will. Selling the house and splitting the money between her and Mark made the most sense, but she knew her dad worried about Mark taking his half of the money and blowing it on yet another failed treasure-hunting expedition, or a snake farm, or a Mexican Christmas tree factory, or whatever he had a gut feeling was going to be his ticket to easy street that week. Louise told her dad the plan: give it all to her, make her the executor; she'd sell the house and put Mark's half in a trust. Mark would be upset at first, but once the monthly checks started arriving, he'd calm down. And it would give her a nice tax break. Her dad approved of tax breaks.

How much is it worth?

A lot. Everyone in Mount Pleasant knew that anything with four walls and a roof that didn't leak could get half a million dollars, easy.

Half a million dollars.

Louise didn't want to be thinking about money so soon after her parents had died, but without even trying she started thinking about Poppy's college education, a bigger house with an actual yard where they could get a dog and she could even have another baby, a brother or a sister for Poppy.

No.

She'd seen what had happened between her and Mark, and she'd promised not to do that to Poppy. She saw the damage done to her mom by her brother and he'd been dead for over sixty-five years. Her dad's brothers hated her mom and she knew the rift that had caused left her dad feeling eternally incomplete. It was too late for her and Mark to be brother and sister anymore, but she didn't have to repeat the same mistake with Poppy. One child was more than enough. But this house where they'd grown up could fund a better future for Poppy. It could—

The TV was on again.

Louise hit the brakes and her Kia lurched to a stop in the middle of the street. Through the big bay window in the living room, behind the drawn curtains, a blue light pulsed and flickered. Someone was inside.

Louise cut her headlights and pulled up. She got out and quietly closed her car door, eyes on the curtains and the blue light dancing behind them. She crept onto the front porch and tried the door, but Mark had locked it again. She snuck around back and tried the rear garage door, but he'd locked that, too. She looked through the sliding glass doors that opened into the dining room and could see the TV light in the hall, shifting on the carpet, but she couldn't see who was inside.

She had unplugged the TV. Someone had come into their house, probably a neighbor with a spare key, and plugged it back in and settled into her dad's chair to watch. It made her furious. She wanted them out right now. She examined the lock on the garage door but it wasn't one she could pick, and a strip of wood kept her from jimmying the latch with her library card. She'd have to do this the hard way.

She found the chunk of the Berlin Wall her dad had brought back from their trip to Germany and picked it up with both hands, centered its pointiest point in the middle of a pane of glass above the doorknob, and gave it a poke. The pane made a silvery splitting sound and glass tinkled out of the frame. She held still, listening. No lights went on, no neighbors' dogs barked, no sound came from inside the house. She pulled her shirtsleeve around her hand, reached through the empty pane, unlocked the garage door, and stepped inside.

Quietly, she walked up the three steps into the kitchen.

A woman's voice came from the living room.

". . . Doll Pajama Party here on HSN, and this wonderful Prayerful Little Boy Doll by Leigh Hamilton. I'm going to put him on my lap so you can see how big he is . . ."

Slowly, Louise reached out and picked up the hammer she'd left on the kitchen counter. She hefted it in one hand as she crept toward the dining room in a half crouch, the muscles in her thighs aching, scanning the flickering blue light in the front hall for a person-shaped shadow.

". . . an invitation into the magical world of Leigh Hamilton, and you can see this little-boy doll is praying, he's praying to say whatever wrongs he's done, you'll please forgive them, everyone . . ."

Louise made herself get it over with, walking fast out of the dining room, onto the hall carpet, stepping around the corner into the living room.

"Hey!" she said, to startle whoever it was.

Pupkin sat in the easy chair watching TV, the remote beside him.

A song she hadn't thought of in years popped into Louise's head.

Pupkin here! Pupkin here!
Everybody laugh! Everybody cheer!

She interrupted it, forced it to stop.

Pupkin sat in her dad's chair, watching TV. Her mom's favorite puppet, the one she'd taken everywhere with her, the one she'd used to tell Bible stories to young audiences, the one she'd learned ventriloquism for, the one who had told Mark and Louise bedtime stories, the one who'd been in her life before them, the one she'd had since she was a little girl, the one she'd loved more than she loved them.

The one who made Louise's skin crawl. The one she hated the most.

Pupkin was a red-and-yellow glove puppet with two stumpy fabric legs dangling down from his front and two little nubbin arms. His chalk-white plastic face had a big smiling mouth and a little pug nose, and he looked out of the corners of his wide eyes like he was up to some kind of mischief. His mouth and eyes were outlined in thick black lines and he wore a bloodred bodysuit with a pointed hood and a yellow stomach. Sitting here in the dark with the Home Shopping Network flickering across his face, he looked like he'd crawled straight out of a nightmare.

Louise hated Pupkin, but right now she was scared of him again, the way she'd been scared of him when she was little, because how had he moved? How had he gotten into this chair?

Mark.

Of course. Her back unclenched and her grip around the hammer relaxed. Mark had come in after she'd left, seen the dolls in the garage, and set all this up. He knew how much she hated Pupkin and he knew she'd come by at some point and he wanted to freak her out.

She turned on the hall light. One of the bulbs had burned out. Her dad always replaced bulbs the instant they went dead, but he must have fallen behind because of his ankle.

". . . doll really brings me back to my childhood, and that warm, safe feeling that everything is going to be . . ."

She picked up the remote to turn off the TV, then stopped. It would be better to leave everything the way it was and not say a word to Mark. She wouldn't give him the satisfaction. He'd go crazy wondering if she'd even seen it.

Sitting in Dad's chair, Pupkin looked like he owned the house. He looked like he belonged here more than Louise. He made her feel like an intruder. After all, she'd broken a window to come inside. Pupkin had been here before her or Mark were even born. He'd known their mom since she was seven years old. He'd traveled with her to all her shows while they'd waited for her at home.

Louise hated him.

Before she could change her mind, Louise walked to the kitchen and got a plastic bag from underneath the sink. She came back into the living room and while the dolls all watched she scooped Pupkin up inside the bag and tied the top. Then she took him out to the garage, and under the blank gazes of the Mark and Louise dolls on the shelf, she opened the trash can and dropped Pupkin inside.

If Mark asked where Pupkin was, she'd say she hadn't seen him. Let him wonder what had happened. She turned off the TV, turned out the lights, and closed up the house while the dolls watched her every move.

Back in her hotel room she put the extra lock on her door and Face-Timed Ian as she turned on all the lights, looked inside her closets, looked under the bed.

"Hey!" Ian answered, taken off guard. "I didn't realize you were going to call." He turned offscreen. "Poppy? Do you want to see Mommy?"

Poppy didn't want to see anyone. Ian turned the phone so Louise could see her huddled in a chair in the corner of the guest bedroom of his family's mountain house. Poppy looked like she'd been so miserable for so long that she didn't know what she wanted anymore. Her swollen face and sticky cheeks made Louise's heart squeeze tight.

"Hey, sweetheart," she said, making her voice excited. "How's Maw-maw and PopPop?"

No answer.

"Do you like being in the mountains? Is it cold?"

Nothing.

"Did you have your supper?"

After a long pause, Ian said, "She sat at the table but didn't eat."

"The point is for her to answer," Louise said. Then she used every scrap of maternal willpower left in her body to make her voice sparkle and said, "Do you want me to read you a story?"

Poppy shook her head. Louise felt like they were getting some-where.

"Do you want to say something to Mommy?" Louise asked. "You can ask her anything at all. You can tell her how you're feeling."

Poppy began to pick at her leggings. It was what she did when she wanted to say something important. Finally, she looked up.

"I don't want to have a birthday party this year," she said in a voice so soft Louise almost couldn't hear.

"Why not?" Louise asked. "Don't you want a cake and presents and to see all your friends?"

Poppy shook her head.

"I'll turn six," she said.

"That's right," Louise said. "And then you'll be seven, then eight."

"I don't want to," Poppy said.

"But when you're six you'll go to big-kid school," Louise said. "That'll be fun."

"I don't want to," Poppy said.

"You'll make new friends," Louise said.

"I want to stay like now," Poppy said.

"But when you're older you can maybe get a dog," Louise said, even though she didn't have any intention of actually getting a dog, but any white lie was okay if it would draw Poppy out.

"No," Poppy said.

"You don't want to get a dog?"

"No."

"You don't want to have a birthday party?"

"When I get older," Poppy said, "you and Daddy are going to die. I don't want you to die."

Then she started to cry again.

"Louise," Ian said off camera, and he sounded weary.

"Hey, Poppy, don't cry," Louise said, helplessly, from three thousand miles away. "We're not going to die."

The screen lurched to one side, then lifted and showed her Ian's face from way too close.

"Lying just makes it worse," he said.

"I'm sorry," Louise said, "but I just—"

"You shouldn't have told her about your parents in the first place," he said. "She's overtired. We'll talk tomorrow."

"Wait," Louise said.

He turned off the call.

I'm not a bad mother.

Louise took a hot shower. She tried to think of anything but Poppy, alone and miserable and terrified of her parents dying, and how that was her fault.

What does Mark want to do at the funeral?

It popped into her head right before she fell asleep. What was so important that he wanted to plan? Playing "Stairway to Heaven" on the bagpipes? She remembered he'd said something about "FCP," and that rang a bell, then it popped into her head like she'd never forgotten it:

The Fellowship of Christian Puppeteers.

How many dinners had she spent picking at a piece of Hawaiian pineapple quiche while ignoring her mom's tale of the latest scandal in the good old FCP? There'd been her mom's friend Judi, who giggled at her own jokes and introduced herself as the FCP's "string-puller in chief." Mark would probably invite her and a bunch of other puppet people to the funeral to speak. Before he dropped out of BU, Mark had always liked their mom's puppets, and after that he didn't like much of anything. He'd even liked Pupkin when they were kids, but she knew that Pupkin hated them. Especially her. And now she'd thrown him away and he was going to be so angry and—

Dolls don't have feelings, she told herself, cutting off that thought before it could get out of control. She needed to stay under control.

Chapter 7

Louise stood in front of Mount Pleasant Presbyterian Church and watched a pink-feathered ostrich walk up the front steps and go inside. The sun shone warm and bright for January, and the male ushers wore three-piece suits in Hawaiian prints while the female ushers wore pineapple-print dresses. Old men in suspenders and cartoon-character ties stood on the sidewalk chatting with middle-aged women in fairy wings. There were Panama hats and fascinators and almost every single person wore a puppet on one arm.

"I didn't think it would be like this," Constance said, standing beside Louise.

"He said it'd be like Jim Henson's funeral," Louise said.

Constance shrugged.

"If it was good enough for Jim Henson . . ." she said.

"Exactly," said Louise.

She'd had second thoughts about letting Mark plan the service when she saw the email from the FCP about "gathering for a FUNeral not a funeral" and "celebrating Nancy and Eric Joyner's ascent into GLORY," but Mark had told her he'd make sure it was tasteful. He told her he'd already talked to the minister. He reminded her that the FCP were Christians first and puppeteers second. He'd asked her if she was going to second-guess every single one of his decisions because if that was the case she could plan it herself and he might or might not come. She'd backed off, trying very hard to be the adult.

"What the hell is wrong with these people?" Aunt Honey croaked, rattling up behind them on her rolling walker.

"It's just like Jim Henson's funeral, Meemaw," Constance said.

"Who?" Aunt Honey snapped as Mercy and Aunt Gail helped her over the uneven sidewalk.

"A puppeteer has passed, dear woman," a literal clown in oversize shoes and a rainbow wig said as he slapped past them. "The puppets gather hither to bid her bon voyage."

"See?" Mercy said. "It sounds nice."

"If any of them tries to hug me I'm going to get my gun and shoot them dead," Aunt Honey growled.

Inside the church, a Hawaiian-print-clad usher led them through the roar of sound and colors and feathers and fur to the row reserved for family, and they sat down, the only people wearing dark colors in the room, standing out like a spot of decay. All around them, people stood in tutus and tiaras, top hats and canes, mustaches waxed to extravagant points, single-sequin beauty marks pasted to cheeks. Someone in the balcony strummed a ukulele and every now and then someone blew a party horn, which was to be expected because they were laid out in every pew, right next to the kazoos.

Everyone wore puppets on their right arms, and all the puppets talked to each other. Monkey astronauts chatted with bear cops, and green pigs hugged purple dragons, one of which actually blew smoke out its nose.

Louise got up and pushed her way to the table of framed photos at the front of the church. Her mom and dad at puppetry conventions, her mom and dad in the audience at puppet shows, loading puppet cases into their car, unloading puppet cases out of their car. If you slowed down from a fast run around Louise's mom, she'd have you loading the car.

The focal point of the table was a green marble Kleenex box and Louise realized it was the urn she'd picked out. Mark had insisted that their mom and dad wanted to be cremated and no one could find any instructions to the contrary, and when Louise had called Stuhr's and they'd told her that the contract Mark had signed was nonrefundable, she'd Googled it and discovered that plenty of families interred cremains in a burial plot. So, cremation it was.

Behind the urn stood two framed caricatures of her parents. Her cartoon dad peered through thick glasses at blackboards displaying equations clearly written by someone who didn't know math. His bristly mustache hung down to his chin, and it must've been a recent drawing because he wore the ankle boot on one foot. A bunch of bears dressed like gangsters posed in the background and Louise figured the artist meant them to be the Chicago Bears.

"Wrong bears," she said to herself.

Her mom's caricature sported a crazed grin, and on her right hand, of course, she wore Pupkin with his matching smile. Louise wondered if he should have gone to the crematorium with her mom, but the thought of forcing her dad to share an urn with Pupkin's ashes for eternity made her breath feel tight in her chest. Pupkin was hopefully in the back of a garbage truck by now on his way to the dump. She felt a pang of guilt about what she'd done, then smothered it. She never wanted to see his creepy grinning face again.

Behind her mom and Pupkin, the caricaturist had drawn every single one of her mom's puppets. Forty years of puppetry filled the frame: Monty the Dog from *A Stray in the Manger*, Danny the Imagination Dragon, Cosmic Starshine, Meow Meow and Rogers, the Inside-Out Man, Judge Goodsense, Flossy Bossypants, Mr. Don't, Pizzaface, Sister Whimsical, Deuteronomy the Donkey . . .

"Louise," a man said behind her.

She turned to face the only other person who looked like he wasn't about to lead a chorus of "Puff the Magic Dragon." He wore a white cassock and had a red heatstroke face, and he squinted at her through tiny glasses. He thrust out his hand. "Reverend Mike. This is certainly a change from our usual congregation."

He smiled at the mayhem.

"Thank you for having us," Louise said, scanning the crowd. "I'm sorry about the craziness, but my mom . . ."

"Wonderful craziness," Reverend Mike said, clutching her hand in his sweaty paw. "Just like your mother. It's what she would have wanted."

Then Louise saw Mark stride up the aisle wearing seersucker shorts, a seersucker jacket, and a red tie. To Louise's horror, he also wore sandals.

"The man of the hour!" Reverend Mike said, and scuttled off to greet Mark.

Everyone seemed to know him. Louise saw Judi, string-puller in chief of the FCP, give him a hug. Puppet people shook Mark's hand and showed him their spinning bow ties, and he shook their puppets' hands, accepted their furry hugs, laughed loudly at their jokes. Louise felt like a guest at an event starring Mark Joyner. It was the same way her mom always made her feel when she came to Louise's school.

"May we all be seated?" Reverend Mike's amplified voice said over the mic, his face barely clearing the pulpit.

Louise drifted over to the drab family pew as everyone found their seats and Reverend Mike beamed at the assembly.

"Make a joyful noise unto the Lord, all ye lands," he said. "Serve the Lord with gladness: come before his presence with singing."

Right on cue, a puppet barbershop quartet sang "This Little Light of Mine." Louise looked at her program but the names all piled up in a meaningless jumble so she let the service wash over her as one puppeteer after another took the mic and told stories about her mom. Sometimes their puppets told the stories. One puppet mouse told a very long story about how his friend Meow Meow had lost her voice and it made him very sad. One puppeteer sang her tribute, another read a poem, and one old man with an enormous white beard and ponytail delivered his tribute via body music, slapping his hands rhythmically across his chest, sides, and cheeks to produce a surprisingly expressive series of percussive snaps and pops.

Louise stared at the marble Kleenex box, trying to convince herself that her mom and dad were actually inside. That the woman who did puppet shows about the dangers of drugs and the glory of the Lord, that the man who had explained the mathematics of perspective to her, lay mixed together in a pile of ashes, like something you'd sweep out of the grill, put in a bag, and throw in the trash.

A man with plastic iguanas sewn onto the shoulders of his green plaid jacket got up and began to tell a story about him and Louise's mother filling in for two drunk puppeteers at a convention without a script. People laughed a lot at that one.

When Mom and Dad had moved back to Charleston they'd had to raise a two-year-old and a newborn on a research assistant's salary. Their mom had been an actress for seven years so she didn't have any savings, and any help from Dad's family caused more problems than it solved. Their only asset was the house Nancy had inherited from her family, and it was almost twenty-five years old. Their baby clothes were hand-me-downs from Constance and Mercy, their plates and glasses came from Goodwill, their meals mostly came out of boxes, they didn't go to movies, they didn't own a TV, so their mom made do with what she had, which was Pupkin. He was the only thing she brought to the marriage besides the house.

Pupkin told them stories about his adventures in Tickytoo Woods, and their mom built backdrops for his tales out of tissue-paper trees with egg-carton mountains and rivers made from recycled plastic wrap. She created friends for Pupkin out of paper bags, and for years, every pair of white socks they owned had faces drawn on the toes because they doubled as puppets.

Someone told Nancy she should do her puppets at the church's kindergarten, so she got a book about ventriloquism out of the library and developed an act where she explained Bible stories to Pupkin, who always repeated them back wrong. Soon they were paying her ten bucks for a day's worth of story times, then she took over the Children's Sermon, then other churches began hiring her, and she started buying supplies to make more puppets, which allowed her to charge real fees, which let her hit the puppet convention circuit, which led to more shows, which led to bigger puppets, which led, eventually, to here.

Every single person in this room, every story, every song, every memory, it all started on the floor of a house without enough furniture, with her mom desperately trying to entertain two little kids with nothing but a threadbare glove puppet she'd had all her life and whatever she could find in the trash.

Suddenly, Louise wanted to tell Mark how she felt, she wanted to see if he felt the same way, she wanted to share this feeling with the only other person in the world who would get it. She turned to look for him in the pews, which is when Reverend Mike said his name.

"And now Mark Joyner, son of Nancy and Eric, would like to end our service with a special moment of song."

Mark stood, and somehow he'd found a guitar. He walked to the front of the church, noodled with the strings, and said, "My mom and dad loved this song. I know they'd be happy to hear it today."

He strummed a couple of open chords, then launched into "The Rainbow Connection." Louise hadn't heard him sing since high school. His voice sounded rough, and it cracked a little, but it was strong and sincere, and when he got to the second chorus, he called out, "Everybody," and the crowd of two hundred puppeteers joined in. Then Mark said, "Kazoos only," and everyone picked up their kazoos and the whole church vibrated as hundreds of people buzzed the entire next verse. Louise felt like someone had punched her in the face. It was absolutely one hundred percent perfect.

She wasn't going to fight with Mark anymore. She shouldn't have fought with him in the first place. She would not let the house come between them. In fact, she wouldn't even put his half of the sale in a trust. He was an adult and he deserved to be treated like one and if he wanted to spend his share of the money on a treasure-hunting expedition, who knows? Maybe he'd be lucky this time. It wasn't her life. It wasn't her money. Half of it belonged to him.

The song ended and she clapped as enthusiastically as everyone else, and then it turned into a standing ovation, and she felt like Mark deserved it. He trotted down the aisle, slapping high fives with puppets and puppeteers alike, and Reverend Mike got up and said, "The *Lord* your God is in your midst, he will rejoice over you with gladness, he will exult over you with loud singing. Go now, and exult in this world with loud singing of your own!"

The room erupted into cheers, the balcony started a kazoo rendition of "When the Saints Go Marching In," and someone threw confetti that drifted down through the sanctuary, tumbling and sparkling in midair. Party horns blared and party poppers popped like it was New Year's Eve as Louise stood and went after her brother.

"I'll meet y'all at the car," she said to her family, sidestepping down the row.

Louise pushed her way through the crowd of dragons and dinosaurs and furry weird things with long arms and red mouths and Ping-Pong ball eyes jamming the aisle, and finally reached the porch where Mark stood, shaking hands, cracking jokes, and she put one hand on his shoulder.

He turned, and when he registered it was Louise his face immediately went blank.

"Let's have it," he said. "It wasn't appropriate, it wasn't tasteful, it was right for Mom but not for Dad, I screwed it up."

"It's exactly what Mom and Dad would have wanted," Louise said. "You were great."

Mark didn't know what to say.

"Cool," he said. "It's weird you didn't say anything, though."

"I'm sorry," Louise said, ignoring his dig. She could be the adult, even if he couldn't. "I'm embarrassed by how I behaved last week. I don't know what got into me, but I overreacted and I'm not proud of it, and it wasn't fair to you. I shouldn't have gotten physical in the front yard. This has been a lot for both of us, but especially you. So, I'm sorry."

Mark looked at her blankly for a long moment, and then he smiled.

"It's okay," he said. "You always needed everyone looking at you."

"I didn't do it for attention," she said, wanting him to understand. "I did it because I was upset."

"Right," Mark said. "You and Mom, always causing drama."

"That's not fair," Louise said, reminding herself to be the adult.

"Like when you ran away from home." He smiled.

"When I went to college?" she asked.

"A year early."

Louise took a deep breath. People jostled her from behind as they pushed past. She made herself look Mark in the eyes. He acted however he wanted. It didn't mean she had to respond.

"You did great today," she said. "This was a perfect service, Mark. Mom would be proud."

So many people packed into Aunt Honey's for the reception Louise could feel the house sway on its pilings. In all the noise and chatter she felt dazed and slow to react, like she was coming down with a cold, so she opted for iced tea instead of wine, then got trapped on the front porch with so many people talking at her that she wished she'd chosen wine instead. What Mark had said haunted her:

It's weird you didn't say anything, though.

Should she have? Why hadn't she? Because she hadn't wanted to fight with Mark, or ask Mark, or talk to Mark, but she should have. Her parents had died and she hadn't publicly said good-bye. She felt unsettled. She felt unfocused. She wished she could go home to Poppy. She felt so tired.

"It would have been nice to hear a traditional hymn is all I'm saying," a woman who was an elder at the church with her mom said to her. "Just a little 'O God, Our Help in Ages Past' or 'Guide Me, O Thou Great Jehovah.' But I'm sure your mother loved it today."

A man in a tweed jacket with a yellow knitted tie took her hand in both of his and wouldn't let go.

"Reed Kirkly," he told her. "I taught with your father, and I wanted to say that he was a great thinker and even though he could be a little bit, shall we say, dogmatic on the subject of tariffs, his research on Soviet wheat production opened a lot of eyes and it mattered. It mattered!"

Mrs. Stillwell in her mom's book club, wearing a loud floral print dress and a pink straw hat, held her by both shoulders.

"Your mother was such a fun lady," she said. "She was so much fun to be around. She was so much fun, we all wanted to be more like her. She was so! Much! Fun!"

Louise looked at all these people talking at her, telling her about her own parents, about her dad's research, his love of the Chicago Bears and Chicago hot dogs, about how much fun her mom was, and how much fun her puppet ministry was, and the Bible stories she told their children with that funny-looking little puppet and how much fun that was, and Louise watched herself nod and smile, and she wondered why she hadn't said anything at her mom and dad's funeral.

She hadn't felt this tired since she'd had Poppy. All she wanted was to be alone, or with her cousins, just someone who actually knew her parents the way they really were, but instead she had to perform like a little puppet.

Her phone buzzed with a text from Ian.

POPPY ONLY SPEAKING IN BABY TALK. WET THE BED LAST NIGHT. MOM KNOWS A CHILD PSYCHOLOGIST WHOS GOOD.

Her phone buzzed again.
THOUGHT YOU SHOULD KNOW, he added.

Louise started to type back "absolutely not," that she'd be home in a week, that Ian's mother didn't get to make these decisions for Poppy, but before she could get further than ABSO someone grabbed her shoulder.

"Lulu?" Constance said in her ear. "I need to borrow you for a minute."

She had a glass of wine in one hand and a sweaty can of Coors in the other.

"What?" Louise asked, feeling pulled between Constance and the text.

"I don't want to do this," Constance said.

"What's going on?" Louise asked, trying to focus and be present. "What happened?"

"Mark's been bothering Brody since the accident," Constance said. "And Brody's been putting him off and putting him off, but Mark is insisting on talking to him right now."

Louise tried to catch up.

"Brody, your husband?" she asked.

"Brody, my husband," Constance repeated.

"Why does Mark need to talk to Brody?"

"To go over the wills."

"Why?" Louise asked.

"He probably wants to know what he gets."

"No," Louise said, "I mean, why is he asking Brody?"

"He's an estate lawyer, right?" Constance said. "He asked your dad to get someone else to do it because he's family, but, well, Brody gave him a family discount and you know your dad."

Louise knew her dad. His cheapness was legendary. He called it "understanding the value of a dollar."

"So Brody has their wills?" Louise asked.

"He wanted to email them to you guys next week," Constance said. "But Mark kept after him and Brody kept saying after the service, after the service, and then Mark practically attacked him the second he got here, saying now was after the service, and he went on about getting his own lawyer and, well, I'm sorry. Brody didn't even have time to get a drink."

Louise heard the roar and chatter swirl around her as people talked about the service and Mark's song, told stories about her parents, and made chitchat over their cremains as Aunt Honey's house swayed on its pilings.

"Lulu?" Constance asked, trying to make eye contact.

Louise thought about the estate, and cleaning out the house, and all the paperwork she'd have to find, and putting it on the market, and splitting it with Mark, and escrow accounts, and Realtors, and shutting off utilities, and her dad's retirement plan, and Social Security, and she felt so tired.

"Okay," she told Constance, ripping off the Band-Aid. "Where are they?"

She had wanted some time after the funeral to adjust to her parents being gone before dealing with all this money stuff, but she was a mom. Nothing happened on her schedule.

Chapter 8

Constance closed Uncle Claude's office door behind Louise, muffling the chattering, buzzing roar of the families, and neighbors, and faculty members, and FCP officers, and distant cousins, and professional storytellers that were packed into Aunt Honey's house. Still, the buzz of their voices made the pine-paneled walls vibrate.

Mark sat in Uncle Claude's black leather swivel chair behind his Texas-size desk, underneath a pair of longhorn horns mounted on the wall. On the front of the desk sat a small sign that read *The Big Kahuna*. Brody sat on the shiny black leather couch, his knees up by his face, and he stood up fast when Louise and Constance came in the room. Constance handed him his sweaty can of Coors.

"Thanks," Brody said, taking it. "Hey, Louise."

He gave her a one-armed hug.

"I'm so sorry about your mom and dad."

Brody felt enormous. He was ridiculous. Handsome, taller than Constance, friendly. At family events he organized football games with the little kids but never played too rough. He didn't hunt or drink too much and he listened and asked intelligent questions whenever he talked to Louise. She thought he was too good for them.

"Thanks, Brody," she said into his lapel.

He stepped away and gestured to the sofa.

"Please," he said. "I'll stand. Con, can you make sure no one comes in?"

Constance stepped outside, the buzz of voices getting louder, then she closed the door and they dropped off again, leaving the three of them alone.

"Finally," Mark said from behind the desk as Louise perched herself on the edge of the sofa. "Let's get this show on the road."

"I don't need to hear this," Louise said. "I know what I'm going to do, no matter what."

"I'm sure you've got it all planned out," Mark said. "Of course, you think it's fair that you get more because you've got the grandkid."

"Mark, come on," Brody said. "Let's keep it civil."

"I don't hear her denying it," Mark said. "But I might still have kids. Billy Joel had a kid when he was sixty-five."

Brody did a very good job of pretending he didn't have a headache.

"As you both know, I drew up your mom's and dad's wills," he said. "We usually email these and mail a hard copy, but this is a tricky situation because it's two wills and each impacts the other. I want to go over them with you in person to explain everything, and normally I'd wait until a decent interval had passed, but Mark insisted."

"Don't make me the problem," Mark said. "Louise is only here for another week. We don't have time to dick around."

"Like I said," Louise repeated, "whatever Mom and Dad wanted, it won't change any of my decisions."

"Give me a minute," Brody said, tucking his beer in his armpit, pulling out his phone, and scrolling down the screen. "I just want to find the documents. Okay. So. Let me email you both the copies."

Mark hunched over his phone, refreshing it again and again, looking hungry. Louise didn't take hers out. She took a pad off Uncle Claude's desk and a pen out of his cowboy boot pencil holder and got ready to take notes instead.

"Did it come through yet?" Brody asked, pressing the cold beer to his forehead.

Mark kept dragging his finger down his phone until it *pinged*.

"Yeah," he said, tapping the document.

"I'll mail you both hard copies tomorrow, but right now I want to walk you through it," Brody said. "Let's start with your dad's will. If there's something you don't understand or you want me to repeat, just ask, okay? We're family, so I've got all the time you need today."

Brody leaned against the doorframe, balanced his beer on the arm of the sofa, and held his phone out in front of him, ready to address the jury. Mark kept scrolling, his eyes flicking from side to side. Louise got ready for him to explode.

"You two are in the unusual position where Uncle Eric and Aunt Nancy passed almost simultaneously," Brody said. "That has some legal ramifications, so the first thing we need to do is consult the predeceased's testament, that's your dad, and—"

"This leaves everything to Louise!" Mark said, slapping one hand down hard on Uncle Claude's desk.

Louise took a breath.

"Mark, I'd like to take you through this step-by—"

"She gets everything?" Mark barked, and his eyes were wet and bulging. "She abandoned them!"

Louise heard the hurt in his voice and it made her glad about her decision.

"Come on, man," Brody said. "Don't be like that."

"How much stuff do they have?" Mark asked. "The house? Whatever they have in the bank? It all goes to her. I knew they'd do this. I don't even matter."

"You do matter," Louise said. "You mattered to Mom and Dad a lot. You know I'll split everything with you, right? Whatever they say in their wills, half of everything is yours."

"I've been talking to a lawyer at work," Mark said, and Louise knew he meant some lawyer who came into his bar. "He says this is what always happens. Money shows up and everything gets fucked."

Louise shut up because she didn't need to argue with Mark anymore. So many fights, so many frustrations, but in the end, her dad left her in charge because he knew she'd do the right thing by Mark. Whatever time it took, it would be worth it. Her conscience would be clean. And then they would never have to speak again.

"You shouldn't even be their lawyer," Mark said to Brody, who, Louise thought, was demonstrating saintlike patience. "You're family."

"I don't like it, either," Brody said, "but that's what they chose, and I have a responsibility to make sure you both understand their last wishes. May I continue?"

Louise realized he'd directed that at her because she was the executor.

"Of course," she said.

Mark could cry all he wanted, but Louise's shoulders unknotted for the first time in a week. She felt her bones realign, she sat up straighter, her jaw unclenched. In a few months she'd be done with Mark forever and she'd do it the right way.

"I'll get another lawyer," Mark said.

"That's your prerogative," Brody said. "Now, I wanted to walk y'all through this from the beginning, but since you've skipped ahead, let's pick up there. As you've seen, if your mother predeceased your father, he left everything to Louise. But if your father predeceased your mother, if you'll read the pages you skimmed, he leaves everything to your mother.

That's a normal thing for married people to do, leaving their estate to each other. So in the case that your mother predeceased your father, then everything would go to Louise. But as best we can tell, the opposite happened."

He turned his phone around so they could see its screen.

"According to the accident report we got Friday," Brody said, "your mother's time of death came after your father's, and I'm sorry to sound a bit ghoulish, but sometimes the law requires that we be precise. Apparently, when emergency medical workers arrived on the scene, your mother was still conscious, but your father had already passed. She passed on the way to Roper."

A heavy silence filled the room for a full minute. Even Mark sat still. Brody turned his phone back around and poked at it for a moment.

"So, if you'll look at the second document I sent you," he said. "Louise, you're sure you don't want to follow along?"

"I'm fine," she said.

"Your mother leaves her estate to your father in case she predeceases him," Brody said. "If he predeceases her, she inherits his estate, then she leaves her entire estate, which now includes his, to Mark. One hundred percent."

Another long silence unfolded. Louise waited for the rest of it. Brody looked at her.

"Sometimes a parent will appoint their adult children as co-personal representatives of their will, but in this case she's not only willed her entire estate to Mark, she also decided to appoint him as her personal representative."

There was another long silence while Brody studied Louise.

"Do you follow what I'm saying?" he asked.

Mark did. He leapt out of Uncle Claude's chair and pumped his fist in the air.

"*Yes!*" he shouted.

"This is a funeral, Mark," Brody said. "You can't pump your fist in here."

Louise swore to herself that she would not cry. Her mother had arranged this entire performance to humiliate her, and she would not cry. Her shoulders started to shake. A hot tear slipped down one cheek. She would not cry. She could see her dad, standing against the opposite wall, combing his mustache with his fingertips, looking miserable and apologetic the way he got when he knew he'd done something wrong. She wiped at her cheeks, hard. She would not cry.

Mark did an end zone dance beside the desk.

"How much?" he asked. "How much is it?"

"We'll have to inventory the estate," Brody said, looking like his stomach hurt. "That's something you'll need to discuss with your new attorney, if you choose to retain one."

Louise waited for Mark to say he'd split the house with her. She waited for him to say that of course it belonged to both of them. She waited for him to do what she had done. She had never for a second assumed it didn't belong to both of them. She had even decided not to do the trust. She had been doing the adult thing. She waited for Mark to do the same.

"But if you had to guess," Mark asked, sitting back down and grabbing one of Uncle Claude's pens.

Every kid has the same question for their parents: who do you love more? Your parents could dodge that question all their lives, they could avoid it for years, but eventually, one way or another, the answer came out.

"Mark," Louise said, and he couldn't hear her because he was peppering Brody with questions about waiting periods and escrow and claims against the estate. "Mark!" she shouted, louder than she intended.

He stopped and looked at her. So did Brody.

"I paid for Mom and Dad's urn," she said. It was all she could think of.

"Okay, thanks," he said.

Brody tried to help.

"Normally that comes out of the estate," he prompted Mark.

"Does it have to?" Mark asked.

"Well." Brody clearly didn't want to answer. "No."

"Great!" Mark said. "So I read about title claim insurance online. That'll let me sell the house faster, right? How much does it cost?"

"Mark," Brody said, "she's your sister."

"So?" Mark said. "Mom and Dad left everything to me. All I'm doing is respecting their wishes."

Louise stood up. The roaring voices on the other side of the door sounded louder. She felt the floor buckle under her feet and tilt to one side. Brody laid one hand on her arm.

"Don't!" she said, and he froze.

Then he crammed something small and hard and sharp into her hand. She looked down at the thick white envelope.

"Your mom wanted you to have this," he said, but Louise wasn't listening; she was already grabbing the doorknob and pulling herself out of the room and into the wall of her parents' friends, neighbors, and family. They all looked like strangers to her. Constance, standing to one side of the door, saw her leave the study.

"Louise," she said, but Louise threw herself into the crowd, staggering toward the light coming in through the door to the back porch. "Louise!"

She lurched through the crowd. Feet pounded on the floor. She stumbled into people's drinks. She heard the ceiling collapsing. She felt the floor splintering, boards tumbling into the yard below. She grabbed the handle of the sliding door and hauled it open and stepped onto the back porch with the smokers.

"Excuse me, excuse me," she said, shoving her way down the stairs like she needed to throw up, trying to inhale oxygen through their nicotine fog.

Her head hurt so much she couldn't see. She needed to find her car. She turned to cut beneath the house to the front yard.

"Louise!" Constance grabbed her by the arm and spun her around.

"What!" Louise snapped, breathing hard.

"Brody told me," Constance said and looked into Louise's eyes with her washed-out blue ones. "I'm sorry."

Louise threw herself against Constance's chest and felt her cousin's arms go around her. She'd been going to split it with him. She just wanted to be left in charge so everything got done the right way. She just wanted them to part on good terms, but he hated her.

Louise's tears took her by surprise. She was crying, she was finally crying, but not over her parents. She was crying because there was no one left in her family except Mark, and he hated her so much.

Constance rocked her gently from one foot to the other as Louise cried into her chest.

"We all loved your mama and daddy," Constance whispered, stroking Louise's hair as Louise cried harder. "Sh, sh, sh, sh, it's all going to be okay. It's all going to be fine."

You know, Louise, her dad said, *statistically, and there's a lot of variance in these numbers, but in general, from a strictly scientific point of view, everything turns out okay an improbable number of times.*

Not anymore. Her dad was dead. Her mom had picked her brother. Her brother hated her. There was nothing left here for Louise anymore.

She pushed herself away from Constance, wiping her face. Constance handed her a Kleenex. She blew her nose and almost gave Constance the Kleenex back, then realized how gross that was and bunched it up and shoved it in one pocket. She realized she still had the envelope in her hand.

"Can you go upstairs and get my purse out of Aunt Honey's bedroom?" she asked. "I don't want to be here anymore. I'm going home."

ANGER

Chapter 9

Louise paced her room in SpringHill Suites, from the chair by the window, past the foot of the bed to the bathroom door, then back to the window. She shouldn't still be here. She had planned to come back, change her plane ticket, and go home. She wanted to get to the airport, sleep through the flight, and wake up making the final approach to San Francisco. She wanted to see Poppy. Let Mark have this. Let him have it all. She didn't care anymore.

But the envelope sat on her bed. A small linen-colored square sitting on the pineapple bedspread. One of her mom's envelopes.

"Fuck, fuck, fuck," Louise whispered to herself.

She didn't want to open it. There was nothing her dead mother could say that would not make this worse. The only things inside that envelope were complications. Everything that could be said had been said. All their conversations were over. There was no point in analyzing the past. Her mom had overruled her dad's final wishes and chosen Mark over Louise, and she and Mark were incapable of getting along. The end.

She'd read this note on the plane. Or once she was back in San Francisco. Or never.

She opened the closet, threw her bag on the bed, and started folding her shirts. She looked at the paper square with her name written on the outside in her mom's handwriting. Too little, too late. This was over. The story of her family was done. Nothing could change that. Mark won. No matter what she did, he always won.

She took her funeral dress off its hanger and folded it into her bag. She got everything out of the bathroom, checked the drawers, made sure there was nothing under the bed, then she zipped up her bag and put it by the door. She took another look around the room. Nothing left but the envelope on the bed. She couldn't leave it here or house-keeping would think she'd left it behind by accident and mail it to her. She picked it up, but before she could tear it into pieces, she opened it. She took out the card. She started to read.

She had to.

Louise, it said, and she could hear her mom's voice, she could see her sitting at the dining room table writing this in the purple felt-tip pen she always used. *I asked Brody to give you this letter in case certain situations arose, and if you're reading this, they have.* She couldn't even bring herself to write the word *dead* when writing about her own death.

I am so proud of the life you have built, and I am so proud of the mother you have become. You have so much, and you have earned it through your own hard work. Mark has so little compared to what you have achieved.

Louise felt cold iron stiffen her spine. She kept reading.

I made the decision I did because I know you will be able to take care of yourself and Poppy no matter what happens, but Mark has no one. You have so much, but he has so little. I am also sure that if things are tight with you, all you would ever need to do is ask and he would happily share what he has. After all, he is your brother, and he loves you and looks up to you no matter how he acts. I know you will not be bitter over my doing the hard but necessary thing. Please look after your little brother. I love you always, Mom.

Louise wanted to yell things that weren't words, just enormous angry sounds. She wanted to tear down SpringHill Suites with her bare hands. She tore the letter to shreds. She curled over on herself and fell onto the bed, clenched her hands into fists and pressed them against her temples until they ached. She opened her mouth in a silent scream, then screwed her face into a mask, grinding her teeth against each other until the enamel squeaked.

Mark got everything—*everything*—and her mom somehow thought this was the right thing to do? No split. No fifty-fifty. Everything went to Mark, and nothing went to Louise because Mark deserves it and Louise, well, she can take care of herself. They could not see him the way he really was, the way Louise had seen him all her life.

Louise had joined Brownies as soon as she could. She'd loved the idea of an army of efficient uniformed girls deployed to fix everything wrong with the world. She'd cleaned up at the Pinewood Derby, sold the most cookies, and stacked skill badges down her sash. She became obsessed with first aid. She got so obsessed that she arranged for a paramedic to come and speak to her troop. She'd only stopped going years later after her friends stopped because they thought they were too old.

Mark had joined Boy Scouts and never earned a single merit badge. They finally gave him Tenderfoot out of pity. After a year and a half he quit by just not showing up for carpool one day. The family story became that Louise and Mark had both done Scouting but dropped out because they found it too competitive, and Louise bristled every time she heard that. She liked competition. Mark was the lazy one.

Mark's high school theater career had shown Louise exactly the person he'd become. Aunt Honey had been right, he'd had talent, and their family made good-looking guys. It didn't take more than a single production before the head of the Dock Street Playhouse realized that if he cast Mark as a little brother or best friend he'd steal the show from the sincere triple-threat kid cast in the lead. Mark started getting bigger parts and people kept buying tickets. The theater organized its seasons around Mark's strengths, putting on musicals like *Oliver!* and *Huckle-berry Finn*.

The bigger the parts, the more attention he received, the less he worked. Mark wouldn't get off book until the last minute, and sometimes he never learned his lines at all. He skipped tech rehearsals. On opening night of *Where the Lilies Bloom* he'd walked onstage late for a cue with a hickey on the side of his neck that Louise knew hadn't been there two scenes before.

He got easy laughs by mugging. He upstaged the other actors. Whatever talent he'd had, he was too lazy to cultivate it. When he dropped out of college, their parents paid for his apartment downtown. When he proposed to Amanda Fox, their parents helped him buy the ring. Everything got handed to him on a silver platter.

Louise worked. She didn't skate by with minimal effort. She didn't expect other people to do everything for her. She was that horse in *Animal Farm* that worked and worked until they sent him to the glue factory. She did not quit.

So she went to the business center and printed out the emails from Brody, then sat down inside her room at SpringHill Suites, laid her mom's and dad's wills out on the desk, and began to go through them, line by line.

I, NANCY COOKE JOYNER, a resident of CHARLESTON County within the State of SOUTH CAROLINA, make, publish, and declare this to be my Last Will and Testament, thereby revoking any and all previous Wills and Codicils made by me.

She'd been born Cook but added the *e* to class it up when she went off to Sarah Lawrence to study acting. Louise had spent her childhood hearing about how her mom got assigned to Jill Clayburgh's old dorm room and how she took her speech class with the guy who directed

Fried Green Tomatoes. She spelled *theatre* the pretentious way, with an *re* instead of an *er*, but she did have one thing in common with Louise: Nancy Cooke Joyner worked.

After college she moved to New York and spent four years as a coat-check girl, going to auditions during the day. She never made it on Broadway, but she'd come close. Finally, she heard Chicago had a good theater scene and less competition so she headed out there and met a guy who gave her the biggest part of her life: Mrs. Eric Joyner.

Her dad's family hated her, but that didn't stop her mom. She had so much energy, she had so much optimism, she had so much love for their dad that she made it work. Even on their wedding day, when not a single member of his family showed up at city hall, when they had to ask the people standing behind them in line to be their witnesses, when they didn't get a single wedding present, even that day she made it work. Louise saw it in their only wedding picture, her mom in a white mini-skirt and go-go boots, their dad's mustache impossibly thick and shaggy, busting out laughing at something she'd said. It was a cold, gray day outside some municipal building in cold, gray Chicago, and because of her mom they were having the best day of their lives.

They moved to Charleston for his career and moved back into their only asset: the house where Nancy had grown up. They'd had casserole and hand-me-down years, but her mom had sung show tunes, started her puppet ministry, had Louise and Mark, and acted like this had been the plan all along.

They hadn't been able to afford a TV for the first three years of Louise's life, but it didn't matter. From the time Louise was three, every night her mom put Pupkin on one hand and turned Louise's bedroom into his magical home of Tickytoo Woods. She'd weave elaborate bed-time stories about the Tick Tock Tree and the Bone Orchard, his friend Girl Sparrow, who always rescued him at the last minute, and the spooky Inside-Out Man who lived in the trees. When Mark was born, he'd sit with them, too, and even before he understood the words he'd been hypnotized by their mom's voice, by Pupkin's tricks, by his sister's attention.

During those bedtime stories, her mom and Pupkin filled the room, and if Louise had been able to tear her eyes away from them, she knew that her bedroom walls would have disappeared, replaced by Tickytoo Woods and Sugar Bats flitting through the trees.

At some point after Louise turned five, the stories lost their shine. She embraced brushing her teeth by herself and putting herself to bed. She loved being responsible, she relished her independence, she got addicted to her parents' praise when they told her what a big girl she was. It felt more real than hearing yet another story about Pupkin getting in trouble and finally finding his way back home again thanks to the hard work of Girl Sparrow.

Mark kept listening, though. Mom thought he was fascinated by her elaborate tales of Pupkin's adventures, but Louise knew he just wanted her attention. Mark lived for it. She was his sun, and he orbited around her, soaking up every compliment, following her into theater, embracing all her suggestions.

Until one day, he stopped.

All references in this Will to the Descendants of any person shall mean their naturally born children and/or legally adopted children, unless otherwise indicated, as well as any of their children's naturally born and/or legally adopted children throughout the generations to come.

Mark decided he hated Louise right after he came home from the church ski trip. He had just turned fourteen.

"It's hormones," her dad explained after Mark had gone into her room and crushed all her oil pastels into the carpet.

"I don't know what the big deal is, Louise," her mom had said. "They'll wash out."

That hadn't been the point. The point was that Mark went into her room and broke her stuff all the time and never got punished enough for it. He tore a self-portrait out of her sketchbook, added zits, and taped it to the bathroom mirror with a word balloon coming out of its mouth saying, *I pick my nose.*

He hid Pupkin in her bed, which she hated. He wouldn't flush the toilet in their shared bathroom on purpose. He put one of her bras around Baudelaire, the Mitchells' golden retriever, one Halloween and everyone thought it was hilarious. Not Louise.

She realized she couldn't win, but the one thing she could do was put her head down and work, so she decided to graduate high school a year early. She took AP classes, enrolled in summer school, and lobbied her parents hard to let her graduate her junior year.

She stopped drawing for fun and focused on creating a design portfolio. She gave up extracurriculars and got a ride to the C of C every day after school, where she audited as many CAD, Photoshop, and first-year design classes as possible because they were free for the children of faculty.

"But you're just copying what you see in real life," her mom had said. "Why can't you do your design portfolio *and* still draw things from your imagination?"

"I'm serious about design," Louise had said.

"You're too young to be serious about anything!"

Louise chopped off her hair and dyed it black because she thought it made her look like someone ready to go to college.

"You had such pretty chestnut hair," her mom wailed.

"Brown," Louise corrected her.

"Auburn," her mother said. "You had wonderful auburn hair. Now you look like Edgar Allan Poe's daughter."

In the end, thanks to her dad's persuasion, she did graduate a year early, but her parents didn't get a second to relax because that was when

Mark started talking about BU. It was expensive, their dad told him, but if he wanted to go he could start saving up.

"But you paid for Louise to go to Berkeley!" Mark protested.

"Your sister is paying for her room and board by herself and she got a scholarship," their dad said.

"I'm being punished because I'm not Louise!" Mark said. "This is total discrimination!"

He raged. He argued. He wanted them to foot the entire bill. He got a couple of jobs but couldn't save a cent. He kicked a hole in their bedroom wall. Louise was glad she'd been on the other side of the country for most of it.

Finally, her dad decided it wasn't worth the endless fights, it wasn't worth the holes in the wall, it wasn't worth the slammed doors, and he agreed to pay for Mark's full ride. Louise had wanted to point out the hypocrisy, but she knew that would only make her parents defend Mark even harder. Especially her mom. She always defended Mark, even after he dropped out of BU his freshman year.

I bestow all of my tangible personal property owned by me at the time of my death, including, without limitation, personal effects, clothing, jewelry, furniture, furnishings, household goods, automobiles and other vehicles, along with all insurance policies upon such tangible property, in accordance to those designated in the attached Schedule— Beneficiary Designations.

Mark dropped out the second semester of Louise's junior year, and apparently he made such a mess of things that their mom had to go up to Boston and bring him home. That summer, Louise came back to Charleston and saw the damage.

She'd gotten up early that first morning and crept into the kitchen to get breakfast before Mark woke up, but the second her bare foot hit the linoleum of the dining room floor, she stopped in midstep. Her mom sat at the kitchen counter, back to Louise, slumped over like a marionette with its strings cut.

This woman who'd prided herself on her posture, who declared, "I'm short enough without slouching," slumped over on her stool, so absorbed in what she was doing that she didn't hear Louise.

"Mom," Louise said.

Her mother jumped.

"You scared me," she said, putting one hand over her heart, turning halfway around. Her eyes looked raw around the edges. On one hand she wore Pupkin.

"You two having breakfast together?" Louise asked, walking to the fridge.

Her mom gave a small, cracked smile.

"Pupkin is a good friend," her mom said. Pupkin cocked his head at Louise. "He always picks me up when I'm down."

Louise looked at Pupkin's leering clown face.

"Yeah," Louise said, "he's so comforting."

"You two don't like him," her mom said, "but I've known this little guy for a long time. You and your brother grew up and went off to school. Your dad goes to work. But Pupkin is always here."

Her mom looked thin and her cheeks looked stretched too tight over her cheekbones. For the first time, Louise was aware of her mother's skull beneath her skin. It made her angry that Mark had done this to her.

"You guys need to lay down some boundaries with Mark," Louise said. "Or things are never going to get better."

Her mom gave a deep, lung-rattling sigh.

"You have to be more understanding of your brother," she said. "College was hard for him."

Even then, so depressed she could barely move, when her only friend was her stupid hand puppet, she defended Mark.

SCHEDULE—BENEFICIARY DESIGNATIONS

Beneficiary Name—Mark Joyner

Relationship—Son

Bequeathed Inheritance—All tangible personal property and all policies and proceeds of insurance covering such property, all residences subject to any mortgages or encumbrances thereon, and all policies and proceeds of insurance covering such property

Inheritance Percentage—100%

Beneficiary Name—Louise Joyner

Relationship—Daughter

Bequeathed Inheritance—Art collection

Inheritance Percentage—100%

Her mom bounced back soon enough. She started going to FCP conventions again and booking puppet shows. She had new puppets to show off to Louise every time she came home. She started making her "art" again.

Louise didn't want to sound mean, but what her mom did wasn't art as far as she understood the definition. It was busywork. The excess energy she had now that Mark and Louise were older got channeled into framed cross-stitch samplers that lined the living room walls, an enormous crewelwork Tree of Life that hung over the sofa, string art that hung over the dining room table, watercolors of sunsets and the downtown Market that hung in the halls, little owls made of seashells with googly eyes that lined every windowsill. She went through phases, like her picture-frame phase, which broke down into a mosaic-picture-frame phase followed by a seashell-picture-frame phase followed by a bedazzled-picture-frame phase.

Her mom turned their house into the Nancy Joyner Gallery of Crap with constantly rotating exhibits; a museum of herself, crammed full of art projects and craft projects and paint-by-numbers self-expression. Louise grew blind to it over the years, just like she had to the dolls, but now she thought of all the framed pieces that hung in the house, all the pieces stacked up in the garage, probably more hidden in the attic, so much of it everywhere—her mom's art collection.

She'd never made a single comment about it, except for her sophomore year when her mom took a taxidermy class and brought home her final project: the Squirrel Nativity. It was exactly what it sounded like, a little wooden model of the stable in Bethlehem with Mary and Joseph bent over the manger containing the Baby Jesus, but they were all squirrels. Dead squirrels.

Her mom set it on top of the doll cabinet, stepped back, and asked Louise what she thought.

"It's gross," Louise said.

Her mom rolled her eyes.

"Okay, you don't like the medium, understood. But what about the art?"

Louise looked at the two dead gray squirrels bending over a smaller red squirrel lying on its back in the manger between them.

"Don't you think it's blasphemous?" Louise asked.

Her mom looked genuinely confused.

"How?" she asked.

"It's the holiest moment in Christianity," Louise said. "And you've made them squirrels."

"It's supposed to be funny," her mom said. "I don't think Jesus minds if we laugh a little sometimes."

But what's the point? Louise had wanted to ask. *What's the point of all this crap you keep sewing and painting and gluing and making?*

Twenty years later, Louise finally understood.

Beneficiary Name—Louise Joyner

Relationship—Daughter

Bequeathed Inheritance—Art collection

Inheritance Percentage—100%

The point, she realized, was that for once in his life, Mark wasn't going to win after all.

Chapter 10

As the flatbed truck carrying the bright red Agutter Clutter dumpster rolled into the driveway, Louise took a fake sip from her empty Starbucks cup. She'd been sitting on the porch as the sun rose, trying to think of a funny opening line to defuse the situation so Roland Agutter wouldn't get mad at her.

A lot of people were about to get mad at her.

The truck shuddered into silence, and Roland Agutter swung down from his cab and came across the dewy front yard. Louise stood up and took another pretend sip of her coffee.

"Feels like déjà vu all over again," Roland said, stopping. "If you'll open the front door and the garage, I'll drop my dumpster in the driveway."

Sunlight flashed off the windows of the busted Honda as it rolled to a stop on the edge of the yard and its doors opened.

"I want you to clean out the house," Louise said, "I really do. As far as I'm concerned, you have this job, but before you start I need to go through and take out my mom's artwork."

"Sure," Roland said, nodding before she'd even finished. "It'll take us half an hour to get set up."

"I might need a little longer than that," Louise said.

"Is there a lot of art?"

"The house is kind of full of it," Louise said.

"Maybe you could just pick out one or two of your favorite pieces?" Roland asked.

"I wish I could," Louise said, and lifted the empty Starbucks cup again and sucked air to avoid meeting his eyes. She actually pretended to swallow.

"Am I going to get in there today?" Roland asked. "Your brother called yesterday to make sure I was coming."

"I'm really sorry," Louise said.

Frustrated, Roland looked to the left of Louise, then the right, the roof, then back at her.

"It would help me out considerably," he said, "if you and your brother would iron out the wrinkles in your relationship before calling me again."

"I'm so sorry," Louise said.

Morning sunlight bounced off Mark's truck as he whipped around the corner and stopped on the edge of the yard. He sat for a minute, staring at Louise through the window, and she could see his mind working, trying to figure out what she was doing here, and then it clicked, and his face changed and he came boiling out of his truck, steaming across the yard. She should've eaten breakfast. The coffee burned inside her empty stomach like acid.

"Don't listen to her!" Mark shouted at Roland Agutter. "She doesn't know what she's talking about! This is my house! She doesn't control this!"

Agutter didn't even wait for Mark to reach them. He walked off toward his boys by the Honda to tell them there was no work today. Mark stopped him halfway across the yard.

"Where're you going?" he said, putting one hand on his shoulder.

Roland Agutter yanked his arm away.

"Every time," he said, suddenly furious. "Every. Single. Goddamn. Time. Money shows up and the family tears itself apart."

Mark stood and watched him go. Louise wanted to tell him that was absolutely not what was happening here, that her family wasn't some cliché fighting over an inheritance, it was her brother who was causing all the problems, not her, she'd been willing to split everything fifty-fifty. Instead, she watched Roland Agutter talk to his boys, then swing himself back up into his truck, crank the engine, and rumble away. The Honda followed. The truck engine Dopplered to the end of the block then went quiet as it took the corner and disappeared.

Mark turned on her, full of rage.

"You selfish asshole," he said. "I'm sorry Mom and Dad didn't do what you wanted for once, but they gave the house to me, not you, so you need to butt out."

Louise had rehearsed this moment all morning.

Stand your ground, look him in the eye, don't give an inch.

"You might want to work on your reading comprehension," she said. "Why don't you go over Mom's will again with Brody—"

The instant she said "Brody" Mark started talking over her.

"He's my lawyer," he said. "Not yours. You can't talk to him!"

"No," she said, happy to knock him off-balance again. "He's the estate's lawyer."

"Which belongs to me!" Mark said.

"Turn to the schedule at the back," she said, pulling out her phone. She read from the email, "Beneficiary designations. Page 8. Beneficiary Name—Louise Joyner. Relationship—Daughter. Bequeathed Inheritance—Art collection. Inheritance Percentage—100%."

She gave it a second to sink in.

"So what?" Mark said.

"Do you understand what she meant by art collection?" Louise asked. "It means everything Mom ever made. All her art. All her paintings, her string art, her picture frames, the squirrels. Everything."

Mark's shoulders unclenched and his body sagged.

"Big whoop," he said, trying to sound brave. "You can have it. You're actually doing me a favor."

"Thank you so kindly for your permission, which I don't need," Louise said. "I'll try to hurry, but honestly, if it takes longer than a week I'll have to go back to San Francisco and leave it unfinished. Which means you can't do anything with the house until I come back."

A woman in a red fleece pushing a jogging stroller bounced by. Louise felt trashy, arguing in the front yard with her brother again, a remnant of the old neighborhood. They didn't fit in with these new yoga people.

"The second you leave," Mark said, "I'll get those guys back over to clean it out."

"You could," Louise said, "but I'm going to insist on walking through every room to make sure I got everything. And it might be a while before I can come back to do that. Mom has a lot of art and I'm going to preserve every single piece of it, as per her final wishes, as stated in the Beneficiary Designations of her will, which I'm sure you agree we should both respect. It might take me a year, and in the meantime, you can't sell the house."

"Fuck you," Mark said. "I'm calling Brody."

"Be my guest," she told him.

She knew he'd have to hear it from someone who wasn't her. She watched Mark's back as he stormed off to the edge of the front yard, pressing his phone to one ear. Louise worked in a tech-adjacent field, which made her hyperaware of power dynamics. Waiting around for Mark to finish his call looked weak. She executed her alpha move and got started on the house.

She went around back and reached through the broken pane of glass to let herself into the garage. Then she slapped the doorbell button that raised the garage door, which made a hideous shriek as it rumbled up, letting in daylight. Cold morning air flowed in around her. The Mark and Louise dolls stared dumbly at her from the shelf. She listened, trying to hear the TV, but all she heard was silence from the house.

Next to the dolls she saw a lampshade her mom had painted with starfish, a set of Mom-made clay bookends shaped like pink seahorses, and a white kitchen garbage bag holding the papier-mâché masks her mom had made during her mask phase. Without even looking hard she spotted a stack of unframed canvases and realized they were the oil portraits her mom had painted of the entire family that everyone had deemed too hideous to hang inside the house. Mark's was the only one that didn't make him look like a prematurely aged gnome baring its teeth and snarling.

Louise looked behind the portraits and saw another white bag of her mom's needlepoint throw pillows and five cardboard boxes labeled *Christmas*, which she knew was only one stockpile of handmade ornaments.

Normally, a job like this would prompt Louise to start a list, but today she had to fight her urge to organize. Today she'd be inefficient. Today she felt grateful for the enormous amount of stuff filling every corner of their house.

Step one: do a walk-through and count the art. Don't touch it. Just count it.

She stood on the steps to the kitchen door and braced herself, then walked inside for the first time since the day she arrived, walked past the hammer on the counter and made herself go into the living room.

The easy chair sat empty. The TV was still off. She ignored the rows and rows of silent dolls and focused on the art: the crewelwork Tree of Life over the sofa, the nine framed cross-stitches on the far wall (four of flowers, three Charleston scenes, one elephant balancing on its front legs, one juggling clown), the three more framed cross-stitches beside the doll cabinet, the yarn art Mount Fuji next to the bay window.

The screen door squealed, a key crunched into the front-door lock, and it swung open to reveal Mark, framed by the sun. They looked at each other, both of them back in the house where they grew up for the first time in years.

"So Brody agreed?" Louise asked.

Mark didn't answer, which meant yes.

"I don't like coming in here anyways," he said. "It's got bad vibes."

He rammed his hands into his pockets, hunched his shoulders, then relaxed them.

"Good," Louise said.

"Good," Mark said.

He started to turn like he was going to walk away, then stopped.

"What's your point?" he asked.

The point was that he crushed all of her oil pastels into her bedroom carpet. The point was that he'd kicked a hole in her parents' bedroom wall and they hadn't made him pay to get it fixed. The point was that her mom had a whole tough-love thing for Louise and let Mark do whatever he wanted and never face any consequences. The point was that she was supposed to look after him and give him everything and never complain, but no one was looking after her. That was the point.

She furrowed her forehead.

"I just want to respect Mom's wishes," she said.

"You hated Mom."

That took her by surprise.

"I didn't hate Mom," she said, voice getting high-pitched with genuine irritation. How dare he say that? It wasn't even close to true. They had a complicated relationship, but she didn't *hate* her.

"You always made fun of her art," he said.

"I never made fun of her art," she said. "I work in design because of her."

"You glued googly eyes to the toilet and said it was her masterpiece. You even put a little museum placard next to it."

"I was thirteen."

"You know she locked herself in her room and cried when you did that."

"I've got a lot to do," she said. "I don't have time for this."

"Cool," he said.

She watched him walk away and pull a camp chair out the back of his truck and set it up in the front yard. Then he came back to the screen door.

"I'm just going to be over here keeping an eye on things," he said. "So you don't accidentally on purpose take something that doesn't belong to you."

"Okay, Mark," she said sweetly.

She watched him drift across the yard and settle in his chair, and Louise figured if the new neighbors didn't think they were trashy before, they did now. Mark began to play on his phone and Louise turned to confront the house full of years and years of her mom's art.

Louise wanted to blow through the rooms, strip them of art, stack it in boxes, go down a list of important paperwork, grab all the family photos, but she needed to slow down. She needed to be inefficient. She needed to not be herself.

She made herself count all the string art hanging over the dining room table: the three-masted schooner on its blond wooden plaque, the owls, the mushrooms, the butterflies, the big wave, the sunset, the reverse silhouette of a cat, the yin-yang sign. Their strings were clotted with dust because her mom was an artist, not a housekeeper.

She went into the living room and scanned the dolls lining the shelf, and the back of the sofa, and the top of the TV, and the doll cabinet, and she decided they were Mark's problem, not hers. Then her gaze landed on top of the doll cabinet and she wondered what she was going to do with the Squirrel Nativity.

It had grossed her out when their mom made it, and the years hadn't been kind. Squirrel Mary and Squirrel Joseph had darkened with age, their fur coming out in patches, their once-fluffy tails now frayed and mangy. They prayed over Squirrel Baby Jesus with withered black paws held in front of their hairless chests, and Squirrel Joseph's wrinkled lips had tightened over time, pulling back to reveal a slice of bright yellow teeth. Squirrel Baby Jesus had gone almost entirely bald, and his tail had become as hairless as a rat's. All of them had lost their eyes and her mom had stitched their hollow sockets shut.

Mark had picked up on Louise's discomfort with it the second it entered the house. He told her he'd seen the squirrels turn their heads one night. He said they were waiting for her to go to sleep and then they'd come crawling down the hall, worm past her lips, and claw their way down her throat. She told him to fuck off, but even today she could feel their sharp, bony claws digging into her soft throat tissue as they hauled their filthy bodies down toward her stomach.

Louise couldn't be in the house with it for another second. She made herself grab it by the sides, the Squirrel Holy Family wobbling so much that for one horrible second she thought they'd snap off and she'd have to touch their bodies to pick them up, and she marched through the kitchen and out to the garage.

The air felt fresh and cold out here. It didn't smell like Yankee Candle and dust. She went to the garbage can, tipped open the lid, and stopped.

Pupkin was gone.

"Hey!" Mark said behind her.

Louise jumped. She turned and saw him staring at her through the open garage door.

pupkin isn't there, he's escaped, he'll be so angry

She dropped the Squirrel Nativity into the can and slammed the lid shut.

"Hey is for horses," she said, a favorite saying of their mom's.

"I know what you're doing." He smiled. "You think I'm going to freak out over how long this is taking and cut you in on the sale."

She locked her face into its blankest expression and asked in an innocent voice, "You're planning on selling?"

"Homeownership is for suckers," he said. "I'm a happy renter."

"Aunt Honey's going to be angry," Louise said. "She thinks you should keep it and rent it out the way Mom used to, or move in."

"Yeah, well," Mark said, "it's my house now, so I don't really care about your opinion."

"Cool," she said. "I'll try to get everything out of here as soon as I can."

Which she had no intention of doing.

"I can wait," he said. "I can wait months. The market just keeps getting better and better."

"Mercy said the bubble's at its peak," she said, using whatever advantage she could find. "You don't want to wait too long."

"Mom left everything to me, Louise. That won't change no matter how much longer you drag your feet."

"Okay," she said, and she couldn't get her face to relax. Her fake smile felt like a snarl.

"You've got a job," Mark said, "and a kid. And you're going to go back to all that in what, a week? A week and a half? By March this house will be on the market and there's nothing you can do about it."

He looked so smug. He thought he could predict everything she was going to do.

"Maybe I'll move here," she said. "Maybe I'll bring Poppy. You want to wait me out? I can bring my daughter here, where the cost of living is cheaper, and I can waste years in Charleston going through this house. You're never selling this fucking place while I'm alive."

Her chest felt flushed, her face felt hot. Mark looked elated.

"So if I split it fifty-fifty you'll pack up and stop pretending you care about Mom's art?"

That stopped her. A fifty-fifty split, and this would be over. They'd reschedule Agutter for next week and it would end. She could go home. She could see Poppy. Everything would go back to normal.

Think of Poppy getting a quarter-million-dollar head start in life, Louise told herself. *And you never have to deal with Mark again.*

She opened her mouth to say something and Mark raised his eyebrows and Louise realized it was a trap. He wanted to see if she'd get greedy and then he'd yank the rug out from under her. He'd never shared anything with her in her life.

"You can't put a price tag on love," she said.

She felt like she'd won. It was a small victory, it was a grubby victory, but it was hers.

Mark flipped her the bird, then noticed something over her shoulder.

"Did you do that?" he asked, and she followed his gaze to the back door and its broken pane of glass. "You broke that window?"

"I didn't have a key," she said.

"I'm charging you for that," he said. "You can't come in here and break my stuff."

He stormed off to his truck and Louise was left alone in the garage with her mom's art and the garbage can and

pupkin

He'd just slid down deeper in the trash, that's all. She could open the can and find him if she wanted, but she didn't want to do that. Then she thought about what else she'd seen in there.

His bag was torn open.

It had torn on something. He hadn't ripped his way out of it. He was a puppet, he couldn't . . .

Mark.

Of course. He'd probably come by and gone to throw something out and seen Pupkin and taken him to mess with Louise. He was going to hide him in her purse or someplace when she wasn't looking. Maybe set him up with the TV again. Fine. She'd go even slower on the art. For once, Mark wasn't going to win. It'd take more than a puppet to get her out of this house.

Chapter 11

Louise stood in her bedroom doorway and looked at Buffalo Jones sitting on her bed, with Red Rabbit, Hedgie Hoggie, and Dumbo above him on their shelf, and realized they were the only things she wanted from her old room. Poppy would love them, and they'd give her a way to tell stories to Poppy about when she'd been little, about Poppy's grandmother, and maybe help her try to explain death again, only better this time.

She gathered them up in her arms and headed out into the sunny front yard.

"Hey!" Mark called from his camp chair. "Where you going?"

"They're mine, Mark," Louise said, not stopping on the way to her Kia.

"No," he said, "they're mine."

"They're for Poppy," she said.

"Did you pay for them or did Mom and Dad?" he asked, pushing himself up out of his chair and lumbering over. "All you get is Mom's art and anything you paid for. If you don't have a receipt, then I'm afraid they belong to the estate, and the estate belongs to me."

Louise's skin flushed hot. She turned, marched back into the house, dumped them on the sofa, got a twenty out of her purse, and went back outside. She balled it up and threw it at Mark. It bounced off his chest and landed on the grass.

"Is that enough?" she asked.

"That's barely beer money," he said, smiling. "I was thinking more like a hundred apiece."

"Four hundred dollars?" she asked. "For my childhood stuffed animals?"

"I wouldn't pay it, either," he said. "I mean, good thing you didn't like them much anyways. You always kept them up on a shelf."

She bent over and picked up her twenty.

"Mom's puppets are her art," she said. "I'm taking those, too."

She didn't want them. She didn't want any of this. Why was she fighting with Mark over this stuff?

Because he can't keep winning everything.

"Good," Mark said. "Less shit I have to deal with."

Anger made her brain buzz inside her skull.

"Why are you acting like this?" she spat at Mark.

"Why're you?" he shot back.

Because I want things to be fair this one time, because you always win everything.

"Because of Mom's will," she said. "I'm respecting her wishes."

"So am I," Mark said.

The two of them stared at each other, breathing hard, and Louise couldn't think of anything to say that he wouldn't boomerang back on her. She turned and went back in the house.

"Nice talking to you," Mark called.

She went and stood outside the door of her mom's workroom. More than anywhere in the house, this was the room that felt the most like her mom's private space, and while she still wasn't ready to go inside, after saying what she'd said about the puppets she felt like she had to look.

Louise threw open the door. It only opened about eighteen inches before it hit a soft wall of puppets. She squeezed her way through the crack. Puppets covered all four walls, dangling from suspended racks made of broomsticks, sitting on dowels on top of the racks; puppets stuffed inside milk crates and piled almost to the ceiling on her mom's worktable. Where there weren't puppets, there were things her mom used to make puppets. Stacks of age-softened cardboard boxes piled high in the corners holding bolts of felt, puppet fleece, gasket rubber, fluorescent pink tulle, Day-Glo fishnet. Behind her mom's worktable, where she cut patterns and trimmed fur, stood her sewing machine, and beside it a metal cabinet of tiny drawers containing eyeballs and eyelashes, fake hair, buttons, feathers, sequins, and paste jewels.

Somehow the workroom contained more stuff than the rest of the house put together. Louise could barely breathe it was crammed so full of puppets, forty years of them stuffed into one tiny room, lining the walls, stacked to the ceiling. It felt too warm, too close, too claustrophobic. It stunk of polyester.

This workroom was her mom's sanctuary. Her safe space. The place where she'd devoted hundreds of hours of her life to making things.

That were all about to go in the trash.

"Let's get you guys counted," Louise said out loud, and the layers of soft puppets lining the walls ate the echo of her words, making them sound small.

The room represented hundreds of hours of her mom's work, hundreds of hours of her life spent creating these things and pretending they were alive. That's probably why her mom liked *The Velveteen Rab-*

bit so much—it was what she spent her life doing: bringing nonliving objects to life.

They're not real. They're just synthetic fabric and plastic. They're only things.

Louise scanned the puppets, some she didn't recognize, but most— like Mr. Don't, Cosmic Starshine, Danny the Imagination Dragon, Pizza-face, Judge Goodsense—she did. To count them she'd have to push her way into the mass of their dangling bodies and shove her way over to the far wall by the window. She got ready to step into this sea of puppet fleece and synthetic fur, and she couldn't. It felt too sad. Could she really throw everything her mom had made away? But what else could she do with them?

Overwhelmed, Louise pulled the door closed. She'd figure them out later.

There wasn't much art to count in the bedrooms, so she decided to kill some time by putting her stuffed animals back on their shelf in her room. She'd find a way to get them out later. She walked into the sun-warmed living room and looked out the bay window. Mark still sat in his chair, guarding the house against her, hunched over his phone.

She gathered up her stuffed animals and took them back to her bedroom, where she put them back on their shelf. She needed to slow down. There were only a couple of paintings in her mom's room and one or two in Mark's bedroom, and that was it, besides the puppets. She checked her phone and it wasn't even noon. She decided to see if her mom had any paintings stashed in her closet.

Louise crossed the hall and stood outside her mom and dad's door, the only one in the house they always had to knock on before entering. Before she could chicken out, she grabbed the knob and turned. It made the sound Louise had heard all her life—a hollow metal rattle with a brief bell note at the end- —and she pushed it open. She hesitated on the threshold. It was the first time she'd been inside since they'd died.

Cold, early-afternoon sunlight came through the windows; her mom's oak-veneer vanity sat next to the door, a thin layer of dust settled over the perfume bottles and her mom's tortoiseshell comb and brush. The bed was made. A few of her mom's chunky, brightly colored oils of fruit hung on the far wall. A single dark sock—her dad's—lay across the foot of the bed. The room looked as final and empty as Louise had dreaded.

When they were little and really sick, her mom had allowed them to sleep in her bed because it was bigger. Louise remembered sick days with the black-and-white TV on the vanity, tucked in, eating Campbell's chicken noodle soup off a tray and drinking flat ginger ale. She wanted to be taken care of so badly. How had she and Mark come to this? Fighting in the yard over nothing, hating each other, arguing over a will?

Louise pushed off her shoes and lay down on their bed, curling up in the middle. The faint smell of her dad's Old Spice and her mom's powder puffed out of the pillows. She hadn't expected this to be so hard. She looked at the still lifes of fruit on the wall, burning with color, thick with oils. She remembered her mom struggling over them. Painting the natural world hadn't come easy to her.

All her life, Nancy had wanted Louise to take her art seriously, but Louise refused. She'd made fun of it, she'd ignored it, she'd even, according to Mark, made her cry over it. Now she and Mark had made it the battleground for all their old resentments, and in the end, like everything in this house her parents had spent years accumulating and saving for and buying and creating, it would all end up in the trash. It would be sold to strangers at Goodwill. Everything would float away, including her and Mark, because after this how could they ever talk to each other again?

And nothing would be left.

"I'm sorry," Louise whispered to the room, still smelling the ghosts of her mom's powder and her dad's aftershave. "I'm so sorry."

She had failed as a mother and now she had failed as a daughter.

Her parents were ashes in a hole in the ground. Her brother had taken the house from her. And she was about to throw everything her mom ever made in the trash. She felt so drained.

She fell asleep.

Louise opened her eyes. The room had gotten brighter, which meant it was after noon by now, and her mouth felt gummy. Some sound had dragged her out of deep sleep. She listened but didn't hear anything. She looked out the open door into the empty hall but didn't see anything. The bed felt so soft, and the air felt cool, but she felt warm and safe, tucked up into herself; her hands between her thighs felt warm, her neck against the pillow felt warm, she didn't want to move.

She let her eyelids slowly lower, staring down her body at her dad's dark sock at the end of the bed. It moved.

In a heartbeat, Louise woke up. It wasn't her dad's sock, it was a small, furry black head coming up over the end of the bed, pointed like a rodent's, like a mouse, like a rat

like a squirrel

The dark gray squirrel scurried two more steps up onto the comforter and raised its nose to sniff the air. There must be squirrels in the attic; that must be why they had boarded up the hatch, and it must have come down through the open vent in the hall and come in here looking for food. Were squirrels rabid?

It looked mangy and the top of its head was missing a patch of fur. Its ears looked chewed. One side of its leathery lips had pulled back and she could see a slice of its yellowed teeth and its eyes were stitched shut and she knew it was from the Squirrel Nativity.

Louise's guts turned to ice. A tiny whimper escaped her lips and the squirrel twitched its head in her direction and Louise realized it was listening. It took another slow, cautious, creeping step forward. It wanted to find her mouth and worm its long, mangy body down her throat and wriggle into her guts.

Quietly she braced herself, careful not to rock the mattress. She tensed the muscles in her left leg to kick the squirrel. She'd kick it, then drop the blanket over it and get outside. The dead squirrel cocked its head to one side, listening, and Louise bunched the muscles in her thigh and suddenly the soft pillow around her throat twitched and moved and the squirrel curled around her neck darted inside the collar of her shirt and scurried down the front of her chest.

Louise screamed, leapt out of bed, not caring about the squirrel at the foot of it anymore, needing to get this thing out from under her clothes. It clawed at her body, her breasts, her belly, her sides, scurrying around to her back, trapped beneath her shirt. She slapped at herself, dancing from foot to foot, screaming "Ah! Ah! Ah!" over and over again, desperate to get it out.

Its dry, sharp paws pinched her belly and she realized it was going down, following her shirt tucked into her jeans, and if it kept going it would come out below her waistband and she panicked, not wanting it to get into her pants.

It felt dry against her skin and light and sharp like some kind of hollow-bodied crustacean, like a crab, darting beneath her clothes. Louise felt its claws pinch her soft stomach again, its small triangular head poking under her waistband like a wedge and she slapped one hand down hard over her gut and trapped it against her, pressing it into her body hard, and something sharper than she could imagine cut deep into her belly. She kept pressing, not letting up no matter how deep it sunk in its teeth.

It thrashed and writhed and tried to get down her pants, and she stuck her left hand into the buttons of her shirt, popping two of them, and yanked her shirt out of the waistband of her jeans and gripped the hard, bony thing and tore it out and hurled it away. It was lighter than she thought. It flew across the room and hit the far wall with a weightless *tap*. Louise turned to run and stopped so fast she overbalanced and fell backward onto her butt. Squirrel Baby Jesus crouched in the doorway, its bald tail twitching. Then its mummified tail broke off in mid-twitch, dropping weightlessly to the carpet. Its stump flickered back and forth as the blind squirrel cocked its head, listening for her.

As silently as she could, Louise rose to her feet and took one long, quiet step to the right, toward the bathroom door. The Squirrel Baby Jesus raised up on its haunches, sensing the air for vibrations. On the other side of the room the Squirrel Mary she'd thrown against the wall turned itself over. One of its front legs hung at a ninety-degree angle. The Squirrel Joseph still crouched on the comforter, and like the one in the door, it raised itself up on its haunches, listening.

Louise froze.

The bathroom door was too far away. She needed at least three big steps to get there and they were faster than her. But it was her only chance. She took another slow, silent step. Underneath the carpet, the floor creaked.

The squirrel on the comforter swung its head in her direction. Louise held her breath. The Squirrel Baby Jesus lowered itself onto all fours and took a slooow step in Louise's direction.

She tried to ease her foot off the carpet as slowly as possible. The squirrel on the comforter lowered itself onto all fours and scrabbled down to the floor headfirst. Louise finally got her foot off the floor. It creaked again. The Squirrel Joseph halfway down the comforter froze. Its tail gave a single convulsive twitch.

Then it came for her. Louise saw the badminton racquets leaning against the wall and she heard Squirrel Joseph's claws racing over the carpet, almost on her, and she scooped up a racquet, flipped it so it faced the ground, and slammed it down, trapping the squirrel between its strings and the carpet.

It twitched, stronger than she imagined, and wrapped its tiny mummified claws around the strings. Louise raised the racquet and the squirrel came up with it, then she slammed it into the carpet again and stepped on it. Something crunched. The squirrel let go. Louise flipped the racquet and brought the edge of its wooden rim down on the squirrel, chopping it in half.

She felt rather than saw the other two burst into motion, streaking at her over the carpet, and Louise dove into the dark bathroom and slammed the door. She heard their dry bodies rattle against the wood on the other side, scrabbling at it with their claws, and she pushed in the thumb lock just as she felt one of them scurry across the knob on the other side of the door.

The shadows on the floor from the crack under the door moved, and she looked down just in time to see a squirrel pushing its long, pointed head through the crack, and without thinking, Louise picked up her bare foot and brought her heel down hard on its dry skull.

She felt it snap like a nutshell through the sole of her foot. It jerked and spasmed for an instant, trying to pull its crushed skull out from under her heel, then went still. She yanked her foot away and looked at the front half of the squirrel's dry, empty husk and caved-in skull, then she turned, leaned over the sink, and opened her mouth to throw up. Her stomach convulsed but only sour air and a long retching belch bubbled up. White stars twinkled in her vision. She stayed like that for a long time, her stomach cramping over on itself.

Finally, she sat on the toilet seat and tried to slow her breathing. When she felt like she could move without going light-headed she turned on the lights, and that was when she noticed the squirrel under the door was gone. Carefully, racquet in one hand, she cracked open the door, heart cramping inside her chest. The door revealed empty carpet, then more empty carpet, then she had it all the way open. The squirrels were gone.

Louise had to know. Still clutching the racquet, she moved to the door and looked down the hall, and a mechanical scream ripped through the house. Louise jumped, then realized it was Mark cutting wood with a power saw. She followed the sound to the garage.

Mark was outside the open back door, chopping a piece of plywood into a patch for the broken glass with his circular saw. Louise stepped over his extension cord and walked to the garbage can. He heard her open its lid.

"You know," he said, "you can mess with Mom's art all you want, but you're going to have to pay for the window you broke."

Louise ignored him. Inside the garbage can lay the Squirrel Nativity. Squirrel Mary and Joseph stood in their prayerful positions like they always did, bent over the red Squirrel Baby Jesus. But Squirrel Mary's dry skull had been crushed and the Squirrel Joseph had a gash in its side revealing its hollow leather interior, a few specks of greasy sawdust clinging to its fur.

"And that badminton racquet doesn't belong to you, either," Mark said, behind her.

They had gotten damaged when she threw the Nativity in the garbage. Those had been real squirrels from the attic in her mom's bedroom. She'd just been mistaken. She hadn't killed them. Squirrels moved fast. She'd only stunned them.

You threw them in the garbage. You made them angry. You made Pupkin angry, too. Where's Pupkin?

"You know, I had this all planned out with Agutter's guys," Mark carried on, behind her. "They were going to deal with all this shit because they weren't emotionally attached to it. Then you fucked it all up. What're you even going to do with Mom's art? You're probably just going to dump it all in the trash."

Louise couldn't do this. She couldn't deal with Mark. With this house *with the squirrel nativity, with pupkin*

She turned around.

"You win," she said. "Call Mercy. Sell the house. I'm done."

Chapter 12

Wait, what?" Mark asked, following her out the garage door.

"I'm finished and I'm not coming back," she said.

She heard Buffalo Jones, Red Rabbit, Hedgie Hoggie, and Dumbo from her bedroom, stranded on their shelf.

Louise, don't leave us.

"What happened?" Mark asked.

Louise kept walking down the driveway.

"Nothing happened, Mark," she said. "I'm just done."

Louise, don't leave us behind again.

"What about Mom's art?" Mark asked. "It's so important you were going to move back here."

Don't leave us behind the way you left—

She didn't want to hear it. She stopped by her bright blue rental car and turned to face Mark. She had to go.

"I did it to mess with you," Louise said. "Because you always get everything and Mom never told you 'no,' but I can't anymore. Being here is really bad for my mental health. So you win. It's all yours. I'm done."

"You can't do that," Mark said. "You can't just show up and break windows and dump Mom's art everywhere, then leave me to deal with everything."

Louise . . .

She could.

She slammed the car door and turned the key, and as she reversed down the driveway Mark walked after her, shouting, "You still owe me for that window!"

When she got to the corner she looked in her rearview mirror and saw Mark standing in the street in front of their house watching her go, and he looked very small and very alone.

. . . please . . .

. . . don't go . . .

Louise put on her turn signal and took a left. She didn't look in her rearview mirror again. She got to the light, pulled onto Coleman, and she was gone.

I panicked. There were squirrels in the attic and they got out and I panicked and I never have to go back there again. It's Mark's house now. It's not our family's house anymore. I'm done.

For the first time since Mark had called she felt free. It felt strange to be finished. There would be no new stories, no new memories, no new obligations; her family was part of the past now, and the past was over. It was gone. It couldn't touch her. She never had to go back to the house again. She would never talk to Mark again, beyond some legal stuff. Her life was in San Francisco now. The story of the Joyner family was through.

She got back to her room at SpringHill Suites, pulled up her shirt, and looked at her stomach in the mirror. It was covered with scratches but she'd been moving stuff around all day. Anything could have caused them. She took a hot shower and repeated it to herself inside her head.

it's over it's over it's over it's over it's over it's over

She wrapped herself in a towel and sat on the edge of her bed. Everything felt very still and very quiet for the first time in days. Her head felt empty. She decided to lie back on the bed, just for a minute, and when she opened her eyes the room had gone gray. She picked up her phone to check the time and saw missed calls from Mark, from Brody, from Mercy, and she didn't care. She was more done now than she had been before she fell asleep. All she cared about was Poppy. She needed to hear her voice.

She texted Ian.

HEY—CAN YOU GET POPPY ON FACETIME FOR ME.

He responded:

NOW YOU'VE DECIDED TO PARENT? I'VE BEEN TEXTING YOU ALL DAY. SHE KEEPS ASKING FOR YOU.

She looked at her phone and saw five missed texts from Ian of increasing urgency.

BEEN DEALING WITH MY DEAD PARENTS ESTATE, she texted back, which was a low blow, but if you couldn't use it at least a little bit, what was the point? NOT INTERESTED IN RELITIGATING THE PAST. AM HERE NOW.

He texted back:

5 MINS.

She didn't want Ian to see her in a towel, so she threw on jeans and a T-shirt just as he FaceTimed, and Louise accepted the call. Her chest got tight when she saw how bad Poppy looked.

"Hey, sweetie," she said. "How are you? I've missed you."

Poppy had dark circles under her eyes, her face looked washed-out, and it wasn't the lighting. The corners of her eyes and the tip of her nose had that raw look.

"Are you okay, Popster?" she asked. "Do you feel sick?"

"When you home, Mommy?" Poppy whined in baby talk.

They'd worked really hard to get her to stop doing this, but Louise didn't let her disappointment show.

"Very soon," she said. "But you're a big girl, so you need to understand that I can't be there all the time."

"I'm a baby!" Poppy babbled. "When you come ho-ho?"

Despite the baby talk, Louise smiled, happy to deliver good news.

"I'm coming home tomorrow," she said. "I thought I'd be here for a long time but I changed my mind because I can't wait to see you, so I'm getting on the first plane in the morning and coming home."

Poppy's smile was so big it cracked her face in two. Ian turned the camera toward himself.

"When were you going to tell me?" he asked.

"It just happened," Louise said. "There's nothing here for me anymore, so I'm coming home as soon as I can get a flight."

"Are you coming here?" Poppy asked, sticking her face into frame, speaking in her normal voice now, baby talk forgotten. "Are you coming here now?"

"We're still in the mountains," Ian said, and Louise could tell he was trying to be graceful about the sudden change.

A call popped up from Mark. Louise declined it.

"I'm flying into San Francisco," she said. "You can bring Poppy back tomorrow or the next day."

The image on the screen lurched as Ian took the phone. She heard him say to Poppy, "I'll be right back."

Then the phone showed her the inside of his nostrils and part of his eyes.

"You're really coming back early?" he asked. "This isn't a joke?"

"I'm finding a flight as soon as we hang up," Louise said.

"Thank God," Ian said. "She wet the bed again last night. My mom already has her lined up with this child psychologist—"

"No way," Louise said. "I'm home tomorrow afternoon."

"I know," Ian said, "but, like, hurry? This has been awful."

"Let me talk to her again," Louise said.

The phone lurched back into the bedroom and Ian held the phone out for Poppy.

"I'm coming home," Louise told her. "But I want to see a big girl when I get there. Can you talk like a big girl for me?"

"Come home now," Poppy said in her normal voice.

"It's very far away," Louise said. "It takes me a little time to get there. Do you know how far away it is?"

"A hundred miles," Poppy said.

A hundred was the longest distance that meant anything to Poppy because it was a hundred miles from San Francisco to Ian's parents' mountain house.

"It's a hundred miles twenty times," Louise said. "Do you know how many that is?"

"Twenty," Poppy said.

"It's further than that," Louise said.

She couldn't believe how good it felt to hear Poppy's voice. Louise remembered her second year of grad school when her mom had called one night and Louise had gone on about the interpersonal politics of charette, and finding a paid internship, and she'd finally realized her mom wasn't talking.

"Why'd you call?" Louise had asked.

"I just needed to hear your voice," her mom had said.

Louise wondered what her mom had been going through that night, but she would never know. Not now. Not anymore. Her mom's life was over. Her secrets didn't matter now.

Mark called again. Louise declined.

"You're only twenty miles away," Poppy decided.

"No, I'm one hundred miles, twenty times away," Louise said.

Louise had no idea why she was trying to explain multiplication to a five-year-old, but she remembered how much she'd liked it when her dad had explained things to her, even when she hadn't fully understood.

"Flights are going to be expensive this late," Ian said. "Are you flying Delta?"

"I don't know," Louise said, annoyed he was interrupting this moment and making it more confusing than it needed to be for Poppy. "I haven't looked yet. Poppy, can you imagine one hundred miles twenty times?"

"You're a hundred miles," Poppy declared.

Mark called again. Louise declined, punching her screen hard.

"Why don't we draw it?" Louise said. "Do you have a piece of paper? I've got—"

Bang!

Something slammed into the window behind Louise. She jumped, throwing her phone across the bed and throwing herself forward after it. She scrambled across the carpet on her hands and knees until she reached the other side of the bed, then looked back.

Mark stood outside her window, smacking it with his hands.

"Lou!" he called, his voice muffled through the double-paned glass. "They won't tell me your room number."

"Mommy?" she heard Poppy call faintly from her phone where she'd thrown it.

"Jesus Christ! What do you think you're doing?" Louise said, then realized Mark couldn't hear her through the window. "What do you want?" she shouted.

"Come outside!" he shouted, his voice muted and very far away. "We need to talk!"

She heard Poppy ask Ian where she was.

"No!" she shouted at Mark.

"We need to talk!" he shouted.

"No!" she yelled again.

"Hey!" someone shouted from the adjoining room. "Keep it down."

"It's important!" Mark shouted through the window. He wasn't going away.

Louise picked up her phone and saw Ian's face in close-up as he tried to figure out why the screen had suddenly gone black.

"Hey," Louise said. "Something's come up. Tell Poppy I'll just be a minute."

She ended the call and turned to the window.

"Meet me out front," she shouted.

"Shut! Up!" the man in the adjoining room yelled.

Mark stood on the sidewalk, just out of range of the sliding-door sensor. His hair stuck out on both sides like he'd been running his hands through it. He held his phone in one hand. His gut peeked out from underneath his T-shirt. Louise walked toward the glass, the doors whooshed open, and she stepped into the cold evening air.

"What?" she said.

"I'm not here to fight," Mark told her.

"I'm going home," Louise said.

"I know you don't like me because I'm not successful enough for you," Mark said. "But I'm actually happy with my life. People like me. They think I'm a nice guy."

"It has nothing to do with whether you're successful or not," Louise said. "But if we weren't related, if we met today, we wouldn't choose to be friends. We're different people with different values, and we're also adults who can choose who we want to spend our time with, and right now I'm choosing to go home to my daughter. I really don't care about the house, Mark. Mom gave it to you."

She turned to go back inside.

"I'll give you twenty-five percent," he said.

That stopped Louise.

"Why?" she asked, turning back around.

"I'm not going against Mom's wishes," he said. "She gave it to me, and I'm choosing to give some of it to you even though you hate me."

"I don't hate you, Mark," Louise said. "But I don't want to fight with you anymore. So whatever you want."

"I'm giving you twenty-five percent whether you like it or not," Mark said.

"That's . . ." Louise tried to think of something to say. "That's very generous."

"I'm a generous person," Mark said.

"So," Louise said, "how does this work? You'll put it on the market and send me a check?"

"No," Mark said. "Mercy's going to sell it."

He held his phone out to Louise, screen first. Mercy waved to her with both hands.

"Hey, Louise!" Mercy said from the tiny speaker, scrunching up her nose. "This is so exciting!"

"Have you been on there this whole time?" Louise asked.

"Mark wanted me to speak with you," Mercy said, "because I think this is such an exciting opportunity, but we need you to stick around for a few days."

"Oh, no," Louise said, panic tightening her throat. "I have to go back to San Francisco. I just told Poppy I was coming home."

"And you will," Mercy cheered as if she hadn't heard the last part, "but we need to start getting the house ready first."

"I need you to do the estate stuff," Mark said. "I'm really good at the broad strokes but you're better at all the boring crap."

Louise realized what had happened. She thought about the missed calls from Brody.

"What did Brody say?" she asked Mark.

"Nothing," Mark said, looking so offended Louise knew he was lying.

"What did he want?" she asked.

"Just stuff," Mark said. "A chain of claimants, an inventory of the house, and he said I'd have to fill out this stuff for Social Security, and he asked if I'd talked to the C of C about Dad's pension."

"No," Louise said. "No way. I'm not breaking a promise to my daughter to do your homework for you. I'm going home."

"Then no split," Mark said.

"Louise," Mercy said from the phone, "I told Mark I'd handle the house, but—and this is nothing personal, Mark—I wouldn't touch it with a ten-foot pole if you weren't involved."

"I can talk to other Realtors—" Mark began.

"And you remember what we talked about, Mark," Mercy said. "I'm not helping you sell the house out from under your own sister. You can find another Realtor, but Brody's the lawyer for the estate, and everyone knows I'm your cousin, and they're going to ask me if you're a problem seller and I'll have to tell them the truth."

"I'm not a problem anything," Mark told his phone.

"Anyways," Mercy said, ignoring him, "Mark knows that no matter what the will says, splitting the house fifty-fifty is the right thing to do. See? It all turns out all right in the end!"

"I said twenty-five percent," Mark protested.

"Mark," Mercy said, "it's fifty-fifty."

"Guys," Louise said. "I'm not sticking around. I can't tell Poppy I'm coming home and then turn around and not. Children need consistency and reliability from a parent."

"Mark," Mercy said. "Give Louise your phone."

He hesitated for a long moment, then thrust it at Louise.

"Don't mess with anything," he said.

She took the phone and walked away from Mark.

"I really appreciate what you're doing, but I honestly cannot—" Louise started.

Mercy didn't even let her finish before starting to talk.

"Brody called and he told us what happened with you and Mark. We've been beating up on your brother for hours. Fighting over money is ugly."

Louise closed her eyes. Her breath felt trapped in the top of her chest.

"I don't want the house," she said. "It's not good for me."

"Shush," Mercy said. "A four-bedroom, two-bathroom house on that block just sold for more than seven hundred thousand dollars by a Realtor who could barely spell her own name. I can do better than that for y'all. Fifty percent of seven hundred thousand is more than three hundred thousand dollars, Lulu. That's the difference between a state school and Ivy League for Poppy. That's Spanish immersion and summer camp and Outward Bound and trips to Japan. That's a big leg up for your little girl."

Louise felt the house wrapping its tentacles around her again, dragging her to it, trapping her in Charleston. She wanted this to be over.

"I cannot go back to my mom and dad's house," she said, her words coming out in a rush. "It's bad for my mental health."

"Do you have health insurance?" Mercy asked.

"Through my job," Louise said.

"Then buy some therapy," Mercy said. "Three hundred thousand dollars will change Poppy's life. There is nothing I wouldn't do for my kids and you're like me. Wake up, Mama. This is real life."

"Mercy—" Louise started.

"You're staying one more week," Mercy said, tone turning to sunshine. "And you were going to be here another week, anyways. Nothing bad is going to happen in seven days."

Louise couldn't breathe. She wanted to go home, she wanted to see Poppy, she didn't want her to get sent to this child psychiatrist, but she also wanted to send her to Dinosaur Dig Summer Camp, she wanted to take her to Italy, she wanted a house with a yard. She looked over at Mark, shifting from foot to foot, conspicuously not looking at her, jingling his hands in the pockets of his cargo shorts. She let out her breath.

"What time tomorrow?" she asked.

Then she went inside to tell Ian and Poppy that she had changed her mind and wasn't coming home until next week after all.

It didn't go well.

Chapter 13

Mercy told them she wanted to come by the house around three and do a walk-through, so Louise got there at nine and parked in the driveway.

"You don't need to go crazy," Mercy had said. "Just make sure it's light, it's bright, and it sparkles. Let it put its best foot forward."

Louise watched a yard crew across the street strap on leaf blowers and weed whackers. She checked the time: Mark was fifteen minutes late. The leaf blowers started to roar. A man power-walked past the end of the driveway: Mark was thirty minutes late. Louise couldn't make herself sit still. She got out of the car.

She headed toward the front door, trying to appraise the house the way Mercy would. The roof needed sweeping, the walls could do with a power wash, the screens were still filthy. There was a lot to do, and she might as well get started. She stepped onto the front porch and stopped to hunt for her phone in her purse, and losing her momentum made her think about the dolls.

There were so many dolls in there, waiting for her. Somewhere, in a less rational part of her brain, Louise felt that nothing could look so human and exist for so long without starting to develop thoughts on its own. What did the dolls think about?

They think about you throwing Pupkin away. They think about you throwing the Squirrel Nativity away. They think about you throwing them away. They think about how much they hate you.

She decided to wait for Mark at the front door.

He arrived closer to ten, already complaining.

"You didn't bring coffee?" he asked the second he got out of his truck. "I'm giving you twenty-five percent of the house, so you could've brought coffee and maybe a corn muffin or something."

"Twenty-five percent doesn't make me your maid," Louise said. "Give me your key."

She held out her hand. He didn't move for a long moment, then sighed and hauled a big jangling wad of keys out of his back pocket and worked his front door key off the ring and dropped it in her hand.

She unlocked the main door and walked into the house fast and forceful, Mark following behind. She kept her eyes low, looking for anything twitching or darting or generally acting like a squirrel.

nothing in this house can hurt me, there is nothing in this house but things

She stopped, staring into the living room. The Mark and Louise dolls stared back at her from the other side of the couch with their dead eyes, standing between the arm of the couch and the wall.

"I hate those things," Mark said, then turned down the hall. "I've got to pee."

He must have put them there yesterday after I left. He saw them in the garage and wanted to keep everything the way our mom had it, they didn't climb down off the shelves and come inside to wait for me.

"The house looks fine," Mark said, walking down the hall. "I don't even know why we're here. Mercy won't come until three."

they aren't angry at me

They looked angry.

"This walk-through determines how she'll price the house," Louise said over her shoulder, unable to take her eyes off the two big dolls. "You don't get a second chance to make a first impression."

"I know you love tests," Mark said, "but we're not getting graded on this. What the fuck?"

Louise turned, stepping backward, keeping her eyes on the dolls and Mark at the same time. Mark had his head tilted back and was staring at the boarded-up attic hatch.

"What the fuck is that?" he asked.

"I don't know," Louise said. "Maybe squirrels. Probably squirrels. I think I saw some yesterday. We'll have to get an exterminator."

"Big fucking squirrels," Mark said. "Don't you think? A little bit of overkill?"

"It looks like a typical Dad patch job," Louise said.

"I don't think we should be in here at all," Mark said. "I think my plan was better and when I see things like that"—he pointed to the hatch—"I feel like I was right. Don't you feel the vibes?"

"The only vibe I feel is that we've got less than five hours before Mercy arrives and a lot to do," Louise said, getting her efficient mindset back. "If the house doesn't sparkle, maybe she'll set the price thirty thousand lower. That's seventy-five hundred dollars less for me. That's almost three months of Poppy's kindergarten, so you and me are going to do everything in our power to make this house look normal."

"This is exactly like when we were kids," Mark said. "Louise in her little Brownie Scout Hitler Youth uniform barking orders at everyone."

"That's a really offensive comparison," Louise said. "Mercy specifically said the dolls creeped her out, so those go first. Then we'll get most of this art off the walls."

She could have sworn she felt a rustle go through the dolls.

"Pictures make a room look bigger," Mark said.

"Not this many pictures."

Mark joined her at the entrance to the living room and together they considered the dolls.

"So do we pack them in tissue paper or what?" he asked.

Louise handed him a box of black plastic garbage bags.

"Whoa," he said, jerking his hand away like it was hot. "I can sell them on eBay for a lot of money."

"Fine," Louise said. "We'll bag them up and put them in your truck."

"They'll get damaged," Mark said.

"Then what do you want to do with them?" Louise asked, irritated.

"I had everything arranged," Mark said. "No hesitation, get Agutter, and bang! Done! Now you and Mercy have me all in here and I don't know how I feel about this."

Louise almost argued, but instead she unrolled a garbage bag, tore it off, snapped it open, and made herself walk over to the sofa (closer to the Mark and Louise dolls). She grabbed two clown dolls off the back of the couch. Wanting to touch them as little as possible, she stuffed them in the bag fast. Her hand felt tacky.

"Come on," she said. "Let's go."

"But," Mark said from the living room doorway, "it's all Mom's stuff."

"You're the one who hired the guys with dumpsters," Louise said.

"It's different having to do it ourselves," he said and looked so genuinely upset Louise felt like she had to say something.

"They're gone, Mark," she said, softening. "Someone has to clean up all the things they left behind."

Mark opened his mouth, closed it again, looked into the dining room, then back at Louise.

"I know?" he said. "But this is their house. This is all her and dad's stuff. It's an entire lifetime. They wouldn't want us to throw it in the trash."

"What they want doesn't matter anymore," Louise said.

"It does to me." Mark shook his head. "This is happening too fast. We need to slow down."

"Mercy is going to be here this afternoon," Louise said.

"Once we get rid of this stuff we can't get it back," Mark said. "What if we change our minds? It'll be gone forever."

"We don't have time for this," Louise said.

"I'm not ready," Mark said. "I can't do it."

"Mark." Louise leveled with him, making eye contact. "I don't want to do it, either, but there's no one else."

Mark's eyes flicked around the room, fast and manic.

"Mom and Dad could've done it," he said. "They were grown-ups. We're just . . . tall children."

He looked like he was going to cry.

"Mark." Louise tried to sound gentle. "Don't make me do this alone."

He made fists, then released them, then made fists again, then threw himself across the room and snatched the bag out of her hands.

"I'll hold it," he said.

Louise pitched the rest of the clown dolls in, one after the other. The Harlequin went next, landing on top of the clowns. Then Louise went to the doll cabinet, trying to keep as much distance as possible between herself and the Mark and Louise dolls.

She pulled open the doors and grabbed something neutral: a little ceramic cottage with a thatched roof.

"Wait!" Mark shouted. "Mom got that on the trip to England y'all took when she was pregnant with me. She has a whole collection."

Louise looked into the doll cabinet and saw one other thatched ceramic cottage.

"There's only two," she said.

"Well, yeah, that's as far as she got," Mark said. "I want to keep them."

He took the tiny cottages.

"If you start hoarding things we're never going to finish," Louise said.

Mark put the cottages on the front hall table and came back. He held out the bag. "Okay, pick anything else. Those are the only two things I want."

Louise grabbed an eight-inch plastic king wearing a red velvet tunic and a floppy black velvet hat. Mark closed the top of the garbage bag.

"You're going to throw Henry VIII away?" he asked.

"Yes," Louise said.

"Don't you remember?" Mark asked. "It was the same trip. Mom bought him and all six of his wives at Hampton Court."

He pointed to the six queens lined up on either side of Henry, all clearly part of the same set, wearing stiff outfits featuring a lot of blue satin, green velvet, and gold trim.

"So?" Louise asked.

"Mom knew the whole rhyme by heart," Mark said, wracking his brain. "Catherine, Anne, Jane: divorced, beheaded, died. Anne, Catherine, Katherine: divorced, beheaded, survived."

He grinned, amazed at his powers of recollection.

"How do you remember that?" Louise asked. "You weren't even born."

"I don't know." He shrugged. "I just listened to Mom's stories."

Louise reached into the cabinet and grabbed a Hummel figurine of a little boy wearing lederhosen.

"Lou," Mark said, and she stopped, shoulders sagging. "Don't you remember? When we went to Germany and they took us to that beer garden in Berlin and Dad won for yodeling? It's the Dad yodeling award!"

Louise dropped it into the garbage bag on top of the Harlequin. Mark looked shocked. He reached in after it.

"Hey, wait," he said. "It's a serious memory."

Louise threw Henry VIII and his six wives in on top of Mark's hand.

"Stop it!" he snapped, and she realized he was actually angry. "You can't throw away all our memories!"

"Mark," Louise said. "You have to think of it as a house full of someone else's junk."

"But this isn't someone else's junk." He gestured around the living room at the dolls, the needlepoint on the walls, the pile of *Muppet Show* VHS tapes under the TV. "It's our junk. This is everything we grew up with. You've got a kid. What do I have? Besides this?"

In the silence between them, the high-pitched whine of a weed whacker started up across the street. Louise let it go on for a minute.

"Why don't you take the dolls?" she said, as gently as she could. "We'll put them in your truck and you can take them home and sort through them there. Keep what you want, sell the rest, you can do it at your own pace."

He gave a quick nod.

"Okay."

"We can put them in boxes," she said.

"Bags are fine," he said quickly. "It's fine. Let's just do this."

The dolls stood rigid, waiting for Louise to take them. She felt like a monster. They filled two black plastic garbage bags, and finally the doll cabinet was empty.

"It looks—" she started, but Mark finished for her.

"Wrong," he said. "I feel like we're doing something wrong. Like any minute Mom and Dad are going to come through the front door and Mom's going to flip that we moved her dolls."

They both listened to a leaf blower howl across the street.

"I'm not taking those," Mark said.

He was pointing to the Mark and Louise dolls standing at the end of the couch. Louise had managed to keep them out of her line of sight so far, but now they were the only dolls left.

"Then take them to the trash," she said.

"I'm not touching them," Mark said. "You do it."

Louise stared at them, unable to make herself pick them up. Mark noticed.

"Let's leave them here," he said.

"Mercy said 'nothing creepy' and there's nothing creepier."

"Here," Mark said, grabbing the Booger Blanket off the end of the couch and dropping it over their heads. "How's that?"

The dolls looked even weirder with the old afghan draped over their heads, but Louise didn't know another solution.

"Sure," she said. "You want help getting these bags in your truck?"

"Someone'll steal them," he said. "I'll keep them in the garage."

They dragged the bulging bags of dolls out to the garage, where Louise tripped over his saw.

"Jesus, Mark," she said. "Don't you take care of your tools?"

He'd quit cutting the patch halfway through and left his saw and the plywood on the concrete floor. There was sawdust everywhere.

"It's a project," Mark said.

They dropped the bags against one wall and, inspired, Louise looked around the garage and saw some collages on the plywood shelves. She grabbed them and leaned them against the rolling garbage can. She picked up the oil portraits of their family and put them there, too, then noticed Mark staring at her. "What?"

"Are you throwing those away?" he asked in disbelief.

"That's the Goodwill pile," Louise said, covering. "Take whatever you want."

Mark picked up the oil portrait of their dad, which gave him a skin condition and a lazy eye.

"This is the only picture we have of Dad," he said.

"Except for the hundreds of photos we have of Dad," Louise said. "And Mom's clay bust of Dad, and the puppet version of Dad she made for his birthday."

Mark didn't say anything for a second, and then:

"You don't want to go back in the house, either," he said, a statement, not a question.

"What do you mean?" Louise asked, annoyed he was so perceptive. "We need to clean up the garage, too."

"Mercy doesn't care about the garage," Mark said. "You're putzing around out here because you don't like it in there any more than I do. The house feels wrong. After you left yesterday I swear I heard something in the attic. I booked out of here."

squirrels, it's only squirrels, normal natural everyday squirrels

"We need to get an exterminator for the attic," Louise said.

"We can stay out here," Mark said.

"No," Louise said. "We need to get it ready for Mercy. Let's do the kitchen—"

"But—" Mark began.

"Together," Louise said.

They went in the kitchen and flipped on the lights. Nothing happened. Louise opened the fridge. It stayed dark and felt warm.

"The power's out," she said.

"Hang on," Mark said, and went back into the garage.

Louise scanned the fridge shelves and saw leftovers in Tupperware containers, a scrap of butter on a clear glass plate, half a turkey sandwich carefully wrapped in Saran Wrap. That stopped her.

Her dad had eaten half of that sandwich, then put it aside for later when he got hungry, but he died before he ever got hungry again. Now he'd never finish his sandwich. The strength went out of Louise's legs and she sank into a crouch, one hand on the fridge door.

She remembered her dad's stollen.

Every year after Thanksgiving, her dad took over the kitchen and baked stollen bread for everyone at work. Even after he retired, he still did it every year for the neighbors. The loaves were tiny and misshapen, they never rose correctly, and they looked lumpy and malformed, but to Louise they had always been magical. She mostly just picked the icing off the top because she hated the taste of the candied fruit folded into the dough, but she loved its colors—jade green, ruby red—and as a kid she'd helped to wrap each loaf in crackling plastic wrap and tie it with a bow of green yarn with a name tag attached. For two weeks, the whole house smelled like baking bread and hot icing.

That's what she wanted to smell right now. Something comforting and alive. She wanted to smell her dad. She didn't want to smell Yankee Candle and carpet cleaner and dust anymore.

Louise closed the fridge and went to the sink for a glass of water. She grabbed a clean glass, and before she could turn on the faucet she looked in the drain.

An eye stared back up at her.

Round and white, it peered up out of the dark hole. Louise stopped breathing. Then she saw the blue fleece around it and realized it was one of her mom's puppets. How had it gotten in the sink? She needed to get it out before it broke the garbage disposal.

Louise reached into the cold drain. The slimy rubber mouth of the O-ring swallowed her forearm to the elbow, and her fingertips brushed wet puppet fleece, heavy with greasy water. She pulled at it but it wouldn't budge. She felt around and her soft fingertips danced along the sharp, heavy blades of the disposal. The puppet had gotten wrapped around them and stuck fast. Using her fingertips, Louise slowly unthreaded it from around the blades, and suddenly the disposal roared into life.

Noise filled the kitchen as she threw herself backward, her wrist bruising on the edge of the drain as her arm whipped out of the vibrating hole. Her feet went out from under her and she sat down hard on the linoleum. The garbage disposal roared at her from the sink.

Mark stuck his head in from the garage door.

"I flipped the breaker back on," he said, then walked across the kitchen and shut off the disposal. "Hey, where'd you find one of Mom's puppets?"

Louise didn't move. She stayed on the floor clutching the wet puppet in one hand.

"Let's wait for Mercy outside," she said.

Chapter 14

Mercy pulled in behind Mark's truck, booping her horn, waving at them from her seat.

"Look at y'all," she said, picking her way across the front yard in her heels to where they stood in the open door of the garage. "Busy bees! You haven't been working all morning for me, have y'all?"

"Yes," Mark said.

"We have to clean it out anyways," Louise said.

"I know," Mercy said, stopping and letting her shoulders slump theatrically. "It's so depressing. Going from the house you grew up in to just a musty old headache. It's hard, y'all. I've seen it. Oh, my word."

She'd caught sight of the family oil paintings stacked against the garbage cans.

"Is that you?" she asked Louise. "What happened to your skin?"

"Mom was learning how to paint," Louise said, feeling inexplicably defensive.

"Isn't that the big lesson?" Mercy said. "We're all holding on to too much junk."

"You want to go in the front?" Louise asked.

"Let's go!" Mercy said. "You coming with us, Mark?"

"I've got to patch this window," he said, but Louise knew he wanted to stay outside.

She didn't push it. Right now, she had to keep up with Mercy, who was already on the front porch.

"I'm so excited!" she cheered, disappearing inside.

Louise caught up with her in the living room as she framed a shot with her phone.

"It really does look so much better"—she lowered her voice to a stage whisper—"without all those creepy dolls."

Mercy snapped another picture.

"This living room is precious," she said and pressed her fingertips against the wall it shared with the kitchen. "I wonder if this is a supporting wall. A lot of people want to go open plan."

The Booger Blanket lay on the floor. The Mark and Louise dolls were gone.

A shriek ripped through the house from the garage as Mark started chopping plywood again. Mercy's flash flickered and the dim room strobed white. Louise felt a sickening pressure in her gut.

"I love the light this house gets," Mercy said. "Once all the old things go and it gets repainted, you're going to think we added a window."

All along, Louise had assumed Mark was moving things, but Mark had been with her all morning. Maybe she'd turned her back for a minute and he'd moved the dolls, but where? She hadn't seen them in the garage. And he was the one who draped the Booger Blanket over them because he didn't want to touch them. She thought about the Mark and Louise dolls watching TV, about Pupkin watching TV, about Pupkin vanishing from the garbage can. About dead squirrels squirming beneath her shirt.

"Lulu?" Mercy said from behind her. "I asked if you knew what was under here."

Mercy crouched in the hall, one palm pressed to the wall-to-wall carpet. Louise tried to focus on Mercy's question, but she kept looking in every corner for the dolls, for squirrels, for Pupkin.

"Lulu," Mercy said, snapping her fingers. "Hello?"

don't you feel the vibes

the house doesn't feel empty

i feel like we're doing something wrong

Louise felt herself getting sucked into Mark's world of vibes and gut feelings and intuition. She forced herself to focus on Mercy. She forced herself to focus on what mattered: getting the house on the market, getting back to San Francisco, getting Poppy back to normal.

"Wood?" Louise said. "I think?"

"Good," Mercy said. "We can tear this ugly old carpet right out. Everyone does hardwood in high-traffic areas now."

Mercy strode into the dining room.

"I thought whoever bought it would just tear the whole place down," Louise said, following, trying to focus on Mercy while looking down the hall, into the kitchen, behind the dining room table for the dolls.

Mercy looked everywhere, too, measuring the house with her eyes, seeing a future renovation snapping into place around them. Another high-pitched shriek of the circular saw tore out of the garage. Louise forced herself to think about the sale. Mercy walked to the patio doors and looked out across the backyard.

"A developer would do a teardown," she said. "But a developer is not the right buyer in your case. Four bedrooms? Two baths? We want to sell to a family. Look at that backyard. Any buyer is going to put an extension on the back and still have plenty of space. Your parents let their outdoor areas go underutilized."

Louise made herself glance out back, trying to see it the way Mercy might: a vast patch of dirt and weeds with a dead pecan tree in the middle, cut off from the neighbors by overgrown bamboo. It looked toxic.

"They weren't really yard people," Louise said apologetically as Mercy walked past her, headed for the hall. "Mark was going to build them a deck once, but he quit before he even started."

"That was Aunt Honey," Mercy said from the hall. "She told your mom she couldn't stand anyone changing her sister's old house and you know how your mom always listened to her. She did y'all a favor, too. That big empty backyard is going to light up some eyes."

Louise followed Mercy into the hall and caught a glimpse of the boarded-up attic hatch. She tried to distract Mercy from looking up.

"So what steps do we need to take?" she asked. "In your opinion."

Louise knew Mercy loved giving her opinion.

"We need to focus on making this house the best house it can be," Mercy said, peering into Mark's old bedroom and taking another flash picture. "We need to brighten this space. Allow it to breathe, make it appeal to the senses."

Mercy opened the workroom door. The puppets kept it from opening more than a crack.

"There's a ton of puppets in there," Louise apologized again.

"They have to go," Mercy said. "You guys grew up around them, so you think they're normal, but puppets creep people out even more than dolls."

"We're getting them out today," Louise promised, following Mercy down the hall.

Something directly overhead thumped lightly on the floor once, purposeful and deliberate. Louise's shoulders twitched and she stopped, waiting to see if it would happen again.

"There's a lot to do here," Mercy said, "but I see high six digits if we do this right."

maybe something just fell over

Louise started down the hall after Mercy, and over her head in the attic whatever it was thumped again, then again, then again, one time for every step she took, staying right over her head, following her down the hall, and she recognized the sound—footsteps. Something in the attic was pacing her. Something small.

"People used to move in and renovate," Mercy continued as Louise stopped walking. Horribly, the tiny footsteps stopped, too. "But these days everyone wants to move into a big white box with marble on the countertops and stainless steel in the kitchen and they'll pay through the nose. I've seen little doo-doo places not even in this neighborhood cover everything with Benjamin Moore off-white, do a gut renovation, and go for almost seven figures."

Louise had to start walking again or it would look weird. She started and the footsteps followed her to join Mercy, who was squatting in front of the wall.

"Why is this vent open?" she asked, examining the hole in the wall. "Is there an HVAC problem?"

"So stupid," Louise said, and the silence overhead was worse than the footsteps. "I knocked it off, but we'll get it replaced. The heating and air work great, though."

"The fluff is the fluff," Mercy said, standing, her knees cracking. "But motivated buyers want to know the nitty-gritty: how old is the heat pump? How old is this roof? Do you have a termite—"

Something slammed into the floor of the attic directly overhead. Popcorn sifted down from the ceiling and trickled down the back of Louise's collar.

"A termite?" Louise prompted.

"Letter," Mercy finished. "Down here you should also have a—"

Something rolled across the attic floor directly overhead and Louise's shoulders hunched. She didn't want to be in this house anymore. Mercy raised a finger and pointed to the ceiling.

"Do y'all have squirrels?" she asked, and Louise felt the scratches on her stomach squirm.

"Maybe?" she said.

Mercy scanned Louise's face, reading it from left to right, then flicked her eyes to Louise's parents' bedroom door.

"You're going to have to get an exterminator," she said. "And find the termite bond. It'll tell you about moisture. Let's see the primary suite."

She opened the bedroom door and walked right in.

"Normally, I'd wait until spring to put a property like this on the market," Mercy said over her shoulder. "But I would not hesitate to list this place immediately once you address the fundamentals."

Louise took a step, shoulders tensed for more sounds from the attic, but there was only silence. Her shoulders unclenched and she joined Mercy in the bedroom.

"Exterminator, paint job, check the foundation, the heat pump," Mercy said. "Definitely do something about those squirrels."

"Shit!" Louise barked.

Mercy stopped and looked at Louise, who had frozen, eyes locked on the corner of the bedroom where the Mark and Louise dolls stood in their little Victorian outfits.

"That is exactly what we don't want happening with a potential buyer," Mercy said. "You have to get *all* those things out of here."

Louise couldn't move. Had Mark put them in here? Was this some shitty practical joke? She realized Mercy was looking right at her.

"Have you noticed a *vibe* in this house?" Mercy asked. "Everything feels a little off, doesn't it?"

Louise forced herself back to reality.

"No," she said. "I just forgot they were there."

get the house on the market, get back to san francisco, get poppy back to normal

"Well, they are unsettling," Mercy said, then started taking pictures of the room again.

Louise made herself scoop the black sock off the end of the bed and took it to her mom's walk-in closet, opened the hamper full of their dirty clothes, and tossed it inside. The sight of the clothes they'd never wear again made her inexpressibly sad. The thought of having to wash them, then fold them and put them away, only for them to never get worn again, made her depressed. This all felt like too much. She couldn't deal with these dolls and the attic, and her parents' lives stopping in midsentence.

"There's a buying bubble in Old Mount Pleasant," Mercy continued, walking to the bathroom, "and people from up north will pay absolutely anything for a new roof and good bones, but it's got to be bright and white."

Mercy took a flash picture of the inside of the bathroom.

"Now, this is what I call a primary bath," she said, flipping on the lights.

Nothing happened.

"Sorry," Louise apologized quickly, feeling like she hadn't done her homework. "It's probably the bulb. I meant to get more done. I'm sorry."

Mercy turned, and she didn't look like a Realtor, she looked like their cousin again.

"It's okay," she said. "I'll help you guys get it all set up, okay? It's just me, Lulu. Come look at this."

Louise made herself cross the carpet and joined her at the bathroom door and saw Mercy framing up a shot of the built-in vanity with her phone.

"This thing is huge," she said. "That means there's so much more room in here once it comes out."

Something inside the vanity knocked on the doors. Three small, swift raps.

let me out

Mercy and Louise stared at the vanity. The small of Louise's back prickled with sweat.

i shouldn't have come back here, i should have gone home last night

She had to get out of here. She couldn't handle this house and its noises and her parents' half-eaten sandwiches and their dirty clothes and all these dolls. She realized she wasn't speaking, just staring at the closed vanity doors. She made herself turn to Mercy, the tendons in her neck creaking.

"Pipes," she said, and gave Mercy a big smile that looked only a little bit manic. "It's just air in the pipes."

Mercy gave her an understanding smile in the gloom.

"Let's go talk to Mark," she said, and walked out.

Louise followed, willing the sound in the attic to stay quiet, trying not to feel the Mark and Louise dolls' eyes boring into her back. As she reached the hall she heard it again behind her, coming from inside the bathroom.

knock, knock, knock

let me out

She caught up to Mercy in the backyard as Mark screwed the plywood square over the broken glass in the garage door. She almost broke her neck tripping over his saw again.

"I'm not saying you have to," Mercy said as Louise joined them. "I'm saying it's an option."

"Don't try to upsell me," Mark said, dropping his screw gun in the dirt. "I've done my research."

"So, what do you think?" Louise asked, dreading the answer.

"The house is great," Mercy said, and she seemed bright and cheerful, as if nothing had happened. Louise heard birds chattering in the dead pecan tree. Things felt so much saner in the backyard. "We need some paperwork, and to find out when your parents last had their roof done, but this is an easy sell. Once it clears probate I think it'll take me two weeks to get you real offers from serious buyers—"

Louise wondered if she had been the only one to hear those sounds.

"—but I'm not going to handle this listing," Mercy finished.

"What?" Louise asked.

"What the fuck?" Mark asked. "We've been busting our asses all day because you were coming over. You made me give twenty-five percent of it to Louise."

"Fifty percent," Mercy said. "The house has issues, and I've learned from experience you do not want to put a problematic piece of real estate on the market. Not if you want to keep your reputation."

"What issues?" Louise asked, but she knew.

"I told Louise to leave the art up," Mark said. "Bare walls make rooms look smaller."

Mercy ticked off the points on her fingers.

"The weird noises in the attic, whatever was in the bathroom vanity, you freaked out way too much over those dolls, and the place has some seriously weird vibes."

"I told you we meant to get more done before you got here," Louise said.

"I'll come right out and say it," Mercy told them. "Strange noises, bad vibes, your mom and dad recently passed— Your house is haunted and I'm not selling it until you deal with that."

"Holy shit," Mark said.

"That's . . ." Louise tried to think of the right word. "That's crazy."

And it did feel crazy. Really crazy.

i'm not crazy

"You're upset," Mercy said. "I get it. No one likes bad news. But my business is houses, and half of selling a house is psychological. Can't you guys feel how off this place is?"

"Yes," Mark said.

"No," Louise said.

"I'd be a fool to ignore my gut," Mercy said. "It's no big deal. I've handled two problematic properties before."

Louise felt like her cousin had betrayed her. Turned on her. Become the enemy.

"This is in really bad taste," she said. "Our parents just died."

"This can't come as a total surprise. Your family's always been weird."

"Why does everyone keep saying that?" Louise asked.

"There's clearly something here you need to deal with," Mercy said. "But there are people who can help. You get a blessing, do a cleansing, they're real discreet. They understand how publicity can affect the sale."

"Who does it?" Mark asked.

"I used Mom," Mercy said.

Louise remembered that her aunt Gail had a guardian angel named Mebahiah who watched over her and helped her find good parking spaces.

"Oh my God," she said.

"Exactly," Mercy said. "She's super churched up and, honestly, all she'll ask y'all for is a donation because they're building a new adult education center. What's the downside, Louise? Let's say you don't believe it's haunted, fine. You still get a nice feeling of closure. Both troubled properties I handled wound up getting five percent over asking after they got cleansed."

"Is it Mom and Dad?" Mark asked, his voice low. "Is that who's in there?"

Mercy turned into their cousin again, not a Realtor.

"I wish I knew," she said and laid a hand on his arm. "I'm sorry, Mark."

"Do you think—" Mark started, and swallowed hard. "Do you think we can see them?"

Louise knew she needed to head this off. It was dangerous to even think for a second that dead didn't mean forever.

just a chance to see them again, even for a second

"I think we might consult another Realtor," she said. "No offense."

"None taken," Mercy said. "But they're going to say the same thing. Your house is haunted, and you can't put it on the market until you deal with that. Even if you find someone who'll list it, these things have a way of coming back to bite you."

She fished her car keys out of her purse, hugged Louise, who made her body as stiff as possible, then she gave Mark a long hug, rubbing his back.

"I've got to get to another listing," she said. "But you guys think about it and let me know. Mom'll be happy to do it, especially for family. She loves being needed."

They followed her through the garage and stood in the driveway as she got in her car, gave them a fun little *boop* on her horn, and drove away.

Chapter 15

E very time," Louise said. "Every single time."

"I know," Mark said. "One step forward, two steps back. You think this house is going to be a real windfall and then—boom— it's haunted."

"I'm talking about you!" Louise said, backing away, putting some grass between herself and Mark. "Every single time you tell me something, or I give you the benefit of the doubt, or I try to help, it comes back and bites me in the ass. Every! Single! Time!"

"Whoa," Mark said. "Last time I checked I'm doing you a favor by giving you twenty-five percent of the house, which is not required of me by law but which I am doing because I'm a good guy. So if by *biting you in the ass* you mean *giving you a lot of money*, then yeah."

"You'd think I learned my lesson," Louise continued. "That being in this house is not good for me. That being here is not healthy. But you beg me to help with the paperwork and here I am again, up to my neck in bullshit. You and Mom really know how to play me like a pipe organ. I'm a thirty-nine-year-old woman and I'm still falling for it. I'm pathetic."

"What did Mercy see in there?" Mark asked, looking back at the house.

"Mercy freaked because something fell over in the attic and there was air in the pipes in Mom and Dad's bathroom that made them bang," Louise said. "It's no big deal."

When she said it like that, out there in the front yard, it definitely sounded like no big deal.

"I've never heard the pipes bang," Mark said.

"It happens in houses all the time," Louise said.

"Was it random banging or did it sound guided by conscious thought?" Mark asked.

"It was banging," Louise said.

"Could it have been Morse code?" Mark asked. "There's a long history of spirits communicating by tapping on tables."

"Our house," Louise insisted, "is not haunted."

"I've been telling you there's weird vibes," Mark said. "I can feel it in my gut. Mercy felt it, too. We aren't alone here."

"Yes, we are!" Louise said.

"Methinks thou doth protesteth too much," Mark said.

"Quoting Shakespeare doesn't make something true," Louise said.

Mark's eyes got wide.

"You saw something in there yesterday," he said, realizing. "That's why you ran out of there! Was it Mom and Dad?"

Louise would not let this house be haunted. Everything had a rational explanation, you just had to keep looking. The squirrels she thought she'd seen, the noise in the pipes, the noises in the attic, the boarded-up hatch, the Mark and Louise dolls, Pupkin disappearing from the trash, the hammer, the cane, the car accident. Everything always had an explanation. She'd learned that from her dad. The other things, the dangerous things, the dolls getting angry and squirrels attacking her by themselves and bad vibes, all of that had been her mom. And Mark had been so close to their mom.

Louise made her shoulders unclench.

"It's an emotional week," she said in her reasonable adult voice. "Go home and we'll call a new Realtor in the morning. The second Mercy hears we're talking to someone else she'll run back over here and list the place."

Mark shook his head.

"I'm not selling the house," he said. "You can lock up."

He started trudging across the grass to his truck.

Louise felt an enormous rage expanding inside her skull.

He tricked me! He made me come back and get involved and exposed me to all this, and now he's walking away. It's not fair!

The problem was this house. They'd been children here and so they reverted to childish behavior the second they came back. If the house was haunted it was haunted by memories, by old fights, by Mark's unresolved stuff with their mom and dad. She was an adult. She had a child of her own. Her goal was securing Poppy's future. She would not let this fall apart. She took a deep breath and went after him.

"Mark!" Louise called.

He stopped on the other side of his truck and watched her come across the grass. The house faced east, so this late in the day the setting sun was behind it, leaving the entire front yard in shadow. The houses on the side of the street behind Mark were lit gold by the late-afternoon light.

"Mark," Louise said. "Do you actually think Mom and Dad's house is haunted? Like, do you believe it has actual ghosts inside?"

"Yes," he said.

"I am not trying to insult your intelligence," Louise said. "I get that the house feels weird. It feels weird to me, too. And what Mercy said plays into our emotional vulnerabilities, but ghosts don't exist."

"I can't sell the house, Louise," he said, shaking his head sadly.

"Then let me do it," she said. "You don't even have to be here."

"Who do you think is haunting the house?" Mark asked. "It's Mom and Dad. Mercy said the only way to sell it is to get someone to banish their spirits, but where do they go? If we banish Mom and Dad's souls, what happens to them? Do they stop existing? I can't be responsible for ending our parents' existence."

Louise pressed her palms against the hood of Mark's truck so she wouldn't clench them into fists.

"Mom and Dad's ghosts are not in there," she said.

"I'm going to let the house sit for a few years," Mark said. "Maybe their energy will disperse naturally."

Louise couldn't hold it in anymore.

"Bullshit," she said. "Bullshit! This is like college! This is like the deck! This is like every single project you ever started and then quit in the middle because it got too hard or you have a fear of completing things or whatever it is that's been holding you back all your life! You made a commitment to me! And Poppy!"

"I didn't know our parents were still in the house!" he shouted at her from the other side of his truck.

"They're not!"

"How do you know? There are more things in heaven and earth than are dreamed of in your philosophy."

"Don't you fucking quote Shakespeare at me," she said. "There are true things and there are false things, and there are no in-betweens. There are facts, like houses and car accidents and cremation, and there's bullshit like ghosts and vibes and exorcisms. And if you start getting the true things mixed up with the false things, you're fucked!"

"Mercy and I think this is true," Mark said. "So does Aunt Gail, apparently. You're outnumbered."

"Reality is not a consensus!" Louise said. "We don't all get a vote!

And Aunt Gail believes the vial of water she got from the river Jordan cures her headaches, so maybe she's not the best example."

The setting sun threw a long slash of molten yellow along either side of the house, but the front yard was fuzzing out, the air turning a thick gray.

"The second you showed up you started telling me what to do," Mark said. "From the minute you arrived you've been bossing me around. But the fact is that I'm the executor and I've decided not to sell the house."

"This is where we grew up. It's not *The Shining*."

"It's *Shining*-adjacent," Mark said in the gloom. "If you could admit that maybe you don't know everything, you wouldn't be raising Poppy alone."

"Look what you're doing!" Louise said. "When you don't like the way a conversation is going you deflect with personal attacks. You're like some kind of emotionally abusive octopus entangling everyone in your word tentacles."

"You should talk to your therapist about your choices of imagery," Mark said. "Pipe organs, octopuses—it's very revealing."

"I don't have a therapist," Louise said.

"That explains a lot."

"You're doing it again! I don't need relationship advice from a grown man who works in a bar and believes in ghosts."

"Says the woman with zero life," Mark said. "The point is, you act like you know everything about everyone but you don't listen to anybody. You just talk at people and tell them what to do."

Louise's skull squeezed itself so tight she thought it would implode.

"You promised me," she said, bearing down on him. "You said we were going to sell this house, and I stayed because I needed the money for Poppy. You don't get to change your mind in the middle."

The light had almost vanished completely from the street. Everything felt cold and indistinct.

"You've got my key," Mark said. "Don't forget the back door."

He opened the driver's-side door and his interior light came on, and for the first time Louise saw how bad he looked. His eyes were wet and his face was bloated. He was leaving because he couldn't handle their parents being dead. He couldn't let go of them. She needed to reach him. He got in his truck and pulled his door closed.

She remembered what she'd learned from her mom about manipulating children. She remembered the ceramic hot dog.

Louise threw open the passenger's side door and said, "Wait! Don't move!"

She left it open behind her and raced into the gloomy house, ran down the hall, past the workroom, past the open vent, into her old bedroom, where she grabbed the huge ceramic hot dog off her desk. She heard the coins inside give a metallic shift as she picked it up. It was heavier than she expected, and it made her right shoulder groan and her wrist bend like it might break. She lugged it back outside and dropped it on the front seat of Mark's truck.

"Dad's Hot Dog Fund," she said, a bit winded by how heavy it was.

"So what?" Mark asked, sitting behind the wheel.

"It feels pretty full."

"Whee," Mark deadpanned.

"There's probably fifteen or twenty dollars in there," Louise said. "You know what that means?"

"It means we have between fifteen and twenty dollars," Mark said.

"It means Pizza Chinese," Louise said, because she knew no Joyner could resist Pizza Chinese. "Come on, Dad wouldn't want us to let specie go to waste. Stay for dinner. We'll do Pizza Chinese and say goodbye to Mom and Dad the right way."

Her mom had lied to keep them from getting a pet. Louise lied to Poppy to keep her from watching *PAW Patrol* on Sundays because "that's when the characters sleep." She would lie to Mark to get him to sell the house.

"I don't want to banish Mom and Dad's souls, either," Louise said, pulling on everything she'd ever seen in movies. "So let's have a final Pizza Chinese in the old house and ask them peacefully, in a spirit of love, to pass on to the other world. We can help them understand it's time to let go and walk into the light."

Mark considered the hot dog, then looked up at the house, then back at her. Louise kept talking, trying to remember an article she'd read about grief and healing.

"Pizza Chinese is our family's ritual, and it's as powerful as any cleansing ritual Aunt Gail might do. We'll share our memories with them, remind them of our love, and then suggest that they no longer need to be tied to this plane. That we'll be okay without them. That it's time to let go and pass to the other side."

Mark jingled his keys for a minute, flipping his truck fob back and forth across his knuckles hard, then stopped.

"I'm supposed to be the stupid one," he said, "but even I know that you don't go back in a haunted house after dark."

"It's where we grew up," Louise said. "The only things here are memories, and those can't hurt us."

"I wouldn't be so sure about that," he said.

But he didn't turn his key, and he didn't start his truck, and he didn't drive away, and she knew. She had him.

Chapter 16

For their mom, nothing beat the stretch of holidays that started at Halloween and came to a climax on New Year's Eve with Pizza Chinese. That night, the Joyners hosted a party in every room. For once, their mom didn't cook; instead she and their dad ordered Chinese food and pizza—everyone's favorite foods—in enormous quantities, and it had come to be known as Pizza Chinese.

People packed the house, wandering the rooms with a slice of pizza in one hand and a foam plate sagging with sweet-and-sour pork in the other. Their dad's entire department came, their mom's puppet friends, people from church; Mark and Louise invited their friends and hosted their own private parties in their rooms. Everyone stayed up until three in the morning drinking supermarket champagne that made their dad speak in a ridiculous French accent.

It was the greatest night of the year—all the fun of Christmas, New Year's, and birthdays rolled into one enormous party centered around two of the world's greatest foods. No Joyner could resist its siren song. Not Mark. Not as a final farewell to the spirits of their parents.

Mark went to pick up their order while Louise fixed the dining room, trying to make the house look as non-haunted as possible. She turned on the lamps in the living room. Two of them were burned out and she couldn't find any spare bulbs, so she scavenged bulbs from Mark's old bedroom.

The overhead kitchen light had developed a flicker, so she left it off and turned on the stove light instead. She turned on the chandelier over the dining room table, but only three bulbs still worked and she couldn't find any more chandelier bulbs, so she grabbed the desk lamp from her bedroom and sat it on the counter, which fixed the dimness problem but made the shadows in the dining room look all wrong. Somehow, she'd succeeded in making the place look more haunted.

The front door banged open and Mark stood in the doorway, four bulging bags of Chinese food dangling from his hands, pizza boxes balanced on his arms, a four-pack of sixteen-ounce tallboys hanging from one finger.

"Some help?" he demanded.

She took the pizza.

"Why do the lights look so creepy?" he asked, slinging the bags onto the kitchen counter.

"It's just burned-out lightbulbs," Louise said as she started unpacking the food. "It's no big deal."

The two of them did the dance they'd performed hundreds of times in this kitchen, Mark grabbing plates, Louise getting silverware, reaching over each other, sidestepping around each other, pausing for one to close a drawer before the other opened a cabinet.

Finally, she grabbed a roll of paper towels while Mark squeezed around the dining room table and dropped into his chair. It creaked as he leaned back on two legs to rest against the wall. Louise sat and noticed they'd automatically taken the chairs they'd sat in their entire lives:

her back to the kitchen, Mark with his back to the wall. If they were still alive, her mom would sit on her right, at the end of the table closest to the phone, and their dad would sit with his back to the patio doors.

Between them Pizza Chinese covered the table. In the center sat a Luna Rossa pizza box containing a small black olive, onion, and green pepper pizza with extra cheese (Louise's). Beneath that sat another box containing a small Hawaiian barbecue chicken pizza (Mark's). Beneath that sat a box containing a small sausage and Canadian bacon buffalo pizza (also Mark's). The boxes were stacked because there was no more room on the table with all the white clamshells displaying sweet-and-sour pork, fried shrimp, egg rolls, crab rangoon, General Tso's chicken, pork lo mein, broccoli and shrimp, chicken wings, and barbecue spare ribs. They'd ordered so much the restaurant had given them enough napkins and chopsticks for twelve.

"Well," Mark said, raising his beer and his voice like he was addressing an audience. "Mom, Dad, this is for you. We're here for a final Pizza Chinese in your house. We invite you to attend because we love you and we want you to enjoy the night and remember all the special things that happened here."

Louise waited for him to continue, then realized he expected her to follow, so she popped her beer and raised it in a toast.

"We love you," she made herself say to the empty house.

"We welcome you to our table," Mark continued like he was in a play. "Because it's your table, too. Let us share these final moments before you move on to your next reincarnation. Cheers!"

He took a sip and Louise followed his lead. Over their heads, something thumped against the attic floor. Mark looked terrified and excited, wiping beer from his chin.

"That's what she heard!" He looked at Louise. "Isn't it? That's what Mercy heard in the attic?"

Louise wanted to say it was squirrels and she'd seen squirrels in their parents' bedroom earlier and had to stun them with the badminton racquet, but she remembered Poppy's future.

"I guess they liked your toast," she made herself say.

Mark raised his beer to the location of the thump.

"Welcome," he said, then he turned to the table before him and put on their dad's fake French accent. "The pupu looks especially tempting tonight."

The desk lamp on the counter threw the same weird, unforgiving light across Mark that it threw over the wall behind him. The skin on his neck hung loose and his cheekbones and jawline were buried beneath poorly shaved excess weight. His thinning hair stuck out in all directions. The pair of jackpot cherries tattooed on the side of his neck looked tired.

The food looked cheap and greasy. With only two of them there, the house felt cold and empty and Louise realized this would be the last time she'd ever eat a meal at this table. This was probably the last time she'd ever eat a meal with her brother. When this was over they would drift apart, and the Joyner family would be over. But her family wouldn't. She would always have Poppy.

"So what happens now?" Louise asked.

Mark slid his Hawaiian pizza out from the middle of the stack, flipped it open, and pulled out a slice.

"Mom and Dad will show us," Mark said, using his chopsticks to pile pork lo mein on top of his pizza. "Our job is to be open to whatever happens."

Mark folded his slice of pizza around the lo mein like a taco and brought it to his mouth. A few brown strands of noodle hung out of the end, glistening with grease. They jiggled like worms as Mark took an enormous bite.

"S'good," he said, through a mouthful of food.

Louise made herself try a piece of radioactive-orange sweet-and-sour pork. As a kid it had made her mouth water. Now it tasted like soggy breading in a sauce that came from a jar. She swallowed as quickly as she could, but it left a waxy coating on the inside of her mouth.

"So how do we know if Mom and Dad's souls move on tonight?" Louise asked. "What's our metric for success?"

Mark picked barbecued chicken strips off his piece of pizza.

"A haunting doesn't necessarily indicate the survival of the human soul after bodily death," he said, chewing. "There's the stone tape theory of hauntings, which says that powerful emotional experiences leave permanent traces behind. There's basic thermodynamics: energy cannot be created or destroyed. So what happens to the energy generated by intense emotional experiences? It has to go somewhere. That's just science."

Louise couldn't help it. When people used the words *science* and *magic* interchangeably, her skin bristled.

"What kind of energy is that?" Louise asked. "Magnetic, electric, kinetic? Or some other kind of California energy that no one's ever seen in a lab but it's inside us and the redwoods and every form of life on Mother Earth?"

"You're very threatened by new ideas," Mark said, taking a slug of his beer. "But people leave behind traces of themselves after they die: art collections, junk you've got to clean out of their houses, emotional problems they inflict on their kids. Why can't they also leave behind energy? We grew up here, Mom grew up here, this house has been a repository for our family's emotional energy for decades."

Louise felt herself wanting to argue, so she switched gears. She had to stay calm and convince him that they had laid their parents' ghosts to rest. Before she could try a new approach, Mark said, "You know she forgives you."

"Who?" Louise asked, taken off guard.

"One reason our house is haunted might be all your unresolved anger toward Mom," he said.

"Wait," Louise said, sharper than she intended. "You think this is my fault?"

"I mean, there's a tradition," Mark said. "Supernatural phenomena often materialize around sexually repressed women. *Carrie*, *The Haunting of Hill House*—"

"I'm not sexually repressed," Louise said. "And I don't want to talk about my sex life with you."

"Because you're repressed," Mark said. "I offered to stay tonight because I thought it would be good for you. I'm hoping it gives you some closure."

Before Louise could react, her phone alarm went off. Seven o'clock: time to check in with Poppy. She made herself stand up. Sexually repressed? Unresolved anger? She had to stay calm.

"I have to call my daughter," she said, walking to the front door.

Louise stepped onto the front porch. It actually felt warmer outside than it did in the house. She texted Ian.

IS POPPY READY FOR A FACETIME? HOW IS SHE?

She needed to get Mark off this haunted house obsession and get him thinking good thoughts about their family. She needed to give *him* closure tonight. This wasn't about "science," it was about him letting go of the past.

Louise's phone screen started to dim, then lit back up.

NOT A GOOD TIME, Ian texted. SHE DOESN'T FEEL LIKE TALKING TO YOU RN AND I'M NOT GOING TO FORCE HER.

Louise instantly texted back. Her thumbs left greasy marks on her phone.

WHAT HAPPENED? IS SHE OK? WHY DOESNT SHE WANT TO TALK?

Three dots appeared and Louise waited, wiping her fingers on her jeans.

YOU NEED TO DO WHAT YOU SAY YOUR GOING TO DO— SHES UPSET THAT YOU SAID YOU WERE COMING HOME AND CHANGED YOUR MIND. POPPY NEEDS CONSISTENCY AND RELIABILITY.

There was a pause. Three dots. Then:

WE HAD ANOTHER WET NIGHT.

Louise gripped her phone so hard it almost shot out from between her slick fingers like a bar of soap. She didn't want to be here. She wanted to be in California. She needed to be with her daughter, not stuck in South Carolina catering to the whims of her crazy brother and cousin. She took a deep breath.

Everyone else can do whatever they want, say whatever they want, sell the house when they want, talk to me when they want, not talk to me when they want—but I need to stay focused. Someone has to be the adult.

She let out her breath and thought about Poppy's future. She took another breath and held it until her lungs hurt, then let it out in a rush.

I need to get Mark to sell the house.

Nothing else mattered.

Louise made herself breathe deeply for thirty seconds, then went back inside. The house felt dingy and secondhand. Whatever she'd been trying with the lamps, it hadn't worked. Everything stunk of Chinese food and melted cheese. Louise wanted to take a shower, she wanted to go home, she wanted this to be over.

"Everything okay?" Mark asked, chewing, half an egg roll held delicately between his fingers.

My daughter is regressing again because I'm staying here after I told her I was coming home and she doesn't want to talk to me and she's wetting the bed and I have to cater to your whims before I'm allowed to go home and see her, so no, things are not fine.

"Everything's great," Louise said, sitting down.

Mark got up to get another beer.

"Why'd you run out of here yesterday?" he asked from the kitchen.

Louise needed to do something with her hands. She looked for anything resembling a vegetable and picked out a soggy piece of broccoli with her chopsticks.

"Dealing with Mom's stuff felt overwhelming," she said. "I wasn't prepared. It brings back a lot of memories."

She felt the mass of puppets down the dark hall, pressing against the workroom door, eyes never closed, lying in the dark, listening to the two of them talk. She felt the dolls in the garage, rustling and shifting inside their plastic bags. She felt the Squirrel Nativity creeping through the shadows.

Mark closed the fridge and came back to the dining room.

"Aunt Honey told me Mom called the night they had the wreck," he said, edging around the table to his seat. "She said she was taking Dad to the hospital because he'd been 'attacked.'"

"Because he *had* an attack," Louise corrected him, picking up a shrimp and peeling off its breading.

"You go right ahead and trust the hearing of a ninety-six-year-old woman in the middle of the night," Mark said, dropping into his chair. It creaked alarmingly. "But if Mom said he'd *been* attacked, the next question is 'By what?' and that leads to the question we've been avoiding: why'd they board up the attic?"

The last of the breading came free. The little pink nugget between Louise's fingers looked like an albino cockroach. She dropped it on her plate and wiped her fingers on a paper towel.

"I saw squirrels in their bedroom yesterday," she said. "I hit them with the badminton racquet and stunned a couple, but they're probably nesting in the attic."

"I thought we were going to have an honest conversation tonight," Mark said.

Louise felt the conversation starting to go somewhere she didn't like. She tried to keep it on track.

"It's why I left," Louise said. "Those squirrels freaked me out. I thought I killed one."

Mark gave a dramatic sigh.

"Mom and Dad won't be able to move on until the bad energy in this house is laid to rest," he said. "Which means you need to be honest."

"About what?" Louise asked.

"About what you did," Mark said.

"When?" she asked.

"When we were kids," he said. "What you did to me."

And just like that, everything slipped out of Louise's hands.

no, this isn't fair, he doesn't get to do this

"What about what you did to all of us?" she asked, because someone had to push back on his bullshit. "When you came back from that ski trip and started terrorizing everyone all the time, yelling, screaming, breaking my stuff, kicking a hole in Mom and Dad's wall."

How many times had her mom called when she was at Berkeley, sounding on the verge of tears? Louise knew it was because of Mark, but her mom always covered for him. Their entire family always covered for him.

"You were a spoiled brat," Louise said, not very strategically, "who got everything handed to him on a silver platter while the rest of us had to work. And you're blaming me?"

"You don't remember?" Mark asked in an amazed voice. "About what happened here when we were little?"

"I remember you terrorizing this family," Louise said. "I remember you breaking my stuff all the time. I remember you fighting with Dad, and him spending all that money to send you to college, and you dropping out your first semester and coming home and sponging off them."

"You've actually blocked it out?" Mark said, and she hated the pitying expression on his face.

"Blocked what out?" Louise asked, because there was nothing to block out. "You living in an apartment downtown that they paid for? Me finding Mom crying and talking to Pupkin because you were so mean to her she thought he was her only friend? What do you think I don't remember?"

"Why are you so mad at me?" Mark asked, his voice so reasonable and calm she wanted to punch him. "Is it because you feel guilty?"

"Guilty?" Louise asked. "Guilty for what?"

"For what you did to me," Mark said.

"I didn't do anything to you."

"Louise—"

"No!" she almost shouted.

"You—"

"It's not true!" she said. "You're making things up again."

"You tried to kill me," Mark said.

It wasn't true. He was lying. She didn't try to kill Mark.

Pupkin did.

Chapter 17

A child acquires stuffed animals throughout their life, but the core team is usually in place by the time they're five. Louise got Red Rabbit, a hard, heavy bunny made of maroon burlap, for her first Easter as a gift from Aunt Honey. Buffalo Jones, an enormous white bison with a collar of soft wispy fur, came back with her dad from a monetary policy conference in Oklahoma. Dumbo, a pale blue hard rubber piggy bank with a detachable head shaped like the star of the Disney movie, had been spotted at Goodwill and Louise claimed him as "mine" when she was three. Hedgie Hoggie, a plush hedgehog Christmas ornament, had been a special present from the checkout girl after Louise fell in love with him in the supermarket checkout line and would strike up a conversation with him every time they visited.

But Pupkin was their leader.

She'd been drawn to Pupkin by the amount of attention her mom paid to him. Her mom had had him since she was Louise's age, and she seemed thrilled when Louise adopted him as her new best friend. Louise pushed her hand into Pupkin and he'd come alive. She took him on car rides, where he'd look out the window, marveling at the world going by, or they'd sit on the living room floor and tell each other stories, or he'd come with her to the library and help her pick out books. Her mom included Pupkin in every conversation.

"What did Pupkin do today?" she would ask, and listen to Louise's answer.

"Does Pupkin think that sounds like fun?" her mom would ask after Dad announced they were going to the beach or Alhambra Hall.

Louise always interpreted for Pupkin, translating his thoughts for the grown-ups, but they were always his thoughts. She never pretended to be Pupkin, she never acted like Pupkin, his thoughts always appeared perfectly formed inside her head, and if she got them wrong, Pupkin corrected her.

One rainy Saturday night, everything turned bad.

It had been raining all week and the air inside the house felt clammy and damp. Dad had spent the afternoon trying to work while Mom did a music lesson in the living room, and the sound of Louise shaking a bunch of pennies inside a coffee can like a maraca and screaming "Itsy Bitsy Spider" at the top of her lungs while Mark banged an upside-down pot with a wooden spoon probably hadn't made tabulating Soviet grain imports any easier.

They ate early, the JCPenney chandelier over the dining room table barely holding back the shadows, and for the first time, Mark ate with them instead of eating beforehand. Louise didn't like the new change because it made her parents fight. Mark spat a piece of chicken on the floor, and they argued over the five-second rule. Her dad asked why Louise had to eat quesadillas that she clearly didn't like instead of chicken fingers with Mark. Her mom and dad picked on each other, back and forth, until Louise's head hurt.

Later on, tucked up in bed, Pupkin said:

Pupkin doesn't like this. No, no, no. That baby isn't good. He makes everything different. It makes Pupkin angry.

"Stop it," Louise whispered in the dark, because she wasn't allowed to say she didn't like her little brother.

It makes Pupkin so angry, Pupkin said.

"You're scaring me," Louise said.

Sometimes Pupkin gets so angry Pupkin wants to do something bad.

"Don't say that, Pupkin," Louise said, feeling tears trembling in the corners of her eyes, then sliding down her temples. "I love you, Pupkin. I don't want you to be angry. Mark is a big boy now so he can eat at the table. Mommy says it's all right."

Pupkin stayed silent for the rest of the night, but Louise knew he was mad.

At first she thought it was her fault. Every morning, she woke up to find her friends tumbled out of bed, facedown on the floor, and she'd be wearing Pupkin on one hand. When Louise apologized and asked what happened, Buffalo Jones, Red Rabbit, Hedgie Hoggie, and Dumbo all stayed silent, but it didn't feel like a nice silence. It felt like they were too scared to speak. They were scared of Pupkin. Instead of getting angry at him, Louise started getting angry at her other stuffed animals because she was starting to get scared of Pupkin, too.

"Why'd you let him push you out of bed, you stupid rabbit?" Louise asked, shaking Red Rabbit with every word. "You're supposed to stay under the covers. You're a bad rabbit. A bad, bad rabbit."

Then she turned Red Rabbit to face the wall as punishment.

Pupkin woke her up in the middle of the night, pressing himself to her face like a cold, clammy thing, squirming against her all night long, waking her up with all his moving around. Finally, one Monday night, tired and cranky, Louise took action. Because he was the hardest to cuddle, Louise loved Dumbo the most, and when she came back from brushing her teeth and found him on the floor with his head off and

Pupkin sitting where he'd been on her pillow, Louise felt enough anger stab through her body to make her brave.

"You're the bad one!" she hissed, scooping up Pupkin and marching him to her closet. "Nobody else! You hog the bed and push everyone out. Bad Pupkin. You need a consequence."

She shoved him into a plastic bin at the bottom of the closet, then rolled the louvered doors shut, and, using all her strength, stretched a rubber band over the two handles to hold them closed. Then she reattached Dumbo's head and carefully climbed into bed with him cradled in her arms.

Louise woke up in the dark. The orange splash from the streetlight outside made a puddle in the middle of her floor. She heard it again, the noise that had woken her, a gentle clack of hollow plastic, a stealthy rattle of toys from her closet.

Something bumped softly against the bottom of her closet doors. The dark clouded her vision and she saw the slatted doors through a swarm of black flies, but she thought she saw one door begin to rock in and out, testing the strength of the rubber band.

Please hold, please hold, please hold, she thought to herself over and over again, because she knew it was Pupkin and she knew he was very angry. She could feel his anger all the way across the room.

She took her eyes off the closet door, shooting a look at her friends, the only ones who could help her, and all her spit dried up and her mouth filled with sand: they were all facing the wall. They had turned their backs on her. None of them could stand up to Pupkin. Louise was alone.

On the other side of the room, the rubber band snapped and the closet door made a muffled sound as it rolled open on its tracks. She wouldn't look over. She didn't want to see Pupkin. If she saw Pupkin she would die.

I can run to the door, Louise thought. *I'm faster than Pupkin, he doesn't have any bones, his legs are too soft.*

She threw back the covers and sat up, but it was too late.

So fast he was a blur, Pupkin threw himself through the black gap between the open closet doors, fabric body hunched low to the ground, scurrying directly for the bed on his stubby arms and legs. Then he disappeared and she heard a slow creak from the end of her bed and her blankets shifted, slipped, took on weight, and the top of Pupkin's pointed head rose over the end of her bed, and then Pupkin had one soft nubbin hand on her ankle and he dragged himself up her body, his black-rimmed eyes locked onto hers the entire way.

His body moved over hers with a repulsive writhing and it felt heavy. She squeezed her eyes shut as his weight moved onto her thighs, dragged itself over her lap, up her belly and then her bony ribs. He finally stopped and she felt him settle just below her chin, pressing down on her throat, making it hard to swallow.

". . . please . . . please . . . please . . ." she whispered. ". . . please . . . please . . . please . . ."

She had no choice. She opened her eyes. Pupkin's maniacally grinning face stared into hers from two inches away. He had the same little black tongue, the same turned-up nose, the same chalk-white face, but something else looked out at her through those black-rimmed eyes. Something she couldn't control, and Louise knew she was all alone in her room with something truly dangerous.

Pupkin's face writhed and folded from within, and then it made a terrible hollow, crumpling sound and his little mouth stretched open wider than she'd ever seen. Louise had pulled her hands up to her chin to keep them away from Pupkin, and now he leaned forward and gripped the fingers of her right hand with his blunt arms and lowered his gaping mouth over the end of one of her fingers. The inside of his mouth felt so cold. Louise tried to pull her finger away but Pupkin bit down. Hard.

The edge of his mouth applied a continuous, ever-increasing pressure to her fingertip, past the point of anything Louise thought she could stand, but she knew it would be so much worse if she made a sound. She felt her bone compress like Pupkin was going to snap off its tip, then he stopped.

Louise sucked air into her empty lungs and sobbed with relief. Pupkin raised his head, letting her finger slip from his mouth, and it pulsed in agony.

You're going to do what Pupkin says, he told her, *or Pupkin will hurt you.*

Louise was already in kindergarten. She knew that grown-ups only expected one answer when they talked to you in that voice.

"Yes, Pupkin," she whispered.

Pupkin squirmed with pleasure and dragged himself over her throbbing hand, swallowing it up inside the hungry hole in his body, and she felt him flexing and rippling around her forearm, gripping her, holding on tight. Then he lodged himself underneath her chin, nuzzling himself against her neck.

Pupkin's going to have so much fun, he cooed.

At first Louise was scared of what he wanted her to do, but soon she realized that the things Pupkin told her to do were funny. She would nudge Mark from behind while he toddled to the car and he'd go over on his face in the grass and she'd have to help him up. Her mom and dad liked when she did that. They said she was a good helper, and a sweet big sister. One day, Pupkin told her to put her mom's car keys in Mark's diaper. Another day, he got her to pour salt on the plastic tablecloth in the dining room and tell Mark it was sugar. He licked it up, then opened his mouth and thick yellow throw-up poured down his chin and over his coveralls.

To her surprise, the more she did funny things to Mark, the closer

Mark wanted to be. He followed her everywhere. He brought her his toys. He watched her play without talking. He glued himself to her side. She may have belonged to Pupkin, but Mark belonged to her.

Christmas used to be Louise's favorite time of the year. Her dad made his stollen, and even though it never got cold enough to snow, fireplaces burned twenty-four hours a day, and people raked their leaves and burned them in piles in their front yards. Christmas wreaths stood out bright green against red front doors and you could see twinkling trees through living room windows. The smudgy gray days smelling of woodsmoke and burning leaves alternated with bright, clear days smelling like evergreen.

Louise loved Christmas visiting. People lit red-and-white-striped candles and fires and baked cookies, and their houses smelled like fresh wood, warm bricks, pine needles, and butter coming up to room temperature. People gave Louise unbelievable things: Hershey's Kiss cookies and gingerbread trees, cellophane-wrapped candy canes, and cards of the Baby Jesus that played "What Child Is This?" when you opened them. She never believed the next house would give her things, too, but the houses kept giving her more and more things, and Mark didn't understand what to do with his things, so she got twice as many.

The Calvins' presents were the best. The Calvins were very old and didn't have any children of their own, and they'd known her since she was a little baby, so they always gave her something her mom said was too nice. This year they visited the Calvins the day before Christmas Eve, the last visit of the season. That night they'd have cheese toast and tomato soup because her mom was resting for Christmas Eve, when she'd cook all day for supper and then at midnight they'd go for the candlelight service at church. After that they'd go to bed and Santa would come, then it would be Christmas morning, and presents, and then all the cousins would come and stay all day and into the night, and they'd bring covered dishes and she could eat as much as she wanted. The Calvins represented the end of the visits and the start of two days of fun.

Patricia and Martin Calvin lived in a bungalow out at the far end of Pitt Street by the ruined old bridge, on a big lot with a long driveway. To Louise, going to their house always felt like driving to the country, even though they lived less than a mile away. Their mom parked in the drive and turned around over the seat to make sure their hats and gloves were on and their jackets were zipped up, then she let them out and they crunched across the frosted grass and rang the Calvins' doorbell.

Martin Calvin opened the door and let them in. It was warm inside and smelled like Christmas trees, and they had on lamps and a fire, and everything was dim and orange and glowed. Mr. Calvin pulled two boxes out from under the tree with its pulsing green, yellow, and red lights. Louise put Pupkin next to her and carefully peeled off her paper to reveal a Spirograph. She traced the big round letters on the cover of the box with one finger, then opened it to see the hot pink harness, the yellow ruler, the different-size blue tips, each with their own pocket to hold it. Her breath moved up into the back of her throat.

"Thank you, Mr. Calvin," she said. "Thank you, Mrs. Calvin."

"Marty," her mom said, "it's too much."

"Do you like that, honey?" Mr. Calvin asked.

"It's precious," Louise said.

She didn't want to take it out of its box until she was home and could do it carefully and make sure she didn't lose a piece, so instead she just kept opening the box and looking at how everything inside had a perfect place, touching them one after the other, rubbing their smooth edges with her fingertips. Mark got one of those super-detailed Hess trucks people bought at the gas station for five fill-ups and five dollars.

He fell down hard on his bottom and pushed his Hess truck around on the floor. Their mom began to talk in hushed tones with Mrs. Calvin about her health.

"They say they got it all out," Mrs. Calvin said. "They just want to be safe."

"Did you know our backyard froze last night?" Mr. Calvin asked Louise and Mark. "It looks like a fairyland. Have you ever been to fairyland before?"

Louise shook her head.

"Why don't you take your little brother outside and see," her mom said from the sofa. "Make sure you hold Mark's hand the entire time."

"Yes, ma'am," Louise said.

"Then come back in and you can draw a picture of it for us."

That meant they would be here for a while, and Louise liked the feeling of being settled someplace with nowhere they had to go. She pushed herself up and Mark immediately stopped shoving his truck around, clambered to his feet, and took her hand.

"He loves his big sister so much," Mrs. Calvin said. "When you come back I'll make hot cocoa the real way for you."

Louise wasn't sure what the real way was, but it sounded interesting and since it was hot cocoa it had to be good. She helped Mark into his special silver space jacket, then pulled her own jacket on, and of course Pupkin came too, riding her right hand.

They went out the kitchen door and stepped into fairyland.

Later, Louise would know that Mr. Calvin had left his sprinkler on overnight so everything would freeze, but right now she thought she had walked into another world. Icicles dripped from the bare branches of the trees, and ice encased the grass. Sheaths of ice wrapped around the tree trunks, and sheets of ice turned the leaves on bushes into frozen green jewels.

She and Mark carefully crunched across the frozen backyard, breaking off icicles and sucking their tips, which tasted like the metallic Mount Pleasant water that came out of everyone's hoses. They explored the entire patch of frozen grass, and then Pupkin said:

I want to see more ice.

Louise knew where she could find more ice.

Bring the baby, Pupkin said, and Louise reached out and took Mark's hand, then she began to walk, aiming for the trees at the back of the property, and soon they were out of sight of the house. They navigated the frozen, uneven ground between the bare tree trunks until they were at the bottom of the little hollow full of long, yellow grass circling the Calvins' frozen pond. Louise had never seen something this big frozen before. Cold came off its surface in waves and tightened the skin on her face. She and Mark and Pupkin stared at it in awe.

The ice on its surface had frozen wavy and uneven and the center hadn't frozen at all. It showed a jagged patch of heavy black water that looked as cold and dark as outer space. Dirty ice covered the pond in a cloudy layer with branches and leaves frozen into its edges.

I'm an ice-skater, Pupkin said, and with no hesitation Louise stepped onto the ice. She felt the cold coming through the soles of her shoes. She heard its uneven surface give a high-pitched creak beneath her feet.

"I'm an ice-skater," she said and slid a little on her feet.

Her center of gravity wobbled but she didn't fall down. She flexed her knees and slid again. The ice pulled her across its surface, making her feel out of control even though she only went a few inches.

Mark watched, squatting and standing up over and over again in excitement. Then he stepped onto the ice, too. The edge splintered beneath his feet and the heel of his navy blue hand-me-down sneaker dipped backward and turned dark in the water. Louise stepped off the ice into the long, brittle grass and held his hand.

"Step up," she told him, and helped him onto the ice.

He slid a little but she kept him upright with one arm. He steadied.

"You're an Olympic skater," she cheered and let go. He smiled so wide it seemed his cheeks would split open. "Go where it's flat," she encouraged him.

Mark shuffle-walked in tiny slippery steps toward the black star at the center of the ice. He stopped and turned around to Louise.

Go further, Pupkin said.

"Go further, Mark." Louise smiled.

He went a few more steps, then turned again, uncertain, sensing he maybe shouldn't be out this far.

A little more, Pupkin said.

"A little more," Louise said.

He took two more shuffling steps, then turned and tried out a smile. Louise smiled back to encourage him.

Go on one leg, Pupkin said.

"Go on one leg like a real ice-skater," Louise called, lifting her leg off the ground to demonstrate.

Mark raised his left leg an inch off the ice, and with a silvery, shearing crack his right leg speared through the ice and plunged straight down. The black water sucked him in and Mark disappeared. Louise lowered her leg and lifted Pupkin higher so he could see.

Mark's head broke the surface and his arms thrashed, but cold water filled his silver space jacket and dragged him backward and down. He opened his mouth to cry but pitch-black water rushed in and filled it up. While Pupkin kept his eyes on Mark, Louise turned back to the house. She couldn't see it from here, which meant they couldn't see her, either.

Mark jerked and thrashed in the center of the pond like an animal trying to keep its nose above water, then the ripples climbed over his upturned face and the pond sucked him down. Louise kept watching, but he didn't come up again. Together, she and Pupkin watched the surface of the pond until it got still.

Pupkin's cold, Pupkin said.

Louise turned and picked her way back between the trees, through the frozen backyard, all the way to fairyland and the back door of the house. She didn't look back at the pond once. She opened the kitchen door and stepped into the warm house. Immediately it began to thaw her face.

The grown-ups were still talking about Mrs. Calvin's health in the living room. Louise walked quietly behind them and sat down between her Spirograph and the fire. She traced the big letters on the front of the box with one finger again. After a while, Mrs. Calvin noticed her.

"Ready to warm up with some hot cocoa?" she asked.

"Yes, please," Louise said. "May Pupkin have a cup as well?"

"I don't see why not," Mrs. Calvin said. "As long as he doesn't make a mess."

"Oh, no," Louise said. "He's very careful."

Her mom glanced over.

"Where's Mark?" she asked.

Pupkin soothed her. He would help.

Potty, he said.

"Potty," Louise said.

"By himself?" her mom asked.

I don't know, Pupkin told her.

"I don't know." Louise shrugged.

"Mark?" her mom called toward the kitchen, then stood up. "Mark?" she said to the front hall.

She stepped into the hallway and called Mark's name again.

Ask if it has tiny marshmallows, Pupkin told Louise.

"Mrs. Calvin?" Louise asked. "Does real hot cocoa have tiny marshmallows?"

But by then, no one was paying any attention to Louise.

Mrs. Calvin stayed with her and together they watched from the kitchen door as Mr. Calvin came back up the yard, soaked to his waist, carrying Mark in both arms, water streaming from his space jacket in silver streams. Her mom trotted beside him, shouting into Mark's face. Louise had never seen a person's skin turn blue before.

Mr. Calvin and her mom drove to the hospital with Mark while Mrs. Calvin stayed behind with Louise. She didn't speak very much. Louise asked about the hot cocoa but Mrs. Calvin didn't seem to remember that she'd promised. After a while, Aunt Honey came and took her home and stayed with her alone in the house for two nights. When her parents came back from the hospital with Mark, they told Louise she couldn't go in his room.

That first night, she sat in the doorway to her bedroom with Pupkin and listened to her parents' voices from behind their bedroom door.

"She saw her brother fall through the ice," her dad said. "She's in shock."

"Why'd she lie?" her mom asked.

"Maybe she didn't understand what happened," her dad said.

"She didn't understand the difference between her little brother being in the bathroom and at the bottom of a pond?" her mom's voice asked.

She couldn't hear them after that, but it sounded like her mom was crying. But Pupkin was very happy she had done what he said, which made Louise happy, even though they had to skip Christmas.

"We'll do presents in January," her dad explained, "when your brother feels better."

The next day they brought Louise into Mark's bedroom, her mom standing in the door like a prison guard, arms crossed, watching every move she made, as her dad, one hand on her shoulder, guided her to Mark's bed. The humidifier sat on his bedside table, blowing out a big white cloud of vapor. Underneath it, Mark looked small and pale against his circus sheets. He pulled one arm out and laid his hand on top, palm up. Her dad jostled her shoulder and Louise stepped forward, hearing

Mark's breath bubble and rasp in his phlegm-clogged throat. She reached out and held his hand. It felt clammy and feverish.

She listened to his breath. Then she pulled her cold hand out of his hot one and asked if she could go play in her room.

"She's scared," her dad whispered to her mom as Louise squeezed past her through the door.

Pupkin wanted to go to the living room and he started wriggling on the end of her arm. She ignored him. The more he wriggled the less she cared all of a sudden.

She needed Dumbo, who was always good and kind. She crawled up on her bed, one knee at a time, and reached for Dumbo, but the instant her fingertips brushed him his head dropped off, falling onto her bedspread with a thump. She reached for Red Rabbit and he turned away to the wall. Breath hitching in her throat, she tried Buffalo Jones next. He flinched from her and trembled. Hedgie Hoggie curled himself into a ball and whimpered.

"I only did what Pupkin told me," she whispered to them. "I didn't do anything bad."

They didn't answer. Louise didn't know it was possible to feel so alone. She curled herself up on her bed around Dumbo's severed head.

Take me to the living room, Pupkin demanded from the end of her arm.

Louise was bad.

You're silly, Pupkin said. *You aren't in trouble.*

Louise was so bad that her own stuffed animals hated her. They would never trust her again. They would never talk to her again. The only one who would be her friend was Pupkin, and he would pinch her and bite her and hurt her and make her do whatever he wanted. She'd never get to be Louise again. He would take her over and make her be Pupkin all the time.

Bored, Pupkin said, beginning to sound angry.

Louise pushed herself up off the bed and carried Pupkin to the living room, where her dad was grading papers on the couch and listening to a concert on the radio.

"Pupkin wants to listen," she said, and her dad nodded without taking his eyes off the papers in his lap.

"Sure, honey," he said.

She left Pupkin on the sofa and went into the garage. She found a trowel on one of the shelves. She took it into the backyard, where people hardly ever went, and walked to the tree growing in the middle and dug a hole. At first the ground was hard and frozen, but she kept digging and she held her thoughts very close so Pupkin didn't know what she was doing. When she'd scraped out a hole as deep as her entire arm, she walked back inside and picked Pupkin up off the sofa. She marched to the backyard, and when he saw the hole he knew what was coming. He clawed and thrashed and scratched but she clutched him tight in both hands.

No, Louise! he wailed. *You're a bad girl. You're bad, bad, bad, and no one's ever going to play with you again. They're going to leave you behind and move, they're going to leave you behind and forget all about you.*

She didn't listen. She knew what she had to do and she turned off her feelings and made herself do it. Tears streamed down her cheeks. Pupkin howled and screamed as she stuffed him down the hole. He tried to climb out but she scraped dirt onto his face.

When he realized he wasn't getting out, Pupkin began to cry. She scraped the dirt onto him faster until it muffled his mouth because the crying was worse than the screaming. Even after all the dirt was piled in the hole, she could still hear him crying. She stood up and stomped the dirt on top of his grave over and over again until it was hard and flat.

Even then, she could still hear him sobbing pathetically to himself.

. . . please, Louise, why? Why? Please don't leave Pupkin alone, Louise. Please. It's dark down here and cold and Pupkin's scared . . . please . . .

She could still hear him as she walked all the way back across the yard. She made herself ignore his crying. It got fainter. In the garage, she carefully replaced the trowel, and his crying got even fainter as she went back inside the warm house, leaving him behind. And then it was gone.

She sat on the sofa next to her dad and made herself look out the window at the cars going by until it was time for dinner. She didn't let herself think about what she had done. She made her mind blank.

That night, she put her stuffed animals up on the shelf and put herself to bed. They never spoke to her again.

Chapter 18

I wasn't even there," Louise said, turning it into a joke, just another funny sibling story. "You're remembering it wrong."

You're bad, Pupkin shouted inside her head. *You're bad, bad, bad, and no one's ever going to play with you again.*

"How should I remember it?" Mark asked.

They sat across from each other in the unforgiving flat light of the desk lamp. The air in the house felt cold and it had sucked all the heat out of the food: the pizza looked dry and hard, the Chinese food congealed in its clamshells.

"We played in their backyard with the ice from the sprinkler," Louise said, clinging to her story. "And you wandered away to the pond and fell in. I didn't even know where you were."

"That's not what happened," Mark said, voice definite.

You're bad, bad, bad, bad . . .

"You were two," Louise said. "I didn't even know you still remembered it."

"You never asked," he said. "It'd be more convenient if I didn't. No one ever talked about it because it was easier for all of you if it just never happened."

"We were kids," she said. "It was a terrible accident, but things happen when you're little."

"I've waited my entire life for someone to say something about it," Mark said. "For one of y'all to admit it happened. None of you ever did."

"To admit what happened?" Louise asked. "You want a truth-and-reconciliation committee for the time I chipped my tooth, or the time you got a nosebleed because you picked it too much? You wandered away and fell in a pond and it was scary but accidents happen."

"I saw you turn your back on me and walk away," Mark said. "I bet you didn't know I saw that, but I did."

You don't know how fragile this is, Louise thought. *One day your brain just goes* ping *and you fall through the ice and puppets are talking and telling you what to do and when you fall into that world it means your brain is broken and you never get out again.*

"I'm sorry you remember it that way," Louise said, voice tight, "because that must feel terrible, but that's not what happened."

"Stop telling me what I remember!" Mark shouted. His voice echoed off the walls and took on a harsh, metallic edge.

"Mark," Louise tried, putting all the compassion she had into her voice, "memories are funny things—"

"I remember everything being so heavy, I remember the water sucking me down, I remember being so cold my skin burned. I've never been that cold again in my life. I remember opening my mouth to breathe and the pond water tasted like copper. I remember a flash of gray sky, and seeing the edge of the ice, and seeing you watch me drown, and then you turned around and walked away. That's my first memory. You walking away from me while I drowned."

"No." Louise started talking over the end of his sentence. "That's not how it was."

She felt like that cartoon coyote running in midair—the only thing keeping her from falling was the belief she was still on solid ground.

"You didn't think I remembered," Mark said. "You and Mom and Dad thought that if you never talked about it this would go away, but I *remember.*"

"I came right in the house when I couldn't find you and got Mom and Mr. Calvin," Louise said, remembering sitting down beside the fire while grown-up voices murmured reassuringly from the sofa. She remembered opening up her new Spirograph and loving how clean and useful it looked.

Where's Mark?

Potty.

You're bad, bad, bad, bad . . .

"You were five years old," Mark said, relentless. "And you told me to go out on the ice, and when I fell through you left me there to drown. They should have gotten you help for trying to kill me, but instead everyone acted like it didn't happen because Louise is perfect."

Being scared made Louise angry.

"What are you? The lone truth teller?" she shot back. "No one remembers anything from when they were two!"

Mark stripped hard cheese off a piece of pizza.

"I went on a church ski trip when I was fourteen," Mark said, rolling the cheese into a pellet. "We went ice-skating and I stepped out on that frozen lake for the first time and had a panic attack and I. Remembered. Everything. I told Amanda Fox because I had to tell someone. She's the only person who's ever believed me. When I came home I asked Mom and I expected her to say 'I'm so sorry' and for her to get you and you'd apologize and it would all be fine, but instead she told me it didn't happen."

"It didn't happen," Louise said.

"Dad said it didn't happen, too," Mark continued. "But I know what happened. I remember all of it."

"Do you even hear yourself?" Louise asked, making her disbelief as large as possible. "You recovered your traumatic repressed memories on a ski trip and they gave you permission to act out? That's your explanation for being such a dick: I did it first?"

"You said it earlier," Mark shouted at her across the wreckage of Pizza Chinese. "There's true and there's false and I know what I remember is true!"

The silence lasted long after the echo of his voice stopped bouncing off the walls. Finally, Louise spoke:

"And then they sent you to one of the most expensive colleges in the country and you dropped out."

She was not going to let him play the victim.

Mark looked away into the living room.

"I had a rough time my freshman year," he mumbled.

"Yeah, I'm sure it was tough to party so hard," Louise said.

Mark's beer can cracked as his hand tightened around it.

"You have no idea," he said, and his voice sounded like a dog growling. "You don't know anything about me. There's all this stuff in our family we don't talk about. Mom doesn't talk about her family, Dad doesn't talk about his family, and you and I don't talk, period."

This is crazy, it's crazy, he's remembering it wrong, he's lying, that's what Mark does, he exaggerates, he blows things up, turns them into a drama where he's the victim.

Louise inhaled, absorbing all the heavy, cold, congealed grease, letting it fill her sinuses until her lungs felt tight, then she released it all at once.

"Mom and Dad are dead, Mark," she said. "Mom was sad all her life because her parents hated her after Uncle Freddie died. Dad's parents hated him for marrying Mom. You and I don't talk because we're not the same kind of people. There are no dark secrets, no big conspiracies, no haunted house. No one tried to kill you—"

there's no puppet buried in the backyard

"—you're just sad and you don't want to face the fact that they're gone and you never got a chance to resolve your issues with them."

"I'm the one with unresolved issues?" Mark asked. "Emotions happen and you lock yourself in your room. You cling to Dad because Dad doesn't do emotions. You moved as far away from home as you can go and still be in America, you don't talk to me, you skip family events. You don't come for Christmas—"

"I stopped coming because you got drunk and made us go to P. F. Chang's after Mom had been cooking all day and ordered the entire menu and passed out at the table!"

"No one ever says no to you, Louise, because we're all scared you're going to lose your temper," Mark said. "Everyone's desperate for your approval. Mom is. Dad is. I've been waiting since I was fourteen for you to apologize for trying to kill me as a kid. This entire family gaslighted me for years because they didn't want to upset you, and you still treat us like we're not good enough for you. I'm surprised you even came home for Mom and Dad's funeral. That's why I made the arrangements. I didn't think you'd bother to show."

In the silence, Mark pushed his chair back. It hit the wall behind him and he heaved himself up from the table.

"I've got to piss," he said and stormed out of the room.

She heard the bathroom fan go on. She felt too aware of Pupkin's grave in their backyard. She hadn't thought about it for years but she remembered now. She saw herself digging it, she saw herself stuffing Pupkin's screaming body into it, she felt the scratch marks on her hands, she felt the bite mark on the tip of her finger.

"Louise!" Mark shouted from the bathroom.

He sounded scared. The kind of scared that launched her out of her seat and down the hall. Mark stood in the doorway to the bathroom, staring down at the tiles. Louise squeezed around him and her skin contracted tight around her bones.

The Mark and Louise dolls stood like stiff corpses on the other side of the toilet, staring at them in the door. On the wall between them, written shakily in red lipstick:

MARK KOM HOM

Louise saw red lipstick smeared on the Louise doll's hands, the open tube of lipstick smashed on the floor, the tattered end of the toilet paper roll dancing back and forth in the air conditioning, the glittering dead eyes of the two dolls, Mark's chest going up and down fast beside her. She heard the wobble of the bathroom fan.

"Did you do this?" Mark asked, his voice cracking with panic and anger.

She became suddenly self-conscious of how small she was next to him. She met his eyes and he looked sincere and she thought about the dolls moving and the long gap between him turning on the bathroom light and shouting her name and she knew.

"Oh, fuck you," she said, backing away from him, shaking her head. "Nice try, Mark, but fuck you."

His eyebrows met and he looked genuinely confused and then he realized what she meant.

"You think I did this?" he asked, his voice going high-pitched at the end.

"Who else? The ghosts of Mom and Dad?" Louise said, furious that she'd fallen for it.

She thought about her self-portrait pinned to the bathroom mirror, about the dolls in the chair watching TV, about all of it, all the things he'd always done, and here he was, still going through the same sad routines.

"I didn't do this!" Mark said, coming toward her.

"Stay right there," she said, and she meant it. She'd seen Mark lose his temper before.

He stopped, shocked at her tone, then he closed his eyes and she could hear him take a deep breath through his nose.

"I'm getting out of here," he said, opening his eyes. "And you should, too."

"Oooh," Louise said. "Scary."

"Grow up," Mark said. "No matter what you did, I still don't want anything bad to happen to you."

"Oh my God, all this drama," Louise said, then she did an imitation of his voice. "'You tried to kill me, why doesn't anyone love me, you mean I have to work to stay in college, our house is haunted.' You're just like Mom! Everything has to be a big production and you're the star. All because you can't face the fact that your life is sad and empty. Mom is dead. Dad is dead. The house is empty. You're all alone."

Mark blinked like he'd been hit in the face. Then he squared his shoulders.

"Is that what you think?" he asked. "That I'm a failure?"

"I didn't say that—" Louise began.

"Whatever," Mark said, waving her words away. "I'm not as smart as you, but what I do know is that when spooky fucking haunted dolls start writing messages on the wall, you should get the fuck out."

"It's way too late to start playing the concerned brother," Louise said. "You haven't remembered my daughter's birthday, ever. You don't write, you don't call, when I see you, you act like a pig and accuse me of trying to murder you, you gloat over the will at our parents' funeral, and I've done just fine without you for years, so it's a little late for you to start being my brother now."

Without a word, without offering to clean up, without anything, Mark turned and headed for the door. She could not believe he was ditching, but of course he was, because that's what Mark did.

"Am I supposed to think the evil dolls are out to get me?" Louise asked, following him out the front door and into the yard. "That they're, what? Possessed by the spirits of Mom and Dad?"

She followed him to his truck.

"I'm not eleven years old anymore," she said. "You can't scare me with stupid stories about haunted taxidermy squirrels. It doesn't work because I'm an actual grown-up now."

Mark stopped and turned and then he smiled.

"You know what I have to keep reminding myself of?" he asked. "When we snuck out of the house that summer when I was ten."

"I don't remember," Louise said.

"It was when Mom was going to all those puppet conferences and Dad was taking care of us," Mark said. "I think it was July."

"Vaguely," Louise said, wondering how he'd twist this to his advantage.

"You asked if I wanted to do something cool and no one had ever asked me to do anything cool before," Mark said. "Dad went to bed and we were watching *Turner & Hooch*, and when it was over you just stood up and were like 'Come on' and walked out the back door and jumped the fence. It was the middle of the goddamn night and this was after that Satanic Panic thing where those Albemarle chicks got kidnapped and everyone was all paranoid and we weren't allowed out after dark. You blew my mind. The whole neighborhood felt different that night. It felt like we were the only two people left in the world.

"We looked in the Mitchells' windows, we moved the garden ornaments at the Everetts', and then you asked me if I was scared of ghosts and I was like 'No way,' even though I was, so you took me to the cemetery. The moon was so bright and all the shadows were so dark and the headstones were, like, glowing white. You dared me to run through it from one side to the other and I dared you back, and then we both started on opposite sides and ran through it and met in the middle. It was the scariest thing I'd ever done. I never told you, but I almost ditched. The only reason I didn't is I didn't want to leave you alone in a graveyard with the ghosts."

Someone's dog barked once down the street.

"We couldn't see each other when we started running," Mark said. "And I thought maybe the ghosts had gotten you, so when I could finally see you I felt so relieved, and then you tripped over that tombstone and wiped out and farted at the same time and we couldn't stop laughing."

Louise remembered. She saw them, sitting on the ground, acorns and sticks poking her in the butt, the smell of her fart hanging in the humid air, Mark waving his hand from side to side in front of his face, laughing so hard he actually bounced up and down, and she was laughing so hard she couldn't breathe, and she clamped her mouth shut, and that made her fart again, and that made them laugh even harder.

"I'm talking to that sister now when I say don't sleep here," Mark told her. "No matter what, I don't want to ditch you here with a bunch of ghosts. Come back in the morning and get your stuff, then go home. I'm not selling the house. Not for a long time. Whatever energy is here, it's going to need years to dissipate."

He almost looked like he actually cared, and Louise saw her Kia sitting in the driveway and she knew she could ask him to wait while she went inside and turned off the lights and grabbed her bag and got her keys and she could wash away the smell of egg rolls and tomato sauce in her hotel shower.

No.

Louise would not let this house be haunted.

She would not let Mark be the hero of this made-up story.

A puppet hadn't told her to kill baby Mark.

She hadn't tried to kill baby Mark.

He had put the stupid dolls in the stupid bathroom.

There were true things and false things and ghosts were false things.

"Bring me a green tea from Starbucks in the morning," she said. "And then you're going to admit this house isn't haunted and we're going to call a Realtor and put it on the market."

Mark shook his head sadly and got in his truck. It rocked as he settled. He slammed the door. It sounded loud in the nighttime street. His passenger-side window whirred down.

"I'm trying to help," he said.

He looked like a bad actor in one of his shitty Dock Street plays.

"Oh, fuck off," Louise said.

Mark's engine roared to life and the window rolled up. Louise took a step backward.

"Don't forget my tea," she called, but he was already driving away.

His brake lights flared once at the corner, then he was gone, his engine fading away into absolute silence. There were no crickets, no katydids, no dogs barking in the distance. There weren't any lights on at the neighbors'. Louise looked at her Kia. It would be so easy to wait a few minutes, then shut down the house and head back to her hotel. She could shower and come back early in the morning. Mark wouldn't even know she'd left. Then she could tell him that his ridiculous fantasy was just immature nonsense, that he had been wrong about everything, and they could call a non-delusional Realtor, put the house on the market, and she could go home to San Francisco and see Poppy.

But she wasn't Mark. She didn't take shortcuts. Louise did things the right way.

Chapter 19

Louise stood in the dining room. All she could hear was the fan wobbling to itself in the hall bathroom. The smell of cold Chinese food and pizza made her feel greasy, so she grabbed the containers and started scraping them into the sink. There was no point in saving food this bad.

She washed the Chinese food down the drain and ran the disposal, then dumped the pizza boxes in a black garbage bag, followed by the clamshells. She tied the garbage bag shut and lugged it into the garage and left it next to the trash can containing the Squirrel Nativity. She thought about opening the lid to make sure it was still there, but couldn't make herself do it. She hoisted the heavy garbage bag up and set it on top instead. Just in case. She went inside and scrubbed the kitchen counters with spray bleach. She scrubbed the sink. She scrubbed the stove. She scrubbed the plastic tablecloth.

She'd lost control and wrecked everything. She didn't know how she'd get Mark to put the house on the market now. They'd said too many horrible things to each other. She'd let the house turn her into a child again. And Mark didn't even know the worst part of the story.

She scrubbed the table harder, the table where she'd been doing her homework in first grade while Mom made dinner, which smelled like liver. Louise went to her bedroom to get the magazines she needed to make a collage of her family and on her way she passed her parents' open bedroom door. Against their pillows sat Pupkin, smiling wide in the late-afternoon sunlight, eyes cut to the side.

Everything held its breath as Louise stared. How had he gotten out of the hole where she'd buried him? How had he gotten onto the bed? Louise thought maybe she was imagining him, so step by cautious step she approached, aware that she shouldn't be in her parents' room but unable to stop herself. She reached the foot of the bed. She couldn't make herself go any closer.

Pupkin looked brand-new. His yellow tummy looked golden, his hood was the color of a crisp candy apple, his face scrubbed clean. Louise recognized the wear in the black lines around his eyes and mouth and on the tip of his nose, so she knew this was the same Pupkin, but he didn't show any rips where he'd dug himself out of his grave, no scratches on his face where he'd pulled himself out of the ground, no dirt anywhere at all.

Something inside Louise's brain went *ping* and Louise saw herself split into two girls, standing in two identical bedrooms, both wearing the same denim ladybug dress. In one bedroom, Pupkin had come back from the grave. He had come back and he was angry because she'd buried him and left him all alone. She could feel the anger radiating off his body like heat.

In the other room, Pupkin sat, safe and sound, without a speck of dirt on his body, and that was impossible because she'd buried him, and that meant she had never buried him in the first place. She had never buried him in the first place because he had never made her do something bad. She had never done something bad because she had never told Mark to go out on the ice. She had never told Mark to go out on the ice because she loved her brother and she wouldn't hurt him, and puppets didn't talk, and they couldn't make you do things.

Louise looked at the two little girls standing in their two bedrooms, each existing in a different world, and she made a choice, and the sane Louise turned around and walked out of her parents' bedroom into a world that made sense, where puppets weren't alive, and no one hurt their brothers, and sometimes you remembered things a little funny. She left the other girl behind, standing all alone in her parents' bedroom. And she closed the door on that little girl and never thought about her again. Until tonight.

After that day in first grade, Louise had stopped being interested in her mom's stories about puppets. She wanted to be around real things that everyone saw and agreed on like numbers and math and dump trucks and cranes. She only drew things that existed, like schematics and blueprints and elevations and plans. In college, she didn't take mushrooms or microdose acid and only kind of enjoyed the occasional glass of wine, and when she saw a person having a mental health crisis in the street, she gave them a lot of distance and the next time she needed to go down that street she tried to find another way.

She washed her hands in the sink with dish soap, dried them on a paper towel, and turned off the desk lamp on the counter. Shadows pooled in the corners. Then she turned off the stove light, flipped on the hall light, and made herself go to the bathroom door, reach inside without looking, and turn off the light and the fan. She closed the door. Whatever was in there, she'd deal with it in the morning. Then she went to her bedroom and closed the door.

She let out a breath. *Safe.* She skinned off her jeans, folded them up, and put them on her dad's office chair, then she wedged the chair beneath the doorknob, turned off the light, and dashed back to bed in the dark, the cold prickling her bare legs with goose bumps. It felt so cold inside this house. She slipped under the covers and set her alarm for six a.m. The faster she fell asleep, the sooner she'd wake up. She should have brought her toothbrush. She should have taken a shower.

She should have gone back to the hotel.

Louise thrashed out of sleep, then slid back down, riding a storm-tossed ship. One foot felt cold and she woke up to find it hanging out of the bed. She pulled it back under the covers without really waking up. Poppy sat in the middle of her bedroom floor in the glow from the streetlight, playing with Pupkin.

no poppy that's not clean that's dirty you need to put it down poppy give it to mommy

The puppet hole in Pupkin's sleeve dripped lo mein and white rice, but the rice pulsed and she realized it was maggots and the long brown noodles squirmed and she needed to tell Poppy no but she couldn't move as her daughter slowly slid her arm into Pupkin's wet, rotten puppet hole and Louise bolted up alone in the dark in the after-echo of shouting "Stop!"

She was sitting up in bed, arms braced behind her, her voice still bouncing off her bedroom walls, lips still buzzing, her throat raw. She panicked, not recognizing the shadows in this room, then remembered she was in her old bedroom. She was okay. She was safe. Nothing could hurt her. It had only been a dream.

The bedroom door stood open.

Every muscle in her body locked. She didn't move. She scanned the room and her vision swarmed with black spots as she tried to see into the shadows. Something on the other side of the room, something low to the floor, inhaled quietly, wet and thick.

Something alive was in the room with her.

i put the bag on top of the garbage can, the squirrels couldn't get out, i closed the bathroom door, i put the chair under the knob

Louise slowly lay back, making an action plan. She needed her pants and her phone. Then she could grab her keys and get to her car. She didn't need her shoes. She needed to get out of this house. She shouldn't have stayed here alone. As quietly as she could, Louise reached down for her phone and something grabbed her hand.

"Ah!" Louise cried, and she tried to pull her hand back but the thing held on, yanking her arm, wrapping itself around her wrist, cold and wet and alive. It clamped itself around her hand and squeezed so hard she felt blood pulse in her fingertips.

Louise leapt to her feet and whatever it was came with her, a heavy lump clinging to the end of her arm, rippling and alive. It gave a single muscular pulse and slid a few inches up her wrist. Louise drew her hand back and flung her arm forward, hard, and her forearm got lighter and something flew across the room and thudded into the wall and bounced into the streetlight's splash of light in the middle of the floor.

Pupkin.

you left me all alone you left me behind you tried to forget about me you left me in the dark

Impossibly, without anyone moving him, he bent forward and climbed unsteadily onto his little nubbin legs. The empty sleeve of his puppet hole hung behind him like a tail. He puffed up his chest and turned his face to her and they looked at each other.

Pupkin was back. And he hated her.

His little plastic face stretched, his chin crumpled and popped as his tiny mouth opened wide, and he hissed at her. Then he surged forward, coming at her, body hunching and releasing fast, faster than the squirrels, leaving the spill of streetlight and entering the shadows, coming for her feet.

no no no no no no no no no no

She fell back onto her bed and pulled her legs up after her, but Pupkin scrambled up the blankets that hung to the floor. He couldn't touch her, she'd die if he touched her, she couldn't let him touch her, her heart trip-hammered against her ribs, she saw the top of his little pointed hood rise over the side of her bed like when she was a little girl, and Louise made a whimper in her throat like a little girl

i am not a little girl

The thought shot lightning up her spine. She leapt for the open door.

She landed hard on one ankle and lurched to her right, almost falling, but she didn't stop, she heard an angry hiss behind her and heard Pupkin drop to the carpet, and she ran out the door, sweeping up the office chair in one fluid movement behind her and hurling it backward, hoping to crush Pupkin.

She heard the chair *bang* off the wall and *clatter* to the floor and she raced into the hall with nothing between her and the front door but darkness, passing the closed bathroom door, passing the workroom, seeing light from the patio doors on the carpet, and something sliced into her shins.

She went down hard, reaching forward to break her fall, and her palms hit wooden bars, then carpet, and she fell in a tangle of sharp wooden edges. She tried to roll over, but her legs were trapped, then she realized: it was one of the dining room chairs, lying on its side. How had . . .

Pupkin had dragged it into the hall. In case she ran.

Fear gave her the strength to pull her legs out of the tangle of wooden rungs. In the dark she stood up, but her bruised feet sent her stumbling. She took a step to steady herself and her foot sank into another trap of wooden rungs and hard edges. She went down hard, landing on her butt. Before she could stand, she heard something heavy galloping down the hall carpet toward her and she struggled to pull her legs out of the chair, then propelled herself backward with her heels and the palms of her hands, and then there was silence and then something hit her hard in the chest like a cannonball.

"Uff!" Louise shouted as the air exploded from her lungs.

She grabbed Pupkin's heavy body with her left hand and pulled him backward, keeping him away from her face, but he clung to her shirt. She grabbed him with her right hand and something stung the ball of her thumb and she yanked her hand away. Her stomach muscles lost their strength and without her hand to brace her, Pupkin's weight pushed her backward until she lay full length on the floor.

The moon shone through the patio doors, showing Pupkin standing on her chest, smiling so sly, smiling so big and secret, and Louise's brain went *ping*.

Auditory hallucinations. Visual hallucinations. Tactile hallucinations. Classic Louise.

She reached her hand out to swat him off, to get him off her body, but he ducked under her arm, filling her vision, and something silver flashed in his mitten, catching the light, and her brain immediately registered *sewing needle* as he plunged it into her left eye.

Instinctively she blinked and her eyelid folded in two in a way it had never folded in her life, like it had a pin sticking out of its middle and it couldn't close all the way and Louise

oh my god there's a needle in my eye pupkin stuck a needle in my eye

panicked and lashed out with one arm and she felt his soft body in her hand, and she squeezed and yanked and felt her collar tear as he clung to it and then she hurled him overhand and she heard him hit the wall between the dining and living rooms, then land on the carpet.

She got to her feet, eyelid fluttering convulsively, putting the chairs between herself and where she'd heard him land. She saw him through one eye, the other eye blurry, swimming with tears. She wanted to close it but her eyelid kept hitting the needle and she could feel the thin silver splinter bouncing up and down inside her eyeball. Liquid flowed down her face.

please let it be tears don't let it be blood don't let it be jelly let it be tears

Pupkin stood in the patch of moonlight from the patio doors, swaying, shifting his weight from side to side. Her left eyelid fluttered like a trapped moth and she couldn't make it stop, and she felt something sliding and she realized her eyelid was pushing the needle farther into her eyeball.

Louise's vision swam, the dark hall and moonlight smeared, and she forced herself to use two fingers to push past her fluttering eyelashes and pinch the small, sharp thorn projecting from the smooth, slippery surface, catching it just as it slipped fully into her eye, and she gripped it between two fingernails like tweezers and drew it out.

Her eyelid, finally free, snapped shut as she threw the needle away, and that's when Pupkin came for her, darting out of the moonlight. Louise should have jumped over him and run for the front door, she should have done anything else, but her nerve broke and she turned and ran for her bedroom and slammed the door, but Pupkin hit it before it closed and shoved his way inside and

auditory hallucinations visual hallucinations tactile hallucinations
cross my heart and hope to die stick a needle in my eye

Pupkin came for Louise at full speed. She saw the closet doors in the splash of the streetlight, the only other doors in the room, and she ran for them, praying she could make it in time, and she fell into her closet, smashing the doors to the side, her right shoulder thudding into the back wall as she landed on the carpet, and she rolled over to see Pupkin running at her on his stumpy arms and legs, hate on his face, and she tried to close the doors, but she knew that this time there was nowhere to go, no escape.

She scrabbled at the louvered slats of the closet doors with her fingertips, bending back her nails, dragging them shut just as Pupkin smashed into them, making the doors rock on their tracks.

For a second she thought she had him as his nubbins skittered and scrabbled through the slats, then another sewing needle spiked into one of her fingertips, drawing blood, and she yanked her hand away. With nothing stopping him, Pupkin slid the door to one side, hissing in fury. Louise heard it rattling back along its track, and Pupkin thrust his face toward her and then something pulled him backward and he flew away from Louise, across the room, into the shadows.

A bigger shadow stood over Pupkin and lightning flashed once indoors, stabbing her in both ears, filling her sinuses with the stink of metallic smoke, and then it flashed again and she heard the flat slap again and in the second lightning flash she saw Mark standing on the other side of her childhood bedroom, holding an ugly black pistol in both hands, pointing his gun at Pupkin on the floor and pulling the trigger over and over again as shredded puppet fabric filled the dark room.

Chapter 20

Louise sat huddled on the floor of her closet, blinded by muzzle flash, her hand over her left eye, hyperventilating gun smoke. Mark said something but she couldn't hear him.

"My eye!" Louise heard her own voice say from far away.

A flashlight clicked on. It swept across the room, catching swirling patterns of smoke, and dazzled her right eye. It came closer. She pushed herself up using the back wall of the closet and stumbled out, shouldering Mark aside. She needed to get to the hospital. She heard someone in another room say that, maybe it was her, and she made it to the hall, flipping the light switch, but everything stayed dark.

Mark came out of the room behind her and his flashlight showed two chairs lying on their sides in the middle of the hall, and Louise stepped around them to the front door, shoved it open, feeling the cold air hit her like jumping into a mountain lake, making for Mark's truck, the rough grass soaking her feet.

She yanked open the door and crawled in. Mark got in on the driver's side and hit the ignition, and for the first time in her life Louise didn't put on her seat belt. They flew down the street and Mark hit his brakes too hard at the corner before remembering to turn on his headlights. He pulled onto Coleman, doing forty-five in a twenty-five zone, and Louise heard herself say, "Pull over."

"What?" Mark shouted from far away.

"Pull over!" she repeated, and she couldn't tell if she said it out loud or not.

Mark yanked the wheel and they slid into the Sea Island Shopping Center and Louise fell out of the passenger-side door, landing on the cold asphalt. She was already crying as her stomach turned itself inside out and Pizza Chinese came up all over the yellow parking line between her feet. The acrid smell of half-digested pizza drifted into her nostrils and she did it again.

"Emergency room," she panted, and her voice sounded closer now. "I need the emergency room."

"What happened?" Mark's voice came down a pipe.

"My eye," she said to the ground, keeping her left eye covered, holding it in her skull. "He stuck a needle in my eye."

"Let me see," Mark said, but she held up a hand, then lurched forward as food started coming up again.

Fireflies swarmed the vision in her right eye. Her body felt weightless and made of plastic. Her stomach felt knotted into a permanent cramp. Something heavy settled on one shoulder and she jerked it away, but then she realized it was Mark's hand.

He pulled her toward him, gently lifting her hand away from her eye.

"I'm blind," she said.

Mark shone his flashlight into her left eye. She flinched and tried to pull away from the glare, but he held her in place with a hand on her chin.

"It's fine," he said. "There's a little blood in the white part, but you're reacting to the light and your pupil is dilated. How many fingers am I holding up?"

"Three?" Louise said.

"Exactly," Mark told her. "You're okay."

Louise tried to put her thoughts together but they didn't fit. She realized she wasn't wearing any pants. She didn't have on shoes.

"I need the emergency room," she repeated. "I need a doctor. I need someone to check my eye. I need a surgeon."

"I know exactly what you need," Mark said.

"Welcome to Waffle House," the waitress said, coming over to their back corner booth and stopping short. "Y'all okay?"

Louise sat hunched in the booth, hand back over her left eye, staring down at the table. Mark had found some sweatpants and flip-flops in his truck, but they were way too big and her T-shirt looked grimy and the collar was torn. Mark was cleaner but he looked like exactly the type of guy who'd go to a Waffle House at three in the morning after shooting a haunted puppet.

"Never better," Mark said. "Louise?"

"I'm blind," she croaked.

"Do y'all know what you'd like?" the waitress asked.

"Louise?" Mark prompted.

Louise stared at the table.

"She'll have an American cheese omelet," Mark said. "Whole wheat toast, scattered, smothered, and covered hash browns."

It was the same order she'd given since she was nine.

"Steak and eggs for me," Mark said. "Make that medium rare."

"Any coffee?" the waitress asked.

"Two," Mark said.

"I'm scared to look," Louise said to the waitress, removing her hand.

She tried to open her left eyelid but couldn't make herself do it. "Is my eyeball still there?"

"Stop it," Mark said.

The waitress almost said something, changed her mind, and headed back to the grill. It didn't pay to ask questions past one in the morning at Waffle House.

"I need a doctor," Louise repeated.

"Would you quit it?" Mark said. "Google says people get injections in their eyes all the time and they're fine."

"I'm not fine," Louise said.

Mark leaned forward and used his fingers to pry open her left eyelid. "What do you see?"

Louise closed her left eye so nothing leaked out.

"Open your damn eye and tell me what you see," Mark repeated.

Louise opened her eye. Light poured in. Her lid fluttered and felt bruised. She saw the laminated wooden table, the plastic menu with bright pictures of happy food, her knife and fork. Floaters flooded her vision, filling the Waffle House, drifting across the walls, but she wasn't blind. She carefully raised her head and looked around, not wanting to dislodge her eyeball, not wanting to feel it run down her cheek.

Waffle House looked cheery and overlit, all yellow and black, and it smelled like hot grill and all-in-one sanitizing solution. The only other people eating were two middle-aged Black men who looked like they were going fishing. It all felt very present and very far away at the same time, like she'd tuned in to the Normal Channel on late-night cable.

"Right now," Mark said, "what you need, for once in your life, is to listen to me."

Louise watched the waitress give their order to the grill man and felt like an alien observing human behavior. She was having a nervous breakdown in Waffle House. Her brains had been scattered, smothered, and covered.

Louise started to giggle. She couldn't help it. This nice, clean res-taurant, everyone acting normal, Mark acting normal, but a puppet had tried to kill her and she wasn't normal anymore. She laughed harder.

"Lulu," Mark said, leaning across the table, "the way you're laugh-ing is actually really, really scary."

"Share the joke?" the waitress asked, clonking two coffee cups down on their table. "Been on since five and I could use a laugh."

"None of this is real," Louise said.

The waitress set down a little crockery bowl of nondairy creamer.

"I hope not," she said, pouring coffee.

"I don't want to be here," Louise told her. "I want to be in the hospital."

Now the waitress stopped. She studied Mark, rifling through the options: Pimp? Abusive boyfriend? Dealer?

"My sister's having a bad night," he said. "Our parents just died."

Some of the starch went out of the waitress's face.

"I'm sorry," she said, relieved there was an explanation. "If you want, we got a Methodist minister who comes in every morning around four thirty and he'll pray with just about anyone."

"Thank you," Mark said.

The waitress walked off, and Louise saw her telling the other wait-ress what Mark had said.

"Real isn't how you're made," Louise said. "When a child loves you for a long, long time, then you become real."

She giggled again. Mark furrowed his eyebrows.

"Get it?" Louise asked. "It's *The Velveteen Rabbit.* It's my favorite book."

She couldn't help it, she started to really laugh now. "I bet it's Pup-kin's favorite book, too."

The two fishermen looked over. Louise smiled and waved. They turned back to their conversation. It didn't matter what she did. Noth-ing mattered anymore. The world was broken.

Mark pushed her coffee closer.

"Drink some," he said. "Stop being scary."

She took a sip and even though it was basically hot, brown water, it grounded her. She stopped laughing. She looked at Mark through the sea of floaters.

"I don't think I'm well," she said quietly. "I think something is really wrong inside me, something I may have inherited from Mom. So I need you to stay with me and keep me safe, and in the morning we need to go to a doctor and I need to get tested for some things. I mean, my eye, but maybe gene testing for pharmacogenetic markers, too, and talk to him seriously about schizophrenia, bipolar depression. We should make a list."

"This isn't about you having a mental illness," Mark said. "This is about us. This is about the way our family is. I think I figured out what's going on."

"Here you go," the waitress said, putting Louise's cheese omelet down in front of her. Then she put Mark's plate in front of him. "Steak and eggs, medium rare. Anything else?"

"That's all for now," Mark said. "Thank you so much."

The smell of the omelet and the fried potatoes and onions covered in melted American cheese didn't make Louise feel sick. It actually made her stomach growl. She took a bite. The food made her feel brave. She felt like she could face the truth, even if Mark couldn't.

"It's genetic," Louise said. "Which means you should probably get tested, too."

Mark smacked the table hard enough to make the silverware jump. Louise looked up at him, startled.

"What does it take," he whisper-growled, "to make someone in this family actually listen to me?"

Louise felt a rush of affection for him.

"You're right," she said, agreeing with him. "Everything you said tonight is true. Our family doesn't face things, we hide from the past, we cover things up when they're not convenient, and so we missed the signs with Mom, her mood swings, her manic crafting. She probably wrestled with significant mental illness her entire life. Her mom probably had to deal with serious depression after Freddie died, and that stuff becomes generational trauma."

Mark stared at her and she wondered if she had said what she meant to say or if it had come out different. She'd have to be careful about how she spoke from now on.

"This has nothing to do with Mom," Mark said, "or Dad. I thought it was their ghosts, but now I realize it has everything to do with Pupkin. I saw him move. He tried to kill you. Those dolls in the bathroom wrote that note on the wall, but the one who's behind everything is that creepy little puppet."

It suddenly sounded really, really funny to Louise. Mark snapped a warning finger at her.

"Don't you fucking laugh at me," he said. "For the first time ever, my life finally makes sense."

Louise took a breath and let it out.

"I'm not laughing at you," she said. "But this is serious. If it's inherited, then I'm worried about it affecting Poppy, too."

She picked up her toast, took a bite, and it stayed down.

"Who stuck a needle in your eye?" Mark asked, and Louise's left eye gave a twinge. She stopped chewing. "You did that to yourself? Who wrote on the wall in the bathroom? You think I did? You think I want to mess with you so badly?"

Louise made herself swallow the hard, dry lump of bread in her mouth.

"I don't think I know what's real anymore," she said.

"I do," Mark said. "Which is why you need to hear me. You're lucky I listened to my gut and decided I was not comfortable leaving you in

211

that house alone after that thing with the dolls, so I parked around the corner. You're lucky I don't sleep too good after a few beers, you're lucky I had my window down, and you're lucky I believe in our Second Amendment right to bear arms, because I heard you screaming and I came in the house and I didn't find you all by yourself trying to stick a needle in your own eye, I found you hiding in the closet while Pupkin tried to tear the damn doors off. I saw him. You saw him. So now that everything's all safe, don't pretend you didn't see it, too."

"There's always an explanation," she said. "That's what Dad always said."

Mark leaned back in the booth.

"How about this?" he said. "For years Mom invested Pupkin with attention and focus and time, and like in *The Velveteen Rabbit*, love brings things to life. She put all her emotional energy into Pupkin, and some of it bled into the others, and as I believe a great man of science once said, energy can be neither created nor destroyed."

"*The Velveteen Rabbit* is not a compelling theoretical framework for the physical universe," Louise said. "It's a children's story."

"So's the Bible," Mark said. "But you got people making laws and killing each other over it every day."

"That's a false equivalency," Louise said. "I don't subscribe to your *Velveteen Rabbit* theory of the universe."

Mark's eyebrows lowered.

"Don't make me sound stupid," he said. "Not after I got you out of that house. Not after I saved you from that puppet. You want to subscribe to something? Try subscribing to this—people leave all kinds of shit behind when they die: clothes, magazines, seashell art, food in the fridge, memories, feelings, emotions, trauma. And, as we're also learning, to our everlasting motherfucking regret, what Mom left behind was Pupkin. She pretended he was real for so long, invested so much of herself in him, got us to act like he was real for so many years, and she dies, and who tells him he's not allowed to exist anymore? Who explains to Pupkin that he's not real now? How's that for a subscription? Can I sign you up?"

"The only thing Mom left behind is some kind of genetic disorder," Louise said.

"She left you mental illness?" Mark asked. "Okay, put that in a jar and show me. Give me your mental illness on a petri dish."

"It doesn't work that way," Louise said. "Mental illness is a complex series of overlapping vectors. It's partially organic, partially cultural, partially psychological."

"Meeeeep," Mark said. "No likes. One star out of five. I will not be reading any further issues of your magazine."

"My explanation is logically consistent," Louise said. "Yours is all magical energy."

Mark waved her words away.

"Louise," he said. "You are neglecting the most important thing of all: the evidence of your senses. You heard things in the attic. You saw the dolls. You saw Pupkin. I saw Pupkin. You touched him. He jammed a needle in your eye. You're asking me to give all that up in favor of your preconceived notions of what can and can't be real?"

Louise felt Pupkin's weight on her chest, saw him lunging at her eye, her eyelid trying to close and hitting the needle, she felt the vibrations in the racquet run up the palm of her right hand, run through her wrist, up her forearm, felt the dead squirrel thrashing beneath its strings.

"I don't know about you," Mark said, "but I'm being presented with a choice between having a serious medical condition and being in extraordinary fucking circumstances, so I'll take option B, but if you want to go down the mental illness route, then really think about what that means. You're having what? A psychotic break? You'll be giving custody of Poppy to Ian for a while, checking yourself in someplace to get help. You'll probably want to let Poppy's teachers know. You'll definitely have to let Ian's family know. You think they won't fight you for custody?"

Louise covered her face with her hands.

"I can't . . ." she said, and couldn't finish the sentence.

"You'd better," Mark said. "Because what happened with Pupkin really happened, and Mercy thinks there's something wrong with our house, and I got some bad news, too."

You're bad, bad, bad, and no one's ever going to play with you again.

"What?" Louise moaned.

"You've spent a long time ignoring what goes on in this family," Mark said. "But it's not safe to do that anymore. Now, here's what's going to happen. I'm going to get another cup of coffee and then I'm going to tell you the real reason I dropped out of BU. You're finally going to learn the truth about Pupkin."

Mark motioned to the waitress, who came over and refilled their cups.

"Y'all doing okay?" she asked.

"We're fine," Mark said.

The waitress looked from Mark to Louise and saw that they were only looking at each other. She shrugged and walked away. Louise watched Mark take a sip of his coffee, put down his cup, and lean back.

"When I went to BU," he said, "the first thing I did was join a radical puppet collective."

BARGAINING

Chapter 21

9/11 woke me up.

Before those planes hit the World Trade Center I'd been in the chute. They start you out in the kiddie plays like *Snow White and the Seven Dwarfs* and *Clockwork Mice*, then I did those church plays for Mom, then you graduate to the adult plays that need children like *Cheaper by the Dozen*, and after that it's all musicals, all the time, you're just aging through the roles in the same carousel of shows: *Oliver!*, *The Music Man*, *Joseph and the Amazing Technicolor Dreamcoat*. You start out playing the little brother and you wind up playing the juvenile lead.

Then came that morning, and every homeroom that had a TV turned them on and we watched the towers go down in big puffs of smoke like a bad magic trick. They sent us home because they didn't know what to tell us. We talked on the phone that night, remember? After we hung up, I stayed up until sunrise thinking, *Everything's different now*.

But it wasn't. Before long they started pretending this new war was just a rerun of World War II, where we were the good guys, they were the bad guys, and we were going to bomb them until the world stopped changing. Then Dock Street called and said they were doing *1776* as a tribute for the troops and I said, "Yeah, I'll audition," but I never showed up.

Nothing made sense, so me and Marcus and Leana Banks started doing shows that didn't make sense. They drove everyone nuts. We did *The Bass Menagerie* and *Breakdance Explosion* and then that high school theater competition banned us from registering because *Breakdance Explosion* had Bonzo the Aborting Clown in it, so we performed it outside the Marriott where everyone was staying and it was all any of them could talk about. They gave us a special award for that.

I had those big fights with Dad about going to BU, but I had to go because it was the only place that let you do a combination theater arts major where you could do acting, some directing, writing, and design, and I needed all that to start my own company because I wanted to get out of Charleston and go somewhere I could make a difference. I knew Dad would give in eventually because he hates conflict. I just had to be willing to fight longer than him.

At first, BU seemed like everything I wanted it to be. It's hard to make friends your first few weeks of college, but not if you're a theater major. By the time classes started, we were taking over whole tables in the dining hall and hanging out in each other's rooms. We'd all read the same books, we'd all seen the same movies, we'd all played the same parts, we were all extroverts.

I hated us.

Derrick Andrews was my Scene Study teacher and he was a fussy little ginger who couldn't wait to break out his Shakespeare voice and show us how a scene should really be played. Derrick didn't want to question what it meant to stand on a platform at one end of a room pretending to be Macbeth when everyone could clearly see you were standing on a platform at one end of a room pretending to be Macbeth. He didn't want to interrogate language or turn *Death of a Salesman* into a slapstick comedy. To him, theater was an office job that just happened to take place onstage. The sad thing was, everyone in the program wanted to grow up to be like him.

I found some people like me, mostly in the playwrights program. We started our own company and our first production was *House of Corn*, a partially improvised soap opera set in the McMansion of the biggest corn growers in Kansas. It didn't matter that none of us could find Kansas on a map. We did an episode a week and twelve people came to the first. By the time we did part six we had almost four hundred people in the audience. The teachers hated what we were doing, but everyone else was having a great time. We had sex scenes, fight scenes, stunts, blood—it felt alive.

And the morning after that last show, I woke up with the horrible realization that I'd reached the end. Dad was spending all this money to send me to school, but the only show that felt alive to me was the one I'd written and directed, and I could do that at the College of Charleston for half the price.

I didn't know how to tell Mom and Dad that after just two months, the thing I'd fought so hard for, the thing I'd yelled about for a year, wasn't what I wanted to do anymore. I didn't know how to tell them that dropping out meant I was more committed to getting an education than staying in. They'd think I was a flake for the rest of my life.

No one in college cares if you cut class as long as the checks keep clearing, so I hung out in my room for a few days, then on Saturday I headed across the river to Harvard Square to change the scenery, but it turned out to be as depressing as the rest of Boston. Then I heard that drumroll. It was the one crisp thing on that gray, overcast day.

I followed it and found them standing in a brick square near the ART, two street performers in tweed jackets and black turtlenecks with snare drums strapped around their necks, playing a rolling tattoo. What nailed me to the sidewalk were their masks. They were made of papier-mâché and had no mouths and gun-slit eyes, and they erased their humanity but also made them look more than human. They stood on either side of a little white-and-yellow-striped puppet theater with a sign propped up against the inevitable plastic bucket that read, *Organ Presents: The Man Who Could Fly.*

The two drummers didn't acknowledge me or any of the people slowing down to watch, they just stood straight-backed and snapped out their tattoo in complete synchronicity. They stopped at the same instant, did an about-face, and marched backstage. A few seconds later, the curtain cranked open to show a tiny living room with a marionette sitting inside. One of the masked performers returned to the side of the stage with an accordion and squeezed out something whimsical and French that inspired the marionette to flap its arms until it slowly lifted off the sofa and flew. It fluttered around the stage, dipping and rising, as graceful as a butterfly.

About fifteen of us had gathered to watch, and parents pointed out the marionette for their kids.

"See the man fly?" a mom asked her baby. "See him fly?"

The marionette was tiny but painted red so he was easy to spot and he really did look alive. Then suddenly the accordion music stopped with a honk and the player took out a pair of scissors and snipped off the strings controlling the marionette's legs.

It crashed to the ground. Parents around me got nervous. I got interested.

The accordion music started again, encouraging the marionette to get up and fly, which soothed the parents, who decided to stay. The marionette fluttered and twitched and struggled, then it rose into the air again, this time with its legs dangling down, but it still flew, and after a minute you forgot about its legs.

Until the accordion music crashed to a halt again and the masked performer took out his scissors and snipped off the string to one of the marionette's arms. This time the happy accordion music seemed to mock the marionette as it lay in a heap, struggling to rise. I heard a murmur go through the small crowd and people with children began drifting away. The marionette flopped like a gutted fish, rattling like dry bones against the cardboard floor. It threw itself into the air, one arm pathetically reaching for the sky, then it crashed to the ground again.

It began to thrash and flail, then, against all odds, it rose again, its remaining arm pumping hard as its other limbs dangled like deadweight, but it flew! It could still fly!

Then another discordant honk of the accordion, and you knew what was coming next. The remaining parents led their children away, but the kids snuck looks over their shoulders as the masked performer snipped the final strings holding the marionette up and it collapsed in a heap. The accordion music started again, and it was the same tune, but it sounded mean now. The marionette lay motionless on the floor. I wondered what would happen next. Maybe a puppet bird would fly in and lift him up? Or strings made of Hope would drop down and hook themselves onto his limbs? But he just lay there while the accordion music played on. Eventually, the curtains closed. People couldn't get away fast enough.

Everyone else could sense the depressing Eastern European vibes coming from these puppets and stayed the hell away, but not me. I watched the next five performances. Mom's puppets always said "Love me! Look at me!" These guys made puppets that wanted to be hated.

By the time the last show ended I was the only audience member left. Even the homeless people had taken off. This monstrously tall bald dude with a ginger goatee stepped out from behind the curtain and started to take the theater apart while the other one, this girl he called Sadie, went to get their car. Sadie wasn't beautiful, right? She had curly hair and too many tiny teeth and eyes like a fox and a body you won't see in magazines, but she acted like she had secrets and I'm not ashamed to admit I had a full-blown crush on her from the second the tall dude tossed her the keys and she caught them one-handed.

I started talking up the tall dude the only way I knew how: by telling him they were the greatest thing I'd ever seen and giving him all my money. It was only six dollars, but I remembered what we learned from Mom and offered to help them load their car.

Sadie came around the corner in a big old yellow tank of a station wagon and I don't want to be inappropriate but sexy girls in big beater cars is the most beautiful sight created by God. I was more in love with her in five minutes than I'd ever been with anyone in my life.

I helped them load and I never stopped talking and I'm sure everything I said sounded like stammering bullshit, but offering to help must've made a difference because when I said, "Can I work for you?" the tall dude said, "Come up to Medford tomorrow at three. We'll try it out."

He gave me the address, then they drove off and left me standing in a big blue cloud of exhaust in the middle of a drizzle at six o'clock in Harvard Square, feeling like something real had finally happened to me.

Five twenty-three Wheeler looked like all the other houses around Davis Square except it didn't have a Virgin Mary in its front yard or a yellow ribbon tied to its fence. When Sadie opened the door, she didn't smile or anything, she just said, "Come on. Everyone's out back making penises."

The tall guy with the goatee turned out to be named Richard and he was working with another guy named Clark, who had the body of a tapeworm—impossibly long, impossibly pale—with the angular face of a German silent movie star crowned with a vertical explosion of wiry jet-black hair. He wore shoes that had been patched together so many times they looked like they were made out of duct tape, and the genius vibe came off him like BO. If I said Wittgenstein, the dude you're picturing in your head looked like Clark.

And Sadie was right, they were making dicks. Big ones, three to four feet long, then smaller ones that looked like they were built around paper-towel tubes. They had them hanging from the back porch roof like wind chimes, slathering them with papier-mâché, looking like salamis made out of newsprint, which was a relief because I'm not sure I could have handled it if they'd been painted and looked like actual dicks yet. I wasn't that cool.

They showed me what to do and I made penises with them for the rest of the day. They talked to each other and I was happy to listen and soak it all in. It felt good just to be treated like an equal.

The penises turned out to actually be penis missiles, and we needed thirty-five of them for the antiwar march that weekend, where they'd be carried by members of the Radical Fairies. The Fairies had gotten overwhelmed building their costumes and outsourced their penis missiles to Organ because they knew Clark. Each one would carry a penis missile like a magic wand with five of them designated as pall bearers for the big six-footer.

We dried them with blow dryers and painted them white to keep the newsprint from bleeding through their final coats of pink. Richard detailed all the ridges and veins and Sadie went through after him and painted *WMD* or *SCUD* on their sides with black paint.

They told me there was no pressure to show up the next day because they were loading up at five a.m. and it was a hell of a long train ride from my dorm, but when I got back to my room my roommate and his scene partner were hanging out drinking ironic forties of Colt 45 and deconstructing Britney Spears songs. Our country was rushing headlong into a manufactured war where real people our age were going to get their arms and legs blown off in a desert they couldn't find on the map, and our response was to bury our heads in pop culture. I set my alarm for four a.m.

Our penis missiles were the hit of the parade. By the end of the day, my feet hurt and my throat was sore from chanting, but I'd earned my place. Back at 523 they ordered Chinese food, and I sat in the living room listening to them complain about Linda, who they'd seen at the parade. From what I could tell she used to work with them but there'd been some kind of falling-out and she'd split off and formed her own radical puppet collective.

I asked them what was next and it turned out to be another protest. We'd be doing street theater at that one. After that we'd be perform as part of the Big Anarchy Marching Band of the Future American War Dead at another protest. Then it was a commedia in Copley Square called *W-W-W-Where's My WMD?* like W. Bush, get it?

Just like that, I joined the cause.

People make fun of us because we lost, but we tried to turn this ship around. Millions of us around the world, half a million in New York City alone, banging our drums, marching in the streets, shouting "Wake up!" Less than twenty percent of Americans supported that war. No one wanted to send their sons and daughters to die in the desert, but the generals gathered in their masses, right? And look at the world they made.

Twenty years of killing, eight thousand people dead, and then— and I know we're not supposed to count them because they're the wrong color and from the wrong country—but a million people died over there. A million yous, a million mes, a million dads, a million moms.

And for what?

I know we were just a bunch of kids with puppets, but we could've stopped it, Lulu. I really believe we could've, and if that makes me stupid and naive, if you think I drank the Kool-Aid, you're right. But I'd rather think we tried and failed than we never stood a chance.

But honestly? What I really wish? What I really wish is that I'd never met a single one of them. I wish I could take it all back. I wish I'd never gotten involved, because those fucking puppets ruined my life.

Chapter 22

The Man Who Could Fly was cool, but I preferred commedia and street theater. They taught me mask work and juggling and how to eat fire and balance a stepladder on my chin, and I got lots of street time, so every day I got better, but I didn't want to touch their puppets because of Mom. Then they showed me Sticks.

I'd been hanging out with them for about three weeks and done seven or eight shows by then, but I wouldn't do *The Man Who Could Fly*. I wouldn't do any of the puppets. Then one night, we were sitting on the back porch of 523 eating homemade black bread and aioli that Richard made, and the conversation turned to why I didn't like puppets. I told them all about Mom's puppet ministry and they started asking me about her shows and I told them about *A Stray in a Manger* and *The Selfish Giant*, and Clark, man, he opened my eyes.

"Your mom's puppets are watered-down copies of copies," he said. "They're off-brand Muppets. Put real puppets in a church and they'd burn it down. Puppets unleash anarchy. Punch in a *Punch and Judy* show beats his wife, kills his baby, and when they try to exccute him he tricks the hangman into hanging himself. Puppets are about violence. They don't do life lessons, they don't do love."

And I said something like, "Yeah, my mom's shows were pretty fucking stupid," because that's what you do when you want to impress people at college, right? You sell out your parents.

And Clark said, "Puppeteers respect their puppets. Your mom probably did, too. Every puppeteer knows that when they wear a puppet it's live, like a grenade with the pin pulled."

And Sadie said, "Show him Sticks."

I didn't see Clark shake his head. He just took another bite of black bread.

"He should see Sticks," Richard said.

"What's Sticks?" I asked.

Something hung in the air between us, like we'd all been waiting for this important conversation to begin. Clark set down his slice of bread and went inside, but he did it with so little ceremony he might have been going to the bathroom for all I could tell. A few minutes later, the back door rattled open and Clark stepped out with a paper bag. He dumped a pile of wood on the ground in a rat's nest of black strings, and it looked like something he'd found in the garbage, but his hands began to fly over it, straightening a string here, pulling a string there, adjusting a bit of wood.

Then his left hand clutched the wooden H of a marionette's control yoke and the pile of wood and string suddenly looked like a human figure barely carved from a bunch of mismatched wooden sticks, jointed with loops of black thread. Its face was a rough oblong with indentations for its eyes. It had no mouth. Clark held the yoke with one hand and looped a ring connected to a thread over his thumb, and he twitched his hands, the strings went taut, and Sticks lifted his head.

Most marionettes are fussy and clattery. This one felt alive.

Sticks hesitated, turned his head to the side, raised his blind face, and sniffed the air. Then he climbed to his feet and stood on the porch between us. Clark turned invisible. I no longer saw Sticks's strings. He didn't hang like a marionette with his feet barely skimming the ground. Sticks stood solidly on the porch, his center of gravity not in the strings but rooted in his belly. Sticks rubbed his face thoughtfully with one hand, then seemed to catch a scent and turned his blind face toward me. He regarded me and I felt seen, not by Clark but by whatever creature stood on this porch with us. Sadie's leg lay between the two of us, and Sticks gestured and she drew it back, then Sticks walked across the floor and stopped when he reached me, leaned over, and sniffed my jeans.

I remember thinking very clearly, *He's getting used to my scent*, even though he wasn't anything but a bunch of blocks of wood tied to strings.

He reached out his small wooden hand and laid it on my leg. It wasn't Clark manipulating a string to poke me with a piece of wood, Sticks laid his hand on my leg. I stopped breathing. He turned his blind face up to me, and even though I could see the chisel marks that indicated his eyes, somehow he made eye contact.

Sticks trembled between us, vibrating with life, and he placed another hand on my leg, then his foot, then he carefully brought his other foot around and now he was standing on my calf, one hand balancing himself on my knee. He weighed less than a cricket. And I heard Clark say, "A puppet is a possession that possesses the possessor."

Then Sticks flew into the air and the life went out of him and all the tension drained from the porch and there were only the four of us again. Clark hovered Sticks over the paper bag and dropped him in. They all watched to see my reaction.

"Can you teach me how to do that?" I asked.

Clark smiled, and I knew I'd asked the right question.

I overslept and missed Monday's Scene Study class, and Derrick chewed me out for not showing proper respect to my fellow actors, so I decided to skip Thursday's class. In fact, I decided to never go back to his class again. Instead, I went to the library and read everything I could find about puppets.

I read about Bread and Puppet in Vermont and their antiwar puppet shows that ended with the entire audience breaking homemade bread together. I read about Little Angel's *Wild Night of the Witches*, and Handspan Theatre, and Charles Ludlam's *The Ventriloquist's Wife*, and Javanese holy shadow puppet plays, and how puppet shows used to be so dangerous that in sixteenth-century England some cities banned them while other cities paid puppeteers to stay away.

By the time Saturday rolled around, puppets were what I wanted to do with the rest of my life.

Boston is a brown town with a gray sky, and everyone stomps around like they've already had a few and are ready to start a fight, but if you open the right door you fall into puppetland: church basements in Somerville, back rooms in Cambridge, a squat in the South End, a dirt-floor basement in a Malden row house. I landed in a world of card-table bars and five-dollar tickets and a passed hat at the end of every night. Everyone knew everyone else and they'd all worked for Bread and Puppet at some point, then Big Fun Puppets in Boston before it exploded and sent splinters of puppet companies spiraling across the city to form and break up and re-form on fast-forward like single-celled organisms.

Linda, who I'd heard so much about, had been in Organ before she split off to form a feminist puppet collective, Raw Sharks, with her best friend, Chauncy, then Chauncy came out and left Raw Sharks to form a lesbian puppet collective committed to direct action called Smash Face, but now there were rumors it was splitting up over the war. The fact that Organ had spawned one, and now two, more puppet collectives made us feel like we had a lineage, it made us seem important.

We worked all the time. We staged street shows about the CIA selling heroin they bought from the Taliban, performed commedia at afterhours bars where Harlequino looked for WMDs in patrons' bras and up their butts, and no one in Boston marched against the war without one of our puppets in their parade. Most importantly, Clark, Richard, and Sadie taught me how to work the street.

No one tosses you a buck because you elevate their spirit. They toss you a buck because you're balancing on your head playing "Pomp and Circumstance" on a kazoo and they want to see what you're going to do next. What we did was a little bit carnival, a little bit circus, and a little bit old-time vaudeville. It made everything Derrick had been teaching us feel dead. How could I respect a teacher who couldn't hold a sidewalk crowd or deal with a drunk?

Puppet work and mask work are essentially the same, and it's hard to describe what it's like to wear a mask to people who've never done it, but the second you put on a mask you're not you anymore. Same with puppets. Put one on and your posture changes, your voice alters, and you can feel what it wants, you can feel what it's scared of, you know what it needs. You don't wear the puppet. The puppet wears you.

"A puppet is a device for driving the personality out of the body and allowing a spirit to take control," Clark said. "Puppets have no freedom, but they give the puppeteer freedom. They have no life, but they live forever."

They freed me. I felt like Pinocchio, finally turning into a real boy. I don't know why I lied to Mom about it. Well, I mean, I lied because I fought so hard to go to BU and it turned out they were paying a ton of money for classes I was cutting.

But I could've told her about Organ. Did you know Mom marched against Vietnam? She went to a bunch of protests when she was in New York. She even got tear-gassed in DC. I could've told her about Organ and left out the part about cutting class, but I didn't want her in my life. You know Mom, she gets excited and all of a sudden she's taking over your space and you can barely breathe.

So I made up classes, and rehearsals, and grades. I made up friends and auditions and told her I'd been cast as the lead in a production of *Barefoot in the Park*, and she and Dad actually planned to fly up and see my big star turn in February. I don't know how I expected to handle that. I guess I figured they'd forgive me when I said I wanted to transfer somewhere cheaper and closer to home.

Everyone in Organ had a personal puppet they did solo shows with—for Clark it was Sticks, Sadie had a rat named Dustin she did a ventriloquist act with, Richard had a political rapper with ripped abs called Marxist Mark—and I think I had the idea that I'd use Pupkin to develop my own solo act. I mean, I knew how freaky he looked, and spooky clowns were kind of in the zeitgeist then, you know? Mom must've been thrilled that all of a sudden I was interested in Pupkin again, because when I asked she shipped him overnight. It wasn't until I opened the box that I remembered how scary he looked. Those big black-rimmed eyes staring out of that corpse-white face, and that relentless smile. He looked totally and completely insane. He looked like a grenade with the pin pulled.

When I pulled him out at 523, everyone lost their shit. Sadie told me Pupkin was what Satan had nightmares about, Richard told me he wouldn't sleep in a room with Pupkin in it, but Clark wanted to try him on. The second he slipped him over his hand, he said, "My name's Pupkin, how do dee do? If you all happy, me am happy, too."

And he did it in the exact same high-pitched voice Mom used for Pupkin when we were kids. It's the first time I ever felt my skin crawl. Clark was right—puppets wear you as much as you wear them. You put them on and they tell you who they are. And Pupkin told Clark who he was, and that's when things started to go wrong.

We'd been hired to do a pageant by an elementary school up in Worcester where Clark's mom knew the principal. The deal was that we'd come up and do a puppet workshop in the morning for the kids, then do the pageant right after lunch when they were at their most obedient. We were very enthusiastic about this chance to show off the primal power of puppetry. We were even more enthusiastic about the eight hundred dollars they were paying us.

We spent the weeks leading up to the show building enormous puppets: a Man Who Could Fly with a six-foot wingspan that we'd operate from a ladder, a massive death's-head, a General that stood seven feet tall, built on the frame of an old overcoat with a gun-turret head. We built thirty-five screaming Victim masks, marionette drones, rod puppet missiles. We built an entire National Security Council whose jaws all flapped when you moved one mechanism, and I can only explain our embarrassing overenthusiasm by saying no one had ever paid us eight hundred dollars to do anything before.

Sadie's station wagon barely had room for human beings with all the puppets and masks and props and accordions and stilts we packed inside. Clark rode shotgun, and Pupkin navigated from his right hand. He'd borrowed him from me and, as far as I could tell, he never took him off.

Clark's parents had a rental house outside Worcester on a rural route, and we stopped by there to drop off our stuff before heading to the school. It's hard to describe how depressing that place was except to say that every light fixture was a fluorescent tube and it only seemed survivable because we thought we'd be there for one night.

We headed to the school and taught our workshop on the playground, which looked more like a parking lot to me but, you know, if you thought Boston was depressing, meet Worcester. Clark taught the kids with Pupkin on one hand, and they went nuts for him.

"They're so excited," Mrs. Marsten, the principal, said. "They've never met real actors before."

I was a "real actor." Mom would have loved it.

Mrs. Marsten got a little wary when we introduced the kids to the Victim masks. They were screaming papier-mâché face masks sewn to burlap body cowls we made out of fifty-pound bags used for coffee beans that we bought from this gourmet coffee place for a buck a bag. Once you put on the mask, the burlap cloak covered your body completely and you disappeared into this howling, tragic mask of pain.

"I thought maybe they'd be playing sunflowers," Mrs. Marsten told us. "Or ducks. They love ducks."

The kids loved being Victims, though. They loved hiding behind those masks, hunched over and walking like their legs were broken and they'd lost everything that mattered to them in the world. They loved wailing and crying and rolling on the ground, given total freedom to play sad by the anonymity of the masks.

Right before the kids lined up for lunch, we had them dip their hands in red paint and cover the General's overcoat in bloody handprints. I kind of feel like if Mrs. Marsten had been paying more attention right then we could have avoided a lot of unpleasantness later, but she'd already gone inside and left us with a teacher's aide who kept disappearing to smoke.

Our theater was the gym with a curtain strung halfway across, and we ran around like demons getting ready, then suddenly it was one thirty and the doors opened and kids filed inside, and Mrs. Marsten brought our thirty Victims backstage. We got them into their masks, then Sadie played a snappy drum roll and Mrs. Marsten introduced us.

"Good afternoon, children," she said into her mic, and I thought it showed weakness that she couldn't control her kids without electronic amplification. "We're very lucky this afternoon that Organ Puppet Theater from Boston has come to see us today. They're going to put on a play—"

"Pageant," I muttered.

"—and I don't think any of us has ever seen a puppet show with puppets this big before. Afterward, you'll get a chance to meet the people who made these puppets and you can ask them questions. I know each class has a question, so I'm very excited to hear the answers. But first, what do we do when we have visitors?"

"Listen and keep still," an army of kids chanted.

That's when I knew we'd chosen to do the right show. These kids had been brainwashed. They needed a wake-up call.

"So, let's give a Busy Bears welcome to Organ Puppet Theater!" Mrs. Marsten cheered.

They were still clapping as we lowered our masks into place and wheeled out the Man Who Could Fly. Sadie held up a sign that read *The Man Who Could Fly* and sounded out the words through her kazoo.

Clark marched onstage wearing his six-foot stilts to operate the massive marionette Man, and a buzz went through the audience. I opened the curtains of the tiny stage and the show began. Those kids never stood a chance. By the time we snipped the final set of strings and the Man clattered to the floor like a dead bag of bones, those third graders knew we meant business.

Then we got into the meat of the pageant: a history of the War on Terror, as fabricated and engineered by the CIA and the American military industrial complex. Those kids were fed a daily dose of imperialist American propaganda in everything from their Saturday morning cartoons to their sugar-coated breakfast cereal, so forty minutes of counterprogramming was the least we could do to liberate their minds.

To be honest, we thought the teachers would be grateful.

The kids were absorbed, but by the time we got to the Soviet retreat and the rise of the Taliban using American-supplied weapons, even from inside my mask I noticed the nervous teachers gathering around Mrs. Marsten by the back door of the gym. They looked pretty upset.

In our defense, the kids playing Victims were clearly having a blast, but when we got to the American invasion of Afghanistan and they all got killed in a drone strike, maybe that was too intense. At the climax, Sadie played "The Star-Spangled Banner" slowed down to a funeral march while Clark made his entrance on six-foot stilts, dressed as Death, swooping low over the bodies of the Victims that lay scattered across the stage. Death was the biggest puppet we'd ever made, and he looked absolutely terrifying. In our final tableau we looked like grim beasts standing over a field of corpses while the great grinning skull of Death itself rose above us like a malevolent moon.

That's when one of the kids started to cry. I'm not sure how we could have been expected to know that a significant portion of them had parents deployed overseas. I also feel like maybe the first little girl who started crying might have been looking for attention? Either way, that one crying kid set off a chain reaction, and suddenly there were sobbing kids everywhere. Through the eyeholes of my mask I could see teachers ushering the kids out the back door like the place was on fire while Mrs. Marsten steamed down the aisle toward us.

"Get off this stage," she hissed. "Right. Now."

We bowed and apparently that was the wrong thing to do, because she yanked my mask off and the tie got caught in my hair so I lost a clump. She was pretty pissed. Sadie and I lifted up the side of the General, and Richard crawled out from underneath, and together we watched the last of the kids vanish through the gym doors. An hour ago they'd been treating us like celebrities. Now they were acting like we'd killed Elmo. To be honest, I blamed the teachers for not preparing them better.

Mrs. Marsten disappeared and we realized most of the teachers were gone, so we struck the show and loaded up the station wagon. We still felt pretty good about it, to be honest, and as for the crying kids? If you're making real art, not everyone's always going to like it. By tomorrow morning they wouldn't even remember what they'd been crying about, and maybe a few of them would even start asking questions about American hegemony. Clark went inside to get our check. The sun went behind the clouds and it started getting cold. He came out a long time later.

"They're not paying us," he said.

"What do you mean?" Richard asked.

"I mean there's no check with our name on it," Clark said. "They're saying we traumatized the kids and probably violated the Patriot Act."

"The what?" Richard asked.

"I spent forty dollars on gas," Sadie said.

"You're going to have to eat it," Clark said. "They're pretty angry."

"And for groceries," she added.

"It's fucking unfair," I chimed in.

I felt like the situation warranted profanity.

"I have spent 375 bucks on materials for this show," Richard said. "I have the receipts. Whether they liked it or not, the least they can do is cover our expenses."

The school disagreed. We wound up having a pretty heated public debate with Mrs. Marsten and a few of her storm troopers in the parking lot. We tried to keep the focus on freedom of speech and the resilience of children, while they threw around inflammatory words like *perverted* and *trespassing*. Eventually, someone called the cops.

By the time Mrs. Marsten finished explaining to them that the dispute revolved around payment for a puppet show performed for third graders about American culpability in 9/11, the cops had stopped listening to our side of the story. They made us unload the station wagon. The General was definitely going to need a new coat of paint before we used him again.

Richard tried to explain the difference between glorifying drug use and demonstrating CIA narco-trafficking used to illegally fund American intervention in foreign wars, but the cops had already made up their minds. By the time they finished "searching" our car, there weren't many puppets left we could salvage. On the one hand, it proved the power of puppetry; on the other hand, it was pretty fucking humiliating.

By the time they let us go the kids had long since gone home and the school was empty. We were hungry and numb. Their cruiser followed us all the way to the township line to make sure we left, which was kind of overkill. I looked over at Clark in the passenger seat, and his face was white, his lips pressed together hard. His left hand shook from whatever emotions he was holding in, and he had his right hand tucked inside Pupkin, holding him in his lap.

It gets dark early in the winter in Massachusetts, and by the time we got to his parents' place outside town there was no light left. We went inside and started switching on fluorescents, but the house was freezing. The heat barely worked. Clark didn't say a word to anyone, he just went upstairs to the big bedroom and closed the door. No one talked much. We ate instant mac and cheese and went to bed. I slept on the living room couch and I hadn't felt this cold in a very long time.

I woke up in the middle of the night to pee and on my way back I saw something orange pulsing in the kitchen. I looked out the windows and saw Clark in the backyard with Pupkin on his arm. They'd set the General on fire and were watching him burn, their pale faces glowing in the dark.

The next morning, Clark told us he'd realized what went wrong.

"What went wrong is that we've got a political message and you booked us a show in an elementary school," Richard said.

"What went wrong is we've lost our way," Clark said. "We've gotten lazy. We need to go deeper. We need to do the work. I've spent a lot of time communing with Pupkin and it's got depths that make our other puppets look dead. I want us to stay here. I want us to recommit to core principles. I want us to explore the ideas I'm getting from this puppet."

We were puppeteers. No one thought twice about listening to what a puppet had to say.

"Politics come and politics go," Clark said. "We're puppeteers be-cause we know there are primal forces in Punch and Petrushka and Guignol, destabilizing forces, forces of anarchy we can unleash that challenge the power structures trying to turn us into superpatriots to spread Pax Americana around the world. We need to be bigger than the CNN ticker. We need to listen to Pupkin. This is our moment. If we stay here and do the work, we can come back with something wild and powerful and true. The question is: can the three of you spare a week of your lives for art?"

Of course we could. We pledged to stay for the week and do an intensive company workshop. They'd done retreats here before, so there were supplies in the basement. We'd make new masks, new puppets, and start putting together a new show. A show true to us. A show dictated by the primal power unleashed by Pupkin.

"I already started last night," Clark told us.

He went down in the basement and came back carrying three fully painted masks. They had big black-rimmed eyes, grinning mouths, and chubby white cheeks. They wore smiles that promised mischief and fun. They were Pupkins.

With his face blown up to life size, Pupkin looked wilder, more dangerous, more like a hand grenade with the pin pulled.

"I think it's time," Clark said, "that we got serious about our work."

When you're doing mask work you shape your face to fit the mask. You let go and the mask shows you what to do. It uses your body to pick things up, knock things over, or do things you don't understand, but the point is you surrender to its will. You don't fight it. You let its personality replace yours. The nice thing is, you're not responsible for your actions because you're a vessel for the mask, and the only rule you have to respect is when the workshop leader says, "Take off your mask," you take it off right away.

The problem was, Clark never told us to take off our masks.

For our first session with the Pupkins, he told us he'd set an alarm for five hours. That's a long time to let three masks run riot in a house.

When he finally helped us take them off, my face ran with sweat and it felt good to breathe something that didn't stink like my own breath. Sadie had sweated through her shirt. Richard had an angry red line across his forehead and his eyes were bloodshot.

It's hard to describe what it feels like to wear a mask. You're aware of what's going on around you but it all feels far away. The longer you wear the mask, the more distant the world becomes through your eyeholes. Bits and pieces of time go black because the mask is active and you slip into a semi-somnolent state, but it feels good because you're not in control. Nothing is your fault. You're a puppet.

Like Clark said, "A puppet is a possession that possesses the possessor."

And a mask turns a person into a puppet.

Vague images from that first session filled my head, and if you'd asked me to write down what we'd done, I would have written *played*. What we'd actually done was trash the house. The Pupkins had slashed the pillows on the sofa, and we found stuffing as far away as the edge of the backyard. A Pupkin had gotten into the groceries and stomped most of them to mush on the kitchen floor. One of them had torn every single page out of the phone book and stuffed them in the downstairs toilet.

"My parents are going to renovate this place anyways," Clark said. "Don't worry about it. What's important is that I got an entire pad of notes. You've tapped into some powerful archetypes. This is the beginning of a really vital show. I felt like I was alone in the house with a bunch of monsters. It was absolutely terrifying."

Then he laughed. I'd never seen him so happy.

Clark never took Pupkin off, and he had us wear our Pupkin masks for longer and longer. Our lives turned into bleary dreams punctuated by waking moments when we were cold and sick and felt awkward and uncomfortable. More and more, it felt better to disappear into Pupkin's dreams.

We'd wake up and find the house littered with Little Debbie wrappers, empty candy bags, crushed Entenmann's boxes. We woke up sick to our stomachs with dried icing crusted around the mouth holes of our masks. Pupkin had a sweet tooth, apparently. We filled the basement with puppets Pupkin made, and all of them were of Pupkin. Pupkin mask after Pupkin mask hung from the walls, ranging in size from as small as a bottle cap to as big as a garbage can lid. We woke up encrusted in papier-mâché.

After a few days, we started waking up naked and smeared with shit. Bruises and cuts covered our bodies. Words were written on the walls in Pupkin talk, like *Kakawewe!*, his victory cry. When we were awake we took showers and ate without talking, and Clark always told us, "We're getting great material."

Then we'd put our masks back on and become Pupkin again.

We lost track of time. Holes started showing up in the walls, and my left toes felt broken. Windows got smashed but only in the back where you couldn't see them from the street. We woke up one time to find half the drywall ripped down in the living room and insulation strewn throughout the house. A Pupkin broke the hot-water heater so we started taking cold showers. Eventually, even the water stopped.

It sounds stupid now. Clearly, we were losing our shit. But it didn't feel that way then. It felt like we were doing magic. It felt like we were possessed by forces larger than ourselves. It felt powerful.

Now I realize we were hiding. Hiding from our fuckup at Worcester Elementary. Hiding from the fact that we couldn't stop the war. Hiding from the fact that we weren't going to change the world with our tiny talents. Everyone realizes that at some point, right? It's part of growing up. You realize you're not going to be the star of the show. You realize you're going to be lucky to scrape by and pay the rent. That's when a lot of people go to med school. Or get married. Or decide that hitting the bong first thing in the morning sounds like a great idea. We didn't do anything that bad. We just went to Tickytoo Woods.

Awake, I felt lost and homesick. But then I put on my mask and went home. I'd put on Pupkin's face and wake up underneath the Tick Tock Tree in Tickytoo Woods, and it looked just like Mom used to say. I got to live inside one of her bedtime stories where you can play all day because you're Pupkin, and you don't have to be responsible for anything except having fun all the time. I spent endless summer days in the Bone Orchard, or visiting Away We Go Beach to see the sleepy pirate chickens sail by in their ship. The light was gold and orange and the air smelled like pine. I chased Sugar Bats. I talked to Girl Sparrow. I hid from the Inside-Out Man, who lived in the trees. That winter I didn't live in a shitty, underheated rental house in Worcester. I lived in Tickytoo Woods, and I never wanted to leave.

Being awake started to feel like dreaming, while Tickytoo Woods started feeling real. Waking up felt ugly and awkward, and we didn't know what to say to each other, so eventually the three of us stayed Pupkin most of the time. It just seemed easier.

We lost track of time. We lost days. I remember Clark saying, "This material is amazing." I remember Pupkin on his arm, watching me all the time. I remember how cold I felt when I wasn't in Tickytoo Woods. I remember flashes that interrupted a dream that I wanted to go on forever.

I remember calling Mom from a pay phone while Clark watched me from the car. I told her I was staying with Ashley's family for Christmas. Ashley was my imaginary scene partner in my imaginary Shakespeare workshop. I described his house as a Norman Rockwell wonderland of roaring fireplaces and snow-covered WASP charm. Of course Mom bought it.

"Don't forget to take Pupkin," she said. "You know how he doesn't like to be alone during the holidays."

As December turned into January, I started finding small, greasy bones on the kitchen counter. At first I thought we were hunting when we were Pupkin, trapping raccoons or rabbits, maybe even squirrels. It took a few trips to the convenience store for supplies before I noticed all the *missing-pet* posters.

I went to Clark.

"What are we doing?" I asked.

I felt cold and sick to my stomach, the way I always did when I wasn't Pupkin, but now I felt nauseous, like a heavy ball of something sat in my gut.

"We're getting great material," Clark said.

"Why are there bones?" I asked. "What are we eating?"

"Don't worry about it," he said.

But I did worry about it. My instinct was to become Pupkin again and escape to Tickytoo Woods, but I made myself go outside in my bare feet and I searched the bonfire we'd built out of the kitchen table and chairs the night before. I sifted through the ashes. I found a dog collar.

I should have left then. But we'd gone too far and I couldn't face what we'd done. What I'd done. I found my mask and hid in Tickytoo Woods again. I thought that was as bad as it was going to get.

I remember flashes of what happened next. Noise and chaos, shouting and things breaking. I saw Pupkin in the dark and plates hitting a bright tile floor. I saw a woman crying and screaming at the same time. I saw my arm pulling a phone out of a wall. I saw a Pupkin kicking in a door as a woman pinballed away from him and then came back running, pursued by another Pupkin, the woman clutching a little boy screaming with fear, a Pupkin smashing a television into a wall. I saw Pupkin holding someone's fridge door open, sweeping the contents onto the floor. Eggs dripping from the ceiling, milk and orange juice and nondairy creamer puddled on the fancy tile. I saw the woman sliding down a wall, sobbing, clutching her limp son to her chest, the two of them sitting in the cold air from the open front door, their eyes as empty as dolls'.

When I woke up that time, something sticky had dried on my arms. I tasted it: orange juice. I had egg yolk dried in my scalp. My bare feet were dirty and covered in cuts and I knew who the woman was. I'd seen her before. She was Mrs. Marsten.

I didn't want to think about it. It wasn't me, it was Pupkin. I pulled on my mask again and hid in Tickytoo Woods. But I had to come out eventually.

The next time I did, I was in the basement, wearing greasy jeans, surrounded by Pupkin's faces on the wall, and they were all laughing at me. He was stronger than we were. We'd given him too much. We'd never said no. He didn't have any limits. Whatever came next would be really, really bad.

I had to do something while I was still myself because right at that moment "myself" felt like chasing a slippery bar of soap around the tub and as much as I wanted to run away and hide, in that one moment, in that cold basement, I knew I might never be Mark again. I grabbed the lighter without thinking. I flicked its wheel and touched the flame to the chin of a big Pupkin mask hanging on the wall and held it there until my thumb burned. I was an idiot. Papier-mâché burns fast and the mask was by the wooden stairs and one second I was flicking the lighter, and the next there were flames racing across the wall, from mask to mask, Pupkin to Pupkin, and licking the bottom of the upstairs floor.

I dragged on my T-shirt and limped to the back door. It already felt like there was an open oven at my back. I thought I could go around and warn Sadie and Richard and Clark. My feet were swollen and covered in infected cuts and by the time I'd limped to the front yard I knew I had fucked up bad.

From the front yard, you couldn't see the fire yet, just smoke coming out the broken back windows and orange demons dancing behind the windowpanes. I hobbled up the front steps, and they were hot beneath my feet. I yelled for Richard and Sadie. Maybe I shouted for Clark? I'd like to think I shouted for Clark.

I had to do something but the fire was too hungry and I was too weak and I knew I couldn't save them. I couldn't save any of them. I could barely save myself. I had tried to stop what we were doing, but I hadn't thought it through. My solution was a Pupkin solution, all instinct and emotion. I had set my friends on fire.

I knew that people were going to come and I couldn't face what I'd done because I was a coward and this time I couldn't escape into Tickytoo Woods because all the Pupkin masks were on fire, so I turned and stumbled down the road in my torn T-shirt and filthy jeans, limping on my bare, bloody feet. I looked back and saw a column of smoke rising into the cold blue sky. Rocks dug into the soles of my feet but the fresh air tasted good. I let it run through me like a river, cleaning out the muck, leaving my brain empty, sweeping all my thoughts away. After a while, I heard sirens.

Behind me, tires crunched, slowed down, and a navy blue minivan pulled up alongside me.

"Son, are you hurt?" a big dude with a buzz cut asked.

At the sound of someone calling me "son" I almost burst into tears, but I managed to croak, "Bus station? Please? I need to go home."

He made me sit on a sheet of newspaper in the back because I was so filthy, but as he picked up speed I felt the house and Clark and Organ and Richard and Sadie and Pupkin and the fire and every horrible, unforgivable thing I'd done falling away behind me, losing their hold. A fire engine passed us going the other way.

At the bus station I got out of the van without even saying good-bye. I needed to keep moving forward while I still had the strength. I walked up to the first woman I saw selling tickets and said, "I don't have any money but I need to get home to Boston. I need to get home to my mom."

She set her mouth and scanned the room.

"How much trouble you in?" she asked me.

"A lot," I said.

She did something on her computer and pushed a ticket through the slot at the bottom of her window.

"Bus is in forty-five," she said.

That's when I started to cry.

When the bus arrived she whispered to the driver and he made me get on first and sit in the back. There were only twelve other passengers. By the time we hit the turnpike I was squirming inside my skin. Every time I closed my eyes I saw Mrs. Marsten's screaming face, I heard the fire screeching in my ears, and I'd jerk awake and after a few minutes the hum of the bus would lull me into letting my guard down again and I'd hear fire and I'd jerk awake all over again.

I didn't want to be me anymore. I had left them to die. I couldn't live like this. I wanted to be Pupkin again because then I'd be back in Ticky-too Woods with no responsibilities. My bones felt too big for my skin. When I saw the *15 miles to Boston* sign, I cried because I realized I was stuck being Mark now for the rest of my life. I had to live with what I'd done.

I got off the bus at South Station and out front was a map and I found BU. It was a long way off but I didn't have a choice, so I started to walk. The buildings began looking familiar around midnight. An hour later I walked past security and into my dorm. No one asked to see my student ID, which was lucky because it was somewhere upstate. I got the spare key from the front desk and let myself into my room and took a long, hot shower. Every time I closed my eyes I heard screaming: Mrs. Marsten screaming, the fire screaming, Sadie and Richard screaming.

I fell into bed and blacked out. I had some awareness of my room-mate coming in and going out over the next few days, and sometimes the room was light and sometimes it was dark, and sometimes I was alone and sometimes I wasn't. I remember drinking cold water from the tap. I remember picking up loose change from the floor and buying barbecue potato chips from the machine. It got dark, then bright, then dark, then bright again, and I stopped being hungry and I just lay there and let the world spin around me. Then one day I opened my eyes and saw Mom sitting on the edge of my bed.

"I was worried," she said.

I told her I had mono. I told her I wanted to come home. I think she knew it was more than that, but she didn't ask, and I didn't tell. Both of us were more comfortable that way. She fed me cream of mushroom soup and packed up my room. The next afternoon I officially withdrew from BU.

Then she finally asked the question.

"Where's Pupkin?"

I'd been dreading this. What could I tell her? That he'd burned up-state in Worcester when I killed the people in my radical puppet collective? I did the only thing I could do. I lied.

"I left him at my scene partner's house," I said. "He'll ship him back."

At least that would buy me some time. But Mom wasn't having it.

"Well, call and see if they'll drop him off at the hotel," she said. "We can't leave without him."

I told her I would, but I didn't. I told Mom that no one answered, but I'd left a message and they'd mail Pupkin.

We left the hotel at six p.m. for our ten p.m. flight, which I thought was Mom acting like Dad about getting to the airport early, but when we got in the cab she asked me where my scene partner lived. I'd gone so far into this lie I didn't see any way out. My brain was too bruised to make up an address, so I gave her the only one I knew.

Five twenty-three Wheeler looked dark when we arrived and I felt relieved. They weren't there. I'd knock and nothing would happen and I'd tell her they'd mail Pupkin and then we'd go home and deal with everything later. I just wanted to go home.

"Albert and I will wait while you get Pupkin," she said, because of course she already knew the cab driver's name and that he was a chemical engineer from Nigeria whose sister was a nun.

There was no way out. I got out of the car and Mom watched me cross the street and every step was sheer terror. I went up the porch steps and I kept expecting searchlights to go on and cops to swarm out of hiding and slap handcuffs around my wrists and arrest me for arson.

But nothing happened except I finally stood outside the door again. With no other choice, I rang the bell and waited. Nothing moved inside for a really long time, and I was just starting to feel like I'd made it when the apartment door inside rattled open, letting light out into the hall. I couldn't see who it was through the glass, just a shape coming closer, then the front door opened and Clark stood there, looking at me.

He wore the same shoes, the same glasses, his hair looked the same, but he had no burns, no bandages, no scars. Maybe we'd never been to Worcester? Maybe it had all been a dream?

"Hey," I said.

Over my shoulder he saw the waiting cab and I saw him figure out the entire story in a flash.

"Is everyone okay?" I asked, voice low. "Is your parents' house okay?"

"What do you want?" he asked.

It was like we'd never met.

"The Pupkin puppet that belonged to my mom," I said. "I need it."

For a second he didn't move and I thought maybe it had burned in the fire. I could tell Mom he'd lost Pupkin and she'd be devastated but I'd be free. After a moment, Clark turned and walked into the house, and I could have followed, seen if Sadie and Richard were there, cleared everything up, but at that moment I was having a hard time standing up, so I waited.

After a minute, he came back with Pupkin in one hand. He held him out.

"Did—" I started, and my throat closed tight, and I tried again. "Are Richard and Sadie okay?"

His face didn't change expression, he just dropped Pupkin on the porch and closed the door in my face. I watched him through the glass as he went back into his apartment, then I turned around and walked across the street, Pupkin in one hand.

I couldn't cut it. I wasn't anyone special. I'd been thrown out. I was just Mark who may have killed two people because he was stupid and selfish, and that's who I'd be for the rest of my life. In the streetlight, I looked down and saw Pupkin smiling up at me and I wanted to pull him over my hand and disappear into Tickytoo Woods again. But I made my legs keep moving and got back in the cab.

"That man looked too old to be a student," Mom said as I closed the door.

Before I could answer, she took Pupkin and held him on her lap. "Hello, you," she said.

"He was the TA," I told her.

She talked to Pupkin and the cab driver for the entire ride to the airport. I don't know what she told Dad, but neither of them ever said anything to me about Boston and I never told anyone, and it's like six months of my life never happened at all.

Chapter 23

Louise let the silence last as long as she could out of respect, but then she couldn't hold it any longer. Mark had been talking for a really long time.

"If I don't go to the bathroom right now," she said, "I'm going to wet my pants."

She slid out of the booth as she said *my pants* and sprinted to the bathroom and locked the door. She came back a minute later, feeling a lot better. Sitting under the bright Waffle House lights, Mark looked lost.

"Look at me," he said, leaning forward, his stomach piling up in his lap. "You're not crazy. This really happened. You got attacked by Mom's childhood puppet. He is real. I've seen what he can do. He is the heart of this thing. But I shot it. Pupkin is really dead this time."

Their eyes met. Louise nodded.

"You definitely killed the shit out of Mom's puppet," she said.

She saw Mark's eyes crinkle at the corners and she started to crack.

"Don't make this funny," he said, but it was too late.

They both burst out laughing. Not crazy laughter, but real laughter. It felt good. It made Pupkin feel small. It felt like the things that had happened to them were a family story, shared at last. It felt like they were finally finished.

I should tell him now, Louise thought. *I should tell him about the pond.*

She opened her mouth and the waitress stopped by their table.

"How y'all doing?" she asked.

"Oh, we're great," Mark said. "We're really bonding here."

The waitress couldn't care less. She disappeared before he even finished his sentence. Slowly, they got ahold of themselves.

"Everything you've seen tonight, I've seen it, too," Mark said, his voice sincere and level. "It's not you, it's our family. It's Pupkin."

Louise didn't recognize this man sitting across from her. He hadn't dropped out of BU his first year because he'd partied too hard. He hadn't come home and moped around like a spoiled brat. He'd gotten bitten by the same thing as her, only worse. He needed to know.

But another thought barged into her head, and it made her veins run hot with rage.

What did our mom do to us?

She had brought Pupkin into their lives. She had given him to Louise, and she had given him to Mark, and Pupkin had almost killed Mark twice and now he had almost killed Louise. Her mom must have seen her bury Pupkin that day, then dug him up, then cleaned him until he looked as good as new and put him on her bed, but instead of trying to find out why Louise had buried him in the first place, she'd pretended nothing had happened. When he'd wrecked Mark's life at BU, her mom hadn't asked any questions because she didn't want to know the answers. She'd sacrificed them for Pupkin.

"I'm sorry," Louise said. "I need you to know that I'm so sorry. I'm sorry I thought you were someone you weren't. I'm sorry I hated you for it. I'm sorry I've hated you for years. But why didn't you say anything? You could have told me."

"When?" Mark asked, scraping the side of his fork across his plate, picking up congealing grease on its tines. "All our bonding sessions? All those fun late-night talks while we painted our toenails and drank white wine? Mom was the only person who knew anything had happened, but she never asked me about it. I was ashamed and I was scared. I'm still scared. Do you know how many years I've spent living in fear? We trashed that woman's house. I burned down Clark's parents' place. I don't know what happened to Sadie or Richard. Either of them could show up out of the blue one day and ruin my life. Or not. I don't know which is worse. I live in constant fear and I'm too much of a coward to do something as simple as Google them to find out the truth."

"How've you ignored it for so long?" Louise asked.

"It's what we do," Mark said. "Our whole family functions on secrets."

Louise took a sip of her coffee. It tasted cold and real. Her borrowed flip-flops and sweatpants were real, the too-bright lights in Waffle House were real, the waitress was real. Somehow she had to link this reality to a reality where angry puppets tried to kill them.

Louise watched Mark add sugar to his cold coffee. It could have been a trick of the light, or the way his bangs brushed his forehead, but he looked like her kid brother for a moment. She thought about not saying anything, but then she would have been even more like their mom.

"Mark," she said, "Pupkin told me to kill you at the Calvins' house that Christmas. Everything you remember, it happened—I got you out on the ice, I watched you fall in, I walked away, and when I got back to the house I didn't say anything. Because Pupkin told me not to."

"What?" Mark asked, looking up, his eyes wide.

Louise told him everything. When she finished, Mark's eyes were red. He swiped the heel of his hand across both cheeks.

"Can I get y'all anything else?" the waitress asked, stopping by their table.

"Just the check," Louise said.

"I didn't even remember you had Pupkin back then," Mark said after the waitress left. "I forgot you carried him around everywhere with you. And he talked to you?"

"All the time," Louise said. "Inside my head. And he bit me, and pinched me, and hurt me if I didn't do what he said."

"That's why he hated you so much," Mark said. "You buried him. You left him all alone. And he hated me because he was jealous. It's like the baby of the family when the new baby is born, they think they're going to get replaced. Jesus Christ, Louise, we never talked to each other so we always thought it was just our own dirty little secrets, but this is the story of our whole family."

"Kind of," Louise said.

"Kind of?" Mark exclaimed. "What do you think happened to Mom and Dad? Haven't you wondered about that night? Pupkin was jealous I was going to replace him so he tried to drown me. He got angry at you for burying him and carried a grudge until he had a chance to get you alone. So how do you think he felt when Dad broke his ankle and Mom turned into Dad's full-time nurse?"

The waitress appeared next to their table with the bill in one hand, waiting for a good moment to set it down.

"What do you mean?" Louise asked.

"For their entire marriage, Dad took care of Mom and Mom took care of her puppets," Mark said. "All of a sudden everything's turned upside down and Mom's taking care of Dad and ignoring Pupkin. What if Pupkin got jealous of Dad the way he got jealous of me?"

It fit so neatly Louise could only say, "Oh."

"What if that 'attack' wasn't a fit?" Mark said. "What if Pupkin attacked Dad the way he attacked you, and Mom finally realized things had gone too far? Maybe that's why she took Dad to the hospital in the middle of the night? And Mom's so racked with guilt that she's not paying attention and drives right through the light and here we are, with both of them dead and it's all because of Pupkin."

Louise thought about the hammer on the living room floor. The chip missing from the coffee table. The cane lying in front of the TV.

"Pupkin came first," Mark said. "Pupkin was here before all of us. Pupkin goes all the way back to when Mom was a kid. To Pupkin, the only person who matters is Mom. I mean, why do you think they boarded up the attic? It's not squirrels up there."

Louise couldn't stand the waitress hovering over them for another second, so she looked up and asked, "Can we help you?"

"I just wanted to let you know," the waitress said. "That Methodist minister I talked about earlier? He's here. It sounds like y'all might need him."

Mark and Louise trudged across the freezing-cold Waffle House parking lot in the lifeless gray dawn, headed for Mark's truck. Mark had his hands shoved in his pockets, each of his steps heavy.

"Mark?" Louise said.

He turned. His face sagged with exhaustion and it made her sad to see his little-boy face looking out from behind those watery red eyes.

"I'm sorry," she said. "I'm sorry I wasn't stronger. I'm sorry I never told anyone."

"You were a kid," he said.

An enormous tow truck ground past the parking lot, yellow lights strobing, a minivan hanging from its rear chains.

"It was more than that," she said after it passed. "I was scared Mom and Dad would look at me different and send me to doctors and I wouldn't be myself anymore. And I was ashamed. And it was easier to pretend nothing happened. But this entire time, my entire life, I've always known something was wrong with me. I've spent my entire life scared that if I didn't do everything exactly right, reality would unravel around me and I'd lose myself again. I used to be so scared in that house."

"Now you know how I've felt for the last twenty years," Mark said.

She looked at her little brother standing there in his Dead Milkmen T-shirt and cargo shorts and Tevas, this beer-bellied man she'd known ever since he was shorter than her, the only other person in the world who knew her parents the way she did, the only other person who knew what had really happened at the Calvins' that Christmas, the only other person who knew about Pupkin, who knew about everything, all the way back to the beginning. She needed to reach out to him. She needed to let him know that she didn't think of him any differently now that she knew the worst thing he'd done. Now that he knew the worst thing she'd done.

She didn't know the best way to start this, so she suddenly stepped forward, overcoming years of keeping her distance from her brother, and she held her arms out wide and brought them around his shoulders and pulled his stiff body to hers and gave him a hug. After the first five seconds she wanted to pull away, but she forced herself to keep hugging and after a moment she felt his big arms go around her and crush her body to his, a little tighter than she would have preferred, but that was okay. He needed his big sister and she could stay like this for as long as he wanted.

She squeezed, wanting him to know that everything would be all right.

"It's going to be okay," he mumble-whispered, his breath hot in her ear, patting her back.

"That's right," she said, figuring he had it the wrong way around. "It'll all be okay, Mark."

She gave him another squeeze. He gave her one.

"I forgive you," he said into her ear.

Louise's forehead furrowed. Did he think *he* was comforting *her?* He began to rock her from side to side, so she started rocking him, sending a clear signal that she was the one doing the comforting. He made a shushing sound. Did he think she was going to cry? She needed to end this before it got out of hand.

She gave Mark one quick squeeze, then stepped back and away. He released her and they stood looking at each other in the empty parking lot, a respectable distance restored.

"Feel better?" he asked.

"I hope *you* feel better," she said. "I'm fine."

"I'm great," he said, and then he seemed to realize that this wasn't what he thought it was. His eyes narrowed. "Did you think you were—?"

She cut him off.

"So what do we do now?" she asked. "About the house. I mean, clearly that's not Mom and Dad in there. The bad vibes you felt, all that stuff, that's Pupkin. And you killed him."

"No doubt," Mark said. "I mean, I definitely shot that little fucker."

"You shot him a lot," Louise agreed. "But what about the other stuff? We can't ignore it this time. It's our responsibility."

"The Mark and Louise dolls," Mark said.

"Yeah," Louise said. "Exactly."

She didn't know how to confess that she'd been holding back on the Squirrel Nativity.

"You're right," Mark said, rubbing his hand down his face, from top to bottom. "We have to take care of the rest. We should probably burn the whole place down. That's what they do to haunted houses and cursed shit in horror movies, right? Fire cleanses everything."

"Is that your solution to everything?" Louise asked.

Mark's neck got stiff.

"That's not funny," he said.

"I'm sorry," Louise said, embarrassed, but Mark was already talking over her, grinning.

"That's *really* funny," he said. "I didn't think you had it in you."

Traffic passed on the road, one car, then three, gradually picking up as the morning grew brighter around them.

"It'd be stupid to go back in the house," Mark said. "What's valuable is the lot, anyways. Whoever buys it is just going to tear it down to build something bigger."

"I said the same thing to Mercy," Louise said. "She told me the house actually has a lot of value because it's got a good floor plan. She thinks we can sell it to a family for way more than a developer would pay for the lot."

"Shit," Mark said, and walked in a small circle, swinging his arms. "Shit!"

"I know," Louise said.

"Capitalism's really got us over a barrel," Mark said.

"There's no one else," Louise said.

"Let's call Agutter," Mark said. "He'll do it in an hour."

Louise shook her head.

"Crap," Mark said. "I really don't want to do this."

"You shot him," Louise said. "He's all messed up. Let's burn him and the rest will be easy. There's no way they can take both of us at the same time. We just have to stick together."

Chapter 24

They sat in Mark's truck staring at the dark house, trying to get up the courage to go inside.

"I mean," Mark said, "we just walk in, grab him, take him out back, and throw him on the grill."

"Exactly," Louise said. "In and out."

"I shredded him to hell when I shot him," Mark said. "There's barely any of him left."

"Just scraps," Louise agreed.

Neither of them moved. They stared at the house. A jogger hopped by and Louise wondered what they looked like to him: two filthy people who looked like they'd been awake all night, sitting in a truck and staring at a dark house.

"And Pupkin's the only one you've seen move," Mark said. "Right? You're not holding out on me?"

"And the Mark and Louise dolls," Louise said. "And maybe the Squirrel Nativity. The three of them kind of attacked me before. Sorry."

"Crap!" Mark said, throwing himself back in his seat.

"But I think I killed them."

Louise listened to Mark's cooling engine tick. She looked at the house's plain brick facade, its painted shutters, its dark windows. It looked like a mask her family wore over their real face.

"Do you think it's all of them?" she asked.

"Yeah, well, no," Mark said. "I'm bringing my equalizer."

He lifted his pistol from where it rested on his thigh. She wanted to tell him to put it away before someone called the police, but he had saved her life with it. Her left eye still ached where Pupkin had stabbed it with the needle.

"Here's the plan," Mark said. "It's Pupkin first. We grab him, grill him, then we do the Mark and Louise dolls just to be sure. And the Squirrel Nativity."

"All the dolls have to go," Louise said. "Just to be safe."

"Shit," Mark said. "There's a lot of dolls."

"Let's go," Louise said, and before she could change her mind, she launched herself out of Mark's truck and flip-flopped across the frozen grass, holding her sweatpants up with one hand. Shadows fuzzed the bushes. Cold air goose-bumped her arms. She didn't hear Mark behind her and she couldn't turn to check because the second she turned around, she'd lose her nerve, and after that nothing could ever make her go back inside that house.

Her heart resumed beating when she heard Mark's feet slapping across the grass behind her. He held his gun in one hand, hiding it behind his thigh. At least he was making an effort. Mark opened the screen door, Louise put her hand on the knob, turned it, and they slipped inside.

Louise stood just inside the door, listening. Quietly, Mark eased the door shut behind them, then he stepped around her and crept down the middle of the hall, gun held out in both hands. She cinched her sweatpants tighter around her waist and followed.

She caught up to him in her bedroom, standing in the middle of the floor, staring down at the scorched carpet. Gray morning light oozed through the curtains, enough to see that Pupkin was gone. His stuffing lay everywhere. She felt her cold skin get tight.

"Shit," Mark whispered.

He began to search the room, under her bed, inside the closet. He stepped into the hall and stopped.

"Lulu," he whispered.

He was pointing to the vent hole chopped in the wall. The sharp edge of the metal duct held a scrap of Pupkin's bright yellow fabric. Louise took out her phone and squatted by the vent. She shone her phone light up the air shaft. On a jagged metal seam farther up the duct a few Pupkin fibers waved gently back and forth in the draft.

Upstairs in the attic, something small fell over and rolled across the floor. Their eyes met, wide and white in the gloom. Louise pointed straight up. Mark nodded.

She put on her jeans and shoes so she could move more freely, then she got the hammer from the kitchen counter and gave it to Mark, who stood on one of the dining room chairs Pupkin had used to trap her and pried the boards off the attic hatch as quietly as he could. He handed the pieces down to Louise one at a time, spiked with bent nails and broken screws. She laid them carefully against the wall. When Mark got the last one free he gave her the hammer, and she laid it by the little pile of wood. Mark hooked his fingers into the edge of the attic door and looked down and met her eyes.

Louise nodded. Mark pulled down with both arms and the springs screamed, echoing through the empty attic. He stopped halfway, then yanked it down the rest of the way, letting the springs squawk loudly, once. Then he hopped off the chair with a loud *thump* that shook the framed pictures still hanging on the walls, and Louise folded down the raw wooden stairs and the two of them looked up into the empty black rectangle in the ceiling.

Cold air spilled out of the hole, rolling down the stairs, making Louise's arms shake uncontrollably. Nothing moved. The hall toilet cut on and Louise jumped. The water ran for a second, then shut off. The silence inside the house felt loud. They listened as hard as they could but didn't hear anything.

Mark lit up his flashlight, gun in one hand, and put his foot on the first step, then the second step. The springs groaned and the wood cracked as he climbed up into the attic hatch. Louise made herself climb up after him. The ladder bounced and creaked beneath their combined weight.

The dark attic smelled like sap and raw pine and forgotten things. Louise turned on her flashlight app. If downstairs had been cluttered, this was chaos. She played her light over bright yellow stacks of *National Geographic*, which no one could bring themselves to throw away because of the pictures, piled on top of old luggage they almost never used. A lacrosse stick from Mark's three-month lacrosse career hung from a hatstand, and a pair of Rollerblades Louise used to love sat on an open box of water-damaged theater programs from Mark's old shows. Her light caught the tiny spiderwebs around the Rollerblades' wheels, bleaching them silver. Something bumped against the back of her hand. She jerked away.

Mark held a tennis racquet out to her. She took it, hefted it in her hand, and felt reassured. If it had worked with the squirrel, it would work with Pupkin. They trained their beams on the mountains of junk, the jumbled landscape of the Joyner family's past, and searched for Pupkin.

"Let's start at the end," Louise whispered, pointing her tennis racquet to the far end of the attic, where a louvered hatch let in the steadily brightening morning sun. In the dark it looked as bright as a spotlight.

Clutching his gun and his flashlight with his wrists crossed, like a cop on a cable show, Mark began picking his way down the crowded attic. Louise followed, high-stepping over Playmobil hospital play sets and plastic bags of rolled posters. She kept her head on a swivel, watching behind them, in front, the sides, then behind again.

Mark stopped short, and she plowed into his back. His light rested on a clear space where the beams sloped down and met the floor. The bare boards had been swept and in the middle sat a tiny room. A battery-powered camping lamp sat next to a water bottle and a small cut-glass bud vase with a dead rose inside. A rubber super-bounce ball sat beside it, along with an open tin of marbles, a box of new crayons, and a pad of paper. Next to those sat a shoebox painted to look like a little bed, and in it was a tiny handmade pillow and a tiny knitted quilt, and underneath it lay Pupkin.

They both stared at him, and he stared up, smiling at the ceiling. His body had been shredded by Mark's bullets, leaving him mostly rags, but his head was intact and he still held his shape.

"She made him a bedroom," Mark whispered.

Louise understood. No matter what Pupkin had done, their mom hated leaving her old friend in the dark all by himself, so she'd tried to make him comfortable, she'd tried to give him things to do, toys to play with, a bed to sleep in. But Pupkin hadn't liked being in the dark, he hated being alone, so he'd found a way into the vents and come downstairs, furious at being locked away.

Neither of them moved.

"Get him," Louise whispered.

"Why me?"

"Because you've got the gun," she hissed.

Mark was too scared to take his eyes off Pupkin.

"Then what?" he hissed.

"The g-r-i-l-l," she whispered.

They stood there staring at Pupkin, who stared up at the ceiling.

"Okay," Mark whispered, barely moving his lips. "I'm going to g-r-a-b the P-u-p-k and we're going to make a fast retreat. You go get the g-r-i-l-l going and I'll be right behind."

"Mark—" Louise started.

"One . . ." he whispered.

Louise didn't like this plan but she braced her legs.

"Two . . ."

She hefted the racquet in one hand. She got ready to bash any squirrels.

"Three!" Mark shouted and Louise launched herself over the rolled-up carpet at her feet, hurtling over boxes, racing for the hatch.

From too far behind her, Mark said, "No."

Louise stopped, already halfway down the attic, and turned. Mark stood over the little bedroom, flashlight held on it, pistol still extended, but his arms looked like they were drooping.

"I don't want to," he said, but it wasn't to her.

He was talking to Pupkin.

"Mark?" she called.

He didn't move. She shone her light around to make sure no squirrels were creeping up, then put it on Mark.

"Come on!" she yelled.

Mark didn't respond. He lowered his gun completely and dropped to his knees. The floor shook. Louise winced in sympathy.

"I'm not putting you on," Mark said to Pupkin. Then he listened for an answer and said, "Because you're going to hurt her."

"Her," Louise realized. *He said "her," not "us."* Pupkin didn't want to hurt Mark, he wanted to hurt her.

Mark shook his head as he talked, his arms dangling between his thighs, his back hunched. He looked weak. He looked defeated.

"Mark," Louise said, taking a step toward him.

"Get out of here," Mark said loudly.

"Come on," she said. "Let's leave, okay? G-r-a-b the P-u-p-k and let's leave together."

She took another step toward him. She needed to get her brother out of here. He didn't sound right.

"All the things I did," Mark said, and his voice sounded dull and defeated, "I want to forget. I want to be Pupkin again."

"Mark!" Louise said, and took another step.

"Stop!" Mark screamed, suddenly frantic. Louise froze. She didn't know if it was directed at her or at Pupkin, but Mark had a gun so she didn't move. "I'm not putting you on!"

The cords in his neck stood out as he screamed at the puppet.

"I'm not doing it! I'm not doing it again!" he shouted.

Louise didn't want to move or say or do anything that might push him over the edge.

"Oh, no," Mark moaned, receiving bad news. "Oh, no, no, no. Don't. Don't do that."

Pain filled his voice.

"Mark?" Louise called.

"You need to go right now, Louise," Mark said, talking fast, like he only had one chance. "You need to get out of here. He's got something. He's got something up here I forgot about and he's going to use it to hurt you if I don't put him on."

"Don't put him on, Mark," she called. "You don't have to do what he says. G-r-a-b h-i-m and let's go."

"You need to get out of here right now," Mark said, talking fast, not taking his eyes off Pupkin. "It won't hurt me, but it'll hurt you. You have to go, Louise, *right now*!"

"Mark?" she shouted, her voice cracking, tears of frustration filling her eyes. "He can't hurt us. He's just a puppet."

"It's not him," Mark said, his voice low and flat. "It's Spider."

Louise's brain went white.

When Louise was nine and Mark was six she wanted a dog so badly she couldn't imagine going one more day without one. She'd spend hours with her arms around its neck. She'd let it sleep in her bed. She'd take it to Alhambra Hall and throw a ball for it all weekend. She convinced Mark that he should feel the same way, and pretty soon he had dog fever, too.

If a movie had a dog in it they'd watch it over and over before they had to take it back to Blockbuster: *Turner & Hooch*, *Bingo*, *All Dogs Go to Heaven*. It got to the point where their dad only let them rent one dog movie a week.

At dinner, they steered every conversation toward dogs.

"Vicky's dog, Beaux, sleeps indoors," Louise would say.

"The Papadopouloses have two dogs," Mark would add.

"No dog talk at the table," their dad eventually decreed.

That didn't stop them. They campaigned relentlessly because they figured their parents would give in at some point. Their dad told them he'd be the one who took care of the dog, pointing out that no matter what they said now, they'd eventually get tired of taking it for walks and feeding it.

"That won't happen," Louise said.

"You think that," their dad said while helping them load the dishwasher. "But I've seen it happen to people at work. I'll be the one who winds up taking him out every night."

"Don't you think Meow Meow would feel jealous?" their mom asked, holding up her favorite kitten hand puppet and making it act bashful when Louise cornered her in her workroom.

"No," Louise said. "I don't think she'd get jealous. She's just a puppet."

Their mom made Meow Meow hide her face behind her paws.

"Now you've hurt her feelings," she said.

"No," Louise protested. "You're making her act that way."

"Boo-hoo-hoo-hoo," their mom fake sobbed in Meow Meow's kitty-cat voice. "Why does everyone hate poor Meow Meow?"

Louise and Mark regrouped in Louise's room. Louise threw herself onto her bed. Mark collapsed on the floor.

"We're never going to get a dog," Louise said.

They sat in silence, contemplating this bleak reality. Through the wall, they could hear their mom's sewing machine hammering away, making more puppets.

"What about a spider?" Mark asked. "Clay Estes showed me one they have in their classroom and it was furry like a dog. Spiders don't need walks."

"I don't want a tarantula," Louise said. "I want a *dog*!"

Her need for a dog had been a gnawing, physical craving in her gut, but something about that night's long cry felt cathartic, and the next morning she woke up and her craving was gone. She still wanted a dog, but it didn't feel as desperate. By the time she got to breakfast, she wasn't thinking about a dog at all. That's when Mark showed up with Spider.

"He's my dog but he's imaginary," he declared to everyone at the table. "So no one can have their feelings hurt and I'm the only one who has to take care of him."

It was an intuitive stroke of genius. Their mom always encouraged them to use their imaginations, and now Mark had imagined a dog. She had no choice but to accept it. And, true to form, their mom didn't just accept Spider, she embraced him. She asked Mark what kind of food Spider liked and got a bowl she filled with kibble for Spider every morning for months.

When they went to get hot dogs, their dad would open the back door of the car so Spider could jump in. When they came home from school their mom gave Mark a report on everything Spider had done around the house that day.

Whenever they asked Mark what Spider looked like, it changed.

Sometimes Spider was tan, sometimes he was black, then he had blue fur, and for a while he was every color all at once.

Spider and Mark spent hours in the backyard playing fetch. Louise watched Mark throw his Frisbee, calling to Spider, then the Frisbee would land and after a moment Mark would run over, pick it up, and do it all over again. It made her sad. He could pretend all he wanted, but an imaginary dog would never play actual fetch.

When the bag of kibble ran out, they didn't get another one, and when school started back after Christmas Louise noticed that Spider came along with them on car rides less and less. After a while, she would go months without hearing Mark mention his name. The first summer she came back from Berkeley, Louise felt pangs of nostalgia for their childhoods and she asked an older, angrier Mark where Spider was these days. "Who?" Mark had said.

He'd grown up and left his imaginary playmate behind. Over the years they'd forgotten all about Spider. Pupkin hadn't.

"You need to go right now!" Mark screamed in the attic.

Louise didn't know which way to go. Mark was freaking out and he had a gun. He might hurt himself. He might hurt her. She thought about running over and grabbing Pupkin, but there was no telling what that would make Mark do.

"Mark," she yelled, determined to try one last time. "You need to come with me now!"

He turned his sweaty face toward her, eyebrows raised in the middle, his forehead wrinkled, full of despair.

"Oh, no," he said. "Spider's here."

Louise's stomach dropped.

"Mark," she said. "Please . . ."

"I'm sorry."

She heard it before it even registered, a long, low growl clogged with phlegm, directly behind her left ear. It came from high up the wall, almost over her shoulder. Her veins clamped shut and her heart squeezed itself into a hard ball.

It took all her strength to make herself turn slowly to the left, the growl continuing the entire time. In the dim attic light she saw him and remembered that Spider was imaginary first and a dog second. All her life she'd thought of him as a dog, but of course he was something Mark had made up. Spider could have as many legs as a six-year-old boy wanted. He could be green or red or even blue. He could walk on walls. He could hang from the ceiling. He could even have a mouth jammed with row after row of sharp white teeth, all slimed with spit.

Chapter 25

Louise's arms shot up, too late to protect her face as the teeth came for her, dog breath scorching her forehead, the enormous shaggy head, blunt and awful, darting forward like a furry shark. Her fingers hit the underside of Spider's hairy, muscular jaw and she realized her face was suddenly inside his mouth, his teeth closing around it, and she felt the teeth on his lower jaw tickle the soft skin underneath her chin, his upper teeth nuzzling her bangs, and she knew he was going to peel her face off her skull. Time slowed down and everything happened in half a second.

She jammed the tennis racquet in his mouth from the side. His teeth hit it, the wood splintering, shards spraying her cheeks, and she let her legs go dead and threw herself backward, falling as fast as she could, landing on the stack of *National Geographic*s so hard it knocked the soul right out of her body, and then the magazines were spilling and she slid with them and a millisecond later her head hit the wooden floor with a jarring, hollow knock she could smell. Her vision went black for a moment.

"Spider, no!" Mark shouted from the other end of the attic.

Something heavy landed on her chest, crushing her to the floor, driving the tiny amount of air left in her lungs out, and Spider stood on her—she hadn't even seen him leap—snapping for her face again. She rammed her hands into the long blue fur of his chest and dug her fingers in, pushing him back hard, like she was bench-pressing a car. She barely moved Spider, but it was enough. His jaws slammed shut one thin molecule away from the tip of her nose.

She turned her face to one side, shoving her arms up and out, Spider snapping at the soft meat of her cheeks in a frenzy, a garbled, hungry whine howling out of his throat. Then he disappeared, but she still felt him in her hands, and he reappeared almost instantly, jaws lurching down at her out of nothingness, hot strings of sticky saliva blasting from his mouth and lashing her lips and nose. Claws frantically raked her shoulders and neck, but he stood on her with all four legs and she remembered he had six, and now his two extra legs were digging at her like a spot in the backyard, shredding her blouse, her skin, her breasts, and the unprotected skin of her neck. Her fingers started to slip in his glossy fur. She felt her elbows slowly forced back.

Something hard dug painfully into her left hip and she took a chance. As Spider drew his head back for another strike, she let go with her right hand, looped it around her left hip, and grabbed whatever it was, swinging it forward with all her strength.

Her shoulder muscles burned as she smashed the pink Rollerblade into the end of Spider's muzzle. Her angle was bad so the blow lost a lot of its strength, but it snapped his mouth shut. He let loose an ear-splitting yelp, then drove all six paws into her soft body, drawing beads of blood from her stomach, hips, and chest, and suddenly nothing stood on Louise.

Panicked, she pushed herself up off the floor, scattering boxes and bags, scrambling to her feet. She couldn't see Spider. She whipped her head up and down the dim attic and caught a glimpse of Mark at the far end.

"Run!" he shouted.

She looked for Spider but he'd disappeared. She heard his guttural chain-saw growl from the darkness and saw him in the gloomy space under the eaves, hunkered down where the floor showed pink insulation, preparing for another leap, ass high in the air, chest down low, and he flickered in and out of view, strobing in and out of reality.

"I won't!" Mark shouted from the other end of the attic, maybe at her, maybe at Pupkin.

Louise's chest felt bruised. The back of her skull where it had hit the floor throbbed with her pulse. Acidic coffee and bits of egg stung the back of her throat, and she swallowed hard to keep down her gorge. She had to get away.

She threw a quick look to the right and saw the hatch nearby. She whipped her head back just in time to see Spider disappearing again, but she heard him growling as he reappeared, already flowing into motion. His six legs gathered and bunched beneath his heavy body, muscles rippling beneath his long blue fur, some part of him always moving. Louise didn't want to touch him again, she just wanted to keep him away.

Instinctively, she grabbed a grocery bag of Mark's old comic books and heaved it at Spider. They smashed into his front legs as he charged, the bag bursting open, not doing any damage but upsetting his rhythm, his writhing legs tangling in each other. He spilled onto one side, hitting her old tricycle hard. All the air in the attic contracted once as he hit the floor. Like a roach on its back, his legs whipped and tangled around each other uselessly for a moment, then he flipped himself back onto his feet.

"Don't make me!" Mark screamed from the other end of the attic.

Louise was already bolting for the hatch. Spider uttered a hideous rising growl, climbing higher and higher like it was building toward a yowl. She hurdled boxes, she shoulder-rolled over a weight bench Mark had gotten from their mom for Christmas one year, she landed on her feet and reached for the lip of the hatch to swing down, drop into the hall, then turn and swing the hatch shut on Spider's face, but something hit her between the shoulder blades and Louise lurched forward and felt her center of gravity turn upside down.

She fell out of the attic face-first, hit the stairs hard, tasting blood, then her legs flipped over her head as the stairs bounced her forward, and she hit the hall carpet. Her vision went gray for a second. Something huge flew over her and Spider landed in the hall with a house-rattling thud, and in one smooth, flowing motion he circled to face her, standing on all six legs between her and the front door. He licked his dripping teeth, flickering in and out of sight. She was trapped inside the house. From up the attic stairs she heard Mark arguing with Pupkin.

She couldn't take her eyes off Spider but let her peripheral vision drift, and behind her she saw her parents' bedroom door open. If she could get in there she could close the door and flip the mattress against it to hold it shut.

She let her body drift forward like she was going to run for the front door and saw Spider track her motion, haunches shifting, then she threw herself backward, sliding between the attic ladder and the wall, knocking a shower of framed pictures to the floor, tripping over the dining room chair. Then she was past the ladder, stumble-running for her parents' room.

She hoped the attic steps would slow Spider down, but she felt the wall on her right bend and echo like a drum as he clawed his way up it, and when she stole a look Spider was coming at her, running down the upper third of the wall like it was the floor, diving down on his prey.

Louise aimed for her parents' doorway, but above her she felt rather than saw Spider's mass leave the wall, and she dug in like an Olympic sprinter, pushing her feet hard off the carpet, hurling herself toward the bedroom just as Spider landed on her shoulders.

His velocity took Louise straight down. She didn't even have time to put her arms out to stop her fall. She had a split second to thank her mom for never replacing the wall-to-wall carpet with hardwood floors, then she felt her teeth snap together as she bit carpet. Pinpricks of white light swarmed her visual field.

She didn't give Spider a chance. She propelled herself desperately forward on her arms and legs, yanking her body out from beneath him. She could still make the bedroom door, slam it, brace her legs, hold it shut. She felt four of his paws on either side of her, trapping her underneath his mass, then the other two came down, pinning her to the floor. Louise rolled onto her back and brought her knees up, lashing out at Spider's face, thrashing her legs, aiming for the end of his muzzle, moving too fast for him to bite down.

She drove her heels into Spider's face over and over again, and he retreated, protecting his sensitive muzzle. For a moment she thought she was going to make it and a sob of relief escaped her throat, then his head shot out and his jaws locked tight around her right ankle.

Louise screamed. A ring of teeth compressed her ankle from all sides, grinding into the bone, and Spider whipped his head back and forth. She felt her knee and the socket of her hip almost dislocate. Growling, Spider began to back up, dragging her with him, her injured leg taking all her weight, and she screamed and tried to sit up but she couldn't get any leverage. She hammered at his face with her other foot, driving her heel into his muzzle over and over again, but he just lowered his massive head and took it on his bony forehead.

She dug her nails into the carpet but couldn't stop her motion. The pain in her ankle got worse and she gasped out loud but couldn't suck in enough air to scream, so she just hyperventilated. All the fight went out of her. Her spine stopped sending messages to the rest of her body. Her arms and legs went limp. This was it. Her brother's imaginary dog was going to kill her. She couldn't fight him anymore.

At first she didn't even notice that Spider had let go of her ankle, and then his feet were stepping on her chest, her ribs, her shoulders, one paw stepping on her face and sliding off, hooking her lip as it went. She turned to the side so he didn't tear it off.

Spider walked a circle on her body to face the other way down the hall, and over the blood roaring in her ears she heard him whining, but it sounded different now, frantic and fast, in and out, the unmistakable sound of fear. High-pitched and discordant, whines piling up on top of each other, he wasn't attacking her anymore, he was standing on her to press himself as far away as possible from whatever was in the hall.

He charged away, forcing himself up the wall to her left, and she saw him fade while still hearing his paws thundering down the wall, passing the attic stairs, then losing his grip as he rounded the far corner of the hall. His body slammed into the floor and shook the house and she heard claws on linoleum, she heard wood and glass splinter as he smashed through the door to the garage, then silence.

She didn't want to move. She'd never felt so wrung out in her life, but she raised her lacerated body on its elbows and looked down the hall and saw the dim outline of a man standing in the middle of the dark hall. Mark.

He had his right arm held high, and something on the end of it seemed to dance and squirm. The rest of his body stood still. The writhing upright arm moved, scanning the hall, looking for something, and then Mark stepped out of the shadows and into the weak daylight coming from the dining room. His face hung slack. On his right hand he wore Pupkin.

Pupkin waved at her.

He leered and capered, as animated and vibrant as Mark was motionless and dead.

"Kakawewe!" Pupkin screeched in his high-pitched voice, and it came out of Mark's throat but it was Pupkin's voice. Louise remembered it all the way back to their childhood.

"No," she said.

Pupkin began to sing, dancing from side to side.

"Pupkin here! Pupkin here! What do dee do? Pupkin here!"

Mark took a stiff stumbling step toward Louise. Then another, Pupkin leading the way.

"Pupkin here! Pupkin home! Oh no de do! Pupkin home!" he shrieked like a deranged child.

Louise pushed herself backward along the carpet with the skinned palms of her hands until her back was against the busted vent.

"Mark?" she asked, then forced her voice to carry authority. "Mark!"

He stopped.

"Mark," Louise said, her voice husky in her bruised throat. "Take that off."

"Mark gone, Pupkin now," Pupkin screeched.

"Shut up," Louise said. She realized she was arguing with a puppet and it made her angry. "Take it off or I'll take it off for you. I can't handle this bullshit right now."

Her right knee felt stuffed with broken glass as she put her weight on it. Her spine cracked and popped as she stood up. Her pelvis felt like it had been snapped in half.

"Oopsie doops!" Pupkin said. "Up ne go!"

"Stop it," Louise moaned, bracing herself against the wall, trying to straighten her back.

"Pupkin saves the day!" Pupkin screeched. "Me make Spider go away. Now it's time to play and play!"

Pupkin turned away from Louise and Mark's body followed. He

273

plodded to the end of the hall and turned the corner toward the front door. Louise tried to take a step. She could go out the kitchen. She had to be fast. Her right ankle felt weak but her knees held. She started to move.

From around the corner she heard the unmistakable snap of the front dead bolt flipping shut and it stopped her. Pupkin popped his head around the corner.

"Mean people lock Pupkin away," he said, nodding in time to his words. "But Pupkin back and here to stay!"

He started dancing down the hall toward Louise, followed by Mark's plodding body. She needed to reach Mark.

"Mark, don't let him do this again," she said. "Don't let him take over."

"Bad Louise," Pupkin cawed. "Mean Louise. Lock Pupkin away. Hurt Pupkin. Make Pupkin very, very angry."

"I didn't lock you away," Louise said, taking another step toward them. If she could dodge around them and get to the kitchen she could make it out the garage. Mark seemed practically asleep. Pupkin looked tattered and damaged. She could give them a hard shove and run. "Nancy put you in the attic because you hurt Eric. You made her angry, Pupkin."

"Nancy no play with Pupkin," he said through Mark's mouth. "Pupkin locked up. Pupkin lonely. Pupkin buried. Everyone leave Pupkin!"

They were close now. Louise got ready to give Mark a shove and run.

"Because you were bad," Louise said. "Are you going to be good now?"

"Pupkin always good," he cooed. "Everyone else bad!"

Mark squatted over the pile of wood they'd pried off the attic door and Pupkin rummaged through it.

When he stood back up, Pupkin held something in his nubby little puppet arms. He began to sing his special song.

Pupkin here! Pupkin here!
Everybody laugh! Everybody cheer!
No more bath time! No more rules!
No more teachers! No more schools!
It's time to sing and dance all day,
Pupkin's here to play and play AND PLAY AND PLAY!

Pupkin held the hammer. Mark swung it down and Louise couldn't get her body out of the way with the attic stairs blocking her, so she turned her head and it caught her high and on the left, glancing off her skull, taking a chip out of it, driving a spike through the left side of her face, all the way down to her jaw, sending her spinning into the wall.

Mark stepped forward, coming around the attic stairs, raising Pupkin and the hammer over his head again.

"AND PLAY AND PLAY AND PLAY AND PLAY!" Pupkin screamed over and over again, and Mark brought Pupkin and the hammer down on Louise's skull.

Chapter 26

Louise looked up and two images of Mark holding Pupkin stood next to each other.

He hit me! she thought, over and over again, her brain stuck in a rut. *He hit me! He hit me!*

"Mark, don't!" she screamed.

But her jaw didn't work anymore and the left side of her face felt numb and swollen, so it sounded like, "Muh, duhn!"

"Kakawewe!" Pupkin crowed and wriggled with delight behind his hammer.

Mark loomed over Louise, blocking out the light, filling the hall like an ogre in a fairy tale. Pupkin's hammer came down again from a long way away and Louise jerked her hands up and felt the haft of the hammer smack hard into her right palm with a solid *thwap*. Her arm went dead at the shoulder, buzzing with pins and needles. Pebbles of Pupkin's hard foam stuffing rained down on her face. She tried to curl her fingers around the hammer so Mark couldn't yank it back, but she no longer had a hand, only a claw.

"It's Louise!" Louise tried. "Your sister!"

It came out, "Uh ooese, yuh susuh!"

"It's time to sing and dance all day," Pupkin squealed. "Pupkin's here to play and play!"

The puppet flipped the hammer around with a dexterous shimmy of his stubby little arms and caught it with the claw side facing Louise. It looked like it could punch through her skull with no trouble at all. Louise's joints felt broken and her muscles felt weak, there was no one left to help her, Mom and Dad weren't coming, she was all alone.

He's going to kill you. He's going to kill you unless you do something.

"Spuh hur!" she said, looking down the hall toward the front door with her full attention. "Ud oy!"

Spider! Good boy!

Pupkin looked, too. The most horrible thing about it was that Pupkin looked, not Mark. The little puppet whipped around, cradling the enormous hammer across its body, and looked where Louise was looking, but Mark never took his dull, blank face off her. It was all she needed.

She threw herself down the hall, as far away from them as possible, knocking down the last picture still hanging. She ran for the dining room, jarring her skull with every step, her vertebrae crackling like Bubble Wrap. She didn't know if she was fast enough, but she couldn't risk looking back; she drove herself forward with the balls of her feet, digging her toes into the carpet, pushing hard.

A blow struck her left buttock and she collapsed onto the floor. She couldn't stop, she kept moving her arms, reaching for the linoleum, stretching, and Pupkin brought the hammer down again, shattering the small of her back, and

oh god i am thinking of him as pupkin now

she dragged herself forward and reached the linoleum just as the hammer hit the back of her right thigh, feeling like it gouged a divot out of her skin.

She pulled herself completely onto the linoleum and risked a look back, and they were too close, they were coming. She hauled herself up along the doorway, her eyes glued to Pupkin and his hammer. He gibbered and cooed to himself.

"Mark come home!" he squealed. "Louise go away!"

Mark took an enormous step forward, swinging Pupkin at the same time, and Louise let go of the doorway and fell backward. The claw end of the hammer punched through the drywall where her head had been, sending fragments showering across her face, blinding her. Instinctively she turned, hurling herself toward the kitchen, her vision clearing, seeing Pupkin frantically trying to extract the hammer from the wall.

It came out with a blast of plaster across the linoleum as Louise stumbled forward, bounced off the kitchen counter, and stumble-ran for the shattered door to the garage. If she could get to the backyard she could get to a neighbor, she could outrun them, she could be safe, she could be free, she could live.

The door seemed to be directly in front of her, but then gravity got heavier on the right side of the room as she lost her balance, veering toward the kitchen sink, and she bruised her hip on the counter again, sending her body spinning.

As she did a full three-sixty she caught a lurching, carousel snatch of Mark coming through the dining room entrance, linoleum floor bending beneath his feet, then she kept revolving past him and crashed into the louvered pantry doors with her left shoulder, hearing them splinter and crack, and she bounced herself off them hard, reaching for the garage. So close.

"Fee-fi-fo-fum," Pupkin shrieked, "I smell bloody Louise-eum!"

She fell forward and grabbed the splintered doorframe to stop herself from falling down the three brick stairs, and the brightening morning sun coming through the garage door windows showed her the back door was wide open, leading to sunlight and safety.

Behind her, Pupkin saw she was getting away and gave a terrible shriek that drove itself into her ears like ice picks. Mark shrieked but really Pupkin shrieked because she had never heard a human throat make a sound like that before. It could only have come from a puppet.

Teetering on the threshold of the garage, Louise allowed herself a grim smile of triumph

suck it, you little creep

She took a step forward and something exploded in her lower back, just above her left kidney. The blow shoved her forward, making her step bigger and wider, and as she heard the thrown hammer clatter to the linoleum floor she fell into the garage, missing the steps entirely. She landed on her left leg and the pain from her kidney where the hammer had hit her made that entire side of her body weak, and she stumbled sideways, sprawling, taking giant loping shuffle-steps across the garage, one foot dragging the extension cord Mark had left there for his saw, then she crashed into the shelves on the other side.

Panting, Louise rolled over and it was too late. Mark filled the door, standing at the top of the stairs, but she understood now, it wasn't Mark. It was all Pupkin. And he had the hammer again.

He took three slow steps down and stood at the base of the stairs. To get to the door into the backyard she'd have to pass within arm's reach of him. It was too close. He had won. It wasn't fair.

It's not fair!

Louise knew she couldn't do this alone. It hurt but it didn't matter, she forced her jaw to move.

"Mark," she said, and it made the blood in the left side of her face so tight she felt veins pop. "Please stop, please help me."

Muh, plus stuhb, plus huhp mm.

He plodded across the garage floor. He stepped on the extension cord and she felt the loop of it around her foot go tight. That's how close he was. He was touching something that touched her.

Louise burst into tears.

"Crybaby! Crybaby!" Pupkin singsonged, waving his hammer from side to side like he was leading a parade.

"You did this before, Mark," she said. "In Boston. You can do it again." But her swollen jaw made the words mush.

"No more bath time! No more rules!" Pupkin chanted, and he was so close his shadow slid over her.

"Please, Mark," Louise said. "Help me!"

Mark stopped walking, just a brief hesitation, but Pupkin noticed.

"No, no nony no!" he gibbered, quivering with rage.

He reared up on the end of Mark's arm, clutching his hammer, and he kept rearing, Mark's arm kept moving, and the hammer went flying backward, hit the ceiling and came down fast, narrowly missing the back of Mark's head, clattering onto the concrete hard.

"Louise!" Mark shouted in his own voice, and she knew what he wanted.

Pupkin hissed as Louise lurched forward, arms outstretched to tear him off Mark's arm. She caught Pupkin around the middle, and he whipped toward her, writhing like a snake.

Mark didn't stop her but he didn't help Pupkin, either. Louise slammed her body into him and he took a startled step backward, got his ankles tangled in the extension cord and sat down hard on the concrete floor. Louise landed in his lap.

Pupkin gibbered and howled and leapt at Louise's face. She grabbed him under his armpits and he didn't feel like he had Mark's hand inside of him, he felt like a living body on the end of Mark's arm.

"It's time to sing and dance all day! Pupkin's here to play and play and play and play!" he shrieked, and he hooked his arms and came at her face.

She felt something sharp sink into her cheek—*his teeth???*—as he covered her face, and there was too much of him, moving in too many different directions. His sharp paws scrabbled at her eyes and he pressed her left eyeball until she saw spots and felt it move slightly backward inside its socket, and she realized Pupkin was pressing her wounded eyeball into her skull.

Louise refused to let go. She tightened her hands around his tattered body and leaned back, bracing her feet against Mark's rib cage, pulling hard. Muscles she didn't know she had strained and tore. Her shoulders burned. She hauled backward, trying to shuck Pupkin off Mark's arm.

He didn't budge.

Then he flew at her again, hard and fast, his hard plastic head smashing into her nose, and she felt warm, wet, salty blood pour over her lips and flow down her chin. Pupkin reared back and surveyed his handiwork.

"Kakawewe!" he shrieked with glee and smashed into Louise's swollen nose again.

Everything went away for a moment. A chunk of time had been spliced out and now Pupkin was crawling on the floor, dragging Mark behind him, going for the hammer. Mark tried to hang on to the collages, grabbed at a pile of paint cans, but he had no strength left and Pupkin kept crawling, dragging him behind like deadweight.

Louise shook her head like a boxer, but that made it spin. She felt weak and empty and she heard another noise underneath the buzzing inside her head, the sound of Mark begging and crying at the same time.

"Don't make me! Don't make me! Please, Pupkin, don't make me!"

She knew what he was saying. *Don't make me. Don't make me beat my sister to death on the floor of our dead parents' garage.*

Something loud and high-pitched tore through the air, snapping her out of her daze. Mark had grabbed the nearest thing he could to stop his advance: his circular saw. It lay on the floor, plugged into the extension cord, and he'd pressed the trigger briefly. He turned his wild eyes back to Louise and they were terrified and for the first time since they were kids they understood each other completely.

"Do it!" he shouted.

Pupkin closed his little arms around the hammer.

"Kakawewe!" he screamed and raised himself up in the air like a cobra and came down on Mark's hand with the sound of breaking pencils.

Mark's hand stiffened and flexed and yanked itself back from the saw, turning red.

"Louise!" he screamed, and it was a guttural, ragged scream torn from deep inside his throat.

She threw her shoulders forward, shoved with her bruised legs, and landed on top of Mark, her left hand on Pupkin. She yanked the hammer from his grip, and he tried to hold on to it, surprisingly strong, but she had surprise on her side. She tossed it as far as she could, which was only about three feet, but that was far enough.

Letting out a grunt of effort, Louise threw her right hand over Mark's shoulder and grabbed the circular saw. It was heavy and she let go of Pupkin with her left and hauled herself onto her knees, kneeling on Mark, not caring about his body anymore, treating it like the floor.

She threw out her left foot and pressed Mark's wrist to the floor. Pupkin saw what was in her hand and he screeched and clapped his hands together.

"Whee! Whee! Whee!" he cried.

"Hurry!" Mark shouted and Louise pressed the trigger and the saw screamed to life.

It felt hungry in her hands, it lurched forward, it wanted to cut. It was loud and she didn't know if she could make herself do it, but over its screeching roar she heard as much as she saw Mark screaming, mouth so wide his jaw looked dislocated, face red and sweaty, and she aimed for the infinity tattoo on his right forearm, and before she could stop herself she brought the saw down in the middle of infinity's arc.

It went in fast, like there was nothing there, like it was cutting air, and everything around her misted red and Louise's face went hot. Then it hit bone (*his radius*, her Girl Scout brain said) and the intolerable screeching of the saw went up an octave to an ear-shredding yowl, like the drill at the dentist's office.

The saw juddered and shook in her hands, burning vibrations trying to force her palms open, trying to make her let go, as she pushed the spinning blade through Mark's *radius*. Thick gobbets of fat splattered her face and knuckles and she was screaming and felt hard grains of bone dust settle on her tongue and she pressed her lips together and tasted her brother's blood. Mark screamed and Pupkin screamed with laughter and danced on the end of his half-severed arm, and then the blade was clear of bone, and Louise, resistance suddenly removed, lurched forward.

The saw struck concrete and shot out a shower of white sparks and Louise smelled something burning and she knew it was her brother's bone, and then the saw hit the second bone in his forearm (*ulna*, her Girl Scout brain noted), but it barely slowed the blade down.

Louise leaned forward, putting her weight on it, sparks shooting into her face, blood misting Pupkin's face, the garage full of Pupkin's laughter and her brother's screams, and then she was through and Pupkin fell at a strange angle, and the circular saw shot forward, screaming against the concrete floor, and she released the trigger and everything went quiet except for Mark screaming.

Louise looked at Pupkin and he was still writhing and she told herself that was just a reflex action of Mark's severed arm inside him but he was crawling deliberately toward the hammer, dragging Mark's ragged red stump behind him as it hung from his puppet hole.

She stood up and grabbed him, palms still numb from the saw, and tore him off the end of Mark's arm and ran over and jammed him in the trash can and slammed the lid. Mark's arm was surprisingly heavy in her hand. She looked at Mark, retracting around himself, mouth wide in a silent scream, curling into a fetal ball around his arm stump as it jetted blood across the concrete floor in a high-pressure spray, pulsing to the rhythm of his heart, radial artery splattering the concrete with red like a fire hose.

Louise dropped his severed forearm, whose fingers curled over on themselves when it hit the floor, and knelt beside him, her agonized body screaming in protest, knees popping, bruises blossoming, and she grabbed the extension cord, wrapped it around her knuckles, and twisted it tightly around Mark's stump, getting a hot squirt of blood in the face as her muscles remembered how to loop the cord and twist the ends to make the perfect tourniquet from the Girl Scout handbook.

She had minutes to call an ambulance before Mark bled out, and she couldn't get to a phone while she held the tourniquet tight. She stepped on one end of the extension cord and pulled, and with her other hand she slid her phone out of her jeans and pressed *EMERGENCY*.

Mark tried to get up, mumbling something through blue lips, and she pushed a knee to his chest and held him to the floor, talking over the 911 operator.

"My brother sawed off his arm, we're in the garage." She gave the address, she let the phone slide to the floor, she tightened her grip around the extension cord.

Mark tried to sit up and she leaned on him hard, both hands pulling on the tourniquet. Through his T-shirt he felt cold, his body shaking so hard it might be a seizure. He was going into shock from sudden blood loss. She used one leg to drag a garbage bag full of dolls over and kicked his feet up onto it, elevating his legs.

She gripped the tourniquet so hard she could feel his pulse through it and her knuckles shook with strain and she thought the same thing over and over again:

I'm not going to let you die. I'm not going to let you die. I'm not going to let you die.

Chapter 27

What do you say after you cut off your brother's arm?

To the paramedics, Louise said it was an accident. Mark was cutting wood in the garage and lost control of the saw. It turned out that the paramedics had just come from Walmart, where a police officer had shot off one finger while testing a .22, then shot the clerk in the shin while picking the gun up off the floor, so they were prepared to believe anything.

To the doctors at the emergency room who put stitches in her scalp, X-rayed her skull, flushed her left eye, and told her they didn't see any permanent damage, she said a set of shelves in their garage had collapsed on her in the confusion.

To the police officers at the hospital, Louise gave more details about Mark's "accident," including her concerns about his lack of safety precautions, her suspicions that he may have had a few breakfast beers, and when they still seemed dubious she added the incriminating fact that at a crucial moment during his sawing she may have distracted him by getting crushed under some shelves she stupidly tipped over.

To Poppy, who she called from the parking garage of MUSC, where they'd moved Mark because the downtown hospital was better prepared to handle this kind of injury, Louise didn't say anything. She just wanted to hear her voice.

Surprisingly, it sounded normal.

"Koala bears," Poppy told her. "Polar bears, panda bears, grizzly bears, drop bears, there's a lot of bears."

"I don't think that last one is real, baby," Louise said.

"Yes," Poppy said. "They're in Australia. Uncle Devin said they drop on people's heads."

"I think he's having fun with you," Louise said.

"He showed me a picture," Poppy said.

Louise didn't want Poppy to stop talking. She felt grateful Poppy was talking to her at all and not begging for her to come home, so she didn't argue.

"You'll have to show me," she said.

"When?" Poppy asked.

"I don't know but very soon. Real soon. I'm going to see you real soon. So, what other kinds of bears did you learn about?"

Louise let Poppy's conversation about bears wash over her for a minute.

"Hey, sweetie," she said, walking toward the parking garage elevator. "I need to go. I love you."

"Okay," Poppy said.

"Is everything okay?" Ian asked when he took the phone back. "It's early."

"She sounds good," Louise said, deflecting. "She sounds back to normal."

"Yeah," Ian said. "Maybe talking to the therapist helped. I don't know. My mom's spending a lot of time with her. We had a dry night. What's going on there?"

"I'm getting on an elevator," Louise said, really not wanting to explain Mark's arm to him. "I'll call later."

Louise wound up in a waiting room on the fifth floor. People with morning surgery appointments drifted into the room, and an efficient nurse checked them in, talking loudly over the flat-screen TV showing morning news, which was covering absolutely no stories about a man sawing off his arm in Mount Pleasant. Louise checked in with the nurse, then sat down and felt very alone.

Her joints had stiffened up since the—accident? incident? amputation?—and every time she closed her eyes she saw the infinity symbol on the inside of Mark's forearm right below Pupkin's sleeve pulling back and forth and then a gout of blood covered it and she jerked her eyes open. Whatever they'd shot into her scalp to numb it had worn off and the skin on the left side of her face felt stretched tight. Everything itched. She didn't think she'd sleep, then she did.

She woke with a start. A very young nurse stood over her.

"He's out of surgery," she said.

"Okay," Louise said, speaking around her thick, dry tongue. "What . . . okay."

"You want to wash your face and I'll take you back?" the nurse suggested.

Louise made the mistake of looking in the bathroom mirror. They'd given her wet wipes at East Cooper Medical but she'd missed a misted spray of blood across her neck, and dots of it crusted beneath her chin, and more crusted inside her nostrils. She had dried blood in her left ear and black blood along her hairline. The left side of her jaw looked swollen. Both her eyes were bloodshot.

She bent over the sink to splash water on her face and her head gave a thick throb and her vision blurred. She stood up fast and her bruised spine creaked. She braced herself on the edge of the sink, trying to catch her breath.

What do you say to people after you cut off your brother's arm?

What do you say to your brother?

Scraped cleanish, Louise followed the nurse through the double doors. The nurse wore a fuzzy blanket wrapped around her waist like a sarong, which Louise didn't understand until she stepped into postsurgical recovery and freezing-cold air enveloped her. They kept it at the temperature of a meat locker, which—Louise saw her brother's ragged, bright red stump again, looking like hamburger meat—she supposed it was. Sounds felt muted. Lights had been dimmed in some of the postsurgical alcoves, and the few people she could see moved quietly and slowly, like they were drifting underwater.

The nurse brought her to a dim alcove and slipped through its half-closed drapes. Louise followed. The bed lay beneath a headboard of machines and tubes and tanks and an enormous digital screen tracking red and green numbers that took up almost the entire room. A putty-colored pleather reclining chair had been squeezed in beside the foot of the bed.

Mark looked swollen and gray against the white laundered sheets. His eyes were half-lidded and tracked the nurse as she checked the readout and mashed on the screen over and over with one thumb. There wasn't much room so Louise climbed around the recliner to stand closer. Mark's eyes slid across the alcove and landed on her, but his expression didn't change. Louise couldn't tell if he saw her or not.

Both his arms rested on top of the sheet, making him look off-balance. One ended in a hand, the other stopped just below the elbow in a tight twist of bright white bandages.

"Some people recover from anesthesia quickly and some don't," the nurse told Louise, speaking loudly and clearly. Mark's eyes slid toward the sound. "He seems to be doing fine, though. There may be some confusion. Dr. Daresh will be here shortly and she'll be able to tell you how things went, but right now everything seems good."

"Okay," Louise said, overly aware of Mark's eyes sliding back and forth between them.

"If you need anything we're right out there," the nurse said. Then she raised her voice to invalid level and directed it at Mark. "How do you feel, Mr. Joyner?"

Louise had never heard anyone called Mr. Joyner before besides her dad.

"Unh-huh," Mark said.

"Good." The nurse smiled and slipped through the curtain, leaving them alone.

Mark's eyes stayed where she'd exited. Louise lowered herself into the recliner and it sucked her backward. Attracted by the movement, Mark's eyes slid over to her. Louise felt like the one grimy thing in the clean hospital nook.

"Mark?" she asked.

Mark stared at her, his eyes glistening, and Louise had a sudden crazy-making thought: *What if he's still Pupkin? What if I got it off his arm too late?*

She didn't feel so safe in here anymore.

"You're," Mark croaked.

Louise waited to see if he'd say more. He didn't. After a minute she asked, "What's that?"

His eyes flicked over her shoulder, widened.

"Spi'er," he mumbled.

Spider.

Louise looked behind her chair, up at the ceiling, across the nook. No Spider.

"I don't see him, Mark," she said, not feeling very sure of that.

Mark focused on the curtains at the foot of his bed.

"Spi'er," he mumbled again, his lips sticking together.

His eyelids slid shut, his face went slack, and his chest rose and fell, slow and steady. The big clock over his bed read 12:14 p.m.

Louise didn't see Spider and assumed it was a postanesthesia hallucination. Soon, her eyes got heavy, dropped, and she felt the hammer nick her skull, her stitches throbbed, she heard the hollow coconut sound of metal dinging bone, her eyes snapped open. Mark watched her.

The two of them stared at each other. Louise didn't feel a need to smile, or look concerned, or make any kind of a face. They just looked.

Mark had more gray than blond in his stubble. The gown left a lot of his neck and shoulders exposed and they were covered in thin colorless hairs. He looked stranded, somewhere between alive and dead.

"How do you feel?" Louise asked after a minute.

"Like—" His words ground to a halt inside his dry throat. He cleared it, looked around for someplace to spit, didn't see anything, and swallowed hard. "Like you look."

His voice sounded steadier than she expected.

"What happened?" she asked. She needed sanity. She craved reality. "Why'd you do it?"

Mark furrowed his forehead at her. Louise dropped her voice down low and leaned forward. It made her joints ache in new ways.

"Why'd you put on Pupkin?" she asked.

"He told me if I didn't," Mark said, "he'd let Spider kill you."

He let his eyes drop to the bed and registered his stump. The muscles in his right forearm twitched and the lines around his mouth deepened with pain.

"Hey," Louise said, leaning forward as much as she could. Mark raised his eyes to hers. They were the only living things in his dead, gray face. "Thank you."

Mark almost smiled at that, then he looked concerned again.

"Go," he said, and Louise wasn't sure she'd heard him right.

"Go?" she asked.

"Burn him," he said. "Burn him like we planned."

She remembered the dead look on Mark's face when he had Pupkin on his arm. She remembered what he'd told her about BU and how much it must have cost him to put Pupkin on again. She thought about Pupkin telling her to send Mark out on the ice.

"Burn him," Mark repeated.

It was the only sane thing to do.

"Yeah," she said, and for a moment she just wanted to stay here in this soft, comfortable chair, then she pushed herself to her feet.

She shuffled to the curtains and peeked out. The nurse who'd brought her back sat at the desk between two other nurses. Behind her, Mark sighed. Louise turned.

"It felt so good," he said. He met her eyes. "It felt so good not to be responsible for anything again."

She slipped through the curtain, feeling enormously self-conscious. The nurse looked up from her station as Louise hobbled past.

"Dr. Daresh is on her way for the postsurgical conference," she said.

Louise smiled but didn't stop hobbling. If she stopped she didn't think she'd be able to start again.

"Bathroom," she said.

"Be fast," the nurse said, then looked back down at her screen.

Louise hobbled out of the recovery unit and limped across the waiting room, passed the bathroom, and headed for the elevator, feeling like she was making a prison break. As she waited for the elevator, she wondered if people thought she was a battered wife or a car crash victim. By the time she got to the lobby she didn't care what anyone thought. By the time she got into her cold little Kia she just hurt. Her skin ached. Every bruise felt connected to another bruise.

She didn't remember navigating traffic to get onto the Crosstown, or going over the bridge, or turning onto McCants, but the next thing she remembered she was pulling up outside the house. The paramedics had left the garage door open. She got out and walked directly into its maw and snapped on the light. She didn't look at the enormous bloodstains on the floor. She slapped the door-close button and the door ground shut, hitting the driveway with a bang, making everything inside turn dim.

She got the grill tongs and a white plastic bottle of lighter fluid sitting next to them and went out back. She dragged the rusty green grill they'd maybe used once in her life away from the wall of the house, opened it up, and used the tongs to scatter the old ashes, then built up a mound of sticks she found in the yard. The more she moved, the more it worked the stiffness out of her joints. She sprayed the sticks down with lighter fluid until they glistened.

On the shelf next to where the lighter fluid had been she found a long fire starter. Then she heaved the garbage bag off the trash can and threw its lid open. Pupkin sprawled on his back, smiling up at her, gory and merry, cutting his eyes to one side, mischievous and sly. Mark's blood stained one half of his white plastic face.

Pupkin fun! she heard him sing inside her head.

She picked him up with the tongs.

Wheeeee! Pupkin said.

She didn't look at him as she marched him into the backyard and over to the grill. As they got closer she thought she felt the tongs twitch. She shot a quick look down, and Pupkin was squirming as she walked. He squirmed faster. He put one nubby arm over the end of the tongs and looked up at her.

No, Pupkin said, his voice thick with panic. *Not Pupkin. Pupkin love you!*

She raised the tongs and dropped him on the mound of sticks.

where nancy nancy help, help pupkin please please pupkin love—

She clicked the fire starter and touched it to the wood. The flames looked clear in the noonday sun. Inside her head she heard Pupkin scream, a high-pitched squeal that never seemed to stop, but that was just inside her head. She could ignore what was inside her head.

She picked up the lighter fluid and sprayed his body. The fire shot up in a column that felt like it baked her eyebrows. Louise released the bottle and it gave a wet sucking sound. Pupkin writhed on his back and screamed in the fire. Scream after scream echoed inside her skull. She should have closed the lid. But she didn't. She made herself stand there and watch him burn.

His screams reached a fever pitch, high enough to shatter glass, as tendrils of flame licked his plastic face and his cheeks blistered and bubbled. Louise worried about the fire leaving anything behind and she sprayed the lighter fluid on his face until the bottle sputtered air. Pupkin's screams became clotted and liquid. As the fire made his face run like wax Louise thought she heard inside her head:

nancy please please nancy nancy promise never leave pupkin alone it hurts it hurts it hurts where nancy nancy help pupkin nancy help

Then Pupkin's head melted and revealed its hollow interior in a hole that expanded and erased his mouth, and his fabric body turned to flakes of white ash that rode lazy air currents around the backyard. The screams stopped. A burning stick popped. He was gone.

Louise watched for a long time, then she lowered the lid of the grill and made herself walk back to the garage. She tossed the empty plastic bottle into the garbage, where it made a hollow plastic-on-plastic *thunk*. Then she closed the garbage can and made herself walk into the house.

It felt still and empty. She walked to the hall, wondering if Spider was still around. Or the squirrels. She realized she didn't care. She could handle them now. She folded the steps back up into the attic. The screw holes in the ceiling looked bad. They'd have to fix them before they put the house on the market.

She made herself push open the hall bathroom door. The Mark and

Louise dolls were where they'd left them. They looked empty to her. They looked dead.

Louise made herself walk down the hall into her parents' bedroom. She stood in the middle of their room and made herself close her eyes. Then she listened. She stood there like that for a long time, and finally opened her eyes again.

The house felt empty. No presence. No one in the rooms. Nothing in the attic. No weight of the past. No sense of her mom and dad. It felt like someone had picked it up and shaken out all the people and all the history and left it empty, not a house anymore but a series of boxes, connected by wall-to-wall carpeting, with nothing left inside.

Their house didn't feel haunted anymore.

DEPRESSION

Chapter 28

On her way back downtown, Louise tried to concentrate on what was in front of her: the changing traffic lights, the merge onto the bridge, the exit for Rutledge Avenue, a parking space near the hospital. Somehow she got up to the fifth floor and found the waiting room again.

"We didn't have any beds open," the nurse at the desk told her, "so we kept him in the PACU."

Louise went back. The nurse from that morning stood up as she passed the desk.

"Dr. Daresh couldn't find you," she said. "She wanted to tell you how surgery went and inform you about postsurgical care. I don't know when she'll be available again."

Louise apologized until the nurse lost interest, then she slipped through the curtains over Mark's alcove. He'd cranked the back of his bed upright and sat against it, staring down at his missing arm. When she came in he looked up.

"He's gone," she said.

Mark's expression didn't change.

"I burned him," Louise said. "There's nothing left. Pupkin's gone."

Mark let out an enormous breath and the scrolling lines on the digital monitor beside his bed spiked.

"I need a beer," he said.

Louise felt unutterably sad. They still had the house to sell, but it wasn't their parents' house anymore; it was just a house. It was over. Everything was over. Mark tried to raise his stump but winced, so he pointed at it instead.

"This," he said, "is why I wanted to hire Agutter."

"Are you blaming me?" Louise asked.

"An apology would go a long way," Mark said.

"For what?" Louise asked, not quite believing they were arguing again, but slipping into it like a pair of old shoes.

"They can't reattach it," he said.

"You told me to . . ." She couldn't say it out loud because those nurses could hear everything, so she made a sawing gesture with one hand.

"I thought they could reattach it," he said. "How could you even do that? I couldn't do it to you."

"You were trying to kill me with a hammer," Louise whispered, hoping it would encourage Mark to lower his voice, too.

"You tried to drown me at the Calvins'," he said.

"We agreed that was Pupkin," Louise said.

"So Pupkin's the one who tried to kill you with a hammer," Mark said, "but you sawed off *my* arm."

"Can you keep it down?" Louise whispered. "I had to lie about what happened to a lot of people."

"Yeah," Mark said, "because if they knew what you did you'd be charged with assault."

"Mark," Louise hissed, "are you seriously upset with me because I saved your life, or is this some postsurgical dysfunction because you're pumped up on meds?"

The curtain flapped open and a kid who did not look old enough to be in college swooped in. He wore plum scrubs and sported a very patchy beard behind his Spider-Man mask.

"Hello, hello," he said. "I'm the surgical resident. They're trying to find Dr. Daresh for you, but I just want to bring you up to speed on what she's going to say."

"To be continued," Mark said to Louise.

"Hi," Louise said to the surgical resident.

"You're the"—the surgical resident checked his notes—"sister. Wow, you look terrible. What tore you up?"

"Some shelves fell on me," Louise said.

"That's your story?" Mark asked in disbelief.

Louise made "shut up" eyes at him. The surgical resident didn't blink.

"Heavy shelves," he remarked. "I'm Dr. Santos, and let's take a look at this amputation site."

He examined Mark's wound.

"Nice clean cut," Santos said, and Louise almost said *thank you* but managed to stop herself.

As Dr. Santos rewrapped Mark's arm he delivered a speech to Louise.

"So, I discussed this with Brother but to say it again for Sister," he said. "We were not able to reattach the limb. It hadn't been kept as cold as we would have liked and the possibility of nerve damage was higher than we'd have liked, but, staying positive, with a nice clean cut like this, we can fit you for a very good prosthesis and pretty soon it'll feel back to normal."

"I doubt that," Mark said.

"East Cooper did an excellent job of debriding that wound," Dr. Santos said. "And most of the IVs you've got going now are antibiotics, but it still might pus up. We're going to keep the surgical drain in for a few weeks and in a minute one of the nurses will show Sister how to milk it, which she'll need to do twice a day. We can release you this afternoon, I think, but we're going to give you a prescription for an oral antibiotic and we need you to keep an eye on the site. Any inflammation, swelling, tenderness, fever, you give us a call. But otherwise we'd like to see you back home for your recovery. It's always an adjustment to lose a limb, but I think this is a best-case scenario for sure. I'm going to go find out if Dr. Daresh is on her way."

Dr. Santos swooped out and it was silent in the cubicle for a long time. Louise knew this would be a roller coaster for Mark, full of ups and downs, so she tried to make a joke.

"I have to milk your wound," she said. "I think I'm being punished enough."

Mark looked at her, eyes wide, upset she would even say that.

"I have one arm, Louise."

He didn't speak to her for the rest of the day.

He didn't speak to her for the next five days, really. Occasionally he'd make a comment, usually mean, but that was it. She got him home and he dropped onto his couch, took out his phone, tried to scroll through Facebook, discovered doing it one-handed was hard, and threw it on the cushions. After that, he mostly slept.

Driven by guilt, Louise dedicated herself to his care. She bought the infinite items he needed to adjust to his new life: rings to attach to his zippers, moisturizer for his surgery site, a multichopper for his kitchen even though, after looking at the condition of his fridge, she suspected he didn't cook much.

She tried to make him do PT. She made remote doctor appointments and showed up at his house to do them with him on her iPad, but he complained that his stump hurt too much, or he felt too tired, or he just wasn't feeling it that day.

"You've got to try or they won't be able to fit you for a prosthesis,"

Louise told him after he'd given up on one session in the middle, embarrassed at how he'd acted in front of a stranger who was only trying to help him.

"I don't want a prosthesis," Mark said. "I want my arm."

"I want that, too," she said, "but it's not going to happen. You need to accept reality."

He stood in the middle of his junked-up, overcrowded living room and looked at her with the dull, lifeless look that he seemed to wear permanently these days, and said, "Leave me alone."

Then he turned around and went back to bed. It was 12:45 in the afternoon.

Louise Googled "postamputation depression" and she tried to talk to Mark, she tried to be a patient listener, she tried to get him to do mindfulness meditations she found on YouTube.

"You like all that touchy-feely stuff," she said, standing in his bedroom doorway at ten a.m., talking to him through the funk of body odor and dirty laundry that radiated from his dark sleeping cave. "So I booked an energy worker who says they can help with the phantom limb pain. But you need to shower if you want to be there on time. I'll buy you lunch after."

"Sure," he said, then rolled over in bed, his back to her, and a minute later she heard him snore.

The few times he engaged with her he mostly seemed annoyed that the cut had gone right across the middle of his infinity sign tattoo.

"Just up three inches or down five," he told Louise. "Then I would have either kept it or lost the whole thing."

"The aesthetic integrity of your tattoo wasn't the first thing on my mind," Louise told him.

"What am I going to do with half an infinity sign?" Mark grumbled.

"You've become such a grouch," she said.

"Having your arm sawed off will do that."

Mercy and Constance came by one day and decided to sit in the grassy patch outside his condo to enjoy the sun. Louise set out chairs and made iced tea.

He complained about it but eventually went outside. "I don't want to see them," Mark told her. "I didn't ask for anyone to come by."

"They're worried," Louise said. "They care about you. They're family."

Finally, he agreed to go outdoors.

"Oh my Lord," Mercy said, when she saw his arm. "Saws are so dangerous."

Louise knew this was the part Mark hated the most: having to pretend it was his own carelessness that caused the accident.

"It depends on who's operating it," he said, slumping into a lawn chair Louise had bought for the visit because Mark didn't own any. "I'm already suing East Cooper Medical."

He wasn't actually suing them, but he researched it constantly. A lawyer had cold-called and told him they'd improperly stored his arm, which was why it couldn't be reattached. Mark printed out articles about malpractice. He even talked to a few lawyers, then always refused to follow up because they didn't have a "gladiator mentality," which meant they didn't think he could get as much money from a settlement as Mark thought he should.

"I'm getting a beer," he said, getting up and going inside.

Louise wished he wasn't drinking because he'd popped a pain pill right before their cousins arrived. She'd actually "forgotten" to buy beer when she bought his groceries yesterday, but he'd just gotten it delivered for an eleven-dollar fee.

"So what really happened?" Mercy asked in a low voice after Mark went inside.

"He wasn't paying attention," Louise lied.

Mercy gave her a long look. Constance raised her eyebrows.

"The last time I saw you guys was the walk-through," Mercy said. "The day after I tell you about your . . . compromised-sale situation, Mark saws off his arm and you look like you've been run over by a truck. What happened?"

"What compromised-sale situation?" Constance asked.

"I'll tell you later," Mercy said, not looking at her, focused on getting the truth out of Louise.

"Mark had a few beers for breakfast and was cutting wood," Louise said. "I stood up on the shelves to get something down and they fell over on me. I think that's what distracted him."

Mercy considered Louise for a long moment, then shook her head.

"We're family," she insisted with conviction.

Louise wanted to tell her, but there was family and then there was family. Pupkin, Spider, what she'd had to do to Mark—that was Joyner family business.

"You've seen those shelves," Louise said, feeling bad. "They're really unstable."

"If you ever want to talk, I'm here," Mercy said quietly, then raised her voice to a normal level. "What're y'all doing with the house?"

"We decided not to sell it right now," Louise said at a normal volume. "It's not going anywhere. We'll probably try again when it comes out of probate."

"Well," Mercy said. "That'll make Meemaw happy, at least."

Mark didn't come back outside and finally Louise went in and found him sitting on the couch looking at his phone, holding a beer between his thighs.

"You're not coming back out?" she asked.

He shrugged.

"I'm not feeling great."

She looked at him for a long time and realized there was no point in arguing. She wasn't his mother. She went outside to tell her cousins. As they walked back to their cars she saw Constance interrogating Mercy.

"*What* compromised-sale situation?" she demanded in what was, for Constance, a discreet whisper.

It wasn't all bad. Louise just had to make it through the week. Mark wasn't her child, he was a grown man who was responsible for his own decisions. And every day she crossed off on the calendar was another day closer to going home.

She knew this was the beginning of the end for both of them. Mark would get better or he wouldn't. They still had some paperwork with Brody, and then would sell the house in about a year, but it wasn't their parents' house anymore, it was just a house, and Louise knew that after they split the money they'd call a little more than usual, then they'd call a little less, then it would be texts, then there would be longer and longer between texts, and then it would be over.

She and Mark were too different. Without something holding them together—living in the same town, Mom and Dad, children the same ages—they would drift apart. She'd try to visit Charleston more often to see Aunt Honey and the cousins, and of course she'd get dinner with Mark when she came in, but something that had started with their parents' car accident had ended with burning Pupkin, and whatever extra connection they'd had felt like a burned-out lightbulb now.

It didn't make her as sad as she expected. She was okay. Things changed. Now she just wanted to go home. She needed to see her real family.

Mark didn't even show up at the airport to say good-bye. Instead, he texted:

SORRY—SICK

She was actually impressed that she'd rated two whole words. Besides, he didn't owe her anything anymore. Everything that had happened between them felt far away, already turning into a story she'd tell someone one day lying beside them in the dark, or she'd tell Poppy when she got out of college. They'd have a glass of wine together and she'd tell her these things about her mom and Pupkin and Mark and they'd turn the story over between them and wonder what it all meant, then pack it away again like family photos.

She'd booked an early-afternoon flight, paid her extravagant hotel bill, turned in her rental car, paid that extravagant bill, and now she sat at her gate feeling like she'd done her duty to Mark and her mom and especially her dad. He'd be proud of how she'd handled all this: direct, practical, and to the point. She'd seen what needed to be done, and she hadn't flinched from doing it.

She felt anxious about seeing Poppy again. She wanted to get home. She wanted to be landing already. She hadn't had coffee that morning because she wanted to sleep through her flight to get home that much faster. The urge to see her daughter made her physically itch. She couldn't sit still.

She'd decided not to tell Poppy about Mark's arm. Not for a while. Why would she? When she'd called Ian to let him know she was coming home, she'd dreaded having to tell him about Mark's arm, then she'd had a revelation: she didn't need to tell him about Mark's arm at all. When was Ian ever going to see Mark again? Taking the easy way out felt a little like lying, it made her feel a little like Mark, but it also felt like a huge relief. Maybe being a little bit like Mark wasn't a bad thing. A little bit of Mark wasn't the problem. The problem with Mark was that it was never a little bit of Mark, it was always either none at all or way too much.

She slept through her entire flight, and when it landed she felt like a key fitting a lock. She texted Ian with lots of exclamation points and even asked her Uber driver where he was from and how long he'd been in San Francisco to make the ride go faster. She texted Ian again a few blocks from the house and she didn't even dread seeing him, she just needed to get rid of him as soon as she politely could.

Unlocking the downstairs door to her building felt weirdly like she was doing it for the first time. She noticed every single scuff mark in the stairwell, every rip in the hall carpet. She lugged her suitcase up the stairs, which creaked more than she remembered, and through their front door and called, "Poppy! I'm home!" like she was about to burst into song.

She expected to see Poppy sitting cross-legged on the floor drawing, or maybe she'd made a cute *Welcome Home* sign, or she'd be running across the room with her arms out for a hug, but she just got Ian sitting on the sofa instead.

"Hey," he said, looking up from his phone. "Jesus, what happened to your face?"

"Shelves fell on me," she said, putting down her suitcase and dropping her purse on top. "Is Poppy okay?"

"Are you all right?" he asked, coming over, arms out at waist level to give her a hug, imitating a concerned partner. She didn't have time for this.

"It's fine, honestly," she said, sidestepping his proposed hug. "Where's Poppy?"

"She's in her bedroom," he told her. "Slow down. She's fine."

She dodged Ian and semi-ran down the short, creaking hall to Poppy's room and gave two quick knocks on the door.

"Pop-pee!" she sang, pushing it open.

Poppy stood in the middle of her brightly colored rag carpet.

"Kakawewe!" Poppy screeched in a familiar, squeaky voice. "How do dee do?"

Pupkin waved to Louise, dancing from side to side, on Poppy's arm.

Chapter 29

L ouise's skin turned to ice. Sweat erupted from her pores. Her guts hollowed out. Her body caved in. She'd traveled across the country only to run in a circle.

"Kakawewe!" Pupkin screeched, his voice forcing itself out of her daughter's throat. "Pupkin home! Pupkin home! Pupkin home forever!"

Louise heard the scream of the saw, she pictured a fantail of orange and white sparks as it bit into the concrete floor.

The word *no* stuck to her lips, just a moan. Her knees felt weak. Her feet went numb. The shrieking inside her skull went up an octave as the saw bit into her brother's bone.

"Mom made it with her," Ian said from behind her. "The Popster came up with it all by herself. She had a real vision."

"Pupkin here!" Pupkin said through her daughter's mouth. "Pupkin here! How do dee do! Pupkin here!"

Louise held Mark's arm under one foot, crushing it to the floor, steel teeth biting into his infinity sign. She tasted her brother's blood. She began to hyperventilate.

"He's a little creepy at first," Ian said, "but he grows on you. And the Popster loves him to death."

"Pupkin home! Pupkin home!" Pupkin danced from side to side, chanting it over and over again, his voice higher because Poppy's vocal cords were less developed, her lungs smaller, her palate softer. Louise heard Pupkin screaming through Mark's throat, bringing the hammer down on her skull. The left side of her forehead gave a sharp, precise pang.

Her lower body went numb and hot urine squirted between her thighs.

"Pupkin home! Pupkin home!" The puppet danced toward Louise on the end of Poppy's arm, then away, taunting her.

"Lou?" Ian said.

She wanted to stop. She couldn't stop. Sticky, hot piss ran down her legs and soaked her socks, puddling in the heels of her shoes.

"Lou!" Ian said.

"Pupkin wants a kiss-kiss!" He pressed himself up at Louise's mouth, leering, contaminating her daughter, corrupting her daughter, her daughter she'd sworn to protect, her daughter she'd failed.

"No!" Louise shouted, way too loud, her wet pants already turning cold. "No!"

She grabbed Pupkin and felt her daughter's arm inside his sleeve. Pupkin felt different, rougher, made of cheaper fabric. She yanked, jerking Poppy's arm with it.

"Lou!" Ian snapped behind her.

"Ow!" Poppy shrieked.

Louise hauled on Poppy's arm, over and over, standing there in her soaking pants, not caring how it looked, needing to get Pupkin off her daughter's arm, shaking it like a pit bull. Poppy made a fist inside Pupkin's body and held on. Louise seized Poppy's elbow, fingers digging in hard, and yanked Pupkin's head backward with her other hand, not caring if she hurt Poppy, just needing to get this puppet out of her house, away from her family.

"Jesus, Lou, stop!" Ian said. "What is wrong with you!"

Poppy started to scream, a single, high, sustained, unbroken note that filled the room and vibrated the walls. Louise chanted "no" with every yank: "No! No! No!"

She dug her fingers into Poppy's elbow harder, her fingers digging deeper—she couldn't afford to show Pupkin an ounce of mercy.

Impossibly, Poppy's scream got higher and Louise felt it vibrating her teeth now. Poppy became deadweight, collapsing to the floor, her mouth yawning wide. Louise felt Pupkin slacken, slip—she almost had him—then something bit into her biceps so hard her left hand opened, and Ian had her by both arms, yanking her away, spinning her toward him.

"What the hell is wrong with you?" he shouted in her face. Poppy's screams turned into sobs and Ian lowered his voice. "You want to leave bruises? Christ Almighty."

He shoved Louise toward the door, putting himself between her and her own daughter. Poppy curled up on her green beanbag, Pupkin cradled against her chest, her entire body folded over him. Ian crouched beside her saying soothing things, one hand rubbing her back, focused entirely on his daughter the way a parent should, leaving Louise standing in the hall in her wet pants, an outsider in her own family.

Pupkin, forgotten by both of them, leered at Louise from the end of Poppy's arm.

"She's going to have bruises," Ian said. "But I think we can keep her home until they heal. We'll just say she got a stomach bug. The last thing we need is Mrs. Li calling protective services."

He stood in the middle of the living room floor, holding a cup of green tea in both hands. Louise sat on the couch in a clean pair of pants, elbows on her knees, hands pressed together, the hands that had left bruises on her daughter, the hands that had sawed off her brother's arm. She thought about Poppy's unblemished young skin with bruises ringed around her upper arm in the shape of her fingers and knew she was going to throw up if she opened her mouth.

Ian sat down beside her, putting her mug on the coffee table with a gentle clack.

"What happened in there?" he asked, sitting close, the way he used to. "I've never seen you like that before."

The second she opened her mouth, all the rotten things inside her would come spewing out all over the floor. She couldn't say a word. She thought she caught a briny whiff of her own urine. Her legs itched.

"You're just jet-lagged," he explained for her. "And I assume you really had to go to the bathroom."

Her stomach squeezed itself into a cramp, then relaxed. She took in a shuddering breath and Ian shifted toward her expectantly, thinking she was about to speak. She couldn't tell him. He'd never understand. Then she realized she didn't have to tell him. She sat up straight.

"Where did it come from?" she asked.

"No, you need to tell me what got into you," he said. "Right now I'm worried about leaving our daughter here because I'm not sure you're in control of yourself."

So this was the price she would have to pay: some kind of forced emotional intimacy to prove she could control herself, to prove she could be left alone with her own daughter. Losing control had given Ian too much power. She couldn't do that again.

"It's a gross puppet my mom had all her life," Louise made herself say, picking her way around the sinkholes in her story. "She used to be obsessed with it. I don't want it here."

"Clearly Poppy misses her grandmother and it reminds her of her," Ian said. "That's sweet."

"Poppy has never seen it before," Louise said.

Never? I'd told my mom I didn't want Pupkin around Poppy. I'd told my mom the other puppets were okay but not Pupkin. I'd protected her. Hadn't I?

"Sure, she has," Ian said. "On a FaceTime or a visit or something, because she had a very clear vision. Mom helped with the head and did the sewing, but Poppy dictated exactly how it should look."

"She can't have it."

"Of course she can," Ian said. "I don't want to sound critical, but you just dropped the entire concept of death on her and left me here to clean up the mess. It didn't get better when you told her you were coming back early, then changed your mind. The therapist helped, and after that Mom started doing craft projects with her. This is what she wanted to make, and it's been smooth sailing ever since. So yes, she can have her weird clown doll and you don't get to be angry about it."

I didn't protect Poppy.

"You're saying this is my fault?" Louise asked, eager to be angry at someone else. "That I'm a bad parent?"

"Jesus, Lou—" Ian started.

"I'm not a bad parent!" Louise said, voice rising. "This isn't my fault!"

"Louise!" Ian snapped. "Whatever associations you have with that puppet, you need to get over them because your daughter is attached to it. You need to be the adult here."

You need to be the adult.

That's why she had to take it away. Poppy would get over it. She'd form an attachment to something else. Kids were resilient. Louise had to find a way to get it off her daughter's arm and destroy it. Could she drug Poppy? Not drug—that didn't sound right—but maybe just give her some cough syrup? And have a replacement puppet waiting when she woke up? Or a puppy? A puppy would make her forget Pupkin.

First she needed to get Ian to leave so it was just her and Pupkin.

"I'm jet-lagged," she said as sincerely as she could. "And I really had to pee. I should have gone as soon as I came in the door but I was excited to see her."

She waited to see if Ian would bite.

"I don't know how I'd act if my parents died," he said, and she felt his hand on her back, rubbing her shoulder blades. She flinched.

"Sorry," she said to his hurt-puppy-dog look. "Some shelves fell on me while we were cleaning out the garage."

He took her right hand and rubbed his thumb over her knuckles.

"Losing both your parents, having to deal with your brother—you're processing a lot of trauma. But you can't take it out on Poppy, Lou."

She hated him calling her "Lou."

"I know," she said. "I'm sorry."

"No apology necessary," he said like a magnanimous king. "You know, I've been wondering what kind of attachment object Poppy would latch onto eventually, and at least this isn't some Disney princess that'll give her body-image issues."

Up until that moment she was worried she'd have to pretend to cry to give Ian the catharsis he needed, but she didn't. The tears came easy.

When would this be over?

It took all the self-control she had not to bite Ian's head off the tenth time he offered to stay the night.

"You're sure?" he said. "It might feel more stable for Poppy if we're both here when she wakes up."

"We both need sleep," Louise said. He'd been there all day and it was full dark now. "Trust me, please? I've been living in a hotel for three weeks. I just need to be in my own home."

"I ordered a bunch of soup and froze it," he said. "It's labeled in the freezer."

She hated soup.

"Thank you so much," she said and hoped that would be enough to get him down the stairs and out the front door.

To her alarm, Ian stepped closer.

"I wish you'd let someone take care of you," he said, voice soft and intimate. "Loss is hard."

Oh, God, she thought. *It's his sex voice.*

"I'll be okay," she said. "Thank you for being here."

"You're not alone," he said.

She felt like she was trapped, performing in one of Mark's awful plays.

"Thank you," she said, "for everything."

Ian went in for the kiss.

Oh God. Pupkin is in my house. Pupkin is on my daughter's arm and my ex is trying to make out with me.

Louise pressed her head to Ian's shoulder so he got a mouthful of hair. She went up on her toes, careful to keep her stomach away from his crotch, not letting her breasts touch his chest, and wrapped her arms tightly around him so he really felt like it was a sincere hug but also so she trapped his arms and kept his hands from roaming.

She let it last for a ten-count, then pulled away, relaxing back onto her heels because now this meant he would go.

"I felt that," he said, making serious eye contact. He took her chin in one hand. "Let's take it slow."

She tried not to scream. Her chest felt full of birds banging against her ribs. Thank God he immediately made his exit, bouncing down the stairs and out the front door. She went to the sofa and pressed a pillow over her face and screamed, muffling the sound, smelling her own hot breath.

After a while, she got control of herself and checked her phone: 10:35 p.m. She had to deal with Pupkin. She had to get rid of him. She had to get him out of her house.

She went to the kitchen and got a white plastic bin liner ready. It would rustle too loud if she took it into Poppy's room, so she spread it open on the counter. She'd sneak in, yank him off Poppy's arm, run in here, drop him in the liner, and even if Poppy woke up, once she had him she'd—what? How would she destroy him? She scanned her kitchen.

She didn't have a grill. She didn't have any lighter fluid. She checked underneath the sink but didn't see anything that might destroy an evil puppet. She stood in the middle of her kitchen, looking from the oven to the stovetop to the knife block to the food processor—and then she saw her Vitamix.

She'd bought it after reading an article about juicing, and she'd used it exactly three times. But she knew it could break anything down into shreds. She'd stuff Pupkin in the Vitamix, add water to soften him up, then switch it on high and grind him into a slurry.

She thought about this Pupkin. His head had seemed lighter and lumpier, and she got the feeling it was made of papier-mâché. His fabric had felt cheap. Her Vitamix would tear him to pieces.

She folded the bin liner and put it away. She didn't need it—he'd go right in the Vitamix. When it was done she'd flush him down the toilet. Then she'd throw out the plastic Vitamix pitcher and get a replacement. She didn't want anything in her house that had touched Pupkin. Except Poppy, of course.

She stood at the lip of the short hall to Poppy's room, took a deep breath, and crept slowly along the wall so the floor wouldn't creak. On her fifth step a board popped, loud as a gunshot. She froze. She listened for the rustling of sheets. Nothing moved behind Poppy's door. She took another step and the floor held, then the final step and she felt light-headed.

The door swung open, smooth on its hinges. Poppy lay in bed, face to the door, eyes closed, looking like a Pre-Raphaelite painting in the golden glow of her goose nightlight. Pupkin was still on her arm. He was sitting up, legs dangling, looking right at Louise, head cocked to one side, waiting for her.

Poppy's eyes were closed, flickering beneath their lids, her lips parted, her breathing deep and regular. Pupkin looked alert. She must have fallen asleep holding him that way.

Louise looked at Pupkin. Pupkin looked at Louise. He didn't move, but she had the crawling fluttery cockroach feeling in her stomach that if she reached for the light switch his head would track her movements.

All she had to do was take three steps and she'd have Pupkin off Poppy's arm before she even woke up—that was the face Poppy made in deep sleep; that was the sound she made when they could pick her up and carry her upstairs and put her in bed without waking her up. She'd have Pupkin off Poppy's arm and in the blender before Poppy could even open her eyes.

She'd lock the door behind her. She'd leave Poppy in here, even if she banged on it and screamed. Sometimes you had to be cruel in the short term, but that was the price you paid for being an adult. You made the hard decisions and hoped that one day your kids would understand how everything you did was for their own good.

She breathed in, gathered all her strength into the center of her stomach, then let her breath flow out and carry that strength into her arms, her legs, her spine. She took her weight off her left leg to step forward, and Pupkin moved. She stopped. He raised one tiny nubbin arm and lowered it, lifted it again and lowered it, waving to Louise, up and down, up and down, again and again, smiling his fixed sly smile.

Bye-bye, his arm said.

Bye-bye

Bye-bye

Poppy didn't move. She stayed asleep, face blank, breathing regular, eyes closed.

Pupkin waggled his head from side to side. He waved both arms. He thought this was a funny game.

All the strength flowed down Louise's legs and into the floor.

Slowly, carefully, she stepped backward out of the room. Quietly, she closed the door and let the latch slide home. Then she sat on the sofa and waited for her hands to stop shaking.

Chapter 30

A steady, piercing *beep beep beep beep beep*.

Louise hauled herself up out of deep sleep and looked around, panicked.

beep beep beep beep beep beep beep beep

The sunlight splashed the wall at the end of her bed like it always did. The angle of the light through the window said six a.m. like it always did. She'd never heard this sound before. Something smelled bad.

It took a moment.

Noise—fire alarm. Smell—smoke.

Fire.

Get Poppy.

She whipped her duvet back, already running, not feeling the cold floorboards beneath her feet. Poppy's bedroom door stood open. Poppy's bed lay empty. Louise didn't slow down, she passed the bathroom (empty) and entered the living room, where the burning smelled stronger and a gray haze hung in the air.

"Poppy!" she yelled.

She heard sizzling and the sink hissing and followed it into the kitchen, where a column of smoke rose from a frying pan on the stove, a blue flame burning underneath, the tap running, gray smoke choking the room, and Poppy standing on a chair at the counter with the cupboards open and ripped-up boxes everywhere and Pupkin on her arm. Louise stepped forward to turn off the burner, her heel slid in a slimy broken egg, and she went down hard on her tailbone, teeth clicking shut.

Poppy burst out laughing in Pupkin's high-pitched voice, which infuriated her. She felt cold, slimy egg yolk on the backs of her thighs. She pushed herself up and snapped off the burner. She turned on Poppy.

"What are you doing?" she barked.

She'd been stirring a bowl with her Pupkin hand, and Pupkin let the spoon drop and turned on her.

"The stove is not a toy," Louise said, feeling like her anger gave her the upper hand. "You do not play with it. At. All."

Spilled flour dotted the counter. Eggshells lay broken on the floor. Butter, milk, bread, almond butter, an avocado, everything Poppy had ever seen her mom pull out for breakfast lay smashed, smeared, spilled, and crushed from one end of the counter to the other.

"Breakfast time!" Pupkin shrilled, dancing from side to side.

Poppy wobbled and fell sideways off the chair. Louise grabbed her and set her on the kitchen floor.

"Pupkin want—" Pupkin began, thrusting himself up between them.

Louise rolled right over him.

"Give him to me right this minute, young lady, or you are in big, *big* trouble."

She didn't give Poppy time to decide. Instead, she reached out and plucked Pupkin off her arm.

That was easy, Louise thought.

Poppy bit her.

She didn't even see her head move. Poppy's mouth caught Louise's hand in midair and her teeth crunched into bone. Nothing hurt like this, the pain sharp and crushing at the same time, shooting up her arm like electricity. Louise's hand spasmed open and dropped Pupkin.

He hit the tile and Poppy released Louise and scooped him up off the floor. Louise felt a wave of relief as the pain stopped, a relief so profound she didn't follow Poppy when she ran out of the kitchen and into the living room, pulling Pupkin back onto her arm.

Louise had a lot to deal with: open the windows and get the smoke out, clean up the kitchen, get the hot pan off the stove. She had to deal with Poppy's bite and this mess she'd made, and she had to turn the fire alarm off before it woke up their neighbors, run cold water on her hand, get Pupkin out of her house—and she had to do it all right now.

She grabbed the handle of the frying pan, the livid bite mark giving a nauseating throb of agony when it got near the heat, and dropped it in the sink with the tap still running. It hissed like an angry snake. She jabbed the fire alarm with the end of the broom until there was blessed silence. She watched it for a moment, daring it to start again, but it clung silently to the ceiling.

She ran cold water on her throbbing hand and wrapped it in a dish towel, then headed for Poppy's room. Standing outside the closed door, she took a deep breath, then stepped into the bedroom, which smelled like strawberry stickers and little girl, ready to be a patient and understanding mom.

"Poppy—" she began, and hit a wall of noise.

"NOOOOOOOOOOOOOOOOOOOOOOOOOOOOOOOOOOOOOOO OOOOOOOOOOOOOOOOOOOOOOOOOOOOOOOOOOOOOOO OOOOOOOOOOOOOOOOOOOOOOOOOOOOOOOOOOOOOOO OOOOOOOOOOOOOOOOOOOOOOOOOOOOOOOOOOOOOOO OOOOOOOOOOOOOOOOOOOOOOOOOOOOOOOOOOOOOOO OOOOOOOOOOOOOOOOOOOOOOOOOOOOOOOOOOOOOOO!"

Poppy's wailing, screaming, howling screeching didn't leave room for Louise. Limbs flailing, words shattering into screams, Poppy transformed herself into a raging tornado, smashing her room. Louise tried to wrap her arms around her, pull her to her body, but Poppy kicked, her legs lashing out too fast to follow, mouth bright red, lungs pushing so much air Louise imagined her vocal cords shredding. Her left thigh ached where Poppy's heel hit her, and Louise decided all she could do was let her scream herself out.

She stepped outside and closed the door. She leaned against it and felt Poppy's screams vibrating through the wood. Her heart clenched and unclenched over and over behind her breastbone, a fist made of muscle. Her breath came high and shallow in her chest. She needed to calm down.

She cleaned up the kitchen. By the time she closed the last cabinet, the noise from Poppy's room had broken into sobs and single screamed "Nos!" By the time she wiped down the counters it was after ten a.m. and all she heard from Poppy's room was silence. She crept down the hall and cracked the door. Poppy lay on her stomach, asleep, face flushed and sweaty, hair sticking to her cheeks, sucking her thumb. Then Pupkin raised his head to look at her and Louise closed the door. She felt very, very alone.

She had kept Poppy safe for so long. She'd protected her from all the stuff between her and Ian, she'd protected her from Mark, she'd protected her from Pupkin and her mom, from the tension between her and Ian's mom; she'd spent years protecting her from all these adults, and this world, and all the meanness out there, but she couldn't protect her from this puppet.

She needed help.

"She almost burned the house down," she told Ian on the phone, speaking quietly and urgently from the front hall, huddled against the door, head turned toward the wood, as far from Poppy as she could get.

"Where is she now?" he asked.

"She's in bed with that puppet, sucking her thumb," Louise said.

"Well, I don't like to hear that," Ian said. "Listen, you've been gone for three weeks. She's dealing with the concept of death. It's going to be a tough adjustment."

"I don't want her to have that puppet."

"I think her behavior has more to do with the lack of stability in her life and less to do with a puppet she made with her grandmother."

Louise tried explain this to Ian in a way that would get him on her side.

"I know I seem crazy about the puppet," she said, "but Mark had that same one when he was a kid, and he formed a really unhealthy attachment to it. So it brings up a lot of stuff for me, because they're the same puppet. I think it would be less loaded if it was something else."

There was silence, which was good. It meant Ian was thinking.

"What'd Mark do with it?" he asked.

"Acting out," Louise said. "Picking fights. He kicked a hole in my parents' bedroom wall."

I cut off his arm.

"Nothing against the guy," Ian said. "But that sounds exactly like your brother, puppet or no puppet. Look, I understand your mom and dad passing is a lot to process, but you've got to be the parent here."

"Ian—" she started.

"You need her to *give* you the puppet if there's going to be any growth."

He wasn't listening. He'd closed the door. She spent the next five minutes agreeing with him just to get off the phone.

Clinging to some semblance of a normal routine, she knocked on Poppy's door and asked if she wanted lunch. She made her almond butter and jelly and carrot sticks with hummus and at least got her to sit at the kitchen table. Louise didn't say a thing about Pupkin. Poppy seemed exhausted and faded, her behavior subdued and mechanical as she hunched over her plate, chewing. She looked pale and her hair hung lank and sweaty around her face. Pupkin watched Louise over Poppy's shoulder, tracking everywhere she went as she loaded the dishwasher. With her back to Louise, there was no way Poppy could see where Louise was, but somehow Pupkin kept his eyes on her at all times.

After lunch she asked Poppy if she wanted to watch *PAW Patrol* on her iPad and set her and Pupkin up on the sofa. Then she went into her bedroom and closed the door to a crack.

She didn't want to make this call, but she needed to talk to someone who understood. She needed to talk to someone who knew what Pupkin could do. She needed to not feel alone in this.

Mark picked up on the eighth ring.

"What?" he asked in a thick voice. He'd probably just had his afternoon pain pill.

"Pupkin's here," she whispered.

There was a long silence over the line.

"No."

It was a simple declarative statement.

"He's here," she said, whispering urgent and fast, one eye on the cracked door. "Poppy made him with her grandmother—"

"Wait, wait, what?" Mark asked, and she heard him trying to follow what she was saying through the haze of his pill. "With *Mom*?"

"No, her other grandmother," Louise said. "Ian's mom. She made a puppet and it's Pupkin and now she won't take it off. She almost set the house on fire."

The pause stretched out so long she thought he'd hung up, but when he spoke there was no argument, no alternate explanation, no demand for proof. She and Mark had been through this together. He knew.

"You have to get rid of it," he said.

"You never told her about Pupkin?" she asked.

"No," he said, and he sounded clearer, more focused now. "I've only met Poppy, like, four times. Why would I tell her about Pupkin?"

Louise listened. *PAW Patrol* sounds played steadily in the other room. "What do I do?" she asked.

It was the first time she'd ever said that to her brother.

"I have to . . ." Mark wavered, stopped, tried again. "I have to think. I need to process this. Listen, don't do anything, okay? I'll call you back."

"Okay," Louise said, and for once she trusted him.

"Louise," Mark said. "Don't . . . don't try to cut it off?"

She saw the image in her head, one foot on Poppy's thin arm, pinning it to the kitchen floor, the good knife in her hand. A wave of nausea made her scalp flush with sweat.

"Never."

"Yeah, well," Mark said. "Never say never. I'll call you back."

For the next few hours she treated Poppy like a ticking bomb. She listened to Poppy whisper to Pupkin. She listened to Pupkin whisper back. She tried hard not to make eye contact with Pupkin. She finally convinced Poppy to lie on her bed for naptime.

Before she left the room, she knelt beside them, Poppy's eyes already sagging closed, and whispered in Pupkin's ear.

"I killed you twice," she hissed, the words barely clearing her lips. "I'll do it again."

She sat on the couch, drinking black tea and trying to stay awake. She couldn't let herself fall asleep. If she did, Poppy might actually set the house on fire. She might find the hammer. She didn't think Poppy would hurt her, but Pupkin would.

Louise sipped her cooling tea. It tasted bitter. She tried to read, but she couldn't concentrate. She kept checking the time. Why wasn't Mark calling back? Had he popped another pain pill? Cracked open a couple of beers? Decided it was all too much and gone back to sleep?

She thumbed through her phone, went through Slack, checked her email, not really paying attention, listening for the slightest sound from behind Poppy's cracked bedroom door.

She must have dozed because her head jerked and snapped forward and now she was hearing low voices from the kitchen. Poppy's bedroom door stood open. Louise got up fast, her back cracking, the stitches in her scalp pulling tight. She was in the kitchen before her brain even slipped into gear. Poppy sat on the floor, her back to the door, and Louise stepped around her to see what she was doing.

"Poppy—" she started.

". . . playPLAYplayPLAYplay . . ." Pupkin singsonged with Poppy's mouth.

Pupkin held the good kitchen knife between his nubbin arms, gouging the point down the inside of Poppy's left forearm. She didn't have the strength to press hard, but she'd raked deep scratches from her wrist to her elbow that oozed sluggish beads of blood. The knife snagged her soft skin, making a fleshy scratching sound in the quiet kitchen. A small drop of blood plopped onto the floor.

"It doesn't hurt," Poppy said in her own voice, gazing at her bloody arm in wonder. Then she looked up at Louise. "It doesn't hurt at all."

Louise moved so fast the knife came out of Pupkin's hands with no trouble, and she threw it, clattering, into the sink. Neither Pupkin nor Poppy resisted when she ran them to the bathroom and sat them on the toilet seat. Pupkin had made his point. He wasn't strong enough to hurt Louise, but he could hurt Poppy.

He watched her clean Poppy's arm and examine the cuts. She looked at the bruises ringing Poppy's biceps. If she took her to the emergency room, there'd be police and social workers and questions, and if she told Ian he'd think she'd done it herself and he'd take Poppy away, so she put disinfectant on the cuts and Poppy didn't even flinch like she normally did. She just stared at her arm like it belonged to somebody else as Louise bandaged the worst scratches.

She carried Poppy back to bed and tried to climb in with her.

"No!" Pupkin screeched.

Louise backed away and sat on the floor, leaning against the door.

What am I doing? I'm fighting an evil puppet for my daughter's life. This is not normal.

Then she thought:

This is my family's fault. Mom made Pupkin. She passed her sickness on to Mark, and now she's passed it on to my daughter. Through me. I did this. She thought about all the other mothers she'd read about who the websites and papers called "crazy." *Maybe they'd only been trying to protect their children, too.*

The pile of covers stirred and Pupkin's head rose above them, grinning at Louise.

What was Pupkin? What did it want from her?

Why not ask?

It took an incredible effort of will for Louise to make herself say the first word. It felt like leaving the land of sanity and entering someplace else.

we're going to tickytoo woods

"Who are you?" she whispered.

Pupkin cocked his head.

"What do you want?" Louise asked.

His grin seemed to get bigger. The way it caught the shadows made his cheeks seem to stretch.

"What do you *want*?" she whispered, barely audible.

She jumped a little when he actually answered.

"Where Nancy?" his squeaky voice said.

It must have come from Poppy. Who was asleep. It sounded high-pitched but thicker, air pushed through vocal cords clotted with phlegm, past sleeping lips.

"Nancy's gone," Louise made herself say.

"Where?" Pupkin asked, leaning forward.

"She's gone away forever," Louise said, feeling light-headed.

"No," Pupkin squeaked, but his voice sounded rougher this time, more animated.

"She died," Louise said, and she wanted to add *You killed her*, but instead she waited to see how he would react.

"Pupkin want Nancy," he said.

"Do you know what 'die' means?" Louise asked.

"No die," Pupkin said. "Pupkin always Pupkin."

"Everyone dies," Louise said.

"No," Pupkin stated. "Nancy hiding and seeking."

Louise tried to think of how to explain death to a puppet.

"Nancy got hurt very—"

Pupkin cut her off.

"Nancy promise!" he hissed. "Never alone. Pupkin good boy, never alone." Pupkin shivered and cooed to himself. He began to stroke himself with his nubbins. "Pupkin good."

"You are good," Louise said. "But you need to go away now."

Pupkin stopped rubbing himself and cocked his head at her. Then he began to giggle.

"Ke ke ke ke ke ke ke . . ." he said and started rubbing his hands over his belly again. "Pupkin home."

One of his nubbins reached up and stroked the side of his face.

"Ke ke ke ke ke ke ke . . ."

Then he slowly sank into the blankets, still watching Louise, stroking one nub along the side of his face, soothing himself. Louise stood up, never taking her eyes off Pupkin, and left the room. In the front hall she called Mark.

He picked up on the first ring.

"I was just about to call you," he said in a rush, and his voice sounded clearer now, more decisive. "I know what to do."

"He wants to know where Mom is," she said. "He thinks she's playing hide-and-seek."

"He's talking," Mark said. "That's good. Write down anything he says. It might be important."

"I can't have him on Poppy's arm for another minute," she hissed. "He cut her, Mark. He got a knife and cut her, and if I try to take him off he'll do it again."

"Come home," Mark said.

It threw her.

"What?"

"You need to come home," Mark said. "We can only deal with him here."

"No," Louise said, shaking her head from side to side even though he couldn't see her. This was a bad idea. She thought about the house, the attic, Spider, the squirrels, the Mark and Louise dolls. She wasn't going near any of them ever again. "Oh, no. I'm not walking into that trap."

"We're out of our depth," Mark said. "So we need an expert. That's what I was going to tell you. I called Mercy."

This conversation kept taking turns Louise couldn't follow.

"What?" she asked again. "Mark, this is my daughter. Mercy sells real estate. Be serious."

"I am being serious," he said. "I don't know anything about talking puppets or possession or ghosts or hauntings, but Aunt Gail? This is where she lives. And family are the people who can't say no. You need to come home."

Chapter 31

The fun started at Security.

"She needs to take her doll off her arm," the TSA guy mono-toned.

"No," Pupkin shrieked. "No! No! No!"

"Hang on, Poppy, it's okay," Louise said sweetly, then lowered her voice to that special frequency only other adults could hear. "Is there anything you can do?"

The TSA agent gave her a look that said *Pampered mothers, spoiled kids.*

"She needs to remove her doll to go through the scanner," he repeated.

"If you could just help me out," Louise pleaded. "She's having a hard day."

"Ma'am, are you going to be a problem for me?"

"What about a pat-down?" she asked.

"No!" Pupkin shrieked. "Pupkin stay! Pupkin stay!"

People looked over to see what this horrible mother was doing to her little girl. Louise felt them noticing the bandages up and down Poppy's left arm, the scratches and bruises on Louise's face, the bite mark on the back of her hand.

"If you could let her keep it on, you'd be doing more for us than you'd ever know," Louise said.

"I'm going to have to ask you to step out of line," the TSA agent said.

What would Mark do?

Inspiration hit Louise.

He'd lie.

"Please," she said, dropping her voice to a whisper. "Her father just passed and he made that for her. We're on our way to his funeral."

The TSA agent adjusted himself in his seat. He looked down again at Louise's ID.

"Can I get a female assist on five?" he said without looking up.

The fun continued on the plane. Poppy kicked the seat in front of them nonstop. She grabbed the flight attendant's skirt when she walked by, causing her to stumble and hurl the tray of water she was carrying down the aisle. Pupkin screamed, "Kakawewe!" at random moments. After the third time, Louise saw people hitting their call buttons and gesturing to the flight attendants, pointing down the aisle toward her and Poppy.

Eventually, the chief flight attendant crouched at the end of the row and whispered through her big smile, "The pilot will land in Salt Lake City and have you and your daughter removed if you cannot get her to behave."

"I'm so sorry," Louise said. "I'm really sorry."

Her nerves fizzed with shame. She turned to Poppy.

"You're embarrassing me!" she snapped before she could think.

She sounded just like her mother.

"Kakawewe!" Pupkin screeched.

Louise felt out of options. Then she realized that if she sounded like her mother, she might as well go all in.

"Pupkin," she said, making eye contact with the puppet, not caring what the flight attendant thought. "If you don't stop, they're going to make us get off the plane and we won't go back to Charleston, and you won't get to see Nancy."

Pupkin stopped and cocked his head at her.

"Nancy?" Poppy asked in Pupkin's voice.

"Don't you miss her?" Louise said. "If you aren't a good boy, you won't get to see her again."

"Nancy . . ." Pupkin cooed.

He behaved for the rest of the flight. Louise hated it. This was the library books being sad all over again, the promise of a dog they'd never get, telling Mark to stay for Pizza Chinese to send off their parents. Mothering, manipulating—sometimes there wasn't a difference. She'd learned that from her mom.

After enduring dirty looks from everyone on the plane, after wrestling her and Poppy's luggage down from the overhead compartment by herself, after enduring a really painful kick in the left shin from Poppy while exiting the aircraft, Louise texted Mark.

WERE HERE

He'd promised to pick them up, but she'd give him five minutes before seeing if there were any rentals. To her surprise her phone lit up almost immediately:

B RT THER

She led Poppy out the automatic doors and into the warm Charleston afternoon, fully expecting to wait at least twenty minutes, but Mark's giant red pickup cruised to a stop in front of them before she'd even put down her bag. She reached up and opened the passenger-side door, but Mark was already out of the cab.

"Hey," he said, bustling around the hood, his missing right arm held away from his body like a penguin wing. "A couple of YouTube videos and I'm driving like . . ."

He froze, staring at Pupkin, who stared back. Poppy's head hung down, her lank hair hiding her face.

Mark let out a long, low "Jesus . . ."

Louise picked up her rolling bag and tried to lift it into the bed of Mark's truck. They had to keep moving.

"Will it be okay back here?" she asked, struggling to get it over the side of his truck.

Pupkin began to sing.

"With a chop-chop here, and a chop-chop there," Pupkin sang, "here a chop, there a chop, everywhere a chop-chop!"

"Louise," Mark said in a dull voice, on the edge of panic.

"Here a chop," Pupkin sang, "there a chop, everywhere a Marky chop-chop."

"Pupkin!" Louise snapped. He surprised her by giving her his attention. "Zip it or no Nancy."

Pupkin stopped.

"Help me," she commanded Mark in the same tone, and he tore his eyes away from Pupkin.

"Yeah, sure," he said, coming around the truck from the other direction, not wanting to get anywhere close to Pupkin.

Inside the truck, away from staring strangers, Louise felt her shoulders unclench. She sat in the middle, between Poppy and Mark, because she didn't want Pupkin anywhere close to the steering wheel. She felt intense guilt not only for having Poppy ride in the front, but also for not having a car seat. She added it to the list of her failures as a mother. Of course, the way Mark was driving didn't help.

"You don't need a special license or something?" she asked.

Poppy began to drum her feet against the glove compartment.

"It's not that different from driving with both arms," Mark said, drifting toward the shoulder. She heard their tires roar over loose gravel. Mark overcorrected in the other direction. "You can get this ball on your steering wheel that helps with turns, but I'm doing great."

He shifted lanes too quickly and Louise's heart lurched. Instinctively she put one arm over Poppy.

"Have you talked to Aunt Gail?" she asked, not wanting to spell it out in front of Pupkin. Then, because she couldn't help herself: "Slow down."

"Don't back-seat drive," Mark said as Poppy began banging her heels harder against the glove compartment. "Can you tell her to stop that?"

Instead of taking her feet off the glove compartment, Poppy thrust Pupkin across Louise and hissed in Mark's face.

"That is not how we behave!" Louise snapped. "Do you want to see Nancy or not?"

Pupkin retreated.

"That works?" Mark marveled.

"Yeah, but, you know . . ." Louise shrugged. You know, how long could she keep manipulating Pupkin this way? "Hey, you need to be in the right-hand lane."

The highway split but Mark stayed on the left, headed downtown instead of veering right toward Mount Pleasant.

"I need to tell you something," Mark said. "They called me because they knew you were in the air."

"Who?" Louise asked, then gritted her teeth as Poppy began to kick the underside of the glove compartment again. "Stop it *now.*"

"Where Nancy?" Pupkin demanded.

"Aunt Honey is in the hospital," Mark said.

Everything looked too real all of a sudden.

I can't lose another one, Louise thought.

"Nancy! Nancy! Nancy!" Pupkin demanded in time with Poppy's kicks.

"What happened?" Louise asked, ignoring Poppy. "Is she okay?"

"Something about her blood oxygen. Mercy called. She said we should go right there."

Not so soon, Louise thought. *I can't handle another one so soon.*

But she didn't have a choice. She would have to handle whatever happened. There was no such thing as too much. There was just more and more, and her limits didn't matter. Life didn't care. She could only hang on.

"Where Nancy? Where Nancy? Where Nancy?" Pupkin chanted.

Louise turned to Pupkin.

"We have to go to the hospital to see Aunt Honey," she said. "Then we'll go see Nancy."

"Nancy!" Pupkin shouted.

"Keep misbehaving and you won't see her at all," Louise said.

Pupkin retreated to the door, keeping his eyes on Louise.

"Mercy said it wasn't too serious," Mark said, "but people say that all the time when someone goes in the hospital, and the next thing you know they're in the morgue."

He swerved too fast to merge onto the Crosstown and Louise heard her suitcase slide across the truck bed behind them and thump into the side. Her skeleton lurched inside her skin.

She couldn't help herself.

"Please don't kill us," she said.

Mark almost ran a red light and had to slam on his brakes at the last second. He almost rear-ended a parked car on Rutledge when he reached for his turn signal with a right arm that wasn't there. He almost sideswiped the little blue Honda beside them when he swung too wide into their parking space. But he didn't kill them.

The hospital was the first place Louise felt like people weren't staring at Poppy's bandaged arm, the stitches in her scalp, or Mark's compression bandage over his stump. When they got to the lobby of Rutledge Tower, Louise had a horrible thought: Aunt Honey, the IVs, the tubes, Pupkin wanting to play. She turned to Mark.

"I don't think she should come up."

"I'm not being alone with her or . . . that thing," Mark said quietly, his eyes pleading.

It didn't matter to Louise. She remembered how ruthless her mom could be when it came to her and Mark. She channeled some of that now.

"No choice," she said. "I can't bring her in."

Sweat beaded on Mark's forehead. All of a sudden, she could smell his BO.

"Make it fast," he said.

Louise knelt in front of Poppy. She didn't like how lifeless and grimy her daughter looked under the bright hospital lighting. She lifted her chin to make eye contact, but Poppy jerked her head away. Louise had to settle for saying, "Be good and listen to your uncle," to the top of her head.

Then she went up.

She got off the elevator on twelve and went to the nurse's station.

"I'm here to see Mrs. Cannon," she said.

"She's in room 1217, but I think she's asleep," the nurse said. "Her daughter's in the family waiting room at the end of the hall if you want to see her."

Louise walked down the hall and into the waiting room, where Aunt Gail sat by herself, reading her Bible.

"Aunt Gail?" Louise asked, picking her way through the chairs. "How is she?"

Aunt Gail stood and gave Louise a quick, hard hug and stepped back. She wore a white-and-gold sweater that had a cartoon of a baby angel hugging itself on the front with the word *Joy!* written underneath.

"Stable," Aunt Gail said. "She was having a hard time breathing yesterday so I went over and stayed the night. She wasn't any better this morning, so the doctor said bring her in. They've put her on the oxygen. Her numbers are back up, and they say that's good, but now we're waiting for someone to come listen to her lungs."

"When do they think she'll get out?" Louise asked.

"Today, they hope," Aunt Gail said and sat down.

Louise sat beside her. She didn't know how to start. They sat in silence for almost a full minute. Finally, Louise felt like she had no choice.

"Are you doing okay?" she asked.

"God keeps me strong," Aunt Gail said.

Louise wished something kept her strong, because whether it was God or good genes or magic water from the river Jordan, Aunt Gail never looked tired. She never got sick. She never complained about feeling under the weather. All Louise felt was under the weather.

"How is that precious little girl?" Aunt Gail asked.

"That's sort of why we came," Louise said, deciding this was her chance.

"She's here?" Aunt Gail asked.

"Downstairs with Mark," Louise said.

"You both flew all this way for my mother?" Aunt Gail asked. "I told Mercy not to make a fuss."

"We're here for Aunt Honey," Louise said. "But we came for, sort of, well . . . I don't know how to put this, but I wanted to speak to you."

Aunt Gail looked understanding.

"It's never too late to have that child baptized," she said. "I can arrange it tomorrow."

Louise took a breath and jumped in.

"Mercy told us that a while back you helped her with a couple of properties she was selling that had some . . . funny stuff going on?"

Aunt Gail's expression didn't change.

"She said there were two houses," Louise struggled forward. "She said they had problems, and you, you know, kind of, prayed for them?"

"They were infested by demonic forces and I blasted them back to Hell." Aunt Gail nodded. "Then she sold them to a couple of Yankees."

Louise felt relieved to be on firmer ground.

"Right," she said. "Well, I don't know how to say this, but we feel like—and Mercy thinks this, too—that our parents' house is . . . the same way, so we wanted to know if you'd do whatever you did for those houses to our house."

"Ask and you shall receive," Aunt Gail said. "Knock and the door will open. What is the nature of the demon you've encountered?"

"We're not even exactly sure it is a, um, demon," Louise said. It was hard saying any of this out loud. "I mean, I've just been kind of worried, and maybe I shouldn't be bothering you . . ."

Aunt Gail laid one hand on Louise's arm.

"Sweetheart," she said, "I once battled a warlock in Summerville. There is nothing you can say that will shock me."

Louise took a breath. She thought about her mother. She did it for Poppy.

"My parents' house is haunted," she said. "That Pupkin puppet Mom always had with her tried to kill me. That little clown puppet she really liked? Do you remember it?"

"No," Aunt Gail said.

"It's got a white face with black eyes and wears a pointy red hood?"

Louise tried. "We get the feeling it's the source of all this because before they were in the accident my mom and dad locked it in the attic, and maybe that's why she took Dad to the hospital in the middle of the night, because it attacked him."

A family with two small children around Poppy's age walked in the door and sat on the other side of the room. Louise wondered if they should go someplace else for privacy, but Aunt Gail just sat there, waiting for her to continue.

"Also, I got attacked by Mark's imaginary dog from when he was six," Louise said. "And some taxidermied squirrels. The key points are that the house is haunted, there's a puppet that seems to be the focus of everything, and I actually"—she lowered her voice—"I actually severed . . . um, cut off Mark's arm to get that puppet off him."

She studied Aunt Gail's eyes for a reaction. Nothing. She struggled forward.

"I haven't told anyone that. He asked me to do it because he was trying to kill me, kind of, he was attacking me with a hammer, but it was really the puppet. And now the puppet is on Poppy's arm and she's just a little girl and it's hurting her and it's making her hurt herself and I don't know what to do, Aunt Gail, and now Aunt Honey's in the hospital, and my parents are gone, and I don't understand what happened, or why they're dead, and I don't know how much more of this I can take. I think I've got a limit and I think I'm getting real close to it and I'm scared of what's going to happen when I reach it because what's going to happen to Poppy and I can't do this alone anymore, I need help, please, I need someone to help me."

Louise couldn't get enough air. Her nose was dripping. She reached up to wipe it and realized her face was wet. She pulled her bag into her lap, blindly searching for a Kleenex.

A hand touched her chin and raised her face. Aunt Gail held a wad of Kleenex she'd magically produced and with the expert touch of a mother, she wiped Louise's tears away. Then she held the Kleenex over Louise's nose and said, "Blow."

Embarrassed to be treated like a child in public, Louise blew. Aunt Gail wadded up the Kleenex and made it disappear, she brushed the hair off Louise's forehead, then she sat back and the two of them looked at each other.

"I'm sorry," Louise mumbled.

"Don't be," Aunt Gail said. "You've lost your mother and father and been targeted by the forces of darkness."

"That's how it feels," Louise said.

"That's how it is," Aunt Gail said. "Let's go see Mama. She's going to be sad that sweet little child couldn't come up, but maybe that'll get her out of here faster. After that, we'll call my girls and see about blasting the Devil out of your parents' house and sending that little haunted puppet straight back to Hell."

Chapter 32

Aunt Gail had everyone assemble on Constance's back deck. Poppy and Pupkin were banished to the yard, where Brody kept them distracted while Aunt Gail had Louise retell her story, step-by-step, and took notes. Mark expanded when he felt like Louise's narrative needed more color.

When they finished, there was silence. A leaf blower started up somewhere on the next block. Louise felt drained. It had been hard to talk about what she'd done to Mark's arm, especially in front of Mark. When she'd gotten to that part of the story, everyone stopped fidgeting and Mark stared down at his lap. Even Aunt Gail stopped taking notes. Now, in the quiet at the end, Aunt Gail closed her eyes and her lips moved soundlessly as she prayed.

"Well," Constance said in the long silence, "I don't know about anyone else, but I need a drink."

Loudly, she pushed back her wrought-iron patio chair and went inside. Her departure woke everyone up. They stirred in their chairs, blinking, taking looks at each other, trying not to stare at Mark's arm. Aunt Gail finished praying and opened her eyes.

"I'm not surprised that your home is infested with demonic forces," she said. "Your mother's puppet ministry trivialized the church. When you move off the path of righteousness you risk being co-opted by the Enemy."

"Mama," Mercy said, "no one likes an 'I told you so.'"

"Hey," Brody said to Louise, trotting up to the rail of the deck, slightly breathless. "She keeps asking about Aunt Nancy. What do I tell her?"

Louise knew she'd have to deal with this eventually, but right now she didn't know any other way to handle Pupkin.

"Tell him," she said, then corrected herself. "Tell her . . . tell *them* that we're going to see Nancy at the house tonight."

Brody almost said something, then shrugged.

"Okay," he said, and trotted back over to where Poppy sat in the grass.

They all watched as Pupkin's head tracked Brody, then cocked to one side as he listened. Louise didn't like the way Poppy's head lolled. She'd gotten a good look at Poppy's face when they arrived, and her eyes had been glassy, her mouth slack, her cheeks gray. She didn't like the way the only part of Poppy that seemed to be alive anymore was Pupkin.

"Cursed dolls are prone to violence and malevolence," Aunt Gail said. "It's their nature. My friend Barb collects them off eBay."

"There are cursed puppets on eBay?" Louise asked, wondering if this was something she was already supposed to know.

"Dolls," Aunt Gail corrected. "I'm not sure if puppets and dolls are the same, theologically speaking, but eBay is rife with them. Barb's calling is to keep them out of innocent hands. On long weekends and federal holidays we spiritually deactivate them."

The sliding door opened and Constance came out with a bottle of wine and a stack of plastic cups.

"Who needs some?" she asked.

"No one," Aunt Gail said. "We need our wits about us if we're blasting these demons back to Hell this afternoon."

Constance looked disappointed.

"And the puppet?" Louise asked. "We're getting it off Poppy's arm?"

Aunt Gail nodded.

"Constance and Mercy assisted me with the other two infested homes," she said. "We'll need everyone there, standing firm, strong in their faith. What denomination are you?"

This last was directed at Louise, who suddenly felt like she'd come home from college and was being asked whether she had a boyfriend.

"I don't really go to church," she said. "Is that a problem?"

Aunt Gail sighed.

"Do you agree that there are forces greater than this world and we are helpless in the face of them?" she asked.

"I, um . . ." Louise said. "I don't know."

"Jesus, Lulu," Mark said, turning to her. "You cut off my arm and you don't know?"

"All right, fine, yes," Louise said.

"Then cling to that and your love for your daughter and we may pass through this fire unscathed," Aunt Gail said.

"I'm an atheist," Mark said.

"Pish," Aunt Gail said, dismissing him. "You're a Presbyterian, just like your parents."

Louise saw Constance suddenly sit up straight, both hands on the arms of her patio chair, eyes on something out in the yard. She turned and saw Brody hunched over on himself, bent double in the middle of the grass. In front of him stood Poppy, head down, hair hanging over her face. Pupkin reared up on the end of her arm and tried to punch Brody in the nuts again.

"Mercy," Aunt Gail said. "Clean out the back seat of the Sedona.

Mark? You're going to follow in your truck. We must handle the curse before we can confront the house. We need to go to Dorchester. We need to see Barb."

"I want Nancy! Nancy! *Nancy!*" Poppy shrieked inside the minivan.

Or Pupkin shrieked. They were getting mixed up in Louise's mind, and that scared her.

She had promised they'd see Nancy later in order to get Pupkin into the car, but halfway through the forty-five-minute drive to Dorchester, he'd had a meltdown, or Poppy had had a meltdown, or both of them had had a meltdown, and she'd had to sit Poppy in her lap and hold her arms while Constance held her legs. Even then, Pupkin thrashed and kicked and occasionally got an arm free and hit Constance in the head. Louise worried what the drivers around them would think, but Mercy seemed to read her mind.

"It's okay, y'all," she reassured them from the driver's seat. "Tinted windows."

Louise smelled the sour stink of Poppy's sweaty hair. She felt Poppy's muscles ceaselessly twisting underneath her skin like snakes. She wanted to look Poppy in the eyes and see some spark of her daughter. She wanted to hear her voice, not Pupkin's voice, come out of her mouth. She needed a conversation about all the different kinds of bears, or sad library books, or even *PAW Patrol*. Poppy had worn Pupkin days longer than Mark had and she was terrified they were too late.

By the time Mercy finally pulled into the wide, flat streets of Dorchester Village Mobile Home Park, Constance and Louise were covered in bruises, but Poppy seemed to have exhausted herself and sat limp in Louise's lap, leaning with the minivan as it took the precise ninety-degree turns of the treeless roads, moving slow, Aunt Gail navigating.

"That's it," she said, pointing across Mercy. "The one with the fun yard."

They pulled up in front of a gray trailer and Louise thought, *Of course.*

Stone deer stood behind its chain-link fence, and behind them sat laughing concrete leprechauns, a St. Francis of Assisi with a bluebird on one finger, a concrete wishing well with the word *Hope* painted on its side, two Jesuses praying in the garden of Gethsemane, a flock of pink flamingos still wearing Santa hats and wreaths around their necks, a three-foot-tall Sasquatch caught in midstride, looking over one shoulder, a little girl bending to smell the flowers and showing her concrete underpants, an orchard of multicolored pinwheels spinning madly in the breeze, three reflecting orbs on pedestals, half a dozen concrete chipmunks and painted snails, and a birdbath with a pedestal made of raccoons standing on each other's shoulders.

"Come on, y'all," Aunt Gail said, getting out. "Make haste."

Cautiously, Constance let go of Poppy's legs as Mercy hit the auto-open button and the door slid back. They got out, Louise holding Poppy, who felt like deadweight. Together, the three cousins followed Aunt Gail up the path between the lawn sculptures and waited while she knocked on the rattling trailer door.

It flew open to reveal Barb.

"Hey, y'all!" she shouted, pulling Aunt Gail violently into her chest.

Barb filled the door. She was Asian, wearing a pink tank top and tie-dyed shorts, and she waved to them with both hands.

"Gail told me y'all were coming!" she cheered. "I'm so excited to meet you!"

Before she could react, Louise found herself and Poppy enveloped in a hug that felt like an airbag going off in her face.

"The mama!" Barb said, shaking them hard.

Then she shoved Louise away and practically skipped to Mark.

"I like a big comfy man!" she enthused, throwing her arms around him and wriggling from side to side. "Look at your flipper!"

Mark started to hug her back, but she pushed him away and ran back to Louise, bending over to face Poppy.

"Look at this adorable doughnut!" she proclaimed to everyone. Then she poked Pupkin with one finger. "We'll talk to you later, mister."

She rose to her full height and said, "We're going to have a busy afternoon, y'all, and I am just full of praise and the Spirit."

Louise noticed that Barb dyed her bangs purple.

"Barb is an expert on cursed dolls," Aunt Gail explained.

"Don't worry!" Barb laughed, seeing Louise's expression. "Dolls and puppets come under the same department as far as the Lord is concerned. I do dolls, I do puppets, I once even did a blow-up s-e-x doll. Now, that one was wild, let me tell you. Come on inside and let's pray together."

She herded them into her trailer, but as Louise put her foot on its front step, Barb dropped a mighty paw onto her shoulder.

"Mama needs to stay out here with baby so we can have a few minutes to compare notes."

"You're not discussing anything without me," Louise said.

"Then Brother can hold on to her!" Barb decided.

Mark lifted his stump and shrugged.

"I've got her," Mercy said.

She took the limp pile of Poppy from Louise's arms, and everyone else filed into Barb's trailer and Barb closed the door.

Louise felt like they'd burrowed into an enormous mountain of dolls. Shelf after shelf of them, up the walls, reaching the ceiling, a wall of tiny bonnets and straw hats and puckered red lips and shiny porcelain faces and clown faces and baby-doll faces, all staring straight ahead with empty, glass eyes. They were lined up along the base of the wall. They were piled up in corners. Fox News soundlessly played on the TV, its light flickering over old country dolls with dried-apple faces, sock monkeys, one-eyed teddy bears, grimy old dolls and crisp new dolls, and charred, burned, and scarred dolls. Their bodies absorbed all the sound, and they completely surrounded the handful of humans in the middle.

Barb tiptoed nimbly between everyone, twisting like a ballerina, picking her way across the room, plucking an enormous thermal cup from beside an armchair and taking a long pull on its gnawed flexistraw.

"I know what you're thinking," she said. "I've got a storage unit where I keep the cursed ones. I'm not going to sleep in a house surrounded by cursed dolls. That's crazy! Now, come on! Huddle up!"

She reached out and gathered them into a loose circle, throwing her arms over their shoulders and pulling them in close. Louise could smell her perfume, something lush, like honeysuckle.

"Listen, listen, listen," Barb said. "Y'all are scared to bits, I get'cha, but you can relax because Big Barb is here." She faced Louise. Her breath smelled like passion fruit. "You're a very lucky lady. Cursed dolls are easy. Same with puppets. They're not really possessed, right? Demons can't possess inanimate objects, but what they do is put a curse on 'em to annoy the heck out of you."

Louise thought she needed to convey to Barb that this required a certain level of seriousness.

"My brother lost his arm," Louise said.

"Right," Barb said. "And that sucks, but to a demon, an arm is nothing. They eat arms for breakfast. Sorry, big boy, but it's the truth. You and Flipperman and your little one have been targeted by a demon, see, and that's the bad news. The good news is that the puppet on your daughter's arm, it's a curse. And Barb? She eats curses for breakfast. I break the curse, find out which demon laid it, then we troop over to Mount Pleasant and Sister Gail blasts that demon out of your home. Sound good?"

"Amen," Aunt Gail said.

"Amen," said Barb. "We're going to take this curse and pop it like a pimple. It'll be easy-peasy, slick and greasy."

Louise squeezed her eyes shut. She had been prepared for anything, but she was not prepared for Barb.

"This is my daughter," Louise said, opening her eyes, fixing them on Barb, trying to convey the seriousness of the situation. "I don't think this is exciting. This thing cut her. It almost set my house on fire! It's not a joke to me!"

She hadn't planned on getting so worked up.

"Barb has high spirits," Aunt Gail said. "But there is no one I trust more with the fate of my immortal soul."

Barb and Louise held each other's eyes for a long moment. Finally, Louise nodded.

"All right," she said.

Barb filled the living room with two big meaty slaps of her hands, making Louise jump.

"Then let's rock and roll!" she said. "But first, I've got a bladder full of passion fruit lemonade that needs a download, and I warn y'all, the walls in here are real thin. You might want to go outside."

Chapter 33

They pushed the coffee table up against one wall and turned off the TV, and Barb cut open the plastic wrap around a pack of water bottles and dropped them on the counter. Everything in her kitchen rattled with the impact.

"One for everyone," she said. "Once we get started you're stuck in your chair and this is thirsty work."

Barb gave up her recliner for Aunt Gail, sat Constance on the couch, and brought in two dining room chairs for Mark and Louise. She took up the second-best recliner, just to Louise's right. With all of them crowded into the living room with the dolls, the trailer felt airless. Louise tucked her water bottle behind the legs of her chair.

"Tell your sister to bring Poppy in," Aunt Gail told Constance.

Constance got up and opened the front door.

"Mercy, come on," she called.

"Want some gum, big boy?" Barb asked, holding out a pack of Nicorette to Mark.

"I'm good," he said.

She extended the pack to Louise.

"No, thank you," Louise said.

"Me neither," Barb said, popping two pieces in her mouth. "But it beats cancer."

Pupkin poked his head into the trailer, examining each of them, then he entered, followed by Poppy. She looked thin and tired and from behind the hair hanging over her face her breathing sounded loud, wet, and raspy. Louise wanted to pick her up, carry her away from all this, take her temperature, give her a bath.

Instead, she forced herself to stay in her chair. These women had to know what they were doing, because she didn't have any other options.

"Sit on the sofa by your sister," Aunt Gail instructed Mercy, and Louise wondered where Poppy was going to sit.

"Mama," Barb said, "put the demoniac in the center of the circle."

Louise realized Barb was talking to her and she bristled. She did not like her daughter being called something that sounded like a cross between *demon* and *maniac*, but she surrendered to Barb, put her arm around Poppy's bony shoulders, and ushered her into the center of the circle.

"This is not a séance," Aunt Gail said, sitting up straight. "I don't truckle with the occult. This is a divine circle of light, a spiritual stronghold built on the faith of believers. Be strong, and let me guide you. There is a demonic presence in this room, caused by that cursed object that has attached itself to our Poppy, and it oppresses her soul."

Poppy looked as lifeless as the dolls staring out from the shelves around her, but Pupkin looked active and alive, listening to Aunt Gail. Louise had a bad feeling Aunt Gail might be outmatched.

"We are going to do what is called Trace, Face, and Erase," Aunt Gail said. "We will spiritually Trace this demon's curse back to whatever unclean entity cast it. Then we will Face it. A demon's first reaction will always be to lie about who they are because that is the way of demons, and it is called the Pretense. But we will push it to the Breakpoint, where the power of God's righteousness will force it to admit its true name. Then the battle will be engaged as we Erase the curse from this puppet and blast it back to Hell. After that, we'll carpool to Mount Pleasant and face the demon in its stronghold.

"This will be strenuous," she continued. "The Enemy will try to crush our spirits by conjuring extraordinary manifestations that will make each of you wish you had never been born. Be strong, trust in the Lord, and stay hydrated. Now, join hands and I will lead us in prayer."

Louise reached out and took Barb's soft, sweaty left hand. She placed her own left hand in Aunt Gail's small, dry right one. They bowed their heads and Barb gave Louise's hand a quick squeeze.

"The light of God surrounds us," Aunt Gail said in a loud, clear voice. "The love of God enfolds us. The power of God protects us. The presence of God watches over us. Wherever we are, God is. And all is well, and all is well, and all is well, amen."

"Amen," Barb said.

Louise took a quick look across the circle and saw Mark had his eyes open, too. He raised his eyebrows. Poppy stood between them, lifeless as a mannequin, but Pupkin stared at Mercy, then turned counterclockwise and considered Aunt Gail, then he turned and looked full at Louise. Then Pupkin moved on to Barb, who made a silent "mwah" kissy-face at him. Then he turned to Mark, who quickly closed his eyes and bowed his head, then Constance.

"By the power of God and my Lord Jesus Christ," Aunt Gail said loudly, "I command whatever demon cursed this earthly puppet to tell me your name."

Pupkin snapped back around to face Aunt Gail.

"By the power of God, tell me your name," Aunt Gail repeated.

"Everyone is Pupkin!" Pupkin sang, and Poppy began to rock lifelessly from foot to foot. "Pupkin everyone! I sing and dance all day long! I live for having fun!"

Louise felt Barb adjust her grip.

"I know your face, Father of Lies," Aunt Gail said. "Tell me your name. The Lord Jesus Christ commands it!"

"Mark!" Pupkin said and it came out "Mawk." Pupkin pointed at Mark. "Pupkin be Mawk!"

Louise saw Mark's shoulders twitch.

"By the power of Jesus Christ, my Lord and Savior," Aunt Gail said, "tell me your name."

"Louise!" Pupkin sang, and now pointed at Louise. "Pupkin Louise."

She wanted to shake her hands free and grab Poppy and make her stop talking this way. She wanted to make her give straight answers. But she had lost her daughter. There was only Pupkin now. She forced herself to stay put. To be strong. To trust her aunt to drive this demon out of her little girl.

"Foul liar!" Aunt Gail said. "Tell me your name! Your defiance is hollow vanity!"

"Nancy!" Pupkin cheered. "Pupkin Nancy!"

Aunt Gail let go of Louise's hand and fished a cross necklace out of the collar of her *Joy!* sweater and stretched it out at Pupkin.

"See the Cross of the Lord!" she said. "Tell me your name, hostile power!"

Pupkin cackled. Then he tilted his head back and crowed, "Kakawewe!"

"Tell me your name, unholy one," Aunt Gail said. "Or I shall bind you with Warrior Angels in a cage five hundred thousand times too small, and sealed with the Blood of our King, Jesus Christ, our Lord and Savior!"

Pupkin turned to Louise, locking eyes with her.

"Pupkin went out one day," he chanted. "To find his friend so they could play. Girl Sparrow was her name, a bird girl good at all the games."

"Reveal your name, I compel you," Aunt Gail shouted.

"Before he set out into the trees," Pupkin continued, tiny eyes glued to Louise. "His mother said—"

From the couch, Mark picked it up without missing a beat, "Pupkin, listen, pretty please. Stay only on the path, my son. The woods are not a place for fun."

Pupkin turned his head toward Mark, who looked terrified.

"If you get lost I'll cry and cry," Mark kept helplessly reciting. "I'll cry so much that I might die."

In the silence that followed, Mark said, "Mom. It's Mom's story. I heard it a million times before bed as a kid."

Mark sagged. Pupkin looked brighter, stronger, more alive.

"By the power of God, tell me your name," Aunt Gail said.

"Pupkin is my name!" he squeaked. "Happy happy is my game!"

Something clanked in the kitchen and Louise jumped, then realized it was just dishes settling in the dish rack. Something shifted in the corner of her eye. Louise looked but only saw row after row of motionless dolls and their dead porcelain faces.

why did we come here? we're surrounded by dolls, we're outnumbered

Barb's hand felt slippery in hers.

this is pupkin's place, these are pupkin's friends

"By the power of God, tell me your name," Aunt Gail said. "Satan? Lucifer?"

"No, no, no, no!" Pupkin chanted.

he's laughing at us, he thinks this is funny

A *clank* as the dishes in the rack settled again, then a clatter as a fork dropped into the sink. Everyone jumped. Barb clutched Louise's hand tight.

"Don't look," Aunt Gail commanded. "It's a distraction. By the power of God, tell me your name! Beelzebub? Leviathan?"

"*No! No! No! No!*" Pupkin said.

Something thumped onto the floor behind her and Louise twisted in her seat. A little boy doll in a sailor suit lay facedown on the carpet.

"Do not look!" Aunt Gail commanded, pulling on her hand, forcing her to turn back to the center of the circle.

On the shelf over the TV, a smiling baby doll tipped over sideways.

"By the power of God, tell me your name!" Aunt Gail shouted at Pupkin. "Belphegor? Moloch? Andras?"

Pupkin laughed.

A teddy bear wearing a corduroy vest and glasses fell off its display shelf and landed faceup on the ground.

Pupkin kept laughing.

Thump thump thump

More dolls fell from the walls, a shower of them tottering, tipping forward, plunging headfirst to the floor. Then, all at once, the rain of dolls stopped. In the silence, Poppy ran up to Aunt Gail and thrust Pupkin into her face. Aunt Gail reared back.

"*Boo!*" Pupkin screamed.

A shiver passed through the dolls, circling them, scraping the walls, some invisible force Louise could feel brush over her body. Then all the dolls hurled themselves to the floor in an avalanche of soft bodies. Everyone tucked their necks in as dolls pelted their backs, ducked their heads as teddy bears thumped onto their heads, hunched their shoulders as a storm of dolls showered down on them.

Poppy fell to the floor, laughing, hugging Pupkin to her chest, rolling from side to side in the pile of dolls, kicking her legs. Aunt Gail's face went white. Her gobble trembled.

"Foul demon . . ." she started.

There was motion on Louise's right and her hand hung empty in midair. Barb threw herself forward and crouched beside Poppy.

"That was very funny!" she said to Pupkin, and grinned.

"Barb!" Aunt Gail snapped, but Barb threw up one hand, palm out.

"I liked that game," Barb said. "Can you do it again?"

Pupkin considered Barb, then Poppy lurched up and slapped her. It cracked sharp and loud in the dim room. Louise recoiled, started to get up, an apology on her lips. She stopped when Barb burst out laughing.

"You're a strong little Pupkin, aren't you?" she said.

Pupkin puffed out his chest. Barb shifted position so her legs were beneath her, half kneeling, half crouching. She reached out and tickled Pupkin under his chin. He squirmed with pleasure.

"Does this strong boy want a treat?" Barb asked.

Pupkin waved his arms excitedly.

"Treats!" he demanded. "Treats!"

Barb reached into her mouth and hooked out her wad of chewed gum, brown and glistening with saliva. She extended it to Pupkin, who tentatively stretched his face toward it, quivering, until Barb met him halfway and rubbed it across his lips. Pupkin cooed with pleasure. Louise's stomach flipped over.

"Where does this strong boy live?" Barb asked in a voice dripping with sugar.

"Tickytoo Woods," Pupkin crooned.

"I bet you're hungry after getting shouted at by mean old Gail." Barb smiled. "I've got a nicer treat for you."

She stretched backward and grabbed a cut-glass bowl of M&M'S off the table by the armchair. She popped a few in her mouth.

"Yummy yum!" she said, grinning and chewing, chocolate squirting between her teeth. She held up a yellow M&M between one massive forefinger and thumb. "Does my brave boy want some?"

Pupkin nodded eagerly and leaned toward Barb. She cupped the back of his head with one hand, then rubbed the yellow M&M back and forth over Pupkin's lips. His body shivered with pleasure.

"Yum, yum!" Barb said.

Then, so slow and smooth Louise didn't even notice until she'd finished, Barb maneuvered Pupkin around until Poppy and Pupkin sat in her massive lap. Pupkin hummed and cooed to himself, rubbing his lips on the chocolate as Barb rocked them both from side to side.

Louise felt sick.

poppy hates chocolate and she especially hates m&m's this is pupkin she's all pupkin now how much of my poppy is left?

"You are a brave boy, aren't you," Barb whispered. "But I bet you get sad sometimes."

Pupkin paused, then went back to his M&M. Friction warmed the chocolate and it smeared itself across his lips.

"Everyone gets sad," Barb said. "Even I get sad. Why are you sad?"

Pupkin slowed his rubbing.

"Nancy," he said.

Louise sat up straighter.

"Do you miss Nancy?" Barb asked.

"She come back," Pupkin said, then stopped rubbing and thought for a moment, then nodded. "We see Nancy soon soon."

"If you miss Nancy," Barb asked, "why did you play mean tricks on her?"

Pupkin twitched his head up, made eye contact with Barb.

"Nancy play trick first," he said.

"But you hurt people she loved," Barb said. "You hurt her husband, Eric, and that made Nancy scared and sad because she didn't understand why you did that."

"No," Pupkin said, and retreated to Poppy's shoulder, hiding in her hair.

Barb dropped the yellow M&M on the floor and plucked a green one out of the bowl. She held it up.

"Greenies are for special people," she suggested.

For a moment, nothing happened, then Pupkin slowly stretched his head forward and began to stroke his lips against the green M&M.

"Why did Nancy deserve mean tricks, Pupkin?" Barb asked, endlessly patient.

"Nancy lock Pupkin away," Pupkin insisted. "Put Pupkin in dark. Pupkin cries and cries but mean Nancy won't help. She only care about Limpy Man."

My dad, Louise realized.

"So what did Pupkin do?" Barb asked.

"Pupkin make him go away," Pupkin said. "So only Pupkin and Nancy now."

"And Nancy got scared when you did that," Barb said. "And she tried to help the Limpy Man and that's when they had an accident and got hurt. Did you want to hurt Nancy?"

"No!" Pupkin shrilled, and Louise thought he was going to stop talking, but he went back to stroking his lips against the M&M again.

"You hurt other people, too," Barb said.

"So?" Pupkin said.

"You hurt Nancy's son," Barb said.

"No care," Pupkin chirped.

"You don't care that you hurt people Nancy loved?" Barb asked.

"Fat Boy," Pupkin said, and his voice got thick and dreamy as he rubbed his lips sensuously against the M&M. "Fat Boy start like Pupkin. Like baby, then grow. He get bigger but Pupkin stay same. Pupkin never get bigger. Fat Boy replace Pupkin. So Pupkin make Fat Boy go away."

"How old are you, Pupkin?" Barb asked.

"Five," Pupkin said, soft, like a whisper. "Pupkin five."

"And have you always been Pupkin?" Barb asked.

Pupkin shook his head.

"What did your name used to be?" Barb asked.

Pupkin stopped rubbing his lips on the M&M.

"Freddie," he said softly, as if he hadn't heard it in a long time. Then louder: "Freddie."

"Oh my God," Mark said.

Barb shot him a look.

"Our uncle Freddie," Mark said, low and urgent. "Mom's brother. He was five."

Barb gestured "shut up" at him, then turned her full attention to Pupkin, but it was too late. Pupkin shoved himself out of Barb's lap, taking Poppy with him. Her head hung to one side like her neck was broken, and Pupkin walked her frantically around the inside of the circle, orbiting Barb, Poppy's free hand slapping each person's leg as she passed.

"No, no, no, no, no, no, no, no, no, no . . ." Pupkin chanted through Poppy's mouth as she walked around in a circle, faster and faster, and Louise pulled her hand out of Aunt Gail's and when Poppy came by again Louise grabbed her and pulled her into her lap.

Poppy thrashed, and Pupkin hit Louise in the face, and her chair went over backward, landing on the dolls, and Louise lost her breath, but she never let go of Poppy. She pressed Poppy to her chest and held her tight, burying her face in her dirty hair.

"It's okay," she said. "It's okay, it's okay, shhh . . . it's okay . . ."

"This isn't a demon," she heard Barb say to Aunt Gail. "It's a ghost."

Chapter 34

Something broke inside Poppy. She lay exhausted in Louise's arms, mumbling nonsense, Pupkin ticktocking his head from side to side to its rhythm. She'd reached the end of some energy reserve, hit some limit, and now Louise held her, slack and feverish, as everyone gabbled around them.

"You said it was a demon," Barb protested. "But it's a ghost and that's a whole 'nother kettle of fish because someone didn't do her homework."

"There's no such thing as ghosts!" Aunt Gail said. "They're all different aspects of the Enemy."

"Does it really matter?" Mercy asked.

"It's a whoooole different ball game," Barb said. "There's no demon named Freddie."

"Freddy Krueger?" Mark asked.

Louise pulled Poppy closer. She felt her feet lose circulation, but she didn't care.

"I'd love it if we only had to worry about a Hollywood movie!" Barb cried. "That would be a holiday on the beach with a cooler of beer."

"Demons know only deception!" Aunt Gail cried. "The true spirits of the dead reside in Heaven!"

Louise barely heard them. Poppy needed to be held. Poppy was letting her hold her. That was her job. Let them talk.

"What does it mean if it's a ghost?" Constance asked, talking past her mother, directly to Barb.

"It means a lot of things," Barb said.

"There's no such thing!" Aunt Gail protested.

Louise hugged Poppy tighter, holding in the scraps of her daughter's personality that still remained, trying to keep them from floating away.

"A ghost remains because it has unfinished business," Barb said.

"It is a demon trying to deceive you!" Aunt Gail protested.

Barb ignored her.

"Something ties it to this earthly plane and keeps it from moving on," she said.

"There are no ghosts in the Bible," Aunt Gail said. "A man dies but once and stands before God. Hebrews 9:27."

"Wait." She heard Mercy trying to make sense of it all. "So Freddie isn't ready to move on? He has unfinished business? He's clinging to this plane?"

Louise wanted to scream at all of them to shut up, to stop arguing, to actually help her daughter. Then Constance did.

"How'd Freddie die, Mama?" she asked.

There was a long pause as everyone waited for Gail to speak.

"He got lockjaw from stepping on a nail," she said. "Up in Columbia."

"So why isn't he haunting Columbia?" Constance asked.

"I was four years old and I wasn't there when it happened," Aunt Gail said. "No one from back then is around anymore."

"Except Aunt Honey," Mark said.

"And she's in the hospital!" Aunt Gail snapped. "We can't bother Mama right now!"

They began to argue, and their voices filled the mobile home, and Louise heard her mom's voice cut through them all.

Your aunt Honey tells stories.

Louise was fourteen, sitting in the front seat of their Volvo with her mom, outside Aunt Honey's house on Easter. Their dad had taken Mark up to Chicago to see his family and it was just the two of them. There'd been a fight in the kitchen between Aunt Gail and Aunt Honey and everything had been tense during dinner. Her mom made excuses to leave before coffee.

"What were they fighting about?" Louise asked, the second they got in the car.

"About Constance," her mom said. "Aunt Honey won't stop saying she flunked out of Wando."

"She transferred to Bishop England because she's dyslexic," Louise said.

"Your aunt Honey thinks it sounds better that she flunked out. She gets it in her head how things should be and then she makes up stories that that's how they are."

"But she got so angry," Louise said.

"Why do you think your aunt Gail got Jesus?" her mom asked. "She turned to the only person big enough to stand up to her mom. Once your aunt Honey decides how something's going to be, that's it. She'll never forgive your father and me for eloping because we deprived her of a big wedding, so she tells people we had one but no one took any pictures. She still thinks we have a dog no matter how many times I tell her Spider is made-up. She's stubborn."

Louise stood up with Poppy in her arms.

"Mark," she said, and everyone stopped talking and looked at her. "We're going to see Aunt Honey."

Everyone looked at Aunt Gail to see what she'd do.

"Louise," Aunt Gail said. "Mama's sick."

"I don't care how sick she is," Louise said. "She's the only one who ever met Freddie, so she's going to tell me everything she knows so I can get this thing off my little girl's arm. Mark, get your damn keys and get in the truck."

The nurse at the station told them they only had half an hour before visiting hours ended at nine, but Louise didn't slow down or listen. She had Poppy in her arms and she was getting heavy and her arms ached and she wanted to put Poppy down so badly, but she would not slow down until they got to the end of this.

She marched down the hall, her shoes squeaking on the spotless linoleum, as Mark apologized to the nurse for his sister, and Louise shouldered open the door of room 1217.

The TV played *Cold Case* or *NCIS* or *CSI* or some kind of detective show, and Aunt Honey sat up, watching. She had a clear oxygen mask over her mouth and nose.

"How're you feeling?" Louise asked.

She set Poppy down in the visitor's armchair.

"I feel like I'm ready to go home," Aunt Honey croaked.

Louise picked up the remote control from her bed and put the TV on mute.

"We don't have long," she said.

"And how's this sweet thing?" Aunt Honey asked, looking past Louise to Poppy.

Mark came into the room. A look passed between him and Louise, then he quietly shut the door.

"Come up here and give me a hug," Aunt Honey said to Poppy. Then she noticed Pupkin looking at her IV tubes. "Don't be scared, it's just medicine."

She took the oxygen mask off her face and rolled over onto one side, holding an arm out to Poppy. Louise stepped between them, close to the bed so Aunt Honey had to look up.

"We have to go in thirty minutes," Louise said. "And there's a lot to talk about."

Annoyance hardened Aunt Honey's eyes briefly, then she smoothed her face out with a smile.

"You can come again tomorrow," she said.

"We don't have time to fuck around," Louise said.

"Lulu," Mark warned her from the door.

Aunt Honey looked up at Louise like she was seeing her for the first time.

"What're you so hot about?" she asked.

"I'm sick of this family and its secrets," she said. "How did Freddie die?"

"Your uncle Freddie?" Aunt Honey asked.

"How did he die?" Louise asked again.

"Oh, sweetheart," Aunt Honey said. "That was a long time ago."

"We need to hear it," Mark said, stepping up beside Louise. "Every detail."

Aunt Honey looked put out. She rolled onto her back and glanced at the soundless TV picture, then over at the black window and the lights of the parking garage. Then she turned back to them and sighed. She started talking in the singsong voice she used when she had to repeat herself for the third time.

"Your grandparents took your mother and Freddie up to Columbia so your grandfather could look at a dry-cleaning business he wanted to buy," she said. "They stayed at the Howard Johnson's because that was a big deal back then, and your mother and Uncle Freddie were playing around the pool and he stepped on a rusty nail. They took him to the hospital right away but he got lockjaw and died."

"Where was our mom?" Louise asked.

"She stayed with me," Aunt Honey said. "I came up and got her. A hospital's no place for a little girl."

Pointedly, she looked at Poppy.

"That's not how lockjaw works," Louise said. "I never looked it up before, but I looked it up on the way here. I don't know why I never did that before, but it takes three days to even show symptoms."

Aunt Honey nodded at Pupkin on the end of Poppy's arm. He was studying Aunt Honey like he was trying to place her.

"I'm glad she kept that," Aunt Honey said.

Louise didn't have time for sentiment.

"It's making her sick," she said.

"It was your uncle Freddie's," Aunt Honey said. "You've heard how my sister threw out everything that belonged to Freddie? She burned all his clothes and toys. She even burned her photographs of him. Then she started asking other people for any snapshots they had. I shouldn't have let her have mine. Your mother rescued that doll from the junk heap and hid it from Evelyn. It's all that's left of her little brother."

Of course it's his, Louise thought. She felt like Aunt Honey had just confirmed that she was on the right track.

"Uncle Freddie didn't die of lockjaw," Louise repeated.

Aunt Honey tore her eyes away from Pupkin and looked up again at Louise.

"A hospital's no place for a little girl," she said. "She's only five. This must be scary for her."

Louise knew what she was doing. They all did it. When a conversation got too close to something a Joyner or a Cannon didn't want to talk about, they made it personal.

"She's here because you're lying," Louise said. "She's here because all of you think that if you don't talk about something, it doesn't exist. Like your sister not talking about Freddie and throwing away everything that reminded her of him. Well, he did exist, and something survived of him, and my mom inherited it, and now it's hurting my daughter. You've lied all your life and now your lies are hurting my little girl."

Aunt Honey leaned forward and appealed to Mark.

"What is eating your sister?"

Before Mark could answer, Louise snapped, "Stop lying and talk to me."

Aunt Honey's face got sharp and her eyes flushed red around the edges as she snapped back.

"I don't do rude," she said. "So maybe I should be talking to your brother. At least he's polite!"

The time to be nice had passed.

"Mom's gone and she never told us the truth," Louise said. "And you've never told us the truth. You are sick and you are old and if you die in here, no one will ever know what happened. This is your one chance to get right with your family and to get right with God."

"It's none of your business!" Aunt Honey shouted, her face white and quivering, one hand gripping the rail on the side of her bed, struggling to pull herself up. "It's got nothing to do with you!"

"It's killing my daughter!" Louise shouted back, leaning down in her face, close enough to smell her skin cream.

Mark put a hand on her arm to pull her back, but Louise shook him off.

"Because you're selling the house!" Aunt Honey said, not backing down, her whole body shaking with the effort of sitting up. "No one said you could do that! This is your own fault!"

"It's not your house!" Louise said. "You're a sick old woman who's scared of change. Stop trying to control everything and tell me what happened to my uncle."

"Your mother let him drown!" Aunt Honey shouted.

She held herself still, no longer shaking, her skin pale yellow, her eyes going dull, then she slowly dropped back against her pillow. She tried to get her breathing under control. She turned her face away.

"Your grandparents went to Columbia and stayed in the Howard Johnson," she said to the window. "They asked Nancy to look after Freddie for a few minutes while her daddy went to the front office and made a long-distance call and her mama unpacked. They told your mother to stay in the little children's wading pool. They told her to look out for her brother. That's how people did back then, but your mama didn't listen. She never listened to anybody but herself. She always had to march to the beat of her own drum. She wandered over to the ice cream place where the man was scooping ice cream and counted the number of flavors because she couldn't believe it when her daddy had told her there were twenty-eight. She told me when she came back there were all these people gathered around the ambulance and my sister was howling like she'd never heard a human being howl before. They took Freddie right to the hospital and I drove up and got your mama out of the waiting room and brought her back home. She didn't understand what she'd done, and so I told her Freddie stepped on a nail, and my sister . . . she went along."

No one moved. Even Pupkin listened. Aunt Honey rolled over and turned her red eyes on Louise.

"How do you tell a seven-year-old child she killed her brother?" she asked. "How could she live with that? That's what we told everyone who mattered, and the people who knew otherwise thought we'd done a kindness for your mother. It ate at my sister. It gnawed her down to the root. That's why she couldn't bear to look at your mother. She tried. She tried to move past it. She tried to concentrate on the child she had, not the one she lost, but it never worked. Just when she felt like she might be starting to heal, she'd think of your mother wandering away to look at those ice cream flavors and she'd have to lock herself away because she was scared of what she might do.

"It was your grandfather's idea to send your mother around. She lived with other people more than she lived at home, and it broke his heart, but my sister could never get back to the way she was with the child who killed her Freddie in the house. Of course they blamed themselves. Of course they felt guilty. But your mother was the one who let him drown, and my sister couldn't let go of that."

Aunt Honey stared at the ceiling, but it didn't look like she actually saw it. Louise felt there was more.

"What else?" she asked.

Aunt Honey shifted her eyes over to Louise without moving her head.

"Don't sell the house," she said. "Please."

Her voice sounded thin as paper. She looked like her life was leaking out of her. Louise made herself hard.

"Why can't we sell the house?" she asked. "There's something you're not saying."

Aunt Honey rolled her head from side to side on the pillow.

"Don't make me," she begged.

Louise leaned over the side of the bed and put one hand on Aunt Honey where she thought her shoulder would be. She made her voice soft and sympathetic.

"You want us to know," she said. "You need to get this out of you, and you're so close. One last secret, then it's over, and you'll be free."

Aunt Honey turned her eyes to Louise. They were steady, her face was hard, but her eye sockets were wet.

"I made a promise to my *sister*," she said, hitting the last word hard.

"Your sister is dead."

Aunt Honey stared at her, expression unchanging, then began to speak. "They had a closed-casket funeral and they were going to bury him in their plot at Stuhr's, but the day before, my sister changed her mind. She couldn't bear to be apart from her little boy. She had Jack bury him out back of the house. That's why they could never move. That's why your mother couldn't build that deck. They'd have to dig holes for any extra house. That backyard belongs to Freddie."

Aunt Honey turned her face away. The loudest thing in the room was Poppy's labored breathing. Louise stood up. Aunt Honey mumbled something, then turned to Louise.

"I made a promise," she said. "The only thing I had left of my sister was the promise I made to her never to say a word. Now I've broken it. You made me break my word to my sister."

"I'm sorry," Louise said.

"No, you're not," Aunt Honey said. "I could have never told and no one would have known."

"Someone would have dug up his bones one day," Louise said.

"People dig up bones all the time," Aunt Honey said, her voice full of contempt. "The world is full of them. You made me break my promise to family."

Louise felt tired. She didn't want to argue anymore.

"We'll move him to Stuhr's," Louise said. "Next to his mom and his dad and his sister. He should be with family."

"What do you know about family?" Aunt Honey asked, staring at her hard.

Chapter 35

Mark and Louise silently walked out of the room, Louise leading Poppy by the hand, Pupkin hanging back, staring at Aunt Honey. They stood in the hall, not knowing what to say or where to go.

"All her life," Mark said. "All her life she must have known something was wrong. She never wanted to talk about death or Freddie because she must've known it didn't add up. Even if it was just a freak accident, she must have felt so guilty that it happened when she took her eyes off her brother. And she never said a word. None of them did. And she clung to the one thing she had to remember her brother by for almost seventy years. Can you even imagine?"

Louise couldn't. She thought about those women—Aunt Honey, her grandmother, her mom—deciding what needed to be done and doing it. They had a hardness she was beginning to think, more and more, she'd inherited. A hardness she couldn't have imagined before she had her own child.

"We have to go to the house," Louise said.

"Why?" Mark asked.

"To find Freddie," she said.

They both looked down at Pupkin, who looked up at them.

"Don't we call the police or something?" Mark asked, but his voice lacked conviction.

Louise adjusted Poppy's hot, soft, unresponsive hand in hers. This is what her daughter's hand would feel like if she was in a coma. This is what her daughter's hand would feel like at the moment of her death.

"We need to do it now," Louise said, "before there's no more Poppy left."

For a moment, it looked like Mark was going to argue, then he nodded.

"Okay," he said.

They had to wrestle Poppy into Mark's truck. She clung to the doorframe, bracing her feet against the seat and pushing backward. Louise was prying her fingers off the frame one by one when Mark let go and stepped back.

"You're going to hurt her," he said.

Louise turned on him in a fury.

"She's already hurt!" she snapped. "Mom's already hurt her! Aunt Honey hurt her! Everyone in this family hurt her! Now, help me!"

He wasn't much help with only one arm, but together they managed to stuff her into his truck. Louise sat Poppy between them to keep her away from the door, but the minute Mark got in Poppy lashed out, shoving herself backward into Louise and kicking Mark in the thigh.

"Hold her!" he said, as Poppy kicked at the steering wheel.

"I'm doing my best!" Louise said, grappling with Poppy, who suddenly seemed to be everywhere, feet flailing at Mark's face, Pupkin pummeling Louise. Finally, she got Poppy in a bear hug, lifted her over herself, and put her own body in the middle, between Poppy and Mark. Her daughter went limp. Louise clicked the passenger-side seat belt over Poppy and made sure it was snug.

One eye on Poppy, Mark started the truck.

"It's a big backyard," Mark said, voice low, as they drove down Ashley.

"I know," Louise said.

"How're we going to know where to dig?" Mark asked, turning onto the Crosstown.

"I don't know," Louise said.

After the first set of traffic lights, Mark spoke again.

"Louise," he said, voice strained, "don't panic, but I need to tell you something."

"What?" she asked, starting to panic.

"Spider's here," he said.

Lighting shot down Louise's spine. She looked around.

"Where?"

"In the back of the truck," Mark said, his eyes flicking to the rearview mirror.

Louise turned and saw the empty truck bed. She kept looking, waiting for Spider to flicker into sight, but he didn't.

"I've seen him a few times," Mark said. "In the hospital after surgery, prowling around outside my place. I thought maybe I was hallucinating, but it's like he's waiting for me."

"We've got bigger problems," Louise said, trying to calm the panic she felt, remembering Spider's teeth around her ankle, his claws raking her back.

They drove onto the bridge, rising high into the night sky, coming around the first roller-coaster turn into the merge lane, then soaring over Charleston Harbor. Poppy fell deeper into a stupor, her head leaning against the door, bouncing along with the road. Her breathing sounded wet and thick, her lungs sounded full of mucus. Her ears had that stale, dirty smell she got when she was getting sick. Louise willed Mark to drive faster. Every minute Pupkin was on her arm, Poppy felt farther and farther away. She could feel her daughter receding with every tick of the clock.

"Mark—" she started.

The cab exploded into wind and chaos. The door-open alarm screamed from the dashboard and Louise turned into a hurricane as Poppy wriggled out of her seat belt like an eel and stood up in the open passenger door.

They were on top of the first span of the bridge and wind blasted through the truck at sixty miles an hour, whipping receipts and paper napkins into their faces, sucking paper coffee cups out the door.

Louise watched for a full heart-stopping second as Poppy threw herself out of Mark's truck. Both her feet left the seat and Louise saw her falling out, and back, toward the hard surface of the road, and she lunged forward and caught Poppy hard around her waist, hanging halfway out the door. She wrapped her arms around her daughter, head and shoulders suspended over the road, and hauled her back inside, feeling pain explode at the base of her spine from the strain.

"Close it!" Mark screamed over the wind.

Louise had both arms around Poppy, who thrashed and kicked and screamed, slamming her body into Louise's chest again and again, and the wind pushed the door into the frame, but the new bridge didn't have any place to pull over, so they drove, passenger door not secured, a high-pitched whistling cutting through the cab, Poppy screaming, trying to get away, trying to throw herself out the door again, battering Louise until gravity got heavier and they came down the last span of the bridge, and then they shifted, leaning dangerously to the right on the final curve, Louise clinging to Poppy, holding her tight, and Mark pulled into the Shell station at the foot of the bridge and everything . . . stopped.

They sat for a minute, lucky to be alive, then Louise reached over Poppy and pulled the door all the way shut and pressed the lock. She sat Poppy in her lap, stretched the seat belt over the two of them, and clamped her arms around her, trapping her in place.

"Jesus Christ," Mark said.

"Let's go," Louise told him.

Mark looked at her, thought about saying something, then reached across the wheel with his left hand and dropped the truck into drive. They pulled back onto Coleman.

He didn't want to stop in case Poppy tried to run again, so he timed the lights, slowing to twenty, to fifteen, waiting for them to switch from red back to green, then punching the gas. Speeding up when they turned yellow. Poppy lay limp in Louise's lap, rocking forward and back with the acceleration. Pupkin stared out the passenger-side window while Poppy's head rolled from side to side against Louise's chest. She felt something wet on her arm. It was Poppy's drool.

She's not even swallowing anymore.

"I can't believe we grew up with a dead body in the backyard," Mark said.

I was so happy you decided to go away for school, Louise remembered her mom saying one Christmas when she was back from college. *I'd leave if I could, but I feel like I'm stuck here.*

Mark rolled slow at a red light, trying not to come to a complete stop. It changed to green and he gunned his engine and took off. For a moment, Poppy stopped breathing. Louise looked down, not knowing what to do. Then Poppy started breathing again with a thick, congested rasp.

"Do we just start digging holes?" Louise asked. "Or do you remember if there was ever someplace Mom told us not to play?"

Mark slowed to a roll, timing the next light.

"Everywhere," he said. "Playing in the backyard was like a punishment."

The light turned green and Mark took off. They were close now.

"What about when you were going to build the deck?" Louise asked. "Did she say anything about where to dig or not to dig?"

"She just told me they changed their mind," Mark said.

"There has to be something!" Louise said. "Think!"

"I don't know, Louise!" he snapped. "Why do you keep yelling at me! Ask him!"

It felt like he'd suddenly snapped on the lights. Louise turned to Pupkin, staring out the windshield.

"Pupkin?" she asked in the nicest voice she could manage. He turned toward her. Poppy's body didn't move. Louise relaxed her throat to keep herself from screaming. "Do you want to play a game?"

Pupkin nodded, eager.

"Do you know how to play hot and cold?" she asked.

Pupkin looked at her for a long moment, then shook his head.

"It's a game," Louise said, "where we try to find something that you've hidden, and when we get closer, you say 'warmer,' and when we get further you say 'colder.' Do you understand?"

Pupkin nodded again, looking up at Louise expectantly.

"Let's say I want to find Pupkin," Louise said, keeping her voice light. She reached her hand toward the steering wheel. "Is Pupkin over here?"

Silence. Cars passed them on the left and Louise saw they were coming to the intersection with McCants, the intersection where their parents had died. She made herself focus.

"Is Pupkin over here?" Louise asked.

"Cold?" Pupkin said through Poppy's mouth.

Louise smiled in encouragement. She reached toward the dashboard.

"Is Pupkin over here?" she asked.

"Colder," Pupkin chirped, more certain now.

Louise reached toward him, then past him to the passenger-side door.

"Is he over here?" Louise asked.

"Colder," Pupkin squeaked, then as Louise brought her hand back, he said, "Warmer . . . warmer . . . warm!"

She made herself poke him in the tummy. Pupkin giggled and cooed.

"Hot!" he squealed.

Louise turned to Mark.

"He's going to tell us where he is," she said, then Poppy exploded in Louise's lap, driving her head backward, smashing Louise in the upper lip with the back of her skull. Louise's sinuses filled with blood and she let go of Poppy, who turned into a tornado, screaming, howling, moving fast. She slipped over the seat belt and lurched across Mark for the driver's-side door.

Louise grabbed her, but Poppy kicked out, shoe catching Louise in the chin. Mark slammed on the brakes and tried to wrap one arm around her, but a hard kick to his stump paralyzed him with pain. A car laid on its horn behind them, headlights filling the cab, then it blasted around them on the left without slowing down. Before either of them could untangle themselves from their seat belts, Poppy had the driver's-side door open and was stepping on Mark, launching herself into the middle of Coleman Boulevard.

"Poppy!" Louise screamed as a white van tore by, swerving to miss her daughter, barely slowing down.

Louise tore off her seat belt, threw open the passenger-side door, and ran, ignoring all the headlights disorienting her, racing after her daughter. Louise ran with the traffic, her right ankle burning, pumping her arms, slowly closing on Poppy, who sprinted up the median at a diagonal, holding Pupkin up high, headed for a thick cluster of trees on the other side of oncoming traffic. Cars blasted past, going the other way, their flashing headlights blinding Louise. If Poppy didn't get hit by a car, she was going to get into the trees and be gone.

Louise poured on a final burst of speed and felt a car just miss her, sending a big wash of air surging into her back, and she used it to take an enormous step forward, reversed course, scooped Poppy up, and fell to her knees on the left-turn arrow painted on the asphalt at the light where their parents had died.

Poppy threw herself from side to side as cars blew by inches away, and Louise, panting, pressed her tight to her chest, holding her as she gulped big lungfuls of exhaust. Poppy threw her head back and howled. All the strength in her body went into that howl, and it rose out of her, a wordless scream of agony, of everything that was too much, pain pouring out of her mouth in a wordless wail, and it wasn't Pupkin's voice; it was Poppy's voice, screaming in a way no child should ever scream, louder than her throat could stand, louder than the traffic, and all Louise could do was hold on to her in the middle of the road while she screamed herself out.

"I know," Louise said, over and over again. "I know, I know, I know."

Finally, Poppy wound down to silence. Louise stood. Mark had pulled up behind them in his truck, hazards clicking. He helped her get in, putting Poppy, limp now, on her lap.

"You okay?" Mark asked.

"No," Louise said, as she buckled in, gripping Poppy with one hand.

Mark looked over his shoulder, then made a right-hand turn onto McCants. As his truck accelerated across the lanes, Louise wondered if the gravel she'd felt digging into her knees had been bits of her parents' shattered taillights, shards of their safety glass.

Mark pulled up in the driveway of their dark house and cut the engine. For a moment, they sat in silence.

Louise looked through the windshield. She'd left this house twenty-two years ago and here she was again. She'd run in a circle. She saw the first day when she arrived in town to bury her parents, she and Mark fighting over the death certificates in the front yard. She saw her cousins playing touch football out there at Christmas, her mom loading the Volvo with her puppet cases, their dad stringing Christmas tree lights. Now, under the harsh silver glow of the distant streetlight, the house looked like something left in the attic too long and leached of all color. It looked like the end of the line.

Mark took his keys and got out. Louise slid out from under Poppy and stood in the driveway with Mark.

"There's a shovel in the garage," she said. "We'll get him to play hot and cold with Freddie's body. I think he'll lead us to it. I think he won't be able to stop himself."

"We're going to need more than a shovel," Mark said. "We'll need a backhoe."

"They buried him by hand," Louise said. "That's how we'll dig him up."

Mark looked through the windshield at Pupkin, staring out at them.

"They're both five," he said in a quiet voice.

"What?" Louise asked.

"Freddie, or Pupkin, or whoever," Mark said. "He and Poppy are both five years old."

Louise looked at her daughter, inert, exhausted, filthy, the only living thing about her the puppet on her arm.

"So was I," Louise said. "When I tried to drown you. I was five years old, too."

"I don't think this is a good idea anymore," Mark said. "What if we dig up Freddie's body and nothing happens? What if it's not here?"

Louise heard Mark's voice shake, and she saw his stricken face in the silver streetlight, his eyes just sockets full of shadow.

"Mark," she said, "if I don't get that puppet off Poppy's arm I'm going to lose her."

Heat lightning flickered once, silently, a long way off over the harbor.

"When he's gone," Mark said, "so's Mom."

"Mom's already gone," Louise said. "This is just one more thing she left behind."

Mark let out a low, shuddering breath.

"Okay," he said. "Okay, let's do it."

A cold wind passed down the street behind them, from one end to the other, rustling the leaves in each tree as it went by. Louise opened the passenger-side door.

"Pupkin?" she asked, hating that she had to call her daughter that name. "Do you want to play hot and cold?"

Pupkin came toward the door and Poppy's body followed. Louise helped them out and the three of them stood in the driveway. The four of them.

"Pupkin," Louise said, "do you remember how we played hot and cold in the car?"

Pupkin nodded.

"We're going to play it in the yard now, but do you know what we're looking for?"

Pupkin shook his head.

"We're looking for Freddie," Louise said, and made her smile as big as she could so she didn't scare Pupkin. "Can you help us play this game?"

Pupkin held still for three long seconds. He shook his head.

"Come on, Pupkin," Louise said, desperate not to let her desperation show.

Pupkin shook his head again. Louise squatted in front of Poppy and looked Pupkin in the eye.

"Nancy is gone," she said. "Eric is gone. Your mother and father are gone. Everyone who remembers you is gone. And it's time for you to be a big boy and go, too."

"No," Pupkin said.

"Who's going to take care of you now?" she asked. "Don't you want to be with your mother and your sister?"

Pupkin slid forward and curled against the side of Louise's neck the way he had when she was a little girl. His body felt cold and heavy, like a slug's.

"You take care of Pupkin now," he said.

Louise tried not to react.

"I'll take care of you," she made herself say. "But if I'm going to take care of you, I need to know where you are. That's why we want to play this game. Do you understand?"

Pupkin uncurled from her neck and looked at her, then up at Mark, his small white face glowing. Nothing happened.

"I don't think—" Mark began, and Poppy ran.

Before Louise could even stand up, Poppy had turned the corner of the house, heading for the backyard, holding Pupkin up in front of her. Louise ran after them. Mark followed.

They came around the side of the house, through the gate, and entered the rustling circle of bamboo that hid their big, bare backyard from the street. Clouds scudded over the moon and the wind rattled leaves all around them. Louise saw the pale shape of Mark's lumber in the blackness of the night. The air had turned cold, drying the sweat on the small of her back, and she shivered as the night air sucked the heat from her body. The wind lashed the trees overhead, making their leaves give a steady roar like the ocean.

Poppy wasn't there, but the back door to the garage stood open.

Mark and Louise walked to the door, and Mark leaned inside and slapped on the lights. Nothing happened. The power was out. Suddenly, it seemed like a really bad idea to go back inside the house. Louise pulled out her phone and made herself poke on its flashlight. She turned it to the door, and its dead white light showed them the inside of the garage.

The two black garbage bags they'd filled with dolls had been torn open and they lay limp and deflated in the center of the concrete floor.

"Oh, no," Mark moaned.

The wind crested and sighed, and from the dark hole where the shattered door led into the kitchen, a giggle floated out.

"Warmer," said Pupkin's voice.

"Are you fucking kidding me?" Mark asked, turning to Louise.

But Louise was already stepping over the threshold and into the garage. Mark stood there, shifting from foot to foot, then he looked over his shoulder, looked back at Louise starting up the brick steps into the kitchen, and he threw himself after her before he could change his mind.

Chapter 36

Louise stood in the dark dining room, lit by the unforgiving white light of her phone, listening to the wind rattle the windows, and she knew they'd made a mistake. It was even colder in here than outside. It smelled like stale grease and flies. And from deeper down the dark hall, she felt something waiting for them.

Mark came up beside her, poked the front of his forehead, and a headlamp switched on. More shadows leapt out of the dark around them, shifting and sliding over the walls as he turned his head.

"He's buried inside the house?" Mark whispered, and even his whisper sounded too loud.

This house had been built right around the time Freddie drowned, Louise remembered. Could you even dig under it? Hadn't it been built on a slab? If they'd buried Freddie and poured concrete on top, the two of them were screwed.

"Warmer," Pupkin's voice singsonged from down the dark hall.

He sounded raspy now, like an old man pretending to be a little girl.

Louise needed to get this over with while there still might be some of Poppy left. She made herself walk deeper into the house.

"Hold on," Mark said, and she heard him opening cabinets behind her.

"Okay," he said, next to her again. He held a frying pan. She gave it a look. "It's better than a badminton racquet."

They walked into the front hall together. Arctic air streamed from the bedrooms, like someone had left the windows open. Louise's skin prickled, the cold putting ice in her blood.

"The fuck," Mark whispered beside her, and she turned and saw the living room.

The dolls had come back. All of them. They'd crawled back into the doll cabinet, Henry VIII and his wives, the yodeling Hummel figurine, all of them back in their places. The Squirrel Nativity stood on top, the German Dolly-Faced Dolls lined themselves up on their display shelf, the clowns sat on the back of the sofa, the Harlequin huddled against one of its arms. They stood where they'd been all their lives, clinging to their old positions, staying where their mom had left them. They weren't ready to be thrown in the trash.

"I'd like to say this is the weirdest shit that's ever happened to me," Mark whispered. "But I have a bad feeling it's going to get a lot worse."

Louise turned back to the hall and forced herself to start walking toward the bedrooms.

"Warmer," Pupkin's voice echoed through the house, seeming to come from everywhere all at once.

Every door in the hall stood open, showing only darkness inside. Mark looked inside his old bedroom and Louise walked over to her mom's workroom door and pushed it open, expecting to feel it bump into the mushy wall of puppets, but it kept swinging until the knob hit the wall. She shone her phone light inside.

Her mom's workroom was empty.

The sewing machine sat by the window, the worktable stood in the middle of the floor, and one of the towers of boxes had tipped over, spilling bolts of puppet fleece across the carpet, but every single puppet was gone. The walls stood bare. The racks hung empty. Mark came and stood beside her, and she heard the hitch in his breath.

"I told you this was a bad idea," he whispered.

They started down the hall, necks on swivels, lights shining everywhere, making shadows stretch and slide, trying not to step on the framed pictures on the carpet. They reached the end of the hall and stood between their parents' bedroom door and Louise's half-closed one. Before they could decide which one to open first, from the other end of the hall behind them, Pupkin squeaked, "Burning up!"

Mark and Louise turned, lights sweeping the hall, and they saw Pupkin standing far away, by the dining room door. Poppy held him up, swaying, weak, feverish, head lolling to one side, her bandaged arm reflecting their lights.

"Is this where Freddie is?" Louise asked.

"You stay," Pupkin said through Poppy's raw throat. "Fat Boy got one arm, he no good for Pupkin. But you stay. You stay and take care of Pupkin and be in Tickytoo Woods forever, and nothing changes, and everything the same, forever ever after."

"Where's Freddie?" Louise asked.

"No stay?" Pupkin asked in a small, sad voice.

"No stay," Louise said. "Freddie needs to go home."

"Freddie home!" Pupkin insisted.

"He wants to be with his family," Louise said.

"Okay," Pupkin said. "Game over."

Something in the dark rooms on either side of them moved, displacing air, and Louise turned toward her parents' bedroom door just in time to see it swinging wide open and a wall of puppets coming down on her like a tidal wave.

An avalanche of puppets plunged toward her, with Mr. Don't in the lead, his Ping-Pong-ball eyes meeting Louise's, his mouth open in a silent scream, and she screamed back, backpedaling across the hall carpet, smashing into Mark as he tried to get away from the puppets flooding from her old bedroom. Screaming puppets came down on them, dropping from everywhere.

Louise dove out of the way, but they buried Mark, wrapping themselves around his legs, his wrist, clinging to his neck and hair, hanging off his stump, tearing the frying pan from his grip. She snatched them off him, flinging them away, but they clung to her hands, wrapped themselves around her arms with their long, ropey limbs, grabbed onto her shirt. She dropped her phone and saw its light go spinning down the hall carpet, drowning behind a storm of puppets.

They needed to get to the front. They needed to reach Pupkin. Louise pulled Mark behind her, feeling puppet arms sliding around her legs, coiling up to her waist, hanging off her back. She made it five steps, but there were too many puppets. They were being swarmed.

She put her back to the wall and tore puppets from her body, flinging them as far as she could. She ripped them from Mark's head. His thrashing headlamp showed flashes of the nightmare all around them: puppets with no legs dragging themselves over the carpet like felt slugs, puppets swinging from the doorframes, puppets hurling themselves toward Louise, their eyes fixed on her, their mouths screaming. The three-foot-long articulated Danny the Imagination Dragon ran across the ceiling upside down, clinging to it with foam claws, wings outstretched. Two five-foot red-and-white-striped candy canes her mom had made for a Santa Claus pageant pogoed toward them from where they'd been hiding in Mark's old bedroom, black mouths flopping open and closed with every hop, and Poppy stood at the end of the hall with Pupkin on her arm, laughing and dancing.

Louise dragged Mark into the bathroom and slammed the door.

Puppets thudded into the other side. She pressed her hands to the wood, holding it shut as puppets frantically hurled their bodies against it, rattling it in its frame. Mark put his back to it, then something scrabbled at her toes, and in the spill of Mark's headlamp Louise saw fur hands and spaghetti-noodle arms whipping through the crack at the bottom of the door, reaching for her feet. She stepped back out of reach, keeping her body weight on the door.

"What do we do?" she cried, on the verge of tears, the panic inside her boiling out of control. "What do we do? There's too many of them!"

They were hitting the door all at once now, their blows coordinated. Each time they hit, Louise felt the door shake in its frame. They were going to get through.

"Oh, Jesus," Mark said beside her, and Louise followed his horrified stare to the other end of the bathroom.

The Mark and Louise dolls stood side by side underneath the window, looking at them with their blank faces and dead eyes. The Louise doll tottered to one side like she was going to fall over, then she caught herself and tottered again in the other direction, and Louise realized she was walking toward them over the tile.

"Oh, Jesus!" Mark said as the puppets slammed into the door behind them again.

The Mark doll took a step toward them now, too, and the two huge dolls wobbled toward them on their doll feet, coming for Mark and Louise. They reached the sink. The way they moved looked wrong. It looked unnatural. It made her want to throw up.

"What do we do?!" Mark shouted in terror beside her. "What do we do?!"

"Hold the door," Louise said, and tore off the Band-Aid.

Without giving herself time to think she stepped forward and scooped up the two dolls by their arms and slung them into the tub. They landed with a heavy double thud. She slid the solid plastic pebbled shower door closed and held it. At Mark's back, the puppets smashed into the bath-room door again, and this time something snapped inside its frame. Louise got to it just in time to brace her hands before they hit it again.

"We have to find Freddie," she said.

"How?" Mark asked. "We're trapped in a bathroom, Mom's puppets hate us, there are dolls in the tub. I think we're fucked."

Puppets slammed into the door again. Whatever had broken in the frame before splintered.

"We don't have a choice!" Louise snapped. "We have to find him!"

"How're you going to find anything?" Mark shouted. "It's like Ticky-too Woods out there."

"Think!" Louise said.

Mark didn't answer. The puppets crashed into the door behind them. This time, the door pushed into the room. Just an inch, but it was enough. They didn't have any time.

"Oh my God," Mark said.

"What?"

"Tickytoo Woods," Mark said as the puppets hit the door again. "I've been to Tickytoo Woods, Lulu, in Boston, when I was Pupkin."

The puppets hit the door again. Louise heard the mounting plate come loose on the knob.

"The Tick Tock Tree where Pupkin takes naps?" Mark said. "In the Bone Orchard? I've seen it. The Tick Tock Tree is a cypress. The Bone Orchard is bamboo. It's where Pupkin always sits at the start of his stories. It's where he does his best thinking."

The puppets hit the door again.

"It's the cypress in the backyard," he said. "With all the bamboo. That's where Freddie is. I know it in my gut!"

Louise didn't like Mark's gut feelings. His gut feelings were how he'd wound up owning a snake farm.

"Trust me," he said as the puppets hit the door again.

Mark's gut feelings were how he'd wound up losing his savings in two treasure-hunting expeditions. Mark's gut feelings were how he wound up investing in a nonexistent Christmas tree factory. His gut feelings had saved him in Worcester. His gut feelings had made him sleep in his truck after Pizza Chinese. His gut feelings had saved Louise's life.

"How do we get there?" she asked.

"Go out the window," Mark said. "I'll hold the door."

Louise hesitated. The puppets hit the door again. It gave a deep splintering crack.

"Go!" he shouted.

She let go of the door as the puppets slammed into it again. This time, Mark's feet slid a few inches. In the tub, the Mark and Louise dolls banged their tiny hands against the inside of the plastic shower door. Louise ran to the window, whipped back its curtain, and tried to push it up.

"It's painted shut!" she said.

"Break the glass!" Mark shouted.

Louise looked around: toilet, sink, soap dispenser, towels, toilet brush. She needed something heavy. The puppets hit the door again. The Mark and Louise dolls pounded on the shower door with their tiny fists. Louise threw the shower door open, hesitated for a split second, then grabbed the Louise doll. It was heavy enough.

"Sorry! Sorry!" she apologized, then rammed it through the frosted glass bathroom window, face-first.

The doll went through the glass with a satisfying silvery smash. Louise held its slowly writhing body like a battering ram and smashed it through two more times, then used it to wipe all the hanging shards from the frame.

Cold air washed in from the backyard. Louise tossed the busted doll back in the tub and made eye contact with Mark.

"Go fast," he said.

She took a deep breath, grabbed the frame, getting glass dust all over her hands, and dragged herself through, going upside down, landing on her hands in the backyard. She dragged her legs out next, and then she was standing.

She looked back into the bathroom. The wind kept her from hearing anything, but she saw Mark jolt forward as the puppets slammed into the door. Then Louise turned and ran.

Chapter 37

A cold wind that smelled like rain screamed through the backyard, whipping the treetops and bamboo. The skin on Louise's arms burned with cold. She had glass dust everywhere. Black clouds closed over the moon. She made herself step through the dark garage door and felt along the shelves until she knocked the shovel off its nail.

She grabbed it and headed outside. Overhead, the wind reversed direction and rattled the high, bare branches of the pecan tree. Around her, bamboo clattered like bones. In the far corner, the stunted cypress thrashed and shimmied in the wind.

Louise ran to it. She hadn't been in this corner of the yard in over twenty years, and it felt dank. Even the wind couldn't wash away the stink of mulch and rotten leaves. The ground looked hard, knobby, and full of roots. She was looking for a five-year-old child the size of Poppy, and she didn't know where to begin or how deep to dig. This was too random. She didn't stand a chance. She couldn't do this.

She had to trust her gut. Like Mark.

Louise made herself close her eyes, take in a breath, let it out, take in another, hold it. The air smelled muddy and moist. She could taste water in it. Far away toward the harbor, thunder rumbled. Louise exhaled and took another breath.

She imagined her grandmother, who she'd never even seen in pictures, walking out into this backyard in the middle of the night, followed by her grandfather, carrying a tin traveling trunk. He stands behind his wife while she holds still, the way Louise is now. Then she points.

Here.

Louise opened her eyes and walked to a spot a little in front and to the side of the tree, hauled her shovel back, and stabbed its blade into the dirt, prying out a chunk of roots. She hacked out another big chunk. A flicker of lightning strobed overhead, showing her the shallow depression she'd started to carve, and she speared her shovel down into the middle of it again and began to scrape out the dirt.

All she could hear was wind. Slashes of light came from a neighbor's backyard floods, hacked into dancing tatters by the bamboo, but otherwise everything was dark. Behind her, in the house, a sudden tinkle of glass cut through the noise of the wind. She didn't stop. She levered out another heavy shovelful of dirt and tossed it aside. Then a huge wave of glass exploded behind her and Louise whipped her head around.

The sliding glass patio doors blew out, pebbles of glass raining on the concrete patio, the metal frame sagging down on itself, and something dark hit the ground and rolled.

Mark.

He sat up, disoriented, shaking his head, dazed. He tried to stand, but his heels only dug uselessly against the ground. She started toward him, then stopped, because behind him, through the shattered patio door, shadows detached themselves from the darkness inside the house and something huge and heavy shoved its way outside, knocking the drooping aluminum frame aside.

Even from here, Louise heard its clumsy feet dragging the metal frame of the sliding doors. She heard them thumping heavily into the ground. The thing stumbled, pulled itself free of the wreckage, glass showering down its back, and then it stepped out of the darkness of the house, and Louise's brain repeated a single word over and over again.

No. No, no, no, no, no, no, no, no, no, no, no, no . . .

A giant humanoid shape, heavy and squat, shuffled forward another step toward Mark. It had a square, rough body, crude arms and legs, and a rudimentary bump for a head, and it was made from puppets. All of them. All of her mom's puppets. Hundreds of them, clinging to each other, arms knotted to arms, legs twined around legs, bodies braided around bodies. The wind blew their fur and hair and yarn and made it dance across their patchwork bulk, their blind, screaming faces and plastic eyes staring in all directions, their mouths hanging open, all of them wrapped together in an angry, senseless mass.

Deuteronomy the Donkey, Danny the Imagination Dragon, Pizzaface, Meow Meow, Jacko the Jester, Rogers, Cosmic Starshine, Mr. Don't, Flossy Bossypants, Sister Whimsical, Monty the Stray in the Manger.

It turned its bulk to face her and Louise felt her brain shut off. The shovel dropped from her numb fingers. It took a step toward her, then another, its body lurching from side to side, overbalancing each time, puppet bodies stretching and contracting like tendons, body rippling as it moved, puppets' mouths jouncing open and closed each time its feet hit the ground.

Behind it, Poppy stepped out from the broken patio doors, Pupkin held high on one arm.

"Kakawewe!" Pupkin cheered in triumph, dancing in the air.

The puppet golem turned toward Pupkin, and Pupkin pointed at Louise. It turned back toward her and began to plod across the yard. Louise looked, but there was nowhere to go. Her hole wasn't deep enough. The thing kept coming. It was at Mark's pile of lumber now.

Her whole life came down to this. Louise grabbed her shovel and slammed it back into the hole, scooping out dirt faster, throwing shovel-fuls aside, her shoulders burning, the small of her back aching. When she looked up, the puppet golem had closed half the distance between them. She looked back at the hole. It was barely any deeper. She didn't have enough time. She had no more choices. She turned to face the golem, gripping the shovel with both hands, holding it in front of her like a spear.

It took two more thudding steps forward and Louise felt her sense of perspective warp. It looked like it should be farther away, but it stood taller than her, taller than Mark, at least seven feet high. Something flickered and died behind her breastbone. She couldn't fight this thing, but even so she braced her legs and adjusted her grip, because she didn't have a choice.

I'm going to fight Mom's puppets, Louise thought. *Four weeks ago I was a product designer with a child and now I am going to fight my mom's puppets with a shovel and . . . oh, God, Mom and Dad, please help me now.*

The thing took another step, and she heard something at the edge of her hearing, voices begging, screaming, gabbling in pain inside her head. Thunder rumbled, closer now, but the screaming in her ears sounded both closer and farther away than the thunder, and that's when she realized it was the puppets; the puppets were screaming.

She knew their names, she had seen her mom make every single one of them, she'd used some of them to perform her mom's shows, and they had been happy for so long, and warm, and safe, and cared for, and now they had lost their creator and grief had twisted them into this deranged thing and she didn't want to do this.

"You're hurting them," Louise called to Pupkin, the wind tearing her words away. "This is wrong. What you're doing is wrong."

The puppet golem took another step and the screaming inside Lou-ise's head made the left side of her face throb, and now it was in striking distance. It swung an arm at her, slow and clumsy, and she stepped back and felt the wind from it brush past her face, as powerful as a passing car. It was too big. It had too much mass. The second it got its hands on her, she was done.

I don't want to hurt them.

She'd tire them out, she thought over the sound of screaming puppets inside her head. She darted to the left, circling the thing, moving away from Pupkin, instinctively leading it away from her daughter, whatever of Poppy there was left, and she swung her shovel at its legs, but her heart wasn't in it, and her blow only clipped its solid bulk and sent Fabio the Fortune-Teller and Mrs. Dizzy Bear spinning into the dirt. The thing lumbered around to face her. Louise kept circling, slashing her shovel at its face to keep it back. She reversed direction, and it turned to follow her, herding her into the corner of the yard. Behind it, Pupkin danced on the end of Poppy's arm. Louise knew she had to hit it. She had to make it stop. It was them or her. She came in low at the puppet golem's legs, brought the shovel back and let it swing, putting everything she had behind it.

The blade thwacked into its right leg and it caught her shovel. Puppet arms swarmed out of its body like vines and wrapped themselves around the blade and held fast. Then it brought its massive right arm down and Louise let go and backed away as it smashed the handle of her shovel in half, and she watched her only weapon fall to the ground.

Something came out of Louise's blind spot and sent her spinning. She'd been hit by a car. Her spit tasted thick. Her body spun completely around in a circle and she fell to her knees, putting one hand on the ground to keep from biting the dust. Through her peripheral vision she saw the puppet golem draw its arm back for another blow.

She staggered up, but it was too close and the thing sent her sprawling in the other direction, crashing into bamboo. Her body felt too heavy. Everything started to get dark around the edges. She knew it was close and she made herself roll away. Its foot thudded into the ground where she'd been.

Louise hauled herself up by the stalks of bamboo. She'd run. She'd run away. She was faster than this thing, but she couldn't see it—where had it gone?—and before she could put her thoughts together, something smashed into her from the right side and her legs stopped working and Louise went down.

She rolled over on her back and tried to stand, but her arms and legs weren't working anymore. She squirmed in the dirt as the puppets loomed over her, blocking out the sky, filling her vision. Louise sensed Poppy nearby, dancing, Pupkin on the end of her arm stretched up to the heavens, singing his song over the sound of puppets screaming inside her head.

Pupkin here! Pupkin here!
Everybody laugh! Everybody cheer!
No more bath time! No more rules!
No more teachers! No more schools!
It's time to sing and dance all day,
Pupkin's here to play and play AND PLAY AND PLAY!

The puppet screams reached a pitch too loud for Louise to process, and her brain fuzzed out to static, and then all she could see were the puppet golem's arms reaching for her, a wide-mouthed dog puppet

monty the stray in the manger

hanging from its elbow, and the puppets loomed over her, bigger than the entire world.

. . . i'm sorry poppy . . .

A single shrill, high-pitched whistle cut through the night. The thing stopped reaching for her and Louise rolled her head to one side and saw that Mark had dragged himself to the base of the pecan tree. His teeth flashed in the dark and Louise realized he was grinning. He brought his fingers to his mouth again and gave another long, shrill whistle. Then Louise heard him call.

"Sic 'em, boy."

For a long moment, nothing happened. Then something slammed into the golem from the side, sending it staggering. The sky above Louise showed nothing but dark clouds. Thunder rolled, nearer now. Louise heard the puppets screaming louder inside her head, and with enormous effort she sat up.

The puppet golem stood stock-still, the vestigial nub of its head pulsing from side to side. Pupkin whipped himself around at the end of Poppy's arm, looking for something, searching the yard . . .

Something hit the golem and shoved it forward. Then it lost half of one arm. Puppets showered to the dirt, wriggling, screaming, and Louise heard Mark shout over the wind, "Good boy."

And she saw him.

Spider.

He tore into the golem, smashing into it, teeth snapping, snarling, ripping, biting, tearing puppets away from its body, all six of his clawed paws lashing out angrily as the blue beast flickered in and out of her vision, crawling all over the thing, swarming up its shoulders, flowing over its chest, catching its head in his jaws and tearing puppets away, flinging them across the yard, winding between its legs, up its back, raking its claws across its face.

The golem stumbled, the puppets screamed, and Louise saw Poppy rear back as if something had exploded inside her head, and she sat down hard on her bottom and didn't move. Louise needed to help her, she needed to go to her, and then she saw Pupkin stirring on the end of Poppy's arm and she knew what she actually needed to do.

With the last strength left in her tortured muscles, Louise forced herself onto her hands and knees and crawled back to her hole. She didn't have her shovel anymore. She shoved her arms in up to their elbows and hauled out dirt. She scraped it out. She lost a nail. As Spider tore the reeling golem apart, puppet by puppet, Louise pulled one handful of dirt after another out of Freddie's grave.

The first cold raindrop hit the back of her neck like a bullet, but she was too exhausted to care. Scattered drops tapped the ground around her, then started sizzling through the bamboo, pattering against the soft cypress leaves, and as the sound of the screaming puppets died inside her skull, the clouds unleashed a biblical flood. Louise hunched over in the dead backyard, rain spiking out of the sky, stabbing into her back like spears, but she couldn't stop digging. She sensed something big coming and she threw her head back and looked.

Spider trotted toward her in the pouring rain, flickering in and out of existence, head lowered, eyes fixed on Louise. Behind him she saw a scattered pile of puppets, still squirming in the dirt as it turned to mud, some tottering up onto their legs to run, then falling motionless after only a few steps. Beyond them, she saw Poppy sitting on the ground, slumped forward, not moving in the hissing rain.

Spider's breath steamed in the cold as he came closer, and Louise's scabs gave a nauseating twinge. He looked at her curiously, and then his enormous maw irised open and his long tongue slithered out and around its edges. She looked down and saw the hole filling up with water; her hands felt as stiff and cold and useless as hooks. It wasn't deep enough. It wasn't nearly deep enough.

She looked up at Spider.

"Dig!" she commanded. He cocked his head to one side and began to growl. "Dig, Spider!" Louise repeated.

This time she leaned forward at the waist and made herself thrust her hands into the icy water and haul up two fistfuls of mud. The skin on her hands screamed in agony.

"Dig!" she commanded and pointed at the hole. "Spider! Dig!"

He stepped toward her and she got ready to close her eyes, and then Spider stopped growling and thrust his two enormous front paws into the water at the bottom of the hole and began to dig. His second set of paws joined in, and then an arc of dirt and mud fountained through the air between his back legs, like a chainsaw biting into the ground.

The flying soil stung Louise's face. She dragged herself out of range and watched as Spider used his six legs to tear his way into the ground as a curtain of rain pounded down on them all.

Something changed in the sound of the dirt flying out of the hole, she heard the sound of claws on something hollow and hard, and Louise shouted, "Spider! Stop!"

He looked up at her curiously, shoulder-deep in the hole, and Louise crawled toward him. At the bottom, half-buried in the dirt, lay a smooth surface. Louise stretched onto her stomach and began to move mud off it, pushing it to one side. The rain flowed down her face, almost drowning her as she dug with her cold, useless hands, working them around the object's edges. She found a handle and hooked both hands around it, and with all the strength she had left she stood up, her back going tight, her spine grinding together, her shoulder muscles tearing, and the dirt held on to the thing, and then it let go and she dragged it out of the hole.

She dumped the tin trunk beside the hole and flopped onto her back, lying there for a moment, gasping for air. The rain came down hard, slapping her in the face and eyes, soaking through her clothes. She rolled over and forced herself to her feet, grabbed the handle of the trunk, and began to drag it toward the dim outline of Poppy through the wall of rain.

Spider flickered in and out of the downpour behind her, watching, and some dim part of her brain acknowledged Mark slumped against the pecan tree, and she felt like she saw his head move, tracking her, but she couldn't be sure.

She trudged across the dirt, rain hissing down hard, making lakes. Poppy came into view, Pupkin still on her arm, resting in her lap. When Louise got closer, Pupkin weakly raised his head. The rain had started dissolving the papier-mâché of his face, making it gummy, peeling it, one layer at a time. He grinned at Louise as the black ink around his eyes ran down his cheeks like mascara.

Louise dropped the trunk between them, then fell to her knees. She hunted blindly until she found one latch and opened it, gritty with rust and dirt. Then she found the second, the third, and finally she grabbed the lid with both hands and forced it back.

Inside lay a child's body, curled around itself. Bones, mostly, but scraps of skin clung to its cheeks and wrists, along with some wisps of pale hair that the rain immediately plastered to its open-mouthed skull, his small hands drawn up and folded delicately beneath his chin, a little boy in faded blue jeans and—this is what stabbed Louise through the heart—a red sweater.

his mother hadn't wanted him to be cold

"It's you," Louise shouted through the rain at Pupkin. "It's you, Freddie."

Pupkin turned his face from the body of the little boy to Louise, then back to the case. The rain beat down on them like clubs. Black paint dripped from Pupkin's chin as his features blurred and disappeared.

"You have to go now, Pupkin," Louise said. "It's time to go home."

Pupkin shivered on the end of Poppy's arm, a sad, peeling wet thing, looking at his own corpse.

"Pupkin no go," he said. "Pupkin stay and play and play . . ."

"There's no one left," Louise said. "They're all gone."

"Pupkin real! Pupkin alive!" he cheered.

"No," Louise said, too exhausted to say more.

"Why?!" Pupkin howled.

"Because when your body gets hurt very, very badly, it stops working, and you die, and that means you go away forever. And that's what's happened to you."

"No . . ." Pupkin whined. "Not fair . . ."

"No," Louise agreed. "Not fair."

The ruined, melting face of Pupkin turned itself to her on the end of Poppy's arm.

"Why?" he asked again, and it was a child's voice, lost, with no way home.

In that moment Louise thought of *The Velveteen Rabbit* and she knew why she had always hated it. Being loved didn't mean you were alive. People loved lots of inanimate things: stuffed animals, cars, puppets. Being alive meant something else.

"Because you're real, Pupkin," Louise said. "And nothing real can last forever. That's how you know you're real. Because one day you die."

Rain smashed down on the three of them sitting in the mud. Finally, Pupkin spoke in a voice so small Louise almost didn't hear him over the rain.

"I'm scared," he said.

Louise dragged herself around the trunk and through the cold puddle forming around them, and she sat down behind her daughter and pulled her into her lap, then reached for the soaked and waterlogged Pupkin on the end of her arm. His face had melted to an unrecognizable lump, but she could still see the faint contours of his eye sockets, his mouth, his chin, his upturned nose. Because she was a mother, Louise gripped his sleeve and slid him off her daughter's arm, then slid him over her own because she couldn't let a child, any child, face this alone.

Pupkin felt cold and wet and heavy, instantly freezing her knuckles to ice, and then she felt his tiny body surge to life, and the rain faded away and the world lurched to one side and spun, and she found herself on her back looking up at the clear night sky streaked with pink glowing clouds.

A gentle, warm breeze ruffled the leaves of the Tick Tock Tree overhead, and Louise sat up and looked beside her and saw a little boy sitting on the grass of Tickytoo Woods. He wore blue jeans and a red sweater. On one arm, he wore Pupkin.

"Where's Nancy?" the boy asked in a child's clear voice.

Louise couldn't speak. She knew this was some kind of hallucination, but everything felt so real and all-encompassing, like it wasn't a vision created by her exhausted brain but a world around her that went on forever and she could walk in any direction and never come to the end.

"I want Nancy," the boy said again.

Louise didn't know what to tell him, and then instinct took over. She remembered how the stories would go, the ones her mother told her years ago.

"She's at the End of the World," Louise said.

"I don't believe you," the boy said. "And Pupkin doesn't believe you, either. The world doesn't end."

"Everything ends," Louise said.

"No, it doesn't," the boy insisted. "Right, Pupkin?"

"Right!" the puppet on his arm chirped in Pupkin's squeaky little voice.

"Why don't you go see for yourself?" Louise asked.

The boy considered her for a minute, then stood up.

"We will," he said. "Come on, Pupkin."

They started to walk away, and then the boy stopped and turned back to Louise.

"What if I can't find it?" he asked, and his voice was colored with worry around the edges.

"You will," Louise reassured him. "You always do. And if you don't,

Girl Sparrow will bring you home. Because you always come home again, Freddie. You and Pupkin. That's how every adventure ends—with the two of you safe at home with Mom and Dad. And your sister."

Freddie puffed his chest up.

"I'm going home," he said.

"You're going home," Louise agreed.

He and Pupkin started off again, and Louise couldn't help herself.

"Freddie!" she called.

He stopped and turned.

"When you see your sister," she said, "tell her I said thank you."

"For what?" Freddie asked.

Louise didn't know. She couldn't find the words. How could she say it? There was too much.

"For everything," she finally said. "Tell her I said thank you for everything."

Freddie shrugged. Then he turned, and he and Pupkin walked off through the Bone Orchard, looking for the End of the World.

Then Tickytoo Woods fell away and gravity pulled her down, and suddenly she was soaking wet and freezing cold again and people with flashlights were everywhere—a jumble of raincoats and visibility vests and ponchos—standing all around her as she cradled her daughter in her lap, a soaking mass of fabric and paper melting into pulp on the end of her right arm. One of the people leaned in and it was Aunt Gail.

"Louise?" she shouted from a long way away. "Louise?"

"I brought him home," Louise said. "I brought Freddie home."

Then she was falling backward and she heard the splash as she came down, and then the whole world went away.

ACCEPTANCE

Chapter 38

Louise crept out of Poppy's hospital room a little before nine the next morning. She felt like garbage but she had too much to do. She needed to see the house. She needed to make sure.

As she pulled up in front of the house, a golden retriever charged past her, running down the block with something floppy and brightly colored in its mouth, and it took her sluggish brain a minute to realize it was one of her mom's puppets. Louise hauled herself out of her car and walked across the yard.

The police were gone, but they'd left yellow crime scene tape behind, tied to the columns on the front porch and wrapped around the side gate. Louise climbed the fence, careful not to tear the tape, and looked at the wreckage in the backyard.

Her mom's puppets lay everywhere, multicolored rags torn to shreds and strewn from one end of the muddy yard to the other. The rain had ruined them. The police and paramedics had walked on them all night and destroyed them beyond repair. Some had been ground into the mud, others had been eviscerated, their scraps and fluff blowing into drifts. The biggest pile of them lay facedown a few feet from the hole that she and Spider had dug. The police had expanded the hole, turning it into a vast pit.

Everything her mom had built, everything she had spent her life creating, everything that meant so much to her, it was gone. The rain and mud and the feet of strangers had destroyed it all. The puppets had been her mom's life. Pupkin had been her mom's life. And now they were gone and so was her mother. Louise began to cry.

She cried because at last it hit her that time only moves in one direction, no matter how hard we wish it wasn't so.

Not fair, she heard Pupkin protest inside her head.

"No," Louise repeated quietly to herself as she wept. "Not fair."

"Excuse me," a sharp voice said behind her.

Painfully, every joint rusty and stiff, tears streaming down her face, Louise turned. A man in a black puffy vest and athleisure pants stood on the other side of the fence holding out his arm. From it, one of her mom's ruined puppets dangled. Louise recognized Meow Meow.

"I don't mean to be rude," he said rudely, "but your trash is all over my yard."

Louise vaguely recognized him as one of the new people living in the Mitchells' old house. They were a finance family from Westchester, or a tech family from the Bay Area, or some career family from someplace like that. She gave him a smile through her tear-streaked face.

"I'm dealing with it right now," she said.

Louise pulled out her phone, found the number in her call list, and tapped it once.

"Mr. Agutter," she said. "This is Louise Joyner from that . . . yes . . . yes, it is early . . . I'm afraid we got off on the wrong foot before. We definitely want you to come back as soon as possible . . . That'd be great. And one other thing? Do you do yards?"

As the hospital cleared Poppy to go home, Louise went down to the car and brought back a duffel bag. She sat on the edge of Poppy's bed, holding it in her lap.

"How do you feel?" she asked.

Poppy coughed and nodded at the same time. Louise put one hand on Poppy's forehead because that's what her mom had always done for her whenever she'd been sick. The doctors said Poppy's lungs were clear and there was a course of oral antibiotics, and Louise had no idea what Poppy remembered, but going home was the first step.

"Are you excited?" she asked.

"Back to San Francisco?" Poppy asked.

"Back to San Francisco," Louise said.

Then she unzipped the duffel bag and reached in and pulled out Hedgie Hoggie and set him on the bed facing Poppy. Then she pulled out Red Rabbit and Buffalo Jones and Dumbo and lined them all up, too.

"These are some friends I had when I was your age," she said.

Poppy's eyes locked onto them.

"What are their names?" she asked without looking up.

Louise introduced Poppy to her childhood friends.

She'd found them in the house, hiding in her bedroom, huddled underneath her bed. She didn't remember seeing them that night in the house, and she didn't think they ever could have done anything to hurt her, and they looked so frightened and alone. She'd gotten them cleaned—spiritually by Barb, who said there was nothing to worry about, physically by Sea Island Suds.

"They're your friends now," Louise said, and Poppy cautiously reached out and pulled Red Rabbit over to her by one ear and tucked him against her stomach, then she reached for Buffalo Jones. "But you'll have to take care of them. They've never been to a city as big as San Francisco before."

When Louise was little, her mom had loved her without reservation, without hesitation, but Louise wasn't born knowing how to do that for someone else. These stuffed animals were how she had first learned to love something that couldn't always love you back. They were how she had learned to take care of something that relied on you completely. They had been training wheels for her heart, and now it was Poppy's turn.

It was up to Poppy to keep them clean and loved and warm and, one day, maybe Poppy would pass them on to her children, or her godchildren, or her best friend's children, or maybe she wouldn't. Maybe she'd get tired of them before then. But no matter what, Louise had done her part. It was up to Poppy now.

They had Uncle Freddie's funeral in October. Louise and Poppy flew in for it and stayed with Aunt Honey, which thrilled her to no end. At first, Louise thought Aunt Honey's warmth was all an act, so she waited until one night after Poppy had gone to bed and poured them both another glass of wine.

"I want to apologize for what happened in your room that night at the hospital," Louise started.

Aunt Honey blew a raspberry.

"I don't even remember," she said, waving one hand in front of her face. "I was doped up on drugs. Let's talk about something that's actually interesting. Do you think Constance is having another baby? Does she look pregnant to you? She's not drinking."

It had taken forever to get a judge to sign an exhumation license to dig up Freddie's empty casket and rebury his remains, and there had been a lot of other legal hurdles to clear, but finally, sixty-eight years after his death, the Joyner-Cook-Cannon family gathered in the grave yard at Stuhr's and laid Uncle Freddie to rest beside his sister.

They gathered around the green open-sided tent in the cemetery, standing by the newly dug hole in the family plot, and everyone had a blast. Aunt Gail led the prayers, and Mark hired a bagpiper to play "Amazing Grace" for reasons no one could comprehend, and even Barb showed up.

"Look at her, she's like a delicious miniature muffin!" Barb said, lifting Poppy in her arms and mashing their cheeks together. "I want to eat her up!"

Louise could tell Poppy had no clue who Barb was, but she liked the attention, so she accepted the hug and treated her like another aunt. It reminded Louise of the way her mom had so easily accepted other people's attention. She remembered how at ease that had always seemed to make them feel.

Each of them threw a handful of dirt on Freddie's coffin, and somehow Brody managed to slip and fall in the hole, although, fortunately, he didn't break anything, and as the service wound down, it turned out that Constance happened to have a bunch of cans of hard seltzer and two bottles of wine in her minivan, and people poured one into the other, and the funeral home didn't seem to be telling them to leave, so they stood around the open grave and kept talking.

Mercy told Louise about a precious little house she couldn't move for love or money because the sellers were in denial that their attic was full of bats. Barb and Aunt Gail read headstones and gossiped about dead people they knew. Constance and Mark got into an argument about evolution while Poppy played hide-and-seek in the tombstones with the other kids. She was finally old enough to play with Constance and Mercy's younger ones, and as their shrieks rang out over the dead bodies lying underground, and Aunt Honey began to deliver a soliloquy about what Freddie had been like as a child, Louise slipped away from the tent and stood over to one side, watching her family.

"Hey," Mark said, coming toward her, holding out an extra can of hard seltzer.

"Hey," she said, taking it. "You feeling okay?"

He looked pale and clammy. Their night at the house had traumatized his surgical site and the doctors had had to shave down some damaged tissue in his right arm. It hadn't been fun.

"It just hurts a little," he said. "And by 'a little' I mean 'a lot' and also 'all the time.'"

They stood next to each other, watching Aunt Honey hold court, listening to the kids playing among the graves.

"Do you think he's happy?" Louise asked.

"Freddie?" Mark asked. "After all that, he'd better be."

"And Pupkin?" she asked.

Over by the tent, Aunt Honey cackled loudly and everyone standing in the circle around her laughed.

"I hope so," Mark said.

"How're the renovations coming?" Louise asked.

Mercy had told them not to expect much from the house. In fact, she'd told them it probably wouldn't sell for a while.

"You find a cadaver in the backyard," she'd said, "suddenly everyone wants to knock a hundred thousand off the asking price. Maybe we'll find someone who's deaf and blind and doesn't read the newspapers, or maybe someone from LA, but I wouldn't get your hopes up that we'll find a real buyer anytime soon."

That hadn't stopped Mark from taking out a loan and starting to renovate. He'd told Louise he needed something to do and there wasn't much of a market for one-armed bartenders.

"Look, we need to talk about something," Mark said.

Oh, no, Louise thought. *I can't take more bad news, I can't—*

Poppy slammed into Louise's legs from behind, face flushed, completely out of breath, panting and laughing.

"Are you having a good time?" Louise asked.

"This is the most fun I've ever had!" Poppy said.

Poppy didn't know what to do with all the joy inside her body. It short-circuited her nerve endings. It made her shake. Her hands clenched into fists and she pressed her face against Louise's legs, then she pushed herself away and charged off after her cousins again, arms and legs flailing. Louise watched her go, then turned and faced Mark.

"Okay," she said. "What is it?"

"We might have a buyer," Mark said.

"What?" Louise asked, struggling to put a sentence together. "How?"

"Mercy said he's some software guy from Toronto. He doesn't care about the thing with Freddie. He's coming down next week to walk through."

"What about the renovation?" Louise asked.

"That's what I wanted to talk to you about," Mark said. "It's pretty much done."

He stood there like a magician who'd just completed a trick, waiting for applause. Poppy came around a gravestone too fast and wiped out hard. Louise winced in sympathy, then watched as Poppy picked herself up, grass stains smeared across the knees of her dress, and kept chasing her cousins.

"That's great," Louise said, turning back to Mark. "That's really great. I mean it."

"You want to see it?" he asked.

Something inside her went cold.

"I . . ." she started and saw Mark's face fall. "I don't know. I almost died there, Mark, and Poppy . . . it wasn't a good place for her."

"If this guy buys, they're going to close fast," Mark said. "You may not get another chance."

"Do you have pictures?" Louise asked.

"It's fine," Mark said, and Louise realized how disappointed he was.

"You know what?" she said. "Let's drive by. If it doesn't bother Poppy, then I'd love to see what you've done."

Louise and Poppy stood in the front hall of the house where Louise grew up, holding hands, taking in the brand-new open-plan living space. It smelled like new carpet and fresh paint.

"I have very good taste," Mark said. "I mean, Mercy helped, but what you're seeing is mostly my vision."

He looked nervous and proud and like he really needed her to like it.

"I'll admit," Louise said, "it looks nice."

Poppy pulled on her hand and Louise looked down.

"Can I go see your room?" she asked.

"Of course," Louise said. "You know where it is?"

Poppy nodded and, clutching Red Rabbit to her side, she walked down the hall to Louise's old bedroom.

"I feel like some appreciative noises would be in order," Mark said. "I have busted my fucking hump on this renovation."

Louise made appreciative noises over the new, bigger hall bathroom, the hardwood floors in the family space, the wall-to-wall carpet in the bedrooms, the venetian blinds.

"It's super on-trend," she said.

He really was good at this. She tried to lay her memories of that last, desperate night over these IKEA fixtures and marble countertops, and they wouldn't take. It didn't look like the same house anymore.

"Mercy asked if I wanted to help her with another place," Mark said as they walked to their parents' old bedroom. "I might. I mean, you know, this was kind of fun."

They found Poppy standing in the middle of her parents' old bedroom. Mark had torn out their dad's closet, enlarged the bathroom, and made a bigger walk-in closet. Louise could barely remember how it had looked before.

"Everything's gone," Poppy said.

Louise nodded.

"It is," she said. "And it's never coming back."

"And Granny and Grandpop?" Poppy asked.

Louise hesitated for a minute, then said, "They're gone, too."

She waited for Poppy's eyes to get teary, for her face to flush, for the beginning of a meltdown.

"Oh," Poppy said, turning it over in her mind. Then she said, "Okay."

She adjusted Red Rabbit and took Louise's hand again.

Mark led them to the kitchen and told Louise about sourcing the marble and what a great deal he'd gotten on the stainless steel, then Poppy had to go to the bathroom and she wanted Mark to take her, so he led her down the hall.

"So, um," he said, coming back. "One thing we didn't talk about is the new asking price."

Louise's heart stopped. Here it came. The bad news. Mercy had told them everyone would want a discount after Freddie.

"What is it?" she made herself ask.

He told her the number. It was big. Bigger than she'd imagined.

"Half of that'll be yours," he said. "That buys a whole lot of future for Poppy."

It took a minute for Louise to absorb what he'd said.

"Thank you," she finally told him. "I mean it. This is all you and it's amazing."

Suddenly, she smelled something behind the paint and new carpet smells, something hot and toasted, and she wondered if Mark had left the oven on, or if he was doing that thing where you staged a house by baking cookies, but the guy wasn't coming until next week. She inhaled again. It smelled stronger now.

It was the smell of baking. It was the smell of stollen baking.

She looked around the bare, cold kitchen and saw that the oven was off, and its digital display flashed *12:00* to itself over and over again. She felt herself wrapped in the scent of warm butter and hot icing, and she inhaled and let it fill her head. She smelled candied fruit and warm sugar. She smelled yeast.

She looked at Mark standing next to her and he had a strange look on his face, like he was listening to faraway music. He met her eyes.

"What . . . ?" he started.

"You know," Louise said, "whenever I used to smell Dad's baking I always felt like everything was going to be okay."

"I . . ." Mark began, and then he just stood there, lost in the smell of their dad's cooking.

They heard the toilet flush and Poppy wandered into the room with Red Rabbit.

"It smells like cookies," she said.

"It does," Louise agreed.

She didn't know if it was energy or vibes or ghosts or memories, or maybe even her dad sending one final message to the three of them, but it didn't matter. For a little while, for the last time, Mark and Louise stood in the house where they grew up and smelled the scent of their dad's stollen baking in the oven.

Finally, Louise said, "We should go."

Mark turned to her, looking stricken.

"Lulu," he said. "Everything else was Freddie, or Pupkin, or whatever, but this . . . it's actually Dad . . ."

She shook her head.

"It's time to go," she repeated.

He swallowed. Then nodded. Then the four of them—Mark, Louise, Poppy, and Red Rabbit—walked out of the house and closed the door behind them.

And after a while, the smell of stollen faded away.

For Louise, it came and went. Sometimes it wouldn't bother her for years, and sometimes it hit hard. The worst was when she dreamed they were still alive and it had all been a terrible mistake. In those dreams, she was still thirty-nine and when she got Mark's call she called home and this time her dad answered the phone and she talked to him and then to her mom and she would wake up glowing. She'd open her eyes and sit up in bed full of energy and actually reach for her phone, and that's when she'd remember they were dead and it would hit her all over again, as hard as it did the very first time.

When that happened, she felt a deep ache inside her chest, like her rib cage was being split open with an axe. When that happened, she needed to call the only other person who knew how this felt. When that happened, she called her brother.

In loving memory

CELEBRATE
THE LIVES AND ART OF

Eric Joyner
&
Nancy Cooke Joyner

ORDER OF SERVICE

Call to Worship—Reverend Michael Bullin

"This Little Light of Mine"
performed by The Doll Wiggler Quartet
(featuring Joshua Bilmes, Adam Goldworm,
Harold Brown, Daniel Passman)

TESTIMONIALS

Miss Mouse in the House & Her Human,
Eddie Schneider

Monsieur Brady McReynolds with
His Friends Jacques & Andre

Valentina "Mrs. Snowball" Sainato

"The Five Penguins"
performed by Susan Velazquez

Jessica "Make a Joyful Noise" Wade

Kitty-Cat Camacho

MUSICAL INTERLUDE

A Tribute to Nancy Joyner in Body Music,
performed by Doogie Horner and His Body

"Candle in the Wind" performed by The Treblemakers

Alexis Nixon	Jin Yu
Danielle Keir	Craig Burke
Fareeda Bullert	Gabbie Pachon
Daniela Reidlová	Lauren Burnstein

TESTIMONIALS

"My Ducky Has Big Eyes" recited by Claire Zion

A Silent Meditation led by Jeanne-Marie Hudson
and Oliver the Ostrich

Emily Osborne and Scarlett Flufflebear

Laura Corless the Dancing Meerkat

Anthony Ramondo and Snocchio

Hosannas and Praise by The Australian Trio

MUSICAL INTERLUDE

Eine kleine Nachtmusik by Wolfgang Amadeus Mozart,
performed by Megha Jain (spoons)

"Where Have All the Flowers Gone" by Pete Seeger,
performed by William Barr (harmonica)

TESTIMONIALS

"I Mime the Body Electric,"
an original poem by Lydia Gittens

A Guided Visualization
by Frances "The Magnificent" Horton and Puppy

Kevin Kolsch and His Dancing Cat, Church

The Original Lounge Lizard (and His Two Frogs),
Davi Lancett

Dr. Ralph Moore and the Three Pigs O'Plenty

Interpretive Ballet by Mr. Giraffe and Friends (Y. S. T.)

A FINAL SONG

"Rainbow Connection" by Kermit the Frog

RECESSIONAL

"When the Saints Go Marching In"
Everybody (kazoo)

We would like to thank the Hendrix Family for the beautiful flowers donated to the sanctuary (Julia, Kat, Ann, David).

The Fellowship of Christian Puppeteers wish to extend their warm gratitude to the Buss Family, who opened their home for so many guests during this difficult time (Barbara, John, Johnny, Leon, Effie Lou).

This service is also dedicated to the loving memory of those who left us too early:

Erica Lesesne, Pete Jorgensen, Aunt Lee, Uncle Gordon, Eartha Lee Washington, Aunt Betty Moore, Joyce Darby, and Scott Grønmark.

――――――――

PLEASE NOTE: The memorial service for Amanda Beth Cohen has been moved to the Fellowship Hall and will take place from 5 p.m.–6 p.m. this evening. If you have any information that may lead to an arrest in this matter, we urge you to contact Detective Ryan Dunlavey at the Mt. Pleasant Police Department.

Sleepy Sermons? Youth Program Yawns?
Your Ministry Needs JOY!
NANCY JOYner and Her God Squad!

With over thirty years of experience as a puppeteer, Nancy's shows bring the Glitz without forgetting the God! Delivering quality puppet shows for adults appropriate for any mainstream house of worship, whatever your Protestant denomination, featuring such classics as:

The Selfish Giant—a lonely giant learns to let love in!

A Stray in a Manger—what one stray mutt saw that first Christmas Eve!

My Friend Danny—an updated but faithful adaptation of Daniel in the Lion's Den!

A Long Way Down—a different perspective on the story we all thought we knew about the Tower of Babel!

She delivers many shows full of learning and laughter aimed at teens!

Smarty at the Party—the smartest kid at the rave is the one who Just Says No!

Happy Helloween—there are more tricks than treats at this unchaperoned shindig!

Dr. Wrong and Mr. Right—sometimes Mr. Right can have a dark side!

Look Up!—we rely on our GPS and phones too darn much, and if we're not careful, they might take us to some unusual places.

Also shows for young children!

Nancy Joyner . . .

★ . . . Taught workshops at over 21 conferences
★ . . . Puppeteer in Residence (2003), Olivet Nazarene University
★ . . . Performed shows in 39 out of 50 states! (And Guam!)
★ . . . Trained by Henry Dispatch and the Story Land Puppeteers!